AUNTY SUSIE'S FABRIC

A Fylde Family Mystery

Kate Laxen

Copyright © 2024 by Kate Laxen

All rights reserved.

No part of this book may be reproduced, or stored in a retrieval system, or transmitted in any form or by any means, electronic, mechanical, photocopying, recording or otherwise, without express permission of the publisher, apart from the use of short quotations in book reviews. Any resemblance to real people, either living or dead, is coincidental.

Creative license was used in the crafting of this story, which means at times it may meander away from the straight path of hard facts, medical or otherwise.

Cover: www.thecovercollection.com

ISBN: 9798343157833

To Jacob.

You've come such a long way.

Contents

1. Michael — 1
2. Aunty Susan — 9
3. Aunty Susan — 20
4. Jacob — 34
5. Michael — 43
6. Jacob — 54
7. Jacob — 62
8. Aunty Susan — 70
9. Aunty Susan — 80
10. Michael — 88
11. Suzy — 93
12. Suzy — 100
13. Suzy — 107
14. Suzy — 118
15. Aunty Susan — 125
16. Aunty Susan — 134
17. Aunty Susan — 144
18. Jacob — 153
19. Jacob — 172
20. Jacob — 180
21. Aunty Susan — 186
22. Suzy — 191
23. Suzy — 197
24. Aunty Susan — 203
25. Aunty Susan — 210
26. Jacob — 220
27. Aunty Susan — 228
28. Jacob — 235
29. Aunty Susan — 240
30. Jacob — 245
31. Aunty Susan — 251
32. Aunty Susan — 261
33. Aunty Susan — 275
34. Aunty Susan — 280

1. Michael

Michael is lost.

He put his phone on the hall table while he was lacing up his boots and forgot to pick it up again, which means he can't ring anyone or consult his map. If he'd stuck to the canal, like he usually does, he'd have been fine. Today, however, he wandered away from the towpath down a side turning that started off as a wide track, covered with a layer of grass that shimmered enticingly in the late afternoon sunlight. In all the times he'd walked down the canal before, Michael had never noticed this turning, and he felt drawn to meander down it almost against his will. Unfortunately, the breadth of luminous green sward gradually became narrower until, eventually, Michael was so tightly hemmed in on both sides by pine trees, birches and small, gnarly oaks, he was forced to walk sideways, which made him wonder if the continuing existence of this woodland path was merely a figment of his imagination. Conscious that there wasn't much daylight left, he decided to turn back. But when he tried to retrace his steps there seemed to be a huge number of crossing points and side tracks, several more than had been there on the way in, and he couldn't remember the exact route he'd taken, let alone reverse it in his head to find his way back to the canal.

'Bloody hell,' he mutters to himself.

Life is difficult enough at the moment, as it is. Returning to England has been much harder than he expected. He got through the summer surprisingly well, mainly because he spent most of it in and around Reykjavik, where he was hosted by the University of Iceland as visiting Professor of Parapsychology. The welcome given to him by his Icelandic colleagues, to say nothing of Iceland itself, with its wide-open spaces and glimmering lakes and the brightness of its skies in the late evenings, made him feel like someone else entirely, not a middle-aged man crippled into borderline elderliness by grief. Now he's back, both in England and inside his true self again, and he's dismayed by the darkening evenings and the gloominess of the cottage he used to share with Reece.

Weekends are particularly unbearable. At first, he tried sitting in his office on Saturdays and Sundays, in an attempt to pretend there was no distinction between these days and the ones that make up the rest of the week, until, one Sunday morning, he bumped into Jamie and Ben, two of his postgraduate students, who both live on campus, and he didn't much like the looks of casual concern they tossed in his direction. The last thing he wants is for his students to recognise him as the basket case he truly is, so he's taken to filling weekends by trudging up and down the canal. He doesn't enjoy these walks very much. The towpath is full of bell-ringing cyclists with a sense of entitlement, and families shoving pushchairs through the mud, dragging reluctant toddlers behind them, together with dogs on ridiculously long leads, totally unaware or not giving a damn that they're blocking the way for people who wish to walk at a brisk pace. But it gets him out of the house, and striding forth feels like a positive action, as though he's crossing a bridge across the aching chasm that cracks open every Friday evening and doesn't close until the following Sunday night. So, he wraps cheese and pickle or egg sandwiches in foil, makes a flask of coffee and sets off. On Saturdays, he walks downstream towards the Wey Navigation and the Thames, and on Sundays he goes in the other direction, towards Basingstoke. Both routes are easy to follow, so he doesn't have to bother with maps, which is handy, because most of the time his brain is too fuddled to make much sense of their wavy lines and contours. He just looks at his watch and when he's walked for two and a half hours, he turns and retraces his steps. By doing that, and adding in lunch and coffee stops, he manages to stay out for a good six hours each day.

He comes to a small clearing, plonks himself down on a log at the edge of it and gazes about. Nothing but trees in every direction. The surface of the log is coated in a layer of damp, mucus-like slime, which starts to seep into the seat of his trousers almost immediately. The temperature is dropping rapidly. Michael's anorak is only really suitable for walking, not for long periods of inactivity, and soon it will be too cold to sit still. Also, he worked up an appetite plunging through the undergrowth when the path tapered out, but he finished his sandwiches and drank his coffee ages ago. Usually, he carries an energy bar and an extra bag of crisps for emergencies such as this, but when he rifles through his backpack, he can't find either of them. He must have forgotten to replace the ones he ate last weekend.

A sprinkling of late afternoon sunlight suddenly dapples the grass in the glade, and a soft breeze passes through the leaves, making them whisper quietly to themselves. Michael closes his eyes, and as he listens to the voices of the trees and tries to work out what they are saying, his mental anguish is soon replaced by an empty drowsiness, coupled with a sense of peace, which rapidly turns to bliss and then expands into full-blown ecstasy. He remains sitting on his log and from a quiet corner of his mind, he observes the familiar unfolding of the early stages of this mental transformation. It's nothing to be afraid of. It happens all the time.

He smiles.

When he opens his eyes again, the sun is so low in the sky it only just touches the tops of the trees and Michael is no longer sitting on the log, but is almost folded in two on the ground in front of it, with one side of his face pressed against the wet grass. A couple of inches away, he can see three bright red toadstools that have thrust themselves upwards through the fallen leaves, *Amanita muscaria*, classified as poisonous, but known mostly for its psychoactive properties. He stares at the biggest one and notes the almost heartbreakingly delicate little frill under its cap and the fact that the spots aren't spots at all, but jagged, irregular oval shapes. Where would it transport him, he wonders, if he were to eat a bit of it? He reaches out, wraps three fingers in a pincer formation around the stipe and pulls at it. The fungus offers no resistance and slides easily out of the ground, as a single, satisfying whole, its base chunkier than its stem and covered in peaty soil. Michael takes a bite out of the scarlet cap and starts chewing.

Nothing much happens at first. From its taste, which is earthy and laced with a faint hint of supermarket mushrooms, there is little to suggest it contains hallucinogenic and potentially toxic chemicals. Michael swallows some of it and then a bit more. Initially, his mind remains comfortably blank. Then, all of a sudden, he's hurled back to the night when he got that call from the hospital. He knows all about past life reviews. He's written papers about them and given keynote speeches at conferences about the way an entire life can be re-experienced by its observer in the time it takes for him to fall from the top of a cliff to the bottom. The series of images running through Michael's head is just like one of those, he realises, apart from the fact it doesn't begin at the start of his life but at the end of someone else's. It's like a film that has been massively speeded up so it can hurtle its way through everything, but still include every single painful moment.

When the re-run has sped beyond Reece's death, rushed through the summer in Iceland and Michael's return to the UK, and reached the point just before Michael decided to divert away from the towpath, it squeals to an abrupt halt and then restarts again at pace much slower than before, almost as slow as real time. He sees himself sitting on the bench where the canal widens out into a flash, eating his sandwiches and gazing absently at three coots and a moorhen bobbing about in the water. Then he watches himself get up, pull his bobble hat down over his ears and start walking again. Michael isn't a vain man. He was once, perhaps. Yes, he definitely had a very high opinion of himself when he was a youngster. But he's way too old for that kind of narcissism now, and he always thinks self-pity an absurd and irritating form of indulgence when he witnesses it in others. And yet the sight of himself cast into the role of a wandering and unhappy man fills him with such tenderness it almost moves him to tears. He doesn't have time to ruminate on this, though, because, suddenly, he is shoved back inside himself to experience the next part of the movie from within. It's only now that he realises he was enticed to take this side turning away from the canal by a sound, a faint tintinnabulation that seemed to emanate from somewhere close to him, but also from a source located deep inside his own head. At first, he thought it might be the tinnitus he often suffers from in the vast, empty silence of his house. But then he remembered. He used to hear this exact sound a lot during his adolescence. Then it stopped, and he never heard it again. Until now.

The external component of the sound seemed to be coming from trees further down the path. Michael was compelled to pursue it, even though he suspected it might be a cruel manipulation, a game devised by his inner self to mock his sadly depleted external counterpart. Then he heard another noise, a ticking from the same direction. The two sounds intermingled with each other, but didn't blend into a single harmonic whole. Instead, they ran along together in parallel, taking it in turn to command his attention, as if they each carried a separate and equally important message. As he progressed, the tinkling and the ticking remained level and constant. They never became louder or closer together, and the note sounded by the tinkling component never varied. He had no way of telling, not having the gift of perfect pitch, but for some reason, he thought it might be middle C.

When he reached the clearing, both sounds stopped abruptly, as if to say *we've led you here, our job is done*, and the final scene of the re-run was the point at which Adrian accepted he was lost and sat down heavily on the log.

He turns until he's flat on his back in the long, wet grass and chews another fragment of mushroom. His trousers and anorak are soaked through and he isn't sure how many bits of toadstool he's swallowed, or why he thought it was a good idea to swallow any. The sky that fills the gap between the highest branches of the trees that surround the clearing is a bright, sunlit blue. Up in the tree tops it's still daytime, but in the area beneath them, a shadowy dusk has fallen. The brief period of ecstasy, followed by complete loss of consciousness means he's had one of his epileptic episodes. During seizures, he's usually aware of his surroundings, more or less, but he can't move or speak, which isn't much of a problem because they tend only last a few minutes. But this time, the first attack must have segued into one of the other types of episodes, the ones that used to be rare but have started to become more frequent over the past few months. These are more severe, and during them he isn't aware of anything. That might explain why he's ended up rolling around in the grass, eating toadstools.

Michael first started suffering from worrying episodes of vagueness was in his first year at university. Then, when he was twenty, he collapsed during a disco in the union bar, and was diagnosed with temporal lobe epilepsy. His condition has never bothered him much, and although his seizures have taken a significant turn for the worse lately, Michael keeps forgetting to take the new medication prescribed for him by his most recent consultant, a younger man who comes across as patronising and has failed to earn Michael's respect. The only concessions Michael makes to his condition are occasional, half-hearted efforts to reduce his alcohol intake and acceptance that it isn't safe for him to drive. This is a nuisance sometimes, particularly now that Reece is gone, although there is a useful train connection between the university and his home, and if he needs to go to places not serviced by the railway, he can usually find a student who will give him lifts for a small fee. Apart from these minor issues, he regards his epilepsy as a good thing, a key that unlocks doors in his mind and makes him aware of things that most other people can't see. Also, particularly in his current stricken state, his seizures provide him with a welcome holiday from his normal self.

It's just that the recovery phase can be a bit sticky, and he often ends up doing stuff he wouldn't normally do, like taking big bites out of toxic fungi.

His mind returns again to the ringing and the ticking, and the way they suddenly seemed to jump out of the shrubbery at the side of the canal. He converts the sounds into a visual image which takes the form of two strands of rope, plaited together and glowing as they pulled him into this woodland clearing. They must have been guiding him towards something important. He has an idea what this *something important* might be, but surely this is wishful thinking? He tries to approach the thing sideways, in case he frightens it away, which would leave him feeling even more lost than he is already, and not just physically, but professionally and emotionally, too. Lost plus lost plus lost. Or is it lost cubed, because each loss has the effect of multiplying the impact of the other losses rather than merely adding to them? And how would he categorise this potential new, extra layer of loss, the one he'll be forced to suffer if the *something important* proves to be an illusion?

Focus, he tells himself. Force yourself to think. At first, logical thought feels awkward and uncomfortable, like scrambling over a high step when you've just broken both ankles. But once he makes it over the top, he slides down the other side with ease and lands in his life's obsession, the conviction that there used to be an extra person living inside his head.

During his professional life, Michael has written many papers exploring the idea that human beings have an outer, active personality and an inner all-seeing one that lives in the non-dominant hemisphere of the brain. Obviously, this wasn't a new idea when he stumbled across it. Most ancient religions speak of the dual nature of man and he's lost count of the number of people who have come up to him at conferences and told him about their own particular mental cohabitee. However, Michael has yet to read about or meet anyone who has been abandoned by their hidden friend and ended up with what feels like half a brain. The creature that lived in the non-verbal side of Michael's head started appearing to him in dreams when he was about thirteen. At first, he confused his angel with the lurid events that took place in his adolescent fantasy world, which, during the early stages of puberty, centred around Marc Bolan, who was represented repeatedly and larger than life in massive posters stuck to his bedroom walls. The boy inside Michael's adolescent head, with his slender limbs, curly dark hair and profound gaze looked a lot like Marc in the beginning, but When Michael moved on to other musical idols, the entity hidden away in his right brain still looked and felt the same. That was the point at which he realised his guardian angel wasn't just a mental construct, but had some kind of independent or semi-independent reality, and was very old and very wise, despite his youthful looks and the playful attitude he often adopted. He seemed to live both deep inside Michael's head, and also in another place at the same time, one that Michael couldn't access.

The name of his protector was Anteros. Michael was certain of this. The original Anteros was one of the Erotes, a group of youthful Gods, usually depicted as winged boys. Had Michael read about the Erotes and named his right-brain companion Anteros, or had Anteros himself somehow let it be known this was what he wanted to be called? Or, more fantastically, was *his* Anteros actually the *original* Anteros, an entity who was real and not mythical? Michael didn't know, but the little god inside his head had been a loyal friend during his teenage years, manifesting mostly in his dreams, but occasionally making his presence known when Michael was awake, to issue warnings or send him specific messages. These communications were always non-verbal and it often took Michael a while to understand what he was being warned against. Sometimes he didn't get it at all, and he suspected this drove Anteros mad with frustration and made him retreat into his lair, where Michael envisaged him sulking darkly and gazing out on the true world in all its swirling chaos, the one he was duty bound to protect his human counterpart from seeing, because it would blow his mind.

The communications Anteros sent when Michael was awake were usually in the form of a noise just like the ones he'd heard today, a ringing that wasn't really in his ears or the ticking of a clock that didn't exist. Sometimes it was loud, but often it was barely audible. If he was with other people when it happened, they never seemed to notice, so he assumed it was entirely internal, even it seemed to come from elsewhere. But the really important thing, the thing he realised only when it was too late, was that he should have paid attention when Anteros tried to communicate with him. One terrible, awful, never to be forgotten summer, when Michael was eighteen, he had neglected to do this and Anteros had flounced off, never to be seen again. Or so Michael had thought.

He heaves himself into a sitting position, and once upright, he hears a rustling in the trees above his head that makes him look up sharply. Something white catches his eye. For a brief instant he's sure it's Anteros, looking as youthful as Michael once was, long ago, and wearing his customary white shift, tied at the waist with a thin leather belt. He seems to be perched on a branch, with his tanned, lightly muscled legs dangling into the drop beneath his feet. Despite the fact that Michael some distance below and his eyesight isn't what it once was, he can see his little god clearly. He can even discern the expression on his face, which is so knowing and so much a part of Michael's private self, he can't bear its frankness, and is forced to look away. Immediately, Michael hears a flutter and glances upwards again, just in time to see a barn owl flit silently across the clearing, leaving behind an inky blue space hemmed in by the tops of the trees and containing nothing but the slender crescent of a new moon.

He stands up, brushes the mud off his trousers and jacket, and leaves the clearing. It's almost pitch dark in the trees and soon he has to stop and lean forward with one hand resting against the narrow trunk of a silver birch so he can vomit over the fallen leaves and pine needles. Probably just as well, he thinks. He has no idea whether the amount of toadstool he swallowed was sufficient to bring about his death, but he doesn't want to end his days writhing in agony and foaming at the mouth, leaving his body to be discovered much later, perhaps by a small dog standing over him, growling and barking until its owner appears. He swipes his hand over his mouth, wipes it on the seat of his wet trousers and continues walking in an almost completely straight line until he reaches the towpath. As he plods home, he feels happier than he has done for a very long time.

But it never occurs to him, even for a single second, to wonder why Anteros suddenly appeared to him like that after so many years.

2. Aunty Susan

Gawain throws a cushion at his brother's head and hoots like a monkey. Jacob catches the cushion and covers his face with it, while the rest of us stare at the big TV attached to the wall. His on-screen counterpart skulks in the background, behind Aimee who is launching into her introductory spiel. I've met Aimee. Jacob brought her along to the last Sunday lunch. She works in admin at the university where he has just registered as a PhD student. Her hair is lime green, cropped very short, and inserted into one side of her nose is a small black disc, which is looks as though it serves a practical rather than a decorative purpose, as a new type of mobile phone, perhaps. One that you operate by twitching your nose.

Anyway, her hair and her face jewellery, and the fact that she is gender fluid don't bother me. Each their own, I always say. But when Gawain and Bartosz were serving up the roast beef and Yorkshire puddings, I accidentally referred to her as *she* instead of *they*, and she refused point blank to cut me any slack, as though I'd done it on purpose. Also, she was unnecessarily specific about the exact status of her relationship with Jacob. She wasn't his exclusive sexual partner or anyone else's, she said, and she did whatever she felt like with whoever she fancied. Jacob hadn't actually said she *was* his exclusive sexual partner. He had introduced her as a friend and hadn't mentioned sex at all. By the time she'd finished her little speech, the poor boy had bright pink circles in the middle of his usually white-as-white cheeks and was unable to lift his gaze from the tablecloth. Gawain and I exchanged a look that didn't need to be put into words, and from that point onwards, I was tempted to refer to her as *it*.

And here she is now, her big, round *in-your-face* face with its heavily made-up eyes beaming confidently at the camera, telling the viewers she doesn't know much about the house behind them, or its former inhabitants. The place is to the south west of London, but she won't be revealing its exact location.

On-screen-Jacob turns and looks up at the house. Before the video started, he told us all he only went on this exploration because Aimee begged him to. Her regular partner couldn't make it, he said, and she didn't want to go on her own. Aimee is what's known as an urbexer. She has her own YouTube channel, which means she spends most of her spare time mooching around in abandoned buildings, anything from tiny cottages and old farmhouses to big, institutional places like hospitals, schools and bankrupt shopping centres, and as she wanders down corridors and in and out of rooms, rifling through any belongings left behind by the people who used to live or work there, she films everything she sees. In the past year or so, *AimeeSeeksandFinds* has developed a sizable following. She even sells hoodies and caps bearing her logo, which is a heart containing what looks like a small bird pecking at seeds, for some reason.

Night has fallen and the two explorers are standing on a pavement in what looks like a suburban street.

'I'm whispering because there are other houses close by,' Aimee says. 'From what I've heard, the neighbours are fed up with the state of the place and with having to call the police to deal with intruders, so we need to be really quiet. Nobody seems to know much about the people who lived here, apart from that they were a bit eccentric and very old. One of them died in the house and the other went into a home soon after. We're not sure if they had any children.'

The camera pans round to show the front of the house, or what you can see of it, which isn't much.

'Look how overgrown the front garden is,' she says.

'From the street, you can only see the roof,' Jacob points out. 'Otherwise, you wouldn't even know the house was here.'

He's found his voice, I think to myself. Good. Unlike Aimee, though, he doesn't have a microphone, so we have to strain to pick up his words. But then Jacob always has an irritating tendency to mumble, as though he's only half-convinced people are interested in what he has to say. Under Aimee's instruction, he shines the powerful torch upwards to show a dilapidated slate roof with several tiles missing. Aimee pushes aside a wrought iron gate, which is barely hanging onto its post by one hinge, and the pair fight their way through a wilderness of overgrown brambles and buddleia to a narrow path that skirts around the edge of the house to the back.

'Did you break in?' Bartosz asks.

'You're only meant to enter a building if there's already an access point, like an unlocked door or a broken window or something,' Jacob says. 'Urbexers have a code of honour about stuff like that, or at least the reputable ones do.'

'But it's ok to go in via windows or doors that have already been shoved in by other people who did actually break in?' Gawain asks.

'As long as they don't do any more damage. Genuine urbexers only want to look around.'

'As in snoop.'

'If the video offends your delicate sensibilities, you could always go and sit in the kitchen until it's finished.'

'Nah. I'm not going to miss your debut on the big screen, am I?'

Jacob hurls a chocolate at his brother from the bowl on the coffee table in front of him. It's a dense, spherical object in a gold wrapper and he puts a fair amount of spin on it. Gawain, who is sitting on the floor, resting his head against Bartosz's left leg, dodges it successfully, and it rebounds off the wall next to my chair and hits my shoulder with the impact of a pellet from a BB gun.

'Boys!' Amanda shouts.

'Yeah, Jacob,' Gawain adds.

'Sorry, Aunty Susan,' Jacob mutters.

I tut, shake my head and bend over to pick up the chocolate, which I unwrap and stuff into my mouth as I watch Jacob and Aimee enter the house through the kitchen door. The lock has already been hacked out, leaving a neat, rectangular gap, and all it takes for them to reach the interior, is a hard shove. The kitchen is dark because the windows are obscured by plant growth, both outside and inside, mostly ivy, which has wound its way in through narrow spaces in the rotting window frames. Jacob tries the light switch, but the power isn't connected, so he shines his torch around while Aimee films and comments. The part of the kitchen nearest to the outside wall is obviously an extension and must have had a sloping roof at one time, but now most of it has caved in over the sink. At the other side of the room, an aga, coated in a mysterious orange crust, squats next to a fridge that turns out to contain nothing much, apart from a few rusty tins of peaches and a three quarters full bottle of milk that has separated itself into alternating opaque beige and clear brown layers. The camera focuses on a small cone shaped object made from blue plastic at the bottom and clear plastic at the top, attached to the wall, close to the aga.

'If anyone knows, what this is, please put it in the comments,' Aimee says.

'It's a tea dispenser!' I say, triumphantly.

Amanda and Bartosz and my nephews all turn to look at me, with expressions of polite interest on their faces, as though they feel sorry for me.

Aimee continues to scan the kitchen.

'We need to find something with a date on it, like a bill or an invoice, so we can work out how long the house has been empty.'

On-screen-Jacob pulls open a wonky draw in a blue, melamine kitchen unit to reveal a mish-mash of perished rubber bands, dried-out biros, a few official looking letters, nibbled round the edges, and a scattering of mouse droppings. Aimee swoops in to have a look, but when Jacob shines his torch into the drawer, she bats it away.

'We don't want to show anything with an address on it,' she says.

The most recent date they find in the kitchen is on a calendar from a local Chinese restaurant, which has been shoved into the same drawer, underneath the letters. Aimee films the calendar. The month is December, twelve years ago.

'That doesn't seem right,' the video version of Jacob says.

Aimee points the camera at him. He stares back at her and shrugs, but doesn't say anything else.

'Go on, genius. Explain.'

'Explain what?'

'Why it doesn't seem right?'

'Everything else in here is a lot older than that.'

Aimee rolls her eyes and draws a deep, *give-me-strength* breath.

'They might not have bothered buying anything new or doing any modernisation for years and years. That can happen when people get older. Obviously.'

At this stage, I'm more interested in the interaction between Jacob and Aimee than I am in the abandoned house. Jacob shouldn't let people speak to him like that. What's wrong with him? I wonder if should have a word. Or perhaps I should mention it to Gawain and get him to say something. He's probably done that already, though, knowing him. They're so thick with each other, these days, even though they seem to fight and quarrel most of the time when they are in the same room.

I tell myself to mind my own beeswax and focus on the video.

None of the downstairs rooms contain anything more noteworthy than tatty carpets, their patterns almost completely obscured by upturned furniture, trodden-in bits of plaster from the ceiling and the contents of various cupboards and drawers left all over the place by other, less scrupulous visitors, searching for valuables probably. A few potentially interesting old books are stacked up near the fireplace, but all of them are covered in spots of white mould so it's impossible to read their titles. Overall, the dire state of the downstairs rooms makes it very difficult to visualise what they must have looked like back in the days when the house was occupied. Maybe that's why I don't notice anything familiar about the place at this point. All I've seen so far is a sad, dark old house that nobody cares about, undergoing a slow and quiet process of decay.

The last of the rooms on the ground floor is little more than an extended cupboard under the stairs and is almost completely filled by a manky leather armchair with a gash running across the centre of its seat, and a long rectangular box on spindly chrome legs. Jacob lifts its big wooden lid to reveal a radio, a turntable, and a rusty metal rack holding a collection of records. They both rifle through the LPs and hold a few up to the camera. A series of rather dull looking men in turtle neck sweaters fill the screen.

'Easy listening classics. Jim Reeves, Andy Williams, Matt Munro,' Jacob says, his voice laced with casual scorn.

Another LP cover comes into view.

'The Black and White Minstrels.' Jacob reads out the words on the album sleeve slowly, as though he's translating them from another language and can't quite believe what he's seeing.

'They used to have a show on the telly,' I find myself saying. 'On Saturdays, after tea. It was incredibly popular.'

Every head in the room turns to stare at me again, this time in horror.

'But they've painted their faces black and put big white rings around their mouths and their eyes,' Gawain points out.

'Why would anyone *do* that?' Amanda adds.

'Nobody thought anything of it in those days. My parents were very keen on them. They wore white gloves and sang songs, and they did that jazz hands thing. Not my parents, the people in the show.'

'What jazz hands thing?' Gawain asks.

He screws his eyes closed and shakes his head to make it clear he doesn't want to know. I'm so amused by the looks of earnest disgust on their faces that I can't resist providing them with a highly animated demonstration. From my chair, I wave my arms about, sing a bit of one of their songs and generally go way over the top. Of course, I find the idea of the Black and White Minstrels every bit as mind bogglingly bewildering and ridiculous as they do. But people weren't as enlightened in the sixties and seventies as they are now, and, like it or not, this troop of singers was what they called a *hit*, particularly with my parents' generation.

'Please stop, Aunty,' Gawain says, wearily, as though I've been making an exhibition of myself for several hours and he's had enough.

The explorers put the records back where they found them and tentatively make their way up the stairs. The first floor isn't quite as dark as downstairs thanks to the halogen glow of a streetlight close to the big window on the landing. However, the space is still full of shadows because the window is partially obscured by a set of moth-eaten curtains. Aimee zooms in on them. Even though they are practically in rags at the bottom, sufficient material remains to make it clear that they feature a series of ovals set against a pink background, each containing a black silhouetted profile of a woman sharply dressed in a pencil skirt and a jacket with wide lapels. In some of the ovals, the woman is holding aloft a cigarette in a long holder, and in others she's got one hand on her hip and is gazing downwards, through the window, as though something interesting is going on around the wheelie bins at the side of the house.

'Probably from the eighties,' Aimee suggests.

'More like the sixties, or even the fifties,' I think.

'Careful on this floor,' Jacob says. His voice sounds muffled as he progresses away from Aimee along the landing. 'The carpet's all spongy. God knows what state the floorboards are in.'

They proceed cautiously, pushing their way through piles of discarded shoes and loops of flowery wallpaper that hang loosely from the damp walls. Then Jacob suddenly veers off to the left into a bedroom at the front of the house and starts shouting something indecipherable. Aimee follows and films her entry into the big room.

'This is one of the bedrooms at the front,' she explains to the viewers as she pans her camera around.

A faint memory, gentle as a nudge from an elbow in a woollen sleeve, registers in a distant part of my brain. At the far end of the room is a big window, un-curtained and bow-shaped, which probably lets in a great deal of light during the daytime. The bare floorboards are splattered with paint and littered with discarded rags, brushes stiffened with paint and empty jam jars, and several huge canvases are propped against the long wall between the door and the window. Gigantic, multi-coloured penises attached to oversized testicles have been daubed across the opposite wall, presumably by later visitors to the house, not its original occupants, and close to the window, an easel, supporting another big painting is positioned to capture the best of the light. Aimee focuses the camera on it.

'Shine the torch on the painting, you melt,' she says.

Jacob moves his light away from the impressive display of phalluses and aims it in a direction that meets with her satisfaction. The canvas is revealed. Thick vertical bands of red, black and green paint sweep down it from top to bottom forming a background across which a few flesh coloured strokes have been added later, with what looks like a much finer brush. Not a single square millimetre of the canvas is unpainted, and yet it looks unfinished somehow.

'What is it?' Amanda asks. 'Are those pink dabs meant to be a head and hands?'

'Dunno,' Jacob says.

'It's full of negative vibes. Like anger or a curse,' Gawain says.

'It's certainly full of paint,' Bartosz adds.

Everyone laughs.

Everyone but me, that is.

Jacob and Aimee pull the other canvases away from the wall and point the camera at each of them in turn, revealing more thick bands of paint, black against red, giving off a sense of manic intensity. They stare at them for a while, and so do we. Then they turn back to the doorway and re-enter the hall. Jacob points his torch towards the end of the hallway. A narrow staircase is caught in the beam.

'There's another floor,' he says.

I get up and leave the room. Somehow, I manage not to run. When I reach the door, Bartosz asks if I want to him to pause the video until I get back, but I say no, I won't be a minute. I make it to the hall toilet and I hover over the basin for a few seconds with my hands resting on the seat. Bartosz's lamb hotpot and treacle tart churn about in my stomach, but when I try to throw up, nothing emerges apart from a small gobbet of saliva. Frustrated, I put the lid down and sit on it to catch my breath. I dab the sweat from my forehead with loo roll, and then, once I've started to get my act together, I apply a fresh layer of lipstick.

I manage to stay in the toilet for exactly the right amount of time, long enough for the part of the video where they explore the attic to be over when I get back, but not so long that Gawain will wonder where I am and come looking for me. When I sit down in my chair again, trying to style it out, as my nephews would say, I glance quickly at the telly, with my eyes half closed. A finale of still shots is passing across the screen, accompanied by evocative and rather tragic piano music, and I'm forced to stare down at my thighs and contemplate the grooves in my green corduroy trousers until it ends. When it finally does, everyone, including me, applauds loudly, and Amanda clicks through to YouTube on her mobile to see if the video has generated any comments. It has, of course, and several of them relate to her little brother's film debut. She reads a few out.

'Who's the babe magnet?'

'Aimee's punching above her weight with that one.'

'Next time can we have an exploration of him?'

'Oh, man,' Jacob groans. A bright pink flush creeps up his neck and face and into the roots of his pale blonde hair.

'What a strange place,' Bartosz says.

'Yeah, it was weird. It had a kind of atmosphere,' Jacob says.

'Are you planning to do more of these, what do you call them?' Gawain asks.

'Explores? Don't think so. Not me, anyway. Aimee and me, we're not like. Anymore.'

While this conversation is going on, I sit rigidly in my chair, hyperventilating sightly, still trying to style it out. Gawain catches my eye and looks away again quickly, but not before he's managed to communicate to me that he's noticed something is amiss. He creates a big palaver about sorting out drinks for everybody, and when he thrusts a double brandy in my direction, he rests the palm of one hand against my upper back. I'm overcome by an intense urge to bat him away and tell him to stop fussing. But this is Gawain we're talking about. When something is afoot with any of us, he always spots it immediately. I find it intensely irritating, but I can't deny that right now, I'm bloody grateful for the brandy.

Later, when I'm back home, he'll ring and demand to know what was wrong with me. Since I had that wretched dizzy spell and was put on blood pressure tablets, even though the actual diagnosis was an infection of the inner ear, he's been on a kind of red alert, as though he expects me to have a stroke any minute. I told him I didn't think the tablets were necessary, but I failed to mention that I didn't even go to the chemists to collect the prescription. He suspects something, though. The only reason he hasn't mentioned it is because he can't work out how to bring it up without sending me into one of what he, Jacob and Amanda call my Highly Indignant States.

I'll need to decide what I'm going to say when he rings. If I tell him I felt unwell during the video, he'll be on my doorstep within the hour and the little backpack he's so proud of, with all its intrusive medical equipment, will *just happen* to be in the boot of his car. On the other hand, if I present him with a watered-down version of the truth or simply make something up, he'll know I'm being evasive, and he'll chip away at me until I've told him everything.

Hang on a minute, though. There must be more than one abandoned home in the UK where a big, north-facing bedroom has been turned into an artist's studio. And those curtains with the silhouettes of the glamorous woman used to be all over the place, not just in houses but in draper's shops and hairdressing salons, and even dentist's surgeries. The LPs in that little room under the stairs don't add up, either. The painters of those canvases, if they really were who I think they were, would never have listened to Andy Williams, let alone the Black and White Minstrels. Druggy, flower power music from the hippie era was more their thing, with an occasional blast of heavy rock. They used to have it blaring out at all hours with the windows wide open. Dad was forced to go round in his pyjamas more than once to complain when Mum was ill and couldn't sleep because of it.

But the more I think about it, the more familiar it all becomes. In the end, I even remember about the LPs. They belonged to Tess's grandad, and that little cubby hole was his living room. I can see him clearly in my mind's eye, with his beer belly and his hair smoothed back and separated into parallel strands with the oily lotion all elderly men used back then. He was a groundsman at the local park, and when he wasn't at work, or doing odd jobs around the house and tending to the garden, he sat in his chair in that little room, listening to his records, with a small cigar sticking out of his mouth. The entire house stank of his tobacco and it stained his fingers brown. Then he died suddenly, from an aneurysm, in that very room. It was Easter. Tess was really upset, and the following summer the garden turned into a wilderness because he wasn't there to look after it. Her parents must have shut the door to his little room and left his possessions to rot. Did they do the same to Tess's room in the attic? Did they spend all the long decades that followed painting those canvases in their big front bedroom, ignoring the fact that, above their heads, Tess's belongings were slowly festering away?

I cup the bowl-shaped glass in my hands, inhale the vapour evaporating from the surface of the brandy and then gulp the liquid down with unseemly haste. Soon, I feel the warmth of it, the Dutch courage, spreading through my limbs, right down to the ends of my fingers and toes. I rummage about in my bag and I fish out my little pearl-framed mirror, a birthday present given to me years ago by the boys and Amanda when they were at boarding school, and I smear my lips with poppy-red lipstick for the second time in ten minutes.

'Where was this place, dear?' I ask, in a casual tone, one of mild curiosity, nothing more.

I might as well have a big sign with the word *fake* written on it, hovering above my head, but Jacob doesn't seem to notice. He sprawls in his chair, long legs stretched out in front of him, unintentionally ready to trip anyone who passes by, and he leaves a gap of several seconds before he replies. Does this mean he suspects something? Probably not. He often hesitates like that, as though he has put questions through a scanner to hunt for hidden meanings before he can formulate a response.

'We're not meant to say,' he says eventually, looking down at the carpet.

'Whyever not?'

'It's another urbexer code of honour thing. Some people like to go along and trash places like that. It's best not to give out locations.'

'I don't think Aunty was planning to go there and smash it up,' Gawain says.

'I know, but..." Jacob scratches the back of his neck and presses his lips together.

Is honour among urbexers the real reason he's reluctant to give away its location? Or is he fully aware that the house is just around the corner from my childhood home? I don't think I've ever mentioned where Davey and I lived as children, not that it's a secret. On the other hand, it isn't far from their old school, so Davey could easily have taken them there on one of their weekend outings. But even if Jacob does know my connection with the area, why is he being so evasive? Surely Davey didn't tell them about Tess and what happened to her?

'Tell her where it is, you complete bell end,' Gawain says.

'Shut up, knobhead,' Jacob replies, casually.

His face has never been as easy to read as his brother's and in any case, he rarely wants to engage with me, not properly. He was always a reserved child, but he became much less communicative after Davey died and he started going to stay with his mother, who by then had teamed up with the pastor of what turned out to be a pretty unpleasant religious community, based in America. In the end, after what was meant to be a gap year, but ended up being much longer, he was rescued by Gawain and Bartosz. Soon after, he had a kind of breakdown, although I'm not meant to know about that.

He gets up, helps himself to a soft drink from the refrigerated cupboard Gawain and Bartosz keep in this man-cave of a room, and sits down again without saying another word.

3. Aunty Susan

Tam bounces about behind me, shrieking in a voice shrill enough to cut jagged lines through brain tissue. Eventually, my niece, who is giving me a lift home, tells her to stop, and Tam resorts to blowing raspberries instead, which is very rude, in my opinion, but less painful to the ears. I feel sorry for Amanda, though. She's so heavily pregnant, she seems to have entered a semi-vegetative state and she's still got more than six weeks to go. The incubation of this particular foetus is an act of pure altruism on her part. For reasons I can't even begin to fathom, she has agreed to be a surrogate for Gawain and Bartosz. I'm not privy to all the intimate details, and I don't want to be, but conception was a DIY affair, apparently, achieved after several failed attempts, not with a turkey baster, but with some ghastly-sounding plastic device with a bulb at one end that Gawain borrowed from his A & E department. They want the baby's sex to be a surprise, so they didn't ask at its twenty-week scan, but the infant will be Gawain and Bartosz's official child, as well as Tam's half-sister or brother, Bartosz's daughter or son and Gawain's niece or nephew. And Jacob's niece or nephew for that matter. And my *great* niece or nephew. Family life can be complicated these days.

    By the time we get to my house, I can feel one of my heads coming on. As I unlock the front door, my phone vibrates in my pocket. A bit keen, I think, even for Gawain. I don't want to speak to him until I've mulled things over and decided on a fobbing off strategy, and after all the wine I drank during lunch, followed by that huge brandy, my brain is in no fit state to plan anything. A rapidly swallowed cafetiere of very strong, Italian dark-roasted coffee with a drop of cream from the fridge partially restores my mental clarity, and by the time I've gulped down three cups I'm ready to face him, which is helpful, because my phone has now vibrated across the kitchen table and is about to leap onto the floor.

    But it isn't Gawain.

'I've bought a van!' Patrick yells in a voice so loud I have to hold the phone away from my ear.

'Are you drunk?'

'No. Are you?'

'No. Well, yes. Possibly. A little. What do you mean you've bought a van? Are you going back to work?'

Until he retired, Patrick was a seller and fitter of bespoke kitchens. Now his son and daughter run the business.

'Why would I be doing that?'

'Because you've bought a van?'

'Not that type of van. A camper-van.'

'A dormobile?'

'Bigger. I think the right name for it is sports utility vehicle, although it's not one of those massive American ones. It's in great nick. There's beds and a kitchenette. And a little toilet. The paintwork needs touching up a bit. I might get it resprayed, but apart from that it's ready to go.'

'Ready to go where?'

'Anywhere you like. I'll bring it round to yours tomorrow morning. You decide.'

'Will it fit in the drive?'

"As long as you move all your pots onto the lawn. I can't wait for you to see it. I've put a box in one of the lockers with a kettle and teabags and everything. You can wire the whole thing up to the electrics if there are any. Otherwise, it's got gas rings and I've bought a cylinder of propane.'

'Gosh.'

The boys and Amanda refer to Patrick as my Not Boyfriend Exactly or NBE. They think I don't know that, in the same way I don't know about my Highly Indignant States. The title came about because I objected to the word *boyfriend* when they attempted to use it. But to be fair, NBE is a pretty accurate description of Patrick's current status in my life.

'You could be a bit more enthusiastic.'

He's right. It's not his fault he's phoned at such a bad time.

'Sorry. I am. It sounds very exciting.'

'I thought we could go for a drive down to the coast. Park up, go for a walk and then make a cup of tea and shut the little curtains. Try out the bed.'

We're not on facetime, but I can still see his grin and the glint in his green eyes. I met Patrick at the Thursday Walkers Group, which

I'd joined with a view to meeting new people when I retired. He'd had the same idea and had turned up in a longish and ancient looking black leather coat, which made him stand out because the other men seem to be engaged in a complicated game of one-upmanship, an important aspect of which involved the purchase of expensive, brightly coloured hiking anoraks with wicking interiors, waterproof coatings and other outdoor-related mod cons. To make matters worse, when it started to rain, he had no hood to put up, so he reached into his backpack and pulled out a beige leather hat with a wide brim. This get-up, together with his slightly bow-legged swagger, reminded me of Clint Eastwood in Pale Rider. I had to bite my lip to stop myself asking where he'd tethered his horse.

A few of the other walkers gawped at him open mouthed when he appeared for that first walk. But he just smiled back at them and then at me in almost, but not quite the same way. We stuck together for most of that day's walk. The rest of the hiking mob are as fanatically competitive about their ambient speed as they are about rain-resistant clothing. They race to get to the top of each hill and then down to the bottom again as quickly as possible, never stopping to admire the view or even take a few deep breaths. We lagged behind that first time and have continued to do so on all the subsequent walks. Patrick said he was surprised each outing didn't end with at least one of them having a coronary. Perhaps it did, I speculated. When I signed up, they said their numbers were going down. He laughed. By the time we reached the pub, most of them had finished their drinks and left, so we had no idea whether they'd all made it in one piece, but it didn't matter. We had plenty to talk about over our brie and cranberry baguettes.

Right now, I'm not really in my *having-a laugh-with-Patrick* headspace, but I agree to his plan, mainly to get him off the phone. By then a couple of missed calls have come through from Gawain. Even though I'm still worried he'll turn up on my doorstep if I don't answer, I prevaricate for another thirty minutes or so, during which I wander around my garden rattling a box of easy-to-digest cat kibble shaped like small fish. Lesley doesn't emerge from wherever it is she's hiding. She's not squatting behind the low wall that separates the lawn from the patio, listening in scornful silence as I call for her, nor is she huddled inside the big tub of compost in the greenhouse. It occurs to me that she might have gone to that bungalow at the entrance to the close, to hang out at the edge of the kidney shaped pond in the garden with the other neighbourhood cats, making the small body of water look like a swimming pool for felines. I walk up and down the pavement, rattling the box of kibble and shouting Lesley's name until I notice a slight but definite shift in the position of a moss green Draylon curtain in Mr Lilicrap's living room window. I realise I'm making a spectacle of myself, so I leave Lesley to her own devices and go home.

As I take my coat off, a text comes through from Gawain.
'Tried ringing. You ok?'
For most texters, this would be a casual message, a few words rapidly put together to ask a simple question. But coming from Gawain, its terseness conveys an almost menacing sense of aggrieved concern.
'I'm fine, thanks.'
'Are you sure?'
'Yes. Enjoy your evening.'
'Okay. Speak later.'
He might be happy to leave it for now, but he won't be prepared to let it go in the longer term. One evening, tomorrow perhaps or later in the week, he'll drop in on his way home from the hospital *just to say hi*. I'll need to get a grip before then, and the only way I'm going to manage that is by facing up to the video and watching it from beginning to end, without flinching or looking away. So, instead of going upstairs, running a bath and tuning into the Archers omnibus, I sit down at the dining table, summon up YouTube on my lap top and find the damn thing.

The first twenty minutes or so are ok. After all, I've seen those before. But when it gets to the bit where they go up to the attic and Tess's room, I have to force myself not to slam down the lid. Jacob shines his torch up into a yawning gap in the ceiling of Tess's bedroom. A considerable amount of water must have poured through that hole over the years. Most of it seems to have landed on the centre of the bed, the middle of which has collapsed onto the floor and is covered by what looks like a homogeneous mass of damp, mouldy grey gunge. But at each end of the bed, you can still make out the remnants of Tess's pink satin bedspread. We used to have picnics on that bedspread in the garden, and one time we pretended it was a magic carpet and bumped our way down the two flights of stairs on it. Like most other parts of the house, Tess's room has obviously been ransacked by intruders searching for jewellery, money and other precious items, and her belongings are strewn across the floor. It feels like both a terrible violation and a waste of time, because none of us had much in the way of expensive possessions in the seventies. The only thing that comes to mind is the silver locket Tess wore throughout that final summer, which was a gift from Ade. When her parents asked her where it came from, she told them she'd borrowed it from me. She never took it off, even when we went swimming in the big pond near the farm or in the pool in Christoff's garden.

Aimee and Jacob have to tread very carefully, because parts of the floor have deteriorated due to the damp, and also because there are long gaps where floorboards have been lifted. Aimee says this has been done by thieves to get to the copper piping. In the end, I'm unable to tear my eyes away from the items cast about everywhere. I'm shocked by their familiarity after so many years, and I keep stopping the video and going back to have a closer look. I recognise a yellow T-shirt, a pair of flared jeans and a furry red jacket with an elasticated waist that Tess bought from C&A with her Christmas money. I find it incredible that these articles still exist in real life and not just as memories. Their continuing presence seems indecent, like leaving a body to decay on the pavement instead of giving it a proper burial. Even if her parents couldn't face clearing her room when they were alive, surely there must have been someone else, an executor or an heir to the estate, who could have come along and sorted it all out? I'm frustrated by the haste with which Aimee and Jacob scan the room. I want them to pick up every single book from the bookcase and read out all the titles through the dots of white fungus, even though I know most of them are about boarding schools, Mallory Towers and St. Claires, and much older ones by Angela Brazil. And how could they both ignore the plush, but faded and grey stump of a leg that can be seen projecting outwards from under the bed. It belongs to a fluffy elephant. He was called Donny, after Donny Osmond.

When the footage finally comes to an end, I switch off my laptop and sit at the dining table staring into space, trying to process what I've just seen. L.P. Hartley was right, about the past being another country, where they do things differently. Now the seventies seem to belong not just to a different country, but another planet, and as for the events of the summer of seventy-six, they began to feel unreal almost as soon as they were over, like a dream or the plot of a novel, something I'd read about and become completely absorbed in, but which, once over, slipped away from my mind with astonishing rapidity. I shifted my focus to sixth form, A' levels, Oxbridge entrance and my entire future, really, and the events of that summer fell away from me as if they were no more significant than the Autumn leaves drifting down from the trees.

Looking back now, my instinct for self-preservation seems cold-blooded, almost psychopathic. Was I ruthless or was I just scared? Or did it all become a blur so quickly because there were parts of it I couldn't remember, that I still can't remember now, after more than forty years? Perhaps I should have talked to someone, but we didn't do that back then. Instead, we bottled things up until we forgot all about them.

I finish moving my pots of winter pansies and cyclamen out of the way just before Patrick appears and reverses his new leisure vehicle into the drive. It looks a brute of a thing, dull green with a band of even darker green around the middle, colours my mother would have described as nunty. Everything vibrates and rattles as we belt down the motorway and the smaller roads that thread their way through the New Forest. By the time we reach the coast I'm the same shade of green as the exterior paintwork. I make a frantic note to myself to take travel sickness tablets before agreeing to be transported anywhere else in this jalopy. After a particularly uncomfortable transit over the top of a small bridge, when the vehicle seems to leave the ground and my stomach stays hovering in the air for several unpleasant seconds, I suggest that the suspension needs to be looked at. Patrick mutters something dismissive about women and their general ignorance when it comes to motor vehicles. Then he stares ahead at the road, whistles *Come on Eileen* to himself and ignores everything else I say. He knows I hate that song.

We end up in an otherwise completely empty car park at one end of Christchurch, close to the sea, and he doesn't recover his good humour until we're half way along the footpath that goes up and then along Hengistbury Head. The day is blustery and wild, but the sea glitters cheerfully in the autumn sun, and I start to feel brighter, too. When we return to the camper van, we manage to set up the dining table, after a false start when we think it's in position and we sit down, only for it to collapse at one side, causing our paper package of fish and chips to slide onto the floor. As we eat, we stare out at the carpark, the sand dunes and the fat white clouds racing across the blue sky, and we wash our lunch down with a cup of tea, proudly made by Patrick with the help of his camping kettle, which he boils on the tiny hob. It takes several attempts before we manage to successfully convert the dining table and seats into a bed, a procedure that almost kills the mood. But once we've worked out how to realign the seat cushions, Patrick draws the swirly purple and orange curtains and pounces. It's like being in a seventies porn movie.

Before I met Patrick, sex was an activity performed by other people, members of a club to which I didn't belong. But now it happens on a regular basis, usually in my spare bedroom, away from the sordid intimacies of the room I sleep in, with its bedside table littered with moisturizers for various parts of the body, dental floss sticks, packets of ibuprofen for aching joints, and the dreadful possibility of that dull fart-like smell that often pervades rooms that have been slept in, to which the regular occupant has become nose-blind. We always keep the curtains open so Mr Lilicrap won't notice and be scandalised. Not that it matters if he is.

At first, I was terribly anxious. I found it impossible to believe I'd still be able to enjoy it after such a long interval. But it turns out you *can* teach an old dog new tricks, and it feels all the more delicious because our congress usually takes place at around three pm, the time that I used to call the dead centre of the afternoon, the time during which for years and years, I'd sat at my desk in my large and dreary office at the end of a very long corridor in Whitehall, wondering how it was possible for the minute hand on the institutional wall clock to slow down and then stop completely. The spell was always broken eventually by the cheerful rattle of Joyce's trolley with its tea urn and its plate of Rich Tea and Sports biscuits, and then later, when Joyce had been put out to grass, by the rapid footsteps of Sadiq or Hassan, the most junior members of my necessarily discrete and unusually skilled team, returning from Pret with a paper trayful of lattes and a selection of gingerbread men and muffins in a small carrier bag. After that, the working day would gather pace again and soon the clock would race forwards until it was time for me to push my way through the commuters on the underground, hope for a train at Waterloo and head home.

Thankfully, I'm free of all that now.

Afterwards, I tend to laugh, partly, because Patrick always looks so pleased with himself. He usually joins in, perhaps because he really *is* pleased with himself, and today we giggle a lot, mainly at ourselves, I think, for still being able to achieve this feat, despite being outside in a carpark, and also because the rusty old camper van creaks almost as much as we do. I sit up and peep through the little curtain, half expecting to see a small gathering of horrified people standing outside the window, including a policeman on a bicycle, Ealing comedy style. But apart from us, the car park is still deserted.

On the way home, it starts to rain torrentially and the spray makes it difficult to see the other cars on the motorway.

'I've got a plan,' Patrick announces suddenly.

I'm instantly wary. Patrick has come up with sudden plans before. Like marriage, which he proposed after going down on one knee while we were waiting for our kebab order to arrive from the new Greek takeaway. Patrick's wife, Bernice, died three years ago and he's been bereft ever since. But we'd only been seeing each other for a couple of months when he popped the question, and I had neither the intention nor, if it came to it, the ability to become Bernice's replacement.

'I'm lost without a woman in my life,' he said.

'You've got a woman in your life.'

'It needs one who's around all the time. I don't mind moving in with you if you don't want to get rid of your house. Or you could move in with me and rent your place out.'

'I don't think so, thank you very much. You're just looking for someone to cook your meals and iron your boxer shorts.'

'I don't wear boxers.'

'You know what I mean.'

He got up and started making his way towards the front door.

'What about your kebab?'

'I've lost my appetite.'

When the food order arrived, I put his portion in the fridge, but he didn't return for over a week, so it ended up in the bin after an unsuccessful attempt to feed bits of it to Lesley. Even so, I'm not about to start any of that marriage malarkey now. I've only ever fallen in love once. It started wonderfully, but ended about as badly as a such a thing could. After that, I never met anyone I felt sufficiently strongly about to change my way of life. And in any case, I was busy. After Oxford, I signed the Official Secrets Act and moved to Berlin while the Cold War was still raging, and when it ended and the dust had finally settled, which took a while, I retreated to my relatively safe corner of Whitehall and anticipated a calmer and quieter future. Perhaps I might have met someone then. But it wasn't to be because my brother went on a work trip to America, believing that Amanda, Gawain and Jacob could look after themselves while he was away. They couldn't, disaster ensued and I was forced to become involved. Davey and I decided to share the cost of a decent boarding school near my house and the initially rather shell-shocked children came to me during the holidays, except when he took them off to a rented cottage by the sea or a chalet at one of the holiday parks. Then, a couple of years later, Davey was run over by a bus on the seafront at Bridlington, so that was it. I was all they had. The three of them kept me very busy for a number of years, I can tell you, with all their ups and downs.

Now, thank goodness, the children are fledged more or less successfully. Amanda is a GP and single mum, Gawain is married to Bartosz and working as a junior doctor, specialising in emergency medicine, and even Jacob, the most troubled of the three, has managed to get a degree and is just about to embark on a PhD. So my life is my own again, and the only way I'll ever become involved with members of the opposite sex is on a friendship basis, with or without benefits. I think it's understandable that my heart sinks to my boots whenever Patrick announces one of his plans.

The traffic ahead of us suddenly slows down, forcing him to slam on the brakes. After a deeply unpleasant glide, during which it's uncertain the camper van will stop before it hits the lorry in front of us, it shudders to an abrupt halt and the engine stalls. Patrick makes a combined sucking and whistling noise, in the way drivers often do when they know they or their vehicle has just screwed up. We sit there, cursing the delay. Then he looks at me.

'A road trip round the coast!'

'Eh?'

'We could start in Cornwall, then make our way through Devon and Wales, spend some of the summer in Scotland, and slowly head back through Northumbria and Yorkshire. And maybe go down to Norfolk, Suffolk. You know. Lots of places. We can decide as we go. Do whatever takes our fancy. It'll be marvellous.'

'Now?'

'Next year. Spring and summer, when it's warmer and the evenings stretch out.'

'You and me?'

'Yes, why not? We've got nothing much to stay at home for. It'll be a laugh.'

'The two of us squashed together in this heap of junk for months on end?'

'There's a tent-type thing. An awning. It joins onto the side for extra space, and we can bring sun loungers and strap a couple of bikes to the back.'

'What about Lesley and my garden?'

'The kids can take care of them.'

'Amanda's rushed off her feet and Gawain will be a father by then. I can't go gallivanting off at the drop of a hat.'

'We'd never be that far away. We could come back home every now and then, to check everything's ok and pick up our post.'

'I don't think so.'

'Don't decide now. Think about it for a bit.'

'I don't need to think about it. It's a bloody terrible idea. Trapped inside this thing, playing scrabble for months on end and wishing the rain would stop so we can get out for ten minutes. Thanks, but it's a no from me.'

'There's other games besides scrabble.'

'Even so.'

I always think it's best to be clear about one's intentions. The worst thing one can do is lead someone up the garden path. But Patrick doesn't seem to appreciate my honesty. In fact, after the scrabble comment, he doesn't say another word. He fidgets about with the ancient radio, which is not digital, and the rock station he finds stutters and spits disjointed sounds into the van as though it's broadcasting from the time when the heavy metal classic it's playing has just been composed. Eventually, the lorry in front starts inching forward again and we do the same, stopping and starting until we leave the motorway. Patrick maintains his stony silence throughout.

'Are you not coming in?' I ask as I clamber down from the passenger seat.

'Nope. I'll see you around.'

His voice sounds strangely constricted, as though his mouth is jammed up with toffee, and as he drives off, I hear him rev the engine twice.

I make another cup of tea and go out into the garden again to look for Lesley, before it gets too dark. Still no sign of her. I vaguely wonder if I should post her photograph in the local Facebook group. It's always full of messages about missing cats, which are never followed up with further posts to say the moggies have been found, either dead or alive, and there are rumours about cat snatchers roaming the area. But I can't think why anyone would want to steal a cat, particularly an unrewarding one like Lesley. Perhaps they all vanish through a portal behind someone's garden fence into another dimension only accessible to animals of a feline persuasion.

When I get back inside again, I look at my phone, half expecting a follow up message from Patrick. Instead, there's a text from Jacob, sent three hours ago. That's odd. He never contacts me directly. On the rare occasions we need to communicate, we do so via his brother.

'Can you call me?'

I ring him immediately.

'What's happened?' I ask.

A maddening silence follows.

'Jacob?'

'Oh!' He says as though he's just woken up and is astonished to find me on the other end of the phone.

'What's happened?' I repeat.

'Nothing. Well, something has.'

Silence again.

'Are you alright, Jacob?'

'Er, yeah. I'm fine?'

'Is it Amanda?'

'Amanda?'

'Your sister. The one who's expecting a baby.'

'No?"

It's like trying to communicate with a ghost at a séance. I take off my glasses and polish them, furiously against the front of my cardigan.

'Please tell me why you texted, Jacob. Start with one word. Then add another and then another. Before you know where you are, you'll have constructed an entire sentence.'

'Sorry. Look. it's about the house. The one in the video.'

Not what I was expecting him to say. My heart rate increases slightly.

'Go on.'

'So, it's on Fieldgate Lane in Larchford? Round the corner from where you and Dad used to live?'

Now it's my turn to pause. Why do most of his sentences sound like questions? A lot of young people seem to speak like that. It really gets on my nerves.

'Are you still there?'

'How do you know where we used to live?'

'Dad took us there a couple of times when he picked us up from school, on our way to that country park down the road. He always wanted to go and look at your old house first. We used to stand in that crescent while he pointed out things like his bedroom window and the little drainage tunnel under the drive where he released snails he'd collected in a bucket. Stuff like that. Then we went to the park and played cricket.'

The country park didn't exist when Davey and I were kids. The other side of Fieldgate Lane was nothing but farmland with fields and woods and lanes that went on for miles.

'Thanks for telling me.'

'No problem.'

'I won't tell Aimee.'

I thought he might laugh when I said that and that if he did, it would break the tension that seemed to be fizzling across the phone from him to me. But he doesn't.

'Aunty, there's something else?'

He says this slowly and carefully, but he sounds surer of himself now.

'Such as?'

'There's something in the house you should see. I wish I'd taken it when I was there, but Aimee would have gone ballistic. If you take stuff and people find out, you can be demonetized.'

'What on earth are you talking about?'

'You don't get paid. It's like being banned.'

'No, I mean what should I see?'

I cast my mind back to the video. He can't mean the clothes or the elephant or any of the other bits scattered across the floor. Have I missed something?

'We found a photo album under the floorboards."

'An album?'

'The thing is, it has pictures with your name written underneath? Even without the writing, you'd still be able to tell it's you. You haven't changed at all. Just got older.'

'Er, thanks, Jacob.'

"I'll go back and fetch it for you."

I remember a photo album. In fact, I can see it in my mind's eye, glossy and lime green, with an outline of a frog on the cover. Tess used a cartridge pen to write people's names under each picture, in a neat cursive script. She was meticulous about that. When a person appeared for the first time she'd put their full name down, and we were the only Fyldes in the phone book. I know because I checked each time a new edition came out, and I always wished we were called something less unusual, like Robertson or Smith.

The last thing I want is for Jacob to go and fetch this document from the past. It should be left there, hidden under the floorboards, waiting to be obliterated when the house finally tumbles to the ground. Damn him. Since I watched the video to the end, I've made a massive effort to stop thinking about that summer, to shove all my memories back into the locked cupboard where they've languished for the past forty odd years. But Jacob's call has brought the house and everything in it back to the front of my mind, not just how it looks now, but also the way it was during the long, hot summer of nineteen seventy-six, with swallows diving in and out of the eaves and unruly yellow roses climbing up the trellis next to the front door.

I come to a swift decision. In order to exorcise all the bad memories, I need to stop behaving like a coward and face up to them.

'Look, Jacob,' I say. 'If you did fetch the album, when would you go?'

'I can't do this weekend. Probably, the Saturday after next?'

'I'll meet you there.'

'You can't! It's not safe. The floors are seriously sketchy? Particularly upstairs.'

'I'm not afraid of a few loose floorboards.'

'It's not just the state of the house, though. What if other people turn up? Sometimes you meet seriously dodgy characters, like druggies sleeping in the beds or gangs of teenagers spraying graffiti on the walls, or robbers.'

'People like that don't scare me. You just have to speak firmly to them.'

'Then they pull out a knife. Or a machete if you're really unlucky.'

'I'll risk it. Anyway, I'll have you to look after me.'

He sighs heavily.

'It's not right, Aunty.'

'If you don't want to be involved, I'll go on my own.'

'Jesus, don't do that. I'll can definitely make next Saturday.'

'What sort of time?'

'It's best to go around dusk, so it won't be completely dark when we first go in?'

'Four-thirty?'

'Ok. Park round the corner near the shops so it's not so obvious to the neighbours.' He hesitates. 'Is there no way I can make you change your mind?'

'No. Not going to happen.'

'Will you do one thing for me then? Or rather not do it?'

'Tell Gawain? I won't do that, don't worry.'

4. Jacob

I run loads. Miles and miles. If I skip even a single day, my body feels kind of snarly and my brainwaves get tangled.

When I was at school, I was the same. I did tons of competitive sports, too. But then I left school, went to stay with Mum at New Sunrise, and it all stopped. Bartosz got me back into it. He said it would help me get into a happier mind space. I was in a piteous state when I first moved in with them. Our branch of the church had just moved back to England from the US, and for me, things had gone from bad to worse. Then, the elders decided I was possessed with demons and needed to be purged, so they gave me a bigger dose of my usual drugs, tied me to a pole and lashed me with a metal whip. It was ferocious and by the time they'd finished, I needed stiches in my back, so someone dragged me to the nearest A&E. It was a horrible shock when I opened my eyes and saw that the doctor taking blood from me and getting ready to stitch me up was my actual brother. It was also awkward as hell, because we'd had a massive falling out eight years previously and hadn't spoken since. What a stupid coincidence! I didn't even know he'd made it as a doctor. Someone from the church took me back to my room at New Sunrise, but eventually, it dawned on me that I should leave. G and Bartosz got me out, which was brilliant, but my demons were still hanging around. Bartosz said running and exercise would help me to deal with them. He knew, because he was invalided out of the army with various injuries, as well as PTSD. Now he works out every single day in the gym he's set up in one of the outhouses, and he's buff as hell.

Today he's running with me. I think he want to know my first proper day at my new Uni went. By the time we set off, night has fallen and out here, in the middle of nowhere, it gets very dark once you leave the area around the house, so we wear head torches. We bomb through the gap in the hedge and along the track in the drizzle, splashing in and out of puddles until our legs and socks are covered in long streaks of muddy water. When the track peters out at the black barn, we turn left down the narrow footpath along the side of the big field. Since I last went this way, the field has been ploughed up and the big clods of soil are difficult to run through. Our trainers quickly get coated in mud and we slip and slide all over the place. We'd planned to go the long way round, down to the bottom of the field, up to the road, along the path in the woods on the other side, and then back to the house. But as soon as we reach the far end of the field, close to the motorway, the drizzle ratchets itself up into heavy rain. We battle on for a few minutes, then concede defeat and retrace our steps. When we reach the barn again, water is tumbling out of the sky in torrents. We go inside to shelter.

Bartosz sits on one of the abandoned hay bales and I sink down onto the concrete floor and cross my legs. These are our default positions, the ones we used to adopt during our counselling sessions. He listened to me for hours and got me to tell him stuff buried so deep I didn't even know it was there.

'So come on then, spill the beans.'

He wipes the moisture off his face with the front of his running shirt.

'What do you want to know?'

'Everything you want to tell me.'

He always says that. His voice is carefully neutral, but his bright blue eyes bore into me and pin me down. Bartosz is my brother's soulmate and I'm into girls big time, but when he looks at me like that, all the tightly wound stuff inside me starts to unfurl and it almost feels like there's some kind of sexual tension between us. At first, back when he began listening to me while I mumbled and cried, I couldn't face that stare. But even though I couldn't look at him, he understood where I was coming from me immediately. His ability to close-read me felt like a massive invasion of my privacy. The only way I could cope was by blinking and looking down at my knees. Even so, it was kind of exhilarating.

These days, I don't feel the need avoid his eyes, at least not very often. He just wants to make sure I'm alright. And I'm totally fine, I really am. I've already been into my new department once before, anyway, to do all the admin stuff and register with the library, which was where I met Aimee. I hooked up with her twice, which wasn't fine. In fact it was a big mistake, particularly the second time. But today was okay or okay-ish. I survived.

'I met the Prof.'

I only applied to this university department because Professor Gossland heads it. In the paranormal world, he's like a God. He didn't interview me for the post, because he was away in Iceland when the applications were dealt with, so today was the first time we spoke.

'It was mental. I was really nervous and I had to wait in his secretary's office until I was summoned. Pauline, that's his secretary, took me to one side and told me to go with the flow and not worry about it. I didn't get what she meant. I knew the Prof had a reputation for being a bit eccentric, but even so.'

'What happened?'

'So, I went in and we shook hands. Then he looked at his screen and started going through my details. *Jacob Field*, he said. I corrected him, told him my surname was *Fylde,* and with that, his face sort of caved in as though he'd swallowed his dentures, and he sank into his chair and stared at me for ages without saying anything. His mouth opened and closed again a couple of times, but no words came out. It was like that film where the main guy has been given something that paralyses him but keeps him awake.'

'What did you do?'

'I stood there, staring back at him, trying to act normal and go with the flow, like Pauline said. After a while, I realised he was kind of gazing through me, at nothing. His eyelids fluttered a bit and I could hear his feet tapping kind of manically on the floor under his desk. I totally lost it at that point and went to fetch Pauline. She came in, took one look at him and said he was having one of his seizures. It happens a lot, apparently. It can be triggered by all manner of things, including social anxiety, which was probably what had caused this one, she thought, although I don't see why someone like him would be anxious about meeting someone like me. I asked her what I should do. She told me to do nothing, just let him come round on his own and don't startle him. Then she left the room and shut the door behind her, really quietly. I went and sat on a chair at the other side of his desk and waited. It took forever for him to come back. I was dying to get my phone out and check my messages, but it felt rude, and anyway, I was worried my clicking might make him jump. Then I heard a running water sound and I thought he'd pissed himself. People do sometimes when they have fits.'

'Had he?'

'No, thank God. It was Pauline filling a kettle in the sink in her office.'

'What did he do when he came back to himself?'

'He rubbed his eyes as though he'd been asleep, then he acted as if nothing had happened and asked me about my PhD proposal. I went over my plan, but it was like I was doing a monologue. I expected him to interrupt me to critique my ideas, point things out or give me advice or something, but he didn't say anything. He nodded a couple of times, but I don't think he was really listening. He kept giving me funny looks, then after I'd rambled on for a bit, he suddenly interrupted me and said my hair and light eyes were very pale and was I an albino? I acted as though I wasn't offended, not that I've got anything against people with albinism. I was just a bit gutted he cared more about the way I looked than what I was saying. I told him I wasn't, and that my blondness was probably because some of my genes come from the Faroe Islands. Then he stood up and said *how charming* and suggested we round up the others and head to the pub. So that's what we did. Or rather, we went to the post-graduate bar. It's called the Seven Spoons, to commemorate a wise woman who doled out herbal remedies from a cave in a wood that used to be on the site of one of the halls of residence. You can still get to her cave through a door in the basement, which is pretty cool. I'd like to go and have a look at that. I'm rambling, now, aren't I? Sorry.'

'No worries. He sounds a bit, I don't know, unwell?'

'He has epilepsy, for sure. But I don't think he's all that bothered about it. He doesn't seem to care what people think of him, but then why should he? Anyway, it turns out he's not going to be my supervisor. He's delegated that role to one of his research fellows, a bloke called Matt Somerville, the one who interviewed me. He wrote a book about contacting the dead via computer. It was almost a best seller. I've read it.'

'Is it any good?'

'It's a great read, but totally unbelievable, unless you think someone can write a handful of sentences to a dead person in Word, leave the programme open on their laptop overnight and find responses written there by an unseen hand when they look at it again the next morning. I tried it myself a couple of times. Nothing happened.'

'You shouldn't mess with things like that.'

Bartosz is a practising catholic. He thinks paranormal phenomena are dangerous and should be left well alone.

'Anyway, Matt made it clear he thinks I'm an arse.'

'No he didn't.'

'He definitely did. He said he got his PhD in Edinburgh. I told him my sister was a medical student and did her GP training there. He looked at me as though I'd said she was a prostitute or something. Like this.'

I frown, open my mouth and transform my face into an astonished grimace.

'After a couple of pints, it was more like this.'

I squash my face down into my neck until it's so wide at the base it almost adopts the shape of a triangle, resting on a double chin that comes from nowhere, and I smile goofily. I know this is an accurate representation of Matt's face, because I've practised it in the mirror. Mimicry is my one and only super power.

Bartosz laughs.

'They all got wasted. The Prof takes the train to work because of his epilepsy, so he doesn't have to worry about being too mullered to drive, and the others live either on campus or within walking distance. I think they've got a serious drinking culture going on, which might be awkward for me. Particularly if I decide to live on campus. I won't be able to use driving as an excuse then.'

I don't drink or do anything else that might be mind-altering. Been there and done that already, in New Sunrise. Mum was instructed by the church elders to keep me drugged up and docile. She did a good job. I didn't know where I was most of the time, particularly towards the end.

'Do you want to live on campus?'

'Not sure. There are a couple of postgrad rooms going spare. One of the team, a guy called Ben, showed me them when we left the Seven Spoons. Ben's almost at the writing up stage. I don't think he likes me much, either.'

Bartosz stands up, stamps his trainers on the hard ground and peers out at the miserable evening.

'You always think people don't like you.'

'They don't, though.'

'Yes they do. Don't be daft. Anyway, come on. We'll freeze if we stay here much longer.'

We jog back to the house. I expect to see G's car parked outside, but it isn't. It niggles me when he's late home from work, even though it happens most evenings, or most mornings if he's on nights. We let ourselves into the utility room at the side of the kitchen. When Bartosz peels off his shirt I try not to look at the intricate tattoos that cover upper body and his arms. I grab a soft white towel from the basket on top of the tumble dryer and wrap myself in it.

'So, who else did you meet?'

'Two other undergrads. Jamie, who's into poltergeist acoustics, and Kirsty. Her work is loosely based around dreams and dream consciousness states. She runs a mindfulness workshop, which I wouldn't mind joining. But she's batshit crazy, too. She asked me where I lived and when I said near Fleet, she stood up, raised her glass and shouted *The Fleet.* The others did the same. Then they all clinked glasses.'

'Why did they do that?'

'They didn't say. Must be a private joke.'

'Was Aimee there?'

'Yeah.'

I walk over to the sink and turn my back to Bartosz as I wring out my socks.

'She kept saying stuff. I ignored her.'

'Stuff?'

'Little digs. She thinks I'm a wimp because I'm not into all that BDSM crap. That last time, when we back to hers, she wanted to tie me up. She's got all these different whips and torture instruments fastened to the wall above her bed. As soon as I saw them, I legged it. When I got back to my car, I had to sit there for a bit before I could drive home.'

'Blimey, Jacob. You should have said.'

'It's fine. No biggie.'

It probably would have been a biggie if I'd let her have her way with the whips, but I didn't, so it's all good.

As I let myself into to the wet room, I hear G's car pulling up outside and the anxious little bird-like creature that lives inside my chest stops fluttering. Later, we sit round the kitchen table, eating Bartosz's signature chicken casserole with Polish dumplings and listening to the wind and the rain lashing against windows. G is five years older than me, but smaller and much darker. Our faces are almost identical, though, so you can tell we're brothers. I watch as he shovels food into his mouth in silence, hunching his shoulders over his plate. He was stuck in a hold-up for an hour and a half on the motorway, just before our exit, within easy walking distance of the house. When Bartosz and I were out on our run, if we'd climbed up the embankment that separates the field from the motorway, we'd probably have seen him in his car, banging his head against the steering wheel. But once he's addressed his hunger, his grumpiness vanishes and he wants to know everything about my day. I repeat it all, but I don't include the part about Aimee and her whips, because G looks exhausted and I really don't want to upset him for no reason. What he really wants to know is whether or not I'm moving out.

'What did you think of the postgrad rooms?'

'Bleak, but they always are until you fill the shelves with books and stick photos on the walls, aren't they? They were bigger than most undergrad rooms I've seen, and they have their own bathrooms. The downside is they've put them on the bottom floor of one of the first-year halls, so the rent is cheap, but you have to act as a warden and stop everything from kicking off among the freshers.'

'Sounds pretty crap to me. How long's the drive?'

'About an hour and forty minutes.'

'That's less journey time than when you were at King's. How often would you need to be there?'

'Probably one or two days per week, if that. You can access most of the library contents electronically and they have zoom meetings. Also, I'm supposed to be travelling a lot.'

'And the other people in your department are all either nutjobs or alcoholics, or both.'

'They're probably not that bad when you get to know them.'

'They're not as nice as us, though.'

My brother was like this when I first went to King's. He said I'd find it hard living in London on my own, after everything. To be fair, he had a point, so I based myself here with G and Bartosz. It's worked out great. I got a job at a local supermarket and saved up to buy a little, second-hand car, and I joined a seriously good cricket club on the outskirts of Guildford. Then I went to university, met loads of girls and got a first. Ok, so I'm still here, at the age of twenty-four, but I pay rent and I help with the housework, and I'm out loads, so I don't think I cramp their style. And I'm their lodger, not their child. Also, there are often other people staying in the house, too, ex-soldiers with PTSD, who use the place as a refuge until they get their lives back together, with a lot of help from Bartosz, so I'm not exactly playing gooseberry.

Even so, I'm not sure they'll want me or anyone else around once their actual, proper baby arrives. Bartosz is going to apply for a parental order and then, because he and G are married and Bartosz is the sperm donor, so is genetically related to the baby, they'll become its official parents. The legalities are sorted, the nursery is finished, they've bought tons of clothes and other bits of kit. They're super-stoked about it all. If it was me, I'd be bricking it. They seem to have forgotten the state Amanda was in after Tam was born. She turned up at the house one morning when G and Bartosz were out. I opened the door to find my sister standing there, her face all shadowy and kind of pursed up. She shoved her way past me, carrying a large holdall. No sign of the baby.

'In the car,' my sister barked. 'She's just gone to sleep. I've left her out of earshot, so I won't hear her when she wakes up.'

Amanda handed me her car keys. She'd parked miles away from the house, right by the gap in the hedge that leads to the lane.

'I can't do it anymore. I haven't slept for three nights. Or is it four?'

With that, she dragged her bag along the hall and up the stairs, found an empty guest room on the top floor and disappeared inside. I ran out to the car. Tam was fast asleep, her dummy, a prop the pregnant Amanda had declared disgusting and an indicator of bad parenting, hanging jauntily out of the side of her mouth, Bogart style. She stank like a farmyard of cow pats and her eyes popped open as soon as I started to detach the car seat. I carried her inside and took her up to Amanda.

I tapped on her door.

'She's awake,' I said.

Amanda didn't answer, so I tapped again. Then she stuck her head round the door.

'Sort her out, then! You're not totally incapable, are you?'

'I've never looked after a baby before.'

'Neither had I. Everything you need is in the car. Deal with it.'

This was back when I'd only just left the church. The scars on my back were still tight and itchy, and a whole load of much worse things had happened to me than being saddled with a baby. So looking after Tam didn't faze me, and anyway, it wasn't as though I had anything else much to do. I took her for long walks, wearing her on my front in a sling. She would fall asleep, her gingery little head lolling against my chest. I'd stay out for as long as I could between feeds to maximise Amanda's rest time and I'd gaze at the sky through the branches of the trees, which were just starting to green up, trying to see patterns in the gaps between the leaves, hoping they would tell me my future, like tea leaves in a cup.

G and Bartosz think parenthood will be easier for them than it was for Amanda. Perhaps it will be. This baby will have two parents instead of one, and in any case, G is one of those people that everything turns out right for, however much he tries to muck it up along the way. And he's experienced at handling babies, too, partly from his job, but also because of me. He was five when I appeared in the world. Mum ran off with Pastor Warren as soon as I was born and G kind of took her place.

Now he's eating caramel cheesecake with a fork.

'This is sumptuous,' he says. 'I haven't eaten all day.'

He catches me looking at him. A familiar signal flashes between us, a quantum of shared understanding. Then we both blink and look away.

5. Michael

Michael puts his pyjamas under his pillow and hangs his dressing gown from the hook on the door of the ensuite bathroom. Several months ago, he told everyone in the department he would never spend another night at 33 Talbot Way. Until now he's kept his word, but here he is, in the room known as the spotty bedroom, with its white and blue polka dot curtains and matching duvet cover.

In paranormal circles, the semi-detached ex-council house in Talbot Way is in competition with a mock Tudor vicarage in Lancashire and a wooden chalet in a holiday park near Cromer for the title of Fifth Most Haunted house in England. Back in the eighties, two girls, aged eleven and thirteen, slept in what is now the spotty bedroom. Reports by apparently reputable researchers claimed the girls had woken at exactly the same time most nights to a kerfuffle caused by Barbie dolls and pieces of Lego removing themselves from a shelving unit near the door and flying through the air to the window at the opposite side of the room, where they plummeted vertically to the ground, in a manner that would be impossible to achieve had they been thrown by human hands. On a later date, another occupant of the same room was supposedly terrified out of his wits one night when a radiator wrenched itself away from the wall and tipped over onto the floor, flooding the carpet with water.

Two years ago, the house was purchased by the Department of Paranormal Psychology at Michael's university, under his direction, for research purposes. Glancing around at his surroundings, he doesn't feel so much as a frisson of fearful anticipation. The muted pastel seascapes on the walls have never once raised themselves off their hooks and tumbled onto his bed, and neither the wicker basket nor the chest of drawers have ever shifted by as much as a centimetre in all the nights he has slept here. In fact, nothing that could be described as otherworldly has ever happened to Michael either here or anywhere else, apart perhaps for the appearance and subsequent disappearance of Anteros. But then, Michael sees

Anteros as a part of himself, a being who, therefore, can be categorised as a natural, rather than a supernatural phenomenon.

The awful truth, the thing Michael describes to himself as his shocking secret, is that his belief in the paranormal vanished a long time ago. This means he has to do a great deal of acting, because it would damage his reputation horribly if people learned he'd crossed the floor and become a sceptic.

The house contains three other bedrooms, all smaller than the spotty room. One of them is just about big enough to accommodate a queen-sized double bed, but the other two are singles. Tonight, they will all be occupied. Ben and Jamie are here, hoping to capture and record more of the bangs, taps and other acoustic phenomena that occur in the house on a regular basis, as well as anything else that might crop up. And the new PhD student is also in residence. As the newbie, he has to sleep in the smallest and least popular room, which is rarely occupied. Back in the sixties this bedroom belonged to teenage girl who became possessed by negative entities that told her to hang herself, or so the story goes. It may be that the room just seems creepy because of its long and narrow shape and the fact that it only has a small window at one end, or it might have something to do with the mysterious smell, similar but not quite the same as human sweat, that accumulates in there when the window is kept closed for long periods of time.

Michael is much too old and too far gone to lie to himself. He's only here at Talbot Way this weekend because of Jacob. When the boy walked into his office and introduced himself, he triggered one of the professor's episodes, because his surname turned out to be *Fylde*, not *Field*. It was a monumental shock, but the resulting seizure probably lasted no more than two or three minutes, and when he came round again, Jacob was sitting in the chair opposite, looking down at the floor and not at his phone, which he'd had the decency not to switch on. He had a little furrow between his pale eyebrows that made him look stern, severe almost, as though he were an aesthete with higher principals than most other mere mortals. Michael had tried and failed to align the boy's features with those of other Fyldes he'd known in the distant past. It's an unusual name, after all. There can't be many of them knocking about. But there was nothing he could pin down, not really.

For a very long time, Michael has experienced the truth of the cliché about policemen, doctors and particularly his students, becoming younger as he gets older. The other day, for example, the guard on his morning train appeared to be a child of around twelve. Jacob is a perfect example of this phenomenon. The boy's CV states that he is twenty-four, which is very young compared to himself, obviously. But he looks a lot younger even than that. On a shelf in his living room, Michael has a book that contains paintings of angels. When he got home after meeting Jacob for the first time, he looked through it to remind himself which of these heavenly beings the youngster resembled so very closely. It turned out to be the angel in L'Annonce aux Bergers by Comerre, the pale and youthful messenger from God, who glows so brightly the shepherds are compelled to cover their eyes.

Ben orders KFC on his phone and the team assembles around the table in the dining area to eat it. Michael decants his chips and popcorn chicken onto a plate and fetches a knife and fork, but the others use their hands and eat directly from the cartons. Furtively, as Michael watches Jacob adding barbecue sauce to his zinger burger and then alternating between eating and licking his fingers, he indulges in a little fantasy in which the boy really *is* an angel who has just descended to earth and is encountering his first takeaway food. As he's thinking this, Jacob suddenly looks up at him and flushes slightly when he realises he's being stared at. Adorable, Michael thinks and he continues to stare.

Jacob turns away from him and looks for something else to focus on. Eventually, his eyes settle on the department's sophisticated recording equipment, which Ben and Jamie have just brought in and left in a heap on the dining room floor.

'Do you often pick things up?' Jacob asks them both.

'All the time,' Ben says. 'Even when we don't actually hear anything ourselves. Although we do hear noises sometimes.'

'Like what?'

'It's probably best if we don't tell you,' Jamie says. 'Then, if you hear anything it will have more validity because you haven't been preconditioned to expect something specific.'

Jamie sounds defensive, Michael thinks. He doesn't like being interrogated by the new boy.

'It always starts after everyone's gone to sleep,' Ben adds.

'So not at a specific time as such?'

'It seems to be related to what we're doing rather than the actual time. If anyone's still up at one in the morning, say, there'll be nothing. But if everyone's gone to bed and the lights are out by midnight, it will probably start soon after.'

'If the equipment picks something up that nobody hears, how do you know it's not an artefact created by the recording process?'

'Because we're not idiots,' Jamie says. 'We've tested different equipment here and still recorded sounds, and we've also set the up same equipment up in different places and got nothing.'

'What places?'

'Erm…our student flats, the Professor's office, and I tried it at my parents' house once,' Ben says. 'I got a single loud tap one night, but we decided it was probably the cat coming in through the cat flap. Also, the knocks we record here have peculiar acoustic properties, whereas the bang at my parent's house home didn't.'

'You mean sound waves that seem to go backwards? I've read about those.'

'Something like that. The recordings have a completely different signature from ones you'd get if you knocked on the walls yourself.'

'What was your first degree, Jacob?' Jamie asks, cutting into the conversation with an awkward change of subject. Michael remembers Jamie asking Jacob about his qualifications when they were in the Seven Spoons. He must have forgotten.

'Neuroscience and Psychology.'

'Where?'

'King's, London.'

'And what's your thesis meant to be about, again?'

He's already asked him that, too.

'Psychological aspects of poltergeist phenomena. Do people who experience poltergeist activity have common characteristics, are they fantasy prone, do they score higher than average on tests for psychic ability? That type of thing. That's the starting point, anyway. I've got some vague ideas about quantum theory and the nature of time that I'd like to develop, too. If I can.'

He sounds incredibly enthusiastic. Long may it last. He also seems completely impervious to Jamie's veiled hostility, but maybe he's being guarded or simply polite.

'Are you psychic then?' Jamie continues.

'I don't think so. No more than anyone else.'

'Have you ever experienced anything?'

'Some weird stuff went down at home a few years ago. Noises coming from the garden and the road outside that me and my brother couldn't explain, but which kind of made sense because of other things that were going on in our lives at the same time. That was partly what got me interested in the first place.'

Jamie leans back in his chair, throws his head back and laughs. Jacob doesn't join in. He doesn't even smile. Michael watches Jacob as he holds Jamie's gaze until Jamie is forced to lean forward and look down at his plate. The boy's no pushover, then. Interesting. Michael would love to hear more about Jacob's experiences, but he doesn't feel he can pursue the topic without making himself seem overly inquisitive, outing himself as it were.

An uncomfortable silence follows.

'I've never heard a thing in this house. Not a sausage,' Michael says, eventually.

Everyone waits for him to expand on this. He feels them watching him, but he has nothing more to say on the subject. He puts down his knife and fork, opens a can of Timothy Taylor's Landlord, pours it into a glass and takes an initial, tentative sip.

'Lovely,' he says.

By midnight, Michael and his students are all in their beds. At ten past one, Michael wakes suddenly from a dream about foxes running about in a dark alleyway, making metallic clattering sounds as they crash into dustbins. He sits up in bed and runs his hand through his sparse, but fluffy hair. Then he hears footsteps running along the landing past his room towards the stairs, bare feet padding lightly against the polished oak floor boards. He goes downstairs and finds the others in the living room. Ben and Jamie are checking the audio equipment, whereas Jacob is staring at the outside wall with his hands on his hips as though he's trying to see through the brickwork. The boy is wearing shorts and a sleeveless top, and his long milky-white limbs light up the dim room. It was worth getting out of bed for this spectacle alone, Michael thinks. He knows he should chide himself for such thoughts, or at least feel embarrassed by them, but he doesn't. Sorry creatures like the one he's become have to take their pleasures where they can. And it's not as though he's perving over Jacob. He's just admiring his beauty.

Jacob looks over his shoulder when he hears Michael walk into the room.

'Did you hear it, Professor?' He asks.

'I'm not sure. I was dreaming about metal bins being banged into, but they're all plastic now. Then I heard you lot running down the hall.'

'There was a huge racket going on, as though someone was dragging furniture across the floor,' Jacob says. 'I thought someone had broken in. But there was nobody here when we came down, and I don't think anything's moved.'

'We've heard sounds like that before, but nowhere near as loud,' Jamie says, looking pointedly at Jacob, who doesn't seem to notice.

'The equipment's picked it all up,' Ben says. He sounds excited.

'Doesn't mean it was paranormal,' Jamie replies.

Jacob goes over to the sofa and tries to move it. It hardly budges and when it does, any sounds it might make are muffled by the thick carpet. He goes over to the dining area and gives the table, which is on a laminate floor, a good shove. It does make a heavy, dragging noise, but once moved, marks are visible on the floor where the legs previously stood, suggesting it had been stationary before. Ben resets the equipment and they all troop back upstairs.

Twenty minutes later, Michael hears loud banging from the direction of the kitchen, as though someone is trying to break in. This time, when he gets downstairs, only Jacob is there, standing in the kitchen, hugging himself and peering through the pane of frosted glass in the kitchen door.

'It's not just me, is it?' He asks.

'I can hear it too,' Michael says. Then he repeats the same sentence twice, because he can't quite believe it. The noises are difficult to describe. Dull thuds come closest perhaps, loud and clearly audible, but muffled, as though they emanate not from outside but from somewhere within the fabric of the building. Michael and Jacob both watch as the disturbance gradually moves from the area around the kitchen door and shifts along the outside wall, before ending up in the dining room, above the fireplace.

Then it stops.

'It's like a noise that feels real, but could be more inside your head than out of it?' Jacob suggests tentatively.

Michael nods. That's exactly what it's like.

'And you can tell it doesn't have the same trajectory as normal knocks. It kind of starts off quiet, get louder and then tips away from you.'

Jacob's voice fades away uncertainly, and the rapping begins again. It moves back along the wall towards the kitchen. At first, it consists of individual sounds, separated by a few seconds. These are soon replaced by double knocks and once they reach the kitchen door, the sounds become clustered into threes, in groups of nine, separated by gaps. Knock, knock, knock, they go. Surely some conscious agent must be responsible. Jacob seems to agree, because he dashes to the door, unlocks it and runs outside. The sounds stop immediately, as though whatever was causing them was trapped in the walls of the building and has now escaped.

When he comes in again, Jacob's feet are wet and droplets of water are making rat tails of his curly blonde hair.

'It's pouring down out there.'

'I can see that.'

'There's no sign of anyone. I ran down the side of the house and onto the street. It's deserted. No cars. Nobody running away. No lights on in any of the other houses. Nothing.'

He locks the door and they wait for a few minutes to see if the knocking will start again. It doesn't.

'I think it's gone,' Jacob says eventually.

'Maybe it will all kick off again as soon as we fall asleep,' Michael suggests. As he heads upstairs, he wonders why Ben and Jamie didn't hear anything this time.

The next morning, they all wake up late. Michael comes downstairs first and has a quick look around. On the rug in front of the fireplace is a teetering tower of books. They definitely weren't there last night when he and Jacob came down to investigate the second set of noises. He counts them and finds there are seven in total, piled one on top of the other, in an arrangement that should be unstable but isn't, with big hardbacks balanced on top of small paperbacks, as though someone has taken care to place them all in the exact positions that would prevent the stack from toppling over.

The discussion that takes place over the breakfast cereal is lively.

'Do you sleepwalk, Jacob?' Jamie asks.

'Er, I used to occasionally, when I was a kid. Not now, though. Not as far as I know, anyway. Why?'

'I don't know, Jacob. All this activity in one night. It's never been as crazy as this.'

'We've had busy nights before,' Ben says.

'Not towers of books,' Jamie insists.

'You think it was me?'

'We can't rule it out, can we? You could have brought the books with you and faked it for all we know. On the other hand, you might have been sleepwalking.'

He holds up his fingers to put imaginary inverted commas around the word *sleepwalking*.

'If that's the case, there should be video footage of me wandering about.'

'Let's have a look, shall we?'

Jamie gets up, disconnects the video recorder from the rest of the apparatus arranged around the room and puts it on the table. He's sure there will be something, that Jacob will be caught faking paranormal phenomena. Michael crosses his fingers under the breakfast table and prays to an unknown god that this won't turn out to be the case. He watches with the others, as all the visual footage taken in the living room the previous night speeds before their eyes. One of the cameras was focused on the area of the living room in front of the fireplace. They see themselves enter the room, then a little later, they watch as Jacob reappears, stands staring at the area around the fireplace, disappears in the direction of the kitchen and then returns a minute or so later and makes wet footprints on the laminate floor. After that, nothing happens until five minutes past six, when the pile of books shows up all at once, between one frame and the next, in an empty room.

'Not me then,' Jacob says.

Phew.

'A pile of books can't just appear like that,' Jamie says.

'It's happened in other poltergeist cases,' Michael says. 'If you believe the testimony of witnesses, that is. I'm not sure it's ever been caught on camera, though. Apart from faked rubbish on social media.'

'Jacob could have interfered with the recording – switched it off, put the books there and then switched it back on again.'

'Anyone else could have done the same,' Jacob says. 'You could have done it, Jamie. To set me up.'

Jacob smirks and shakes his head in apparent disbelief at Jacob's suggestion.

Michael wonders if Jamie would do that. Would he really be so spiteful and insecure that he'd want to make Jacob look like a trickster? He can't have done, though, surely? Every time frame of the footage is accounted for. There are no missing minutes or seconds that might have shown someone entering the room and stacking up the books and the equipment records any stoppages. They all go to look at the wall of bookshelves in the living room, opposite the fireplace, which houses a library of heavy tomes, lighter paperbacks and journal issues, all featuring various aspects of the paranormal. The books are jammed closely together, and there are no odd gaps to suggest some of them may have been removed. The stack consists of old paperbacks by Jackie Collins, together with a large cookery book from the seventies, a medical encyclopaedia and a rather battered, coffee table-sized book containing a collection of large and graphic photographs of naked men in what Michael suspects are homoerotic poses, masquerading as art. He decides to sneak the book into his overnight bag so he can have a proper look later.

'Where the hell did they come from?' Jamie says, as he opens the recipe book on a page with a larger than life photograph of a prawn cocktail, complete with lurid pink Marie Rose sauce.

Ben picks up a paperback and sniffs it. 'Smells mouldy,' he says.

He passes it to Jacob, who also sniffs it, then nods in agreement.

'Maybe they've been in the house all the time,' Michael suggests. 'Stored away in a hidden cupboard somewhere.'

Nobody attempts to explain how the books could have made their way out of their putative hiding place, wherever it might have been, and nobody apart from Michael touches the book with the men. Eventually, they turn their attention back to the noises and soon discover there is nothing to distinguish between the frequency signatures generated by the thumping and furniture-dragging sounds.

'It looks as though they were both the same thing,' Ben says.

Jacob shakes his head. 'They definitely sounded different to me. The first time, I genuinely thought someone was moving furniture around downstairs. There were all these long, dragging noises. The second lot were shorter and more staccato, like knocks or bumps.'

'Or someone could have been outside making that last set of sounds,' Jamie suggests.

'You mean I brought along an accomplice and they stood out there in the rain, until they thought the time was right, then they banged on the wall? Why would I even *do* that?'

'I don't know. You tell me.'

'We've recorded similar sounds before,' Ben says.

'I ran out of the kitchen door when the knocking was still going on. You can see that from the video footage. I didn't even stop to put my trainers on. I went like a bat out of hell, down the path at the side of the house and out onto the pavement. There was nothing. Nobody.'

'He did run out very quickly,' Michael says. 'But as soon as he opened the kitchen door it stopped.'

'We've done loads of experiments where we've banged on the outside walls with all sorts of implements - garden spades, mallets, baseball bats. The recording signatures look completely different when we do that,' Ben says. 'You know that, Jamie.'

Jamie scratches his head. 'Yeah, but, look. I don't know. Something doesn't add up. Particularly about the books.'

'Well, it wasn't me,' Jacob says. 'And when I came down the second time, everything felt really uncanny valley. It's difficult to explain, but I was seriously freaked out. I know that sounds lame.'

'Early hours of the morning. Everything feels strange then,' Michael says.

They all nod at him, respectfully, Jacob included.

When they leave, Jacob offers Michael a lift back to his house. He says it's on his way.

'Were you really scared?' Michael asks him when they drive off.

'Yes. But I'm kind of used to it. The house I live in can get a bit creepy, too, sometimes.'

'Is it old?'

'I think it was built in the mid nineteenth century, but all the rooms have been modernized, so it doesn't have a traditional haunted house vibe. It's more that it's very isolated, at the end of a winding track, surrounded by trees. No neighbours to hear you scream, that type of thing.'

'Do you live with your parents?'

'With my big brother and his husband. My parents are dead.'

Michael wants to ask him much more about his family set up, but again he fears his curiosity might come across as morbid and unhealthy in some way. It's ok, though, because Jacob is happy to volunteer more information without being asked. He tells Michael all about his brother and Bartosz and about the house and the war veterans. He describes the way his brother thinks the building is full of invisible but harmless spirits of the dead, and of people from the future, some of whom aren't even alive yet, and he tells him how they were both sure they heard the sound of a car crashing in the lane outside on the night their mother died after being in a similar-sounding accident.

'Maybe we should do a few investigations at your gaffe,' Michael says.

Jacob smiles. 'That would be so cool. I'd love to borrow the acoustic equipment and see if it picks anything up.'

'You'd have to get into Jamie's good books, first.'

It's still chucking it down outside and the windscreen wipers click quietly as they move from side to side. Jacob is no boy racer.

He drives carefully and takes no risks. But Michael isn't in a hurry. He looks at Jacob's exquisite profile, made stern by his aquiline nose and his slender neck. What a weekend, he thinks. Not only did he spend another night at 33 Talbot Way, after saying he would never do so again, because he didn't believe in ghosts anymore, but he heard the same inexplicable noises as everyone else, and a pile of books appeared from nowhere in the living room while everyone was sleeping. And to cap it all, he's being driven home by a luminous angel.

Michael knows he's still lost and that he will continue to sit at his desk in the Department of Paranormal Psychology doing little more than signing grant application forms and staring into space from early morning until late afternoon. And each evening, when he goes home, he'll still stand in his front room, trapped alone between the four walls like a fly in a spider's web, wondering what the hell to do with himself, and every night he'll still go to bed too early and wake up sobbing because the space next to him is cold and empty when it should be filled by Reese, who was forced to spend the last few minutes of his life alone and bleeding out in the car park at Woking Station, after being attacked by a gang of homophobic yobs, because Michael hadn't wanted to go into London to see the musical Reese was so enthusiastic about.

Yes, Michael thinks, it will take more than the appearance of Jacob in his life and one night of interesting events, whatever their potential significance, to drag him out of his mental quagmire. But he can feel a faint quickening sensation in his belly and a flickering inside his head. Maybe the boy's youthfulness and strange charisma represent a source of energy that can be tapped into, a conduit through which his spark can be re-ignited and all the things lying dormant inside Michael's psyche can be brought back to life, things like his sense of purpose and his awareness of unearthly beings like spirits or ghosts, or perhaps even Anteros. Imagine that.

6. Jacob

When I was a kid, Aunty Susan freaked me out so much, with her shiny red lipstick and her loud, snappy voice, I could hardly bring myself to speak to her. Usually, G had to act as an intermediary between us. She'd ask me a question and my brother would answer on my behalf. If I was feeling brave, I'd nod or shake my head in agreement. If I wasn't feeling brave, I'd press my face into my brother's side and stay superglued to him until she became exasperated by my behaviour and prized us apart. She said I was like a ventriloquist's doll. Now I'm several inches taller than my brother and almost twice as big as Aunty Susan, but I still can't stand up to her, which is why I've agreed to escort her into a dangerous building.

When I get to the row of shops, only a single, very tight parking space is left. I manage to reverse into it in a single, slick manoeuvre, which I decide to take as a good omen. I'm late and in a mild panic in case Aunty Susan thinks I'm not coming and has gone ahead without me. But as I'm parking, I spot her clambering out of her silver mini and putting up a large golfing umbrella. The fluorescent lights from the nail bar across the pavement briefly illuminate her ginger curls, which look both bouffant and rigid. She's all lipsticked up as usual, and her face has that immovable, determined look, the one G, Amanda and I have come to dread. One of my schoolfriends once pointed out that Aunty is a dead ringer for Lucille Ball. I didn't know who she was, but when I looked her up, I was gobsmacked. Aunty S is older than Lucy was at the time of her shows, and is probably way more hardcore than her when it comes to not taking crap from anyone, but they both have the same outraged stare and apparently accidental comic timing.

Once she's finished embracing me in a contactless hug and aiming air kisses upwards in the direction of my face, like a cartoon goldfish blowing bubbles, I have another go at dissuading her from going ahead with the expedition.

'Why don't you stay in the car and let me fetch the album on my own?'

'It's not just the album, Jacob. I want to see the place for myself.'

There must be a shedload of stuff she isn't saying about this house and what it means to her. But I don't ask and she doesn't volunteer any further information. It's difficult to hold a proper conversation, anyway, because it's pissing down again. For the past fortnight the rain has barely stopped. Flood warnings are in place at locations miles away from rivers and canals, and lakes of water have accumulated at random low points on the roads, taking drivers by surprise. G's alpacas have been moved into the utility room because their enclosure is waterlogged. You can't get to the washing machine now without having your neck nuzzled or your legs nipped, depending on who you are and whether they like you or not, which really means whether you're G or not.

To say I've got misgivings about going into this house again is the biggest understatement of the century. The place was close to derelict last time I was here, but now, after all this rain, it's only going to be worse. We run down the road with the shops and turn to the right, past Fieldgate Crescent, then a bit further. It doesn't take long, but by the time we get to the house, my hair and my hoodie are sopping wet. Aunty Susan on the other hand, is more or less dry and snug inside her puffer jacket, under the shelter of her umbrella.

'Do you not own a coat, Jacob?'

'Not really.'

'I'll buy you one. A nice raincoat with a belt. A Burberry if you like.'

'It's okay. Thanks, though.'

Please don't, I plead silently. I'd look like a tall, skinny version of a policeman in a nineteen thirties crime novel. *The Beanpole Detective.* Aunty S has a habit of buying me and my brother what she thinks is desirable clothing, like beige thermal socks and old-man cardigans with toggles for buttons, and one time, after she'd been on a trip to Norway, bright blue peaked caps with *Oslo* written on them in rainbow letters. She usually gets the size right, but little else. G wore his cap once, at a fancy dress party. He was dressed like a waitress at TGI Fridays and he told everyone the letters didn't stand for the capital of Norway, but were an acronym for something camp and outrageous. I can't remember what.

One good thing about the rain, though, is that the neighbours are all inside tucked up behind closed curtains, and passers-by are non-existent, so nobody sees us go through the gate. As we enter the kitchen, I reach into my bag and pull out the two head torches Bartosz and I wore on our run. I switch them both on and hand one to Aunty Susan.

'Put it round your head. Then you'll be able to see, but still have your hands free.'

'Ooh, how exciting!'

Aunty Susan clucks and chuckles as she arranges the thick, black band of elastic around her hair-do.

The beams emitted by the torches are incredibly bright, offering as much, if not more, illumination than the lights in the house would have done, if the electricity had been switched on.

'Take it really slowly and watch where you put your feet. The floors are sketchy as hell, even downstairs. And there's tons of rubbish scattered about. Be careful you don't trip.'

I escort her through all the downstairs rooms and wait while she carefully inspects everything. She doesn't mention that she's been here before, but I already know that from the photo album. Some of the pictures were clearly taken in this house. Now it looks as though she's trying to square the battered furniture, the items thrown around the place and the general squalor with her memory of the rooms as they were when she was last here.

'What do you think?' I ask her.

'It's just a sad old wreck of a place, nothing like it was back then. Could be anywhere. And what's that smell?'

'Damp and mould, probably. We should be wearing masks, in case there are spores.'

'And something sweet and rotten. It reminds me of the time we had mice in the space above the ceiling in Whitehall. The pest control company thought it would be a good idea to chuck poison at them through a vent. It killed the mice alright, but nobody could access their bodies to get rid of them. The stench was terrible. All we could do was wait for it to go away. Took ages.'

'It could be anything. Rats, mice, a cat even. Aimee's seen dead cats in other houses. I don't remember noticing it last time I was here, whatever it is.'

'I can't recall what the house smelled like in the seventies. Not downstairs anyway. But of course, when I was here, I was always in the attic. My friend's room was very aromatic. She loved perfumes. When we were around twelve, it was all musk and patchouli oil, and that gloopy, orangey stuff. What was it called? Aqua Manda, that's it. Then we graduated onto more sophisticated fragrances like Rive Gauche.'

'I can't imagine you being into that kind of thing, Aunty.'

'We used to squirt it over our wrists and in our hair. God knows what other people thought when we came within smelling distance.'

I already know about her friends. I've seen the pictures of them in the album. I even know their names. But I don't say.

'Are you sure you still want to go upstairs? Wouldn't you rather wait for me down here? I'll only be a minute.'

'Absolutely not! I'm not coming all this way without seeing the bedrooms.'

I'm not surprised, but I sigh anyway.

'Well, look, I'll go first. Stay close to me. Hold onto one of the straps of my backpack.'

'Will do. Lead on Macduff.'

'Who?'

'Never mind.'

Two weeks ago, the stairs and the landing were spongy underfoot, but basically intact. This time the stair carpet squelches as we tread on it, and water seeps upwards and soaks our shoes. It's like wading through a bog.

'Don't worry,' she says when I comment on this. 'Just keep going.'

But when I get to the top of the stairs, I halt abruptly and Aunty Susan slams into my back. Her head hits the area between my shoulder blades. She bounces back and almost loses her balance and falls, dragging me with her. But she clings onto my rucksack and manages to right herself. I grab the banister rail. If we'd looked up when we were walking through the downstairs hallway, we might have spotted the long gap in the ceiling and been forewarned. As it is, I came very close to crashing through the hall floor onto the dining room table directly below. The huge chasm stretches ahead, all the way to the end of the landing. I look up and my torch illuminates narrow rivulets of water pouring down the walls from the attic rooms.

'We can't go any further.'

'Let me see.'

Aunty Susan shoves her head under my arm.

'There's still a bit of floorboard over there on the left.' She points her head to provide the necessary illumination. 'We could sidle along with our backs to the wall.'

'We really couldn't.'

'*I* could, with my tiny feet.'

'There's nothing to hold onto. And anyway, God knows what state the attics will be in after all this rain. There were already big holes in the roof last time we were up there.'

She ignores me and cautiously starts making her way down the corridor. 'Here's the source of the stink!' She shouts.

I creep up so I'm standing just behind her and I look over her shoulder. A large chest of drawers has fallen through the gap in the ceiling from the attic floor and landed on a small dog with scruffy white and black fur. All you can see are its head and its front legs. I wonder how it took for the poor thing to die and whether we'd have found it alive and been able to rescue it if we'd come last weekend. Beyond the drawers and the dog, there's nothing but an aerial view of the downstairs hall. I tell Aunty S we definitely can't go any further. She curses a few times, but she seems to accept defeat and she follows me back down the dodgy stairs. But as soon as we get to the bottom, she dashes back outside into the rain, without stopping to pick up her umbrella, which she'd deposited just inside the back door. I realise what she's planning to do, and I follow her quickly, my trainers skating over the moss-covered paving stones.

To the left of the kitchen window is recess with an ornate metal staircase that provides direct access to the balcony outside one of the attic rooms. It might have been intended as a decorative fire escape or perhaps the occupants of the second floor had been lodgers at one time, and the former owner had wanted them to be able to reach their own rooms without having to traipse through the rest of the house. Whatever its original function, the staircase has seen better days. Most of its orange paint has peeled off and the rain-soaked steps look slick and lethal. By the time I reach her, Aunty Susan has already managed to climb half way to the top. I try to grab her round the waist. She resists and the only reason we don't fall backwards together is because she has a tight grip on the stair rail. She breaks free, recovers her balance and continues to climb. I don't attempt to hold onto her again, but I stay close behind, so that if she loses her footing, she'll land on top of me and I'll break her fall. Hopefully.

Suddenly, everything goes to crap. The bolts attaching the staircase to the wall must have worked themselves loose over the years. Several have obviously fallen out completely, and when we're almost at the top, the final few give way. The entire staircase swings outwards from the wall. Each time we try to take another step it sways back and forth, like a dangerous playground ride.

'Let's just stop for a second,' I say.

She ignores me or she can't hear me because of the rain and the ominous creaking. Either way, she keeps on climbing, so I'm forced to follow. At the top is a balcony. It must have had railings at some point, but they're long gone now, and the space in front of this room on the upper floor of the house isn't much more than a small platform, fully exposed to the wind and as slippery underfoot as an ice rink. Aunty S jumps onto it and slides gracefully into the room beyond, through the doorway, which is accessible, thanks to vandals who have smashed the French windows to such an extent that no glass remains in them at all. I leap up the staircase, trip over the threshold and tumble into the room, my fall broken by the ancient, rotting clothes scattered across the floor.

'I can't believe we're doing this,' I say.

'What's your problem?'

She turns to face me and throws a look of bemused innocence in my direction. I'm getting seriously annoyed with her now.

'The problem is, Aunty, we've nearly broken our necks at least twice. And the even bigger problem is, we have to go down again the same way. And going down is going to be harder than going up now the staircase has worked itself loose. There's a serious possibility we'll lose our footing or the entire thing will fall away, taking us with it.'

'Stop catastrophising, Jacob. You always take the dimmest view of life.'

'I'm not. I don't.'

Now I sound like a five year old, trying to defend myself after being told off for defiling her immaculate living room carpet by walking over it in muddy trainers. If G was here instead of me, and had said the exact same words, she wouldn't have accused him of catastrophising. She'd have agreed with him, and in any case, she's got no right to critique me like that after I've put myself out like this just to accompany her into a death trap. I force myself to take a deep breath. Never mind, I tell myself. Rise above it. It doesn't matter. Right now, getting her out of here safely is more important than winning an argument about my negative attitude.

'Why don't you go and stand in the doorway, while I root around for the diary?' I suggest.

She takes no notice, marches into the centre of the room, drops onto her knees and begins rifling through the piles of clothing and all the other bits of rain-soaked seventies tat.

'There's still a bit of a perfume smell. After all this time,' she says.

'Watch where you put your hands. There might be rats under all that lot.'

'Courage mon petit.'

'Jesus, Aunty!'

'Look, Jacob,' she whispers, encouragingly. 'Let's find the album, then we can leave. Before you know it, we'll be back in our cars. I'll treat you to a pub meal on the way home if you like. There's a nice place off the dual carriageway. The Roebuck. Do you know it? They do rather good home-made pies. Ginormous portions and lashings of gravy and mashed potato.'

I'm still close to losing my temper big time, but I think I can sense a hint of artificial brightness in her voice now, which makes me wonder if her apparent confidence is actually bravado. I manage to stop myself telling her that I don't want a mega-large slice of pie, thanks very much, and I crawl over to the long gap in the floorboards under the bed, where I found the album last time I was here. When I look down, water drips into my eyes from my hair. Almost blind, I reach into the hole and try not to think about the rats I've just attempted to scare Aunty S with. The ends of my fingers tingle as they anticipate being nibbled by sharp, little teeth.

Soon, my hand comes into contact with the shiny plastic cover.

'It's still here!'

'Jolly good.'

I reach in and pull it out with one hand. Mission nearly accomplished. All need I do now is put it in my backpack and steer my aunt out of the room and safely down the staircase again. We'll have to be incredibly careful. I'll make her walk behind me, I decide, and I'll tell her to hold onto my waist. And that will be the end of it. Never again will I visit an abandoned house, with or without Aunty fecking Susan.

But I don't have time to put any of this plan into practice. I don't even have time to drag myself out from under the bed.

It starts with a low rumble. At first, I assume it must be coming from a lorry driving past on the aforementioned dual carriageway, which is nearby, so I don't pay much attention. Then, when it doesn't stop, I kind of assume it's thunder in the distance and the heavy rain is ratcheting itself up into a proper storm. I don't know whether Aunty Susan has noticed. I can't see her from my position under the bed, but I can still hear her rummaging about. The sound gets louder and louder, very quickly, and soon I realise it's not thunder, it's something else, and whatever it is, it's going on right here. Next, an ear-splitting and apparently never-ending groan fills the air and the bedroom floor vibrates.

When I was twelve, our school took us on a trip to the Science Museum in London. The best exhibit by far was the earthquake simulator and I was gobsmacked by the juddering of the floor and the rattling of household objects on shelves next to my head. It was totally awesome, and once I was in there, I didn't want to go anywhere else in the museum, not even to the part with the lunar module or the really cool room in the basement where you could eat your packed lunch. I don't know what on earth is happening here, but this attic bedroom suddenly feels similar to that earthquake room, except that the noise is way louder and the vibrations are much stronger. And this time, it isn't a simulation, it's real.

I shout to Aunty Susan and I'm just about to start crawling out from under the bed, feet first, when the single huge moaning sound suddenly splits into a waterfall of other noises: breaking glass, the clattering of roof tiles onto the patio below, the crumbling of brickwork, the snapping of joists and the crash-landing of heavy furniture after it has dropped through empty spaces where floors used to be. A cascade of destruction. I can't move, but I can feel the middle part of the bed, the bit where it dips downwards, touching the small of my back.

Then I fall.

7. Jacob

My eyes are full of light.

I'm flying over a field of neatly mown grass surrounded by pine trees. In the middle, a skinny boy with closely cropped blonde hair and a cricket bat is hitting balls thrown by his father. I swoop down and take possession of him. I'm in the country park, where Dad takes us on weekend outings from our boarding school, twice each term. The game is a big deal, because I'm good at cricket and Dad is praising my batting skills. The only noises are the thwack of the bat and his voice. And my brother's voice, coming from the side of the field. He doesn't like cricket. He prefers to lay down on the grass and soak up the sun. A murmuring builds up inside my ear. It might be the hum of a dragonfly or the burbling of a stream. Either way, I'm on my back now, too, next to my brother, basking in a warm glow. I've never felt so peaceful, and I realise two things. This is what complete happiness feels like, and I've never even come close to it in real life.

Dad says he has to go. He shrugs and smiles apologetically, but it doesn't soften the shock of his departure. He takes the sunshine with him and I feel almost as raw as I did the first time round. I think I shiver, which makes fingertips flutter against my shoulders, light as butterfly wings, as they pull a thin blanket over me. I don't know who or where I am, but I'm grateful for this small act of kindness, and the touch of these fingers is really familiar. A tapestry of new sounds surrounds me, the beep and tick of machines, footsteps on a hard floor and endless chatter. Crowds of people loom close and their voices get louder. Then they recede again, like waves on a beach.

Someone shouts my name and tells to open my eyes. I do as I'm told and feel a liquid creep under my eyelids. It stings. This person has tricked me. Is that me swearing or someone else? I blink. I must have been blind before, but hadn't noticed or cared. Now I can almost see again, albeit through eyes that are half closed and sore.

For a while there doesn't seem to be much else to think about apart from the concept of vision and whether it's a gift or a curse.

Then I come back to myself.

'Sorry,' I say to the nurse.

She appraises me with the unempathetic and calculating eyes of a school bully and then carries on squirting and dabbing. When she's finished, she leaves the treatment bay without saying a single word.

'She's not very nice.'

I can hear the whine in my voice and I feel slightly ashamed about it. Then I notice my brother hovering about by the other side of the bed.

'Oh,' I say.

G does his annoying eyebrow raising and lowering thing, which tells me he could say plenty, but chooses not to, at least not now. Then he strokes the hair back from my forehead. He's taking liberties big time. No way would I let him do this under normal circumstances. But I lap it up. That's how sad I am, deep down.

'You're back, finally.'

He's wearing jeans and his blue sweat shirt, not scrubs. But his NHS lanyard dangles down from his neck. He's off duty then. Only here because of his relationship to me. But unlike most relatives, being the way he is, he can't resist involving himself in the care of the patient.

'I'm in your A&E?'

'They did a CT scan of your head and neck. It was all ok, so they've taken the neck brace off.'

'What neck brace?'

He doesn't respond. He must get pointless questions like that all the time.

'You've got a bit of a gash on the back of your head, but it's not too bad. We'll get you sitting up soon and staple it together. Other than that, it's just scratches and bruises. No broken bones. You were incredibly lucky. The paramedics said it was the bed that saved you. And a clump of bullrush type things.'

'The bed?'

'You were underneath it. In the back garden, on top of a bush, which broke your fall. I don't know what you were doing, going back there, but never mind that for now. At least you're ok.'

I was in a garden? Under a bed? Suddenly, I'm falling again, but inside my head this time. The restful sensation of being nobody and nowhere slips away, and reality reasserts itself with a sickening slam. I remember. Where I was, what I was doing. Why I was doing it. And who I was with.

'I'm going to throw up.'

Gawain hoists me into a sitting position. My head swims and the eye-drop nurse darts through the curtains again to thrust a grey cardboard receptacle shaped like a small bowler hat onto my lap. I heave and retch, but I don't produce much more than saliva. Not surprising, really. I can't remember when I last ate. Clearly, we never made to the pub with the immense pies. Tears form in my eyes and start to run down my cheeks. Nobody says anything. Not even G. They probably think it's due to the eyedrops and the vomiting. I feel the warmth of my brother's palm, pressed flat against my back. Why is he being so nice? He won't be when he knows the full extent of what's happened. I make a big effort to get my shit together, so I can ask the question I need to ask. It feels like trying to catch hold of several lengths of string attached to wild creatures all flying in different directions, and it takes a while before I manage to twist the strings together into a knot that will hold.

'Aunty Susan?'

The words are pebbles in my mouth. It's hard to spit them out. But I have to know. She must be ok, though, surely? Otherwise, G would be different.

'Aunty Susan what?'

"Where is she?"

'Why? There isn't much point getting her to come here. You'll be discharged soon. We should keep you in overnight, because you were out of it for ages. But there's a bed shortage. Ring her when you get home, if you're that desperate to talk to her.'

It takes me a while to explain. At first G thinks I'm still away with the fairies. Then he seems unable to accept what I'm saying, because it should be impossible. But eventually, he gets it. He presses his lips together and a kind of green wash passes over his darkish olive skin, turning it blotchy and pale. He doesn't resort to violence against me. He tends not to do that, except in mock fights, although occasionally, a kind of deep rage flares up between us. One time, he drove me insane with fury and I made a dent in his head with a tennis racquet.

Once he's got the details from me about the location of the house, he doesn't say anything else. The angry demand for an explanation as to why I took Aunty Susan inside a derelict building will be stored up and aired at a later date. He fishes his phone out from his trouser pocket and puts it to his ear. Then he exits the cubicle, without a backwards look.

After a while, another doctor turns up. She apologetically inserts metal staples into my head wound, a procedure that is absolute burning agony, but thankfully only for few seconds per staple. Then Nurse Nasty sorts out my discharge paperwork and hands me a bottle of painkillers. I discover my backpack and trainers under a nearby chair, together with the rest of my clothes which are cut to ribbons, presumably by the paramedics to get them off me. I'm still wearing my boxers, which is something, I suppose. I put my trainers on, without the socks, which are intact but soaked, and I sit on the chair and stare at my phone, wondering if I'm meant to call an Uber and get myself home wearing nothing but a hospital gown, my Calvin Kleins and a pair of soggy Nikes. But after about five minutes, Bartosz comes to the rescue, carrying a holdall.

'You ok?'

'Er, yeah.'

'I've brought you some clean clothes.'

'Thanks. Aunty Susan is…'

'I heard.'

I look at him and try to gauge his mood, but expression on his face is impossible to interpret. I've seen him get scarily angry in a slow burning way, but it doesn't happen very often, and his wrath has never been directed against me. Still, there's a first time for everything, and he does seem a bit distant.

'Where's G gone?' I ask him.

'Where do you think?'

'I need to get back there, too. Can you give me a lift?'

'You've had a bash on the head. You need to rest, mate.'

'How can I when Aunty Susan's missing?'

'The emergency services won't let you anywhere near.'

'I know exactly where she was before it happened. I could help them find her.'

Bartosz gives me a level stare.

We drive there in silence. I desperately want to exonerate myself, explain that Aunty Susan insisted on going to the house, that she said she'd go on her own if I refused to go with her. But my need for absolution is a side issue and wittering on about it now won't help anyone. I'll save it for later, use it as my defence when G has a proper go at me. We park by the row of shops, right behind Aunty Susan's car and close to mine. Not even four hours have passed since we parked there, in what feels like another life. The front-facing part of the property is surrounded by tape, and the road outside is lined with ambulances, police cars and fire engines. A few members of the press have turned up too, including a bloke in a heavy wool coat being followed around by a cameraman and an assistant carrying one of those big furry microphones. There don't seem to be many casual onlookers, though, probably because of the weather. But a couple of people are watching from the upstairs windows of the houses on the other side of the road.

I thought it would be difficult to convince the policeman guarding the front gate that I'm a witness, and that I might be able to help, but he lets me through almost straight away, possibly because of the stapled gash on my head and the mark on the side of my cheek that is rapidly turning into a bruise. Although he lets Bartosz onto the site as well, so maybe he's just fed up of standing there in the cold and the rain, and doesn't care who goes where. Once we're through the gate we see that, apart from a couple of cops with German shepherds on leads, the area at the front is deserted. When I realise the extent of the devastation, my breath exits my lungs as though I've been hit by a bomb blast. The place is little more than a mountain of bricks and rubble. It's crazy to think that this pile of debris was once a house with doors, windows and rooms, that I was in there when it collapsed, and that I'd taken Aunty Susan in there with me. And it's impossible to believe there's a chance Aunty S will still be alive underneath all that masonry.

I sink to my knees and hope the thing scratching at my airways isn't the beginnings of an asthma attack. But Bartosz is having none of it. He grabs me under the arms and pulls me back into a standing position.

'Whereabouts in the house were you when it happened?'
'Round the back. Upstairs.'
Bartosz puts his hands on my shoulders and propels me forward as though I'm under arrest. Turning the corner is like walking out onto a stage from the wings. The entire back of the house, or what's left of it, is so brightly lit you can see every detail. The damage, although still ruinous, is less extensive than at the front. Items of furniture are suspended in mid-air and a couple of the upstairs rooms are almost intact, with fireplaces and pictures still hanging from exposed walls. I spot Tess's bed at ground level. Somehow, it has been thrown clear of the collapsing house and come to rest at an angle. One end is propped against the remains of the metal staircase,

which is still hanging on, despite there being nothing much for it to hang on to, and the other end hovers unsteadily over a thick clump of pampas grass. Despite being weighed down by a portion of wall which has settled on top of it and despite the dip in the middle, the entire bed is still in one piece and still partially covered by bits of the pink satin eiderdown. My survival is totally down to this bed and the way it landed. It's absurd, a bit of dumb luck I don't deserve and will never be able to feel thankful for if Aunty Susan hasn't been dealt a similar hand. I know she's pretty ancient, and we joke about her age-related opinions and all that, but she's too young to die. I'll be condemned to a lifetime of survivor's guilt, and G will never forgive me.

Dogs are sniffing about in the rubble, but they don't seem to be picking up any scents. I think back to when it all started to happen. She was right behind me, so close her fingers must have been within touching distance of the soles of my trainers. Surely she would have been thrown clear, like I was? But she wasn't under the bed. She might have fallen inwards. Maybe the sudden collapse of a house creates a big vacuum that sucks objects into a whirling vortex and crushes them.

Emergency workers are painstakingly edging around the rubble. Every so often they shout and tap, and they make everyone keep quiet so they can listen for a response. G is standing next to three paramedics, watching and waiting, hands clasped behind his head. He's wearing a high viz jacket, several sizes too big for him, with *Doctor* written on the back. He must have found it in a cupboard somewhere in the hospital or in one of the ambulances parked at the front, and managed to wangle his way into an official role as part of the emergency rescue team. Even so, he looks too frantic to be capable of acting professionally.

'What a God-awful mess,' Bartosz says, in a tone that implies the state of the house is entirely down to me.

I scan the back of the ruined building again, more slowly this time, looking for gaps or tunnels in the collapsed brickwork that might lead to air pockets. The remaining structure is fairly open at the top, but the ground floor area is densely packed and compressed by everything that has fallen onto it and disintegrated on the way down. She's got no chance if she's underneath all that.

'Why don't they put ladders up so they can search the top part?'

'They must think it's too dangerous. The last thing they'll want is for anyone else to get hurt.'

I nod and turn away from Bartosz to hide the fact that my eyes have filled with tears again. I stare into the jungle that used to be the back garden, and try to force air into my reluctant lungs. Vertigo hums deep inside my ears as I look down at the paving stones and then up again at the dark wilderness of brambles and overgrown garden shrubs. I squat again and hold my head still to shake off the dizziness. Once it's gone, I'll tell Bartosz he's right. We shouldn't have come. The best thing we can do is leave and let the experts get on with it.

But then I look at the paving stones again and scrutinize them more closely. Some of them are a washed out pink and some are blue, but most are a dull stone colour. I get onto my hands and knees and I turn to face the shrubbery. I hear Bartosz asking me what I'm doing. He sounds miles away. Out of nowhere, I suddenly remember a TV programme G and I were obsessed with during the summer holidays one year. It was about secret agents who had acquired superhuman powers that switched themselves on just at the right time and made them hyper-alert. That's how I feel now. I'm wired and a kind of spidey sense has kicked in. The soles of my feet thrum as though the paving stones are an illusion whose purpose is to hide a drop down the side of a cliff.

The lights are all directed towards the house, so it's impossible to see through or over the barrier of leaves, twisting stems and thorns that lies in front of me. Urbexers often include outbuildings in their videos, but during the explore with Aimee, we didn't go down to the bottom of the garden. Aimee said we'd need to hack our way through the undergrowth, and there probably wouldn't be much to see down there in any case. I wish I'd got my headtorch. It was still attached to me and intact when I was rescued, apparently, but now it's in my backpack, round the corner in Bartosz's car. Nevertheless, I crawl towards the bushes and the thing I knew I'd find is there, right in the centre, a gap, close to the ground. Perhaps it's not some sort of special psychic ability that told me it was here. Maybe I wasn't unconscious when the bed landed and I caught a glimpse of this space then, before everything went dark. It leads into low tunnel, only high enough for a small child to stand up in, probably because the leaves and the branches are weighed down with rainwater. I creep in. The ground is unexpectedly solid. It must be paved, then, a footpath leading from the patio across what once was a lawn, perhaps. As I move, my hands come into contact with empty cans, cigarette packets and plastic bottles. My eyes adjust to the darkness and I begin to see everything more clearly. Other visitors have been down here, so it must lead somewhere. I keep going. Bartosz shouts for me to come back. I ignore him, and he's suddenly right behind me.

'Watch where you're putting your hands,' he says. 'There might be broken glass.'

After crawling for about thirty seconds, we emerge from the tunnel into a small open area. The ground beneath us is covered in rough, bobbled concrete, which scratches our hands and hurts our knees. We both stand up. Inches away from us is a dark wall. I stretch my arm out until my hand touches a slimy, wet surface with vertical grooves running down it.

'Garden shed.'

Its door is open. Tentatively, I step inside, not wanting to clatter into sharp garden implements, like spades or forks, or the blades of a lawn mower. There's a nose-itching smell of fertiliser that takes me right back to the days when we still lived with Dad. He used to be a keen gardener and he had a shed that smelled exactly like this. Bartosz bumps into something light and flimsy that makes a plasticky rattling sound as it rolls away from us.

'Hula hoop,' he says.

I trip over something soft.

8. Aunty Susan

Hospitals are best avoided by people my age. They take one look at you, decide you're an old crock and not worth the effort, and that's it. Off you go to the mortuary at breakneck speed. It happened to Glenda Skelton's gardener. He fell off a ladder when he was pruning an apple tree and sustained a broken pelvis, which was fixable, they said, but then he succumbed to some infection or other, had a stroke and that was it. Curtains. Something similar happened to Molly Beasley's sister. She went in for knee replacement surgery, had an adverse reaction to the anaesthetic and ended up with the mental capacity of a cabbage.

Gawain hitched a ride with me in the ambulance when they got me out of the shed. He says the break in my ankle is a nasty one, a compound fracture, and what's more, my foot was so swollen at first, they weren't sure whether the circulation was blocked, which could have meant amputation. Doctors love telling you things like that. They seem to relish their own honesty. A chronic inability to mince words is something to be proud of, part of their training.

If you ignore my ankle, a few scratches, a minor concussion and the start of hypothermia from sitting in that damp shed for so long, I'm fit as a butcher's dog. I'd sneak out when nobody was looking, call a taxi and get myself home, if I wasn't so infuriatingly immobile. But as it is, I'm forced to stay here, where I'm not only risking an early death due to the incompetence of the medical staff, but also acting as a sitting target for all the virtue signalling numpties whose lives are so empty they can't resist the opportunity to indulge in a bit of hospital visiting. These types appear at the entrance to the ward with no warning, so I never have time to hobble out of sight. Even the wretched vicar turned up yesterday. I'd like to know who told *him* I was here. Today, though, Jacob turns up for the first time since it happened. I'm happy to see him. Until I realise he's brought the sodding photo album.

'It's a bit battered round the edges, but the photos are ok. The rain didn't get to them. I was clutching it when the floor caved in and I had my arms wrapped round it when they found me. Bit of a miracle, really.'

I don't think it's a miracle at all. Just the opposite. What bad luck it survived the collapse of the house. My interest in its contents has evaporated completely, now after all the bother the damn thing has caused. As soon as they let me out of this infernal place, I'll sling it in the recycling bin or light a bonfire in the garden and chuck it on top. I make a supreme effort not to say any of this to poor Jacob, though. One side of his face is covered by a big purple bruise and he has a vertical cut along the back of his head, held together with what looks like bits of metal. I should thank him for rescuing me from the shed and maybe apologise for insisting we went there in the first place, but I can't think of a way to say any of that without sounding *pass-the-sick-buckety*. When I get out of here, I'll go online and send him a chocolate pizza with Thanks or Sorry written on it. Or both. Or perhaps I should transfer fifty quid into his bank account. Yes, that might be best. He's always skint.

'We thought you were still in the house,' he says as he pulls up a chair.

I'm vaguely aware that of a couple of the nurses huddled together around their computers at the other end of the ward are looking across at us, or rather at him. One of them giggles. Jacob doesn't notice or he pretends not to.

'Then, suddenly, out of nowhere, it came to me that you might be in the middle of the brambles so I crawled through them and found the shed. At first, I thought it was divine inspiration, but I must have opened my eyes and spotted your feet disappearing into the bushes when I was under the bed.'

'I saw *you*,' I say.

It's true, I did. It sounds ridiculous, awful even, but at the time I was more bothered about getting away from those paving stones than anything else. I remember thinking he was asleep and being pleased that he'd found shelter under the bed. He looked peaceful so I left him to it. I can't have been in my right mind. Otherwise I'd never have disappeared off like that, would I? I put my glasses on so I can see his face more clearly.

'As long as you're alright?' I ask him.

'Me? Yeah. I was a bit out of it for a couple of days. Slept a lot, but I'm good now. It's G you need to worry about. He's hardly speaking to me and as for you, don't even go there.'

'I wondered why he hasn't been to see me.'

'He's come up a few times when you've been asleep, but he says he's too hurt and betrayed to engage with you when you're awake. And not just because we went to the house behind his back. I heard him going on at Bartosz about how you've not been taking your blood pressure tablets. You've triggered him big time with that one.'

'How does he know?'

'He read your notes.'

'Nosey little bugger. I could get him struck off for that.'

'I don't think you could, Aunty. Anyway, he only did it because he was worried about you. You know what he's like.'

'Yes, well.'

Amanda comes in, too, with books and toiletries, and Bartosz sweeps down the ward some days, bearing coffee from the café in the foyer and Tupperware boxes full of brownies, sandwiches, crackers and little wrapped portions of cheese. I'm more than grateful for these offerings. The tea and coffee served by the hospital taste like brown paper dissolved in tepid water, and the meals are generally cold by the time they reach my bedside. And in any case, they're tricky to eat with the bendy plastic knives and forks they provide.

As soon as Molly Beaseley heard the news she started turning up on a regular basis. She's often accompanied by June Stanford from the British Legion Fund-Raising Committee. I'm not sure whether their visits are down to altruism or because they find the hospital atmosphere exciting, with its potential for drama and the possibility that the dashingly handsome orthopaedic consultant might put in an appearance. He's one of two demi-gods that prance along the ward each morning at around eleven, with their minions trailing behind them. Communication with each of these doctors is challenging for completely different reasons. The good-looking one is way too young for the post, in my opinion, and he's massively over-confident. He speaks slowly and loudly at us patients in a plummy voice, as though we're all imbeciles. The first time I encountered him, he asked me a question, but before I'd finished my reply, he'd moved onto the next patient and I was left sitting there, talking to an empty space. The next time he spoke to me I pretended not to hear him. He probably thinks I'm senile. The other consultant is older and his face is much more empathetic, but words stream out of his mouth in a series of rapid whispers that I can't hear. When I was a small child, there was a lady in our neighbourhood who went shopping with an ear trumpet. She would bellow questions at the butcher, then hold the trumpet to her ear so she could pick his reply. Perhaps if I had one of those, I'd know what was going on.

I don't mind Molly and June turning up so regularly, if I'm honest. It's nice to hear all the gossip, and the first time Molly appeared she'd just been to the cash and carry and she brought me several packs of those small cans of Guinness. I've hidden them in my locker, and in the late afternoon, once the sun is over the yardarm, I've got into the habit of quietly emptying one into my yellow plastic beaker. This is easy to get away with because most of the nurses ignore the patients as much as they can. In fact, they probably wouldn't notice if I sat in the chair by my bed, blatantly swigging the Guiness from a pint glass, its creamy head of froth on show for all to see. Bone idleness is clearly an occupational hazard on this ward, as is clinical obesity, probably because they spend most of their time hovering like swollen crows over tins of Quality Street and boxes of homemade flapjacks. I'm not sure whether it's just the nurses in orthopaedics who behave like this or if the entire hospital is run in the same way. It used to have such a good reputation, too. But their negligence suits me on the whole. I don't like nosy parkers prying into my affairs, and before long, I'm at least half way to total independence, out of bed and able to hop about on crutches. And most importantly, I can get to the bathroom and attend to my lavatorial affairs without any help from anybody.

On the fourth day of my sojourn, Gawain turns up when I'm actually awake. He's in his scrubs and seems out of breath, as though he's just run a marathon. He doesn't ask how I am, probably because he already knows that after reading my notes. Instead, he launches into a rant about how I could have died and how I'm going to need tons of help when I leave hospital.

'And don't think I don't know you haven't been taking your blood pressure meds,' he adds.

'Jacob told me you'd found out about that. And broadcast the information to the world.'

'Ah yes, Jacob, my brother. The one who went through a major trauma, got his shit together and then nearly ended up dead for no good reason.'

The ward isn't much more than a small alcove at one side of a corridor and is only big enough for four beds. The one next to mine is occupied by an overflow patient from the stroke ward. She's propped up on cushions and remains in that position from one day to the next, with her eyes closed and her mouth wide open, poised to catch any flies or wasps that might be zipping about. But the two ladies opposite are orthopaedic patients with all their marbles intact, like me. One of them is knitting furiously and the other is pretending to read the latest issue of Bitcoin Digest, but I can tell they're both listening to every word. Altercations like this don't happen very often, and when they do, it's important to extract as much enjoyment from them as possible. I'd do the same.

'Your bedside manner isn't up to much, darling. There must be a course you could do to improve it.'

'Oh look, just fuck off, will you?'

Gawain delivers this suggestion at a much lower volume than the earlier part of his attack, thank goodness. He sighs, folds his arms and stands staring down at me, biting his lip and shaking his head for an uncomfortably long time, as though he can't decide whether I'm a puzzling clinical conundrum, a monster or a sad old lady deserving of pity. I stare right back at him. Eventually, his beeper goes and he shakes his head one more time and trots away. From that point onwards, he dashes up from A&E and appears at the end of my bed at unpredictable intervals, like a particularly furious little member of the Spanish inquisition. He hurls carrier bags at me, containing clean clothes and food sent by the others, then his pager beeps again and he curses under his breath and runs off. In the end, I learn to recognise the light tap of his trainers on the shiny linoleum as he hurtles along the corridor towards my alcove, and I pretend to be asleep.

Towards the end of the second week of my hospital stay, the situation between us becomes even more fraught. One evening, according to the little menu I've been supplied with, supper is chicken casserole, but the meat, carrots, potatoes and gravy have become glued together in a way that would be impossible to achieve if you tried to do it deliberately, and have formed a rubbery amalgam that refuses to yield to the cutlery or the penknife I keep in my handbag. The only way to tackle it would be to treat it like a large, gummy biscuit, pick it up in one's fingers and alternate between sucking and chomping at it, in the hope it would eventually soften and transform itself into something that resembled food. I push the tray away and nibble a couple of my cream crackers instead, but I polished off the last of the cheese after lunch, so my evening Guinness hits a largely empty stomach. Soon, I'm forced to open a second can for extra sustenance, and after a while, thanks also to the painkillers, I'm sozzled and in desperate need of the loo. I manage to stagger there on my crutches, but on the way back, perhaps because I rise from the toilet seat too quickly, I have a bit of a wobble. I make it back to the entrance to the ward again, but I seem to be moving at an angle, with my head tilted towards my left shoulder. I get myself through the swing doors, but then one of my crutches slips out of my grasp and clatters to the floor, so I'm forced to prop myself up against the sink, with my head resting against the paper towel dispenser, just for a second, until the shakiness dissipates.

Of course, Gawain chooses that very moment to rush into the ward. He grabs hold of me firmly, in what feels like a competent, professional manner, something he's been taught to do. It annoys me intensely, and the sympathetic tuts he throws in my direction don't help. If I wasn't half-pissed, I'd risk lifting my good leg to give him a swift kick on the shin.

'Have they changed your meds?'
'I'm just a bit woozy. Dashed off to the bogs too quickly.'
'You're slurring your words, Aunty.'
'Sod off, you interfering little busy body.'

I think I hear myself saying this out loud, but I'm not sure. He smiles, grimly, and I'm forced to lean on him as we meander slowly back to my bedside. It takes a while, but he's fine with that. It's all in a day's work for him. When we get there, he pushes me into a chair and crouches down so he can shine his blasted torch into my eyes.

'I'll get someone to come and sort you out.'
'You'll be lucky. They all bugger off at this time of night. Anyway, I don't need sorting out.'

I'm sobering up a bit now and I'm fully aware that when I pick up my yellow beaker and neck down the rest of its contents, I'm being slightly theatrical. I don't really fancy the dregs of the inky black beverage anymore, I just want to see how he'll react. He takes the beaker from me mid-gulp and sniffs its contents.

'Would you like one? I've got plenty.'

I reach over and open the door of my locker. It's worth it for the look on his face when he sees the cans. He gasps and slumps onto the bed.

'I don't know what to say.'
'Then don't say anything. It's not as though it's Special Brew and they're only small cans.'
'Where did you get them from?'

'Molly Beaseley. She might be a bit of an airhead, but at least she's tuned in to my actual needs. Not like you bloody medical people.'

Gawain's sorrowful, Jersey-cow eyes, with their ridiculously long lashes, bore into me. For a shaky few seconds, the possibility that he only has my best interests at heart and that I'm a nasty, ungrateful old bint drifts across my mental horizon, like a faint wisp of grey cloud. I wonder if I should say something, offer him - not an apology exactly – but perhaps an acknowledgement of his hurt feelings.

It's too late.

'I give up. Do what you want.'

Three whole days and nights pass before he returns again. The relatively pleasant consultant has just done his ward round. He smiled sweetly, nodded his head a few times more than usual and twittered at me. I couldn't make out a single word.

'You're being discharged,' Gawain says.

'What? When?'

'As soon as they've sorted out the paperwork and your physio appointments. And the drugs. All that stuff. Didn't they tell you?'

'Possibly. Hard to say. Anyway, how do *you* know? Oh no, hang on a minute. You know everything. I forgot for a moment. Silly me.'

'Amanda phoned in this morning for a progress report.'

'There seem to be an awful lot of people talking about me behind my back.'

"Yes, well that's probably a good thing, seeing as you're half-pissed most of the time and don't have a clue what's going on. She's coming in to take you home.'

'Isn't there a hospital minibus I could get?'

'There is, but they'll want you out of your bed and gone from here as soon as you're discharged, then you'd have to sit in the waiting room downstairs for God knows how long. Could be hours. Nobody looks after the people waiting, because they're not in-patients anymore. The toilets are miles away, so the chairs stink of piss and the air is full of cigarette smoke because the no smoking rule isn't enforced. So, even though you're a complete and utter pain in the rear end, Aunty, we don't want you having to put up with all that.'

'You're too kind.'

'You're coming to ours until the plaster's removed and you can get about on your own.'

'I don't think so, thank you very much. Amanda can take me home. I'll be perfectly fine.'

'You wouldn't be,' he says quietly, in a tone that implies the topic is neither up for debate nor particularly interesting.

He leaves without saying anything else. Nothing at all. Not even *see you later*.

*

At first it's not too bad. Bartosz empties the little downstairs room he normally uses as an office and put a bed in it, and there's a bathroom with a sink close by, so I don't have to tackle the stairs. Amanda's a big help with practical issues and when Jacob's around, he often sits at the kitchen table with his laptop to keep me company. I spend most of my days in the kitchen, reading and gazing out at the bird table, and occasionally I heave myself out of my chair and hobble about for a bit, up and down the length of the kitchen and out into the hallway. Bartosz has taken me out in his car twice. One morning we went to my house, so I could pick up my post and a few other bits and pieces, and another day we did a scenic route around the South Downs and parked up for a while at the top of a hill where there's a view of the sea. Gawain, on the other hand, is keeping well out of my way. He's not at home all that much, in any case, but when he is here, he goes to bed early. Bartosz says he's doing extra hours and saving up his leave for the arrival of the baby, but that's just an excuse.

After about ten days, time starts to drag. I've still got another fortnight before the cast comes off and a small roll of fat has started to form around my middle, which has never happened to me before. Also, I'm becoming increasingly addicted to daytime TV. I was quite put out the day before yesterday, because I went to the loo and missed the first five minutes of a show about doing up your house, something I wouldn't be interested in at all under normal circumstances. Clearly, my mental faculties are beginning to atrophy due to lack of use, and I can't help thinking life is moving on and leaving me behind. I'm suffering from that acronym. What is it? FOMO, fear of missing out.

'I'm mouldering away,' I say to the blue tit pecking at sunflower seeds on the bird table.

'That's a bit drastic. Even for you,' Jacob says.

I'd forgotten he was in the room.

'I'm irrelevant.'

He raises his eyebrows and looks faintly amused. That's all I am to him, a comical old aunt who has lost track of reality.

'No you're not. Molly Beasley and that swivel eyed woman with the weird hair, what's her name? They can't keep away. They're like your fan club.'

He's got a point. They both drop in for morning coffee almost every day, heads twitching like inquisitive sparrows, hoping to catch sight of one or other of what they call my captivating menfolk.

'June Stanford. What's wrong with her hair?'

'Those two little horns sticking up at the front. Like she's a messenger from Satan or something? The devil's disciple.'

I can't help smiling. Jacob pushes his chair slightly back from the table and sits upright with his feet pressed to the floor, as though he thinks he might need to get up and run from the room if the conversation takes the wrong turn.

'Can I ask you something, Aunty S?' His tone is cautious.

'You can ask. You might not get an answer.'

'I was just wondering. Why hasn't Patrick been to see you?'

I'm taken aback by Jacob's directness. He's usually so reserved and discrete. Gawain has always been the nosey, interfering nephew.

'He's given me the bum's rush.'

'What, like a sexually transmitted disease?'

I can't tell whether he's joking or not.

'He's dumped me. Molly saw him in the Red Lion having lunch with that tarty woman who used to be in holiday shows on TV. The one that simpers around the new vicar at St. Lukes. She staged a coup to take charge of the flower arranging rota. I can't remember her name. It might be Lynda. If it isn't, it should be.'

'Why?'

'In my experience, women called Lynda are often…'

'No, I mean, why has Patrick ended things?'

'He wanted me to go on a trip with him around the coast.'

'How did that make him dump you?'

'I said I didn't want to be squashed into a tin can with him for weeks at a time. He took it the wrong way.'

'What would have been the right way to take it?'

'Like a man?'

'Maybe you could have been a bit more tactful?'

'I didn't want to mislead him. It's not my fault he's so sensitive.'

Jacob frowns at me.

'No need to look like that.'

'Like what?'

'As though you're judging me. I get enough of that from your brother.'

9. Aunty Susan

One morning a week or so later, whilst I'm eating my Weetabix and trying to ignore the new voice in my head that tells me cereal is only the first course and should be followed by at least one buttered crumpet, Jacob appears at the kitchen table again. But this time he's not staying. He folds a slice of toast in half and posts it into his mouth. Then he drags a purple hoodie over his head.

'Where are my trainers?'

He darts from one side of the kitchen to the other in his socks, which don't match. One is all purple stripes and the other is yellow with an orange heel.

'By the washing machine in the utility room, where you left them.'

He sits on a chair and pulls them on without unfastening the laces.

'I've been summonsed.'

'By your new Prof?'

'By Edinburgh Matt. My arch nemesis. I asked why we couldn't talk on facetime, but he made a series of outraged spitting noises. I thought he'd got Dorothy in his office for a minute. Then he said I have to go in. Like now. For the sake of his blood pressure if nothing else. I don't know why he's got such a short fuse. He'll explode if he's not careful. What a total loser.'

Dorothy is the larger of Gawain's beloved alpacas. She likes to hurl shots of saliva at anyone who gets too close, apart from Gawain, of course.

'Oh dear.'

'This PhD is turning into a nightmare. I can't deal with it.'

'Of course you can.'

'Say a prayer for me, Aunty.'

'Don't be so feeble, Jacob.'

He slams the front door on the way out. The entire house reverberates and then falls silent. I get up and stagger to the hall window so I can watch as he runs towards his car, covering his head with a blue, cardboard folder, because it's pouring down again. He really needs to man up. Gawain and Bartosz coddle him, as though he's a small child who for some reason is entitled to have feelings more delicate than anyone else's. When I was his age, I was flying solo behind the Iron Curtain.

Bartosz has gone out and Gawain is at work. So here I am, on my own with nothing to do. Or rather nothing I want to do. My condition and my immobility bore people now. Molly and June's visits are becoming less frequent, and as far as the boys are concerned, I might as well be a piece of furniture. Even Bartosz has stopped taking me out.

This attitude won't do, I decide. I make a big mental effort to summon up my list of reasons to be cheerful. The day after tomorrow sits at the top of this list, because Amanda is taking me to the hospital to have the plaster removed, which means I can go home. Second on the list is my improving mobility. On dry mornings or in gaps between showers, I've started to venture outside. I usually walk around the perimeter of the house, then I potter down the drive to the gap in the hedge that opens onto the track leading to the road and I look at the gaunt trees on the other side and listen to the song thrush who seems to think it's spring. You can hear the motorway from there, too, which is surprisingly stimulating when you're locked away from the world like I am. Before I go back inside, I like to amble across to the enclosure and say hello to the alpacas. They gaze at me and I talk to them for a bit. The smaller one, Helen, is a good listener. She looks at me sympathetically through her long lashes, which remind me of Gawain's, and she raises her head high in the air with indignation on my behalf as I moan away at her. But I have to stand well back in case Dorothy comes charging out and sprays me with the contents of her salivary glands.

Today, the rain isn't showery in nature. It's a slow and permanent drizzle from a dead sky the colour of pewter, so instead of walking about outside, I'm condemned to parade up and down the hall to the front door and then back again to the kitchen, passing the bookshelves as I go. I try to ignore the fact that the photo album is there, hidden in the middle of an entire shelf of fantasy fiction books that seem to tell the story of a dismal universe populated by giant skeletons. But these paperbacks have matt grey spines and the album is a glossy, eye-catching green, so it's hard to miss. I turn the other way so I'm not looking at the books when I pass, but then I start to obsess about whether or not I can see a vague, lime-coloured reflection on the opposite wall.

When I first came out of hospital, I chucked the album into the recycling bin, under a flattened cardboard box and a leaflet about solar panels. Unfortunately, Jacob came into the kitchen soon afterwards and spotted it.

'You don't want to lose it now, after all the trouble we went to,' he said.

I wished I'd shoved it in the food cannister, under the remnants of the previous night's sausage and baked bean casserole. But he thrust it in my direction, and the expression on his face was earnest and sincere, and he still had a hint of that awful bruise on the side of his face. So I took the album from him. I even thanked him and made an effort to sound enthusiastic. He seemed pleased, which made me feel oddly miserable, and when he'd gone I wedged the damn thing in with the bony monster series. Unsurprisingly, nobody ever reads those books, so I thought it would be safe there.

I cave in and pull the album from the shelf. I decide I'll look at the photos, just once, to get them out of my system. I know they'll upset me, but at least then I'll be able to stop obsessing about them. And in any case, the day that lies ahead of me promises to be so long and empty that even tragedy seems like an attractive diversion. I take the album into the kitchen, settle myself in my usual chair open it on my lap.

Tess started taking photos the Christmas when she was twelve, because one of her presents was an instamatic camera. Instamatic was a misleading description. It wasn't like a polaroid or the cameras we all have in our phones nowadays. There was nothing even remotely instant about the process of taking photos with it. You had to remove the reel of film, making sure you didn't expose it to the light and take it to the chemist's to be developed. Then, anything up to a week later, you'd get these blurry little photos back, which were small and almost square with white borders. Sometimes, only a few of the photos from a reel of film were any good. The rest were hopeless, shots taken with a finger over the lens or accidental views of the photographer's feet, or a really boring view of a field or an anonymous building. I think this must explain why there are so few pictures here, despite the fact they cover a period of more than four years. Also, if I remember rightly, this particular album was dedicated to her friends. She definitely took other photos, of trips abroad when her parents taught on painting courses in places like

Nice or on the island of Elba, for instance. Those snapshots went somewhere else, in a blue album, I think. Yes, that's right. I remember Tess saying the blue matched the colour of the Mediterranean or the cloudless sky. I used to roll my eyes when she said things like that, but secretly, I was more than a little impressed. My parents had never taken us further than Bournemouth for our summer holidays, and we'd never even gone there after Mum died, because Dad didn't like having to close the shop and lose a week's income. Mum had a friend who owned a caravan that sat quietly on its own in a field surrounded by forest, but close to the sea. She took Davey and me there for a week each summer, while Dad stayed behind to run the shop.

In a kind of rapid, emotion-saving first encounter, I flick through the album very quickly and skim over most of the pictures without looking at any of them properly. But when I get to the four snaps on the final page, which must be the last ones ever taken, I freeze. I try to tear my eyes away from them, but I can't. The backdrop to all of these four photos is the porticoed entrance to Fieldgate Hall. It's the night of the end-of-summer party, a huge event, held annually by Christoff's parents, with a disco in one room, a jazz band in another and fairy lights in the garden. I'm in two of the pictures, wearing the knee-length cheesecloth dress from Chelsea girl I bought with money I'd earned working in Dad's shop during the holidays, and a pair of strappy sandals that once belonged to Mum, but which I'd hidden under my bed after she died. My feet had only just grown big enough for me to wear them without accidentally kicking them off. My smile is that of a girl with nothing whatsoever to hide, a girl with no clue about anything. I was happy then, more or less. Not as cheerful as I had been at the beginning of the summer, before Tess came back from Italy, but not as devastated as I would be a few hours later.

In one of the shots, I'm standing with Donna and in the other I'm with Tess, who has suddenly grown tall and willowy. Tess, with her long chestnut hair and her white sleeveless dress that flowed around her ankles and accentuated her tan. Tess, who pretended not to notice how all the boys kept glancing or even staring at her and a fair few of the dads, too. In the other photos she's with Ade, who is two years older, several inches taller and about century more glamorous and sophisticated than Donna, myself or even Tess. The pair are slightly turned towards each other, and Ade is holding both Tess's hands in his. The expressions on their faces as they gaze into each other's eyes makes the photo look posed and professional, like the pre-wedding shots couples put on social media nowadays.

The reason I'm so astounded about this set of photos is that I've never seen them before, and I can't work out how they could possibly have made their way into this album. I remember Tess fishing the camera out that evening and snapping away, then getting someone else to take the ones that include her. But who took the film to be developed and put the photos in the album? And who left the album in Tess's bedroom? It definitely wasn't me, and if Donna had done it, she'd have told me. I look at the photos again, more closely this time. Is it my imagination, or do we all look slightly stiff and awkward? Do our smiles seem vaguely false, as though some of us are acting and the rest of us have worked out something is going on, but we don't know what, and are trying to pretend everything is ok? No, I don't think so. We were just nervous and very young, not used to big formal occasions, and my judgement is tainted, because of what happened later.

I can't bear to look at these final photos any longer, so I flick back to the beginning of the album. Tess must have got someone else to take the earlier snaps because she's in them all. The first is of Donna, Tess and me sitting cross legged in a row on paving stones with our backs resting against a pale sandstone wall, in our yellow checked summer dresses, Clarke's sandals and beige, nylon socks, which, infuriatingly, only reached half way up our calves, however often we tried to pull them up to our knees. It must be the end of our first year at St. Ursula's. Donna, Tess and I started there when we were eleven. Before that, we went to the local primary school. Most of the other girls at St Ursula's had been there since they were five, which made us incomers. That alone was enough to make them hostile towards us, but each of us also had our own individual bull's eye stamped on our backs.

Donna was teased for being short and fat, which wasn't fair, because Patricia Rumbelow, who was widely regarded as Top Dog of our form, had a much bigger bum than she did, and even a second chin. But Patricia was a verbal abuse specialist, so she got away with it. I automatically qualified as a loser because my mum had just died. And my shoes didn't help. Dad ordered them specially from one of his suppliers and said they were just like the ones ladies in the police or the army wore, as though that was a point in their favour. If Mum had still been around, she'd have had a quiet word with him and I'd have been allowed to choose my own footwear, within reason. But as it was, I had to turn up on my first day wearing long, narrow lace ups with no heel and no decorative features whatsoever, in a shade the other girls described as dog-shit brown. It didn't help that on the very same day, Rosalind Bentall had wowed everyone by turning up in black leather, knee-length platform boots. Of course, she was sent home with a letter addressed to her parents, but it didn't matter. Her grooviness, as we called it then, was established, and for the rest of her time at the school Rosalind was Patricia's number one sidekick.

Tess got the worst of the bullying. It's difficult to remember exactly what she was like back then, because she changed so much in the years that followed. Her parents were artists, who lived a bohemian lifestyle, and Tess had turned up at St Ursula's wearing a random grey skirt, navy jumper and blazer purchased at the last minute by her mother in the charity shop next to the building society. The jumper was threadbare at the elbows and had a gold border around the V, instead of a white one, the cuffs of the blazer were frayed and the skirt hem hovered unevenly several inches below her knees, which was a recipe for disaster in an era when we all wore our skirts about two inches down from the tops of our thighs. But worst of all, her tie wasn't even a St Ursula's one. It was the one worn by the boys who went to the grammar school in Froehampton.

By the time those first summer pictures were taken, though, things had improved. Donna, Tess and I stuck together and agreed not to react to anything the others did or said, so they soon got bored with us. A few other things helped, too. Donna improved her reputation by being seriously good at lacrosse and netball, and Tess acquired the correct uniform, thanks to Donna's mum, who called on Tess's parents, tried to explain that the outfit Tess wore to school was a problem, got nowhere, and ended up going into Guildford and buying the whole lot for her. As for me, I endured the relentless comments about my shoes until the Friday afternoon of the second week, when I walked home through the park and kicked them off, one by one, into the boating lake. I tripped happily home in my plimsols, which I'd brought with me and told Dad someone had stolen the shoes. As if anyone would want them! But he believed me and I needed new shoes urgently, so it was quicker to let me choose a pair myself from the shop than send off for replacements.

I turn the page and we jump forward in time to Christmas, 1974. I'm sure it's as late as that because in the first photo, I'm standing next to Davey in front of a large, silver Christmas tree in what it clearly our living room and he's several inches taller than me, even though I'm fifteen and he's only eleven. The previous Christmas he was shorter than me, but then he had a massive growth spurt. His resemblance to Jacob is astonishing. I've never really noticed much of a similarity between them before, probably because soon after the photo was taken, Davey put on weight and became much more solid, and of course, although Davey was also fair, Jacob's hair and eyes are much lighter than his were. I'll have to show him this photo. I might even take it out of the album and give it to him. In another picture on the same page, Donna, Tess and I stand with our arms linked, in front of the same tree, beneath the paper chains we'd painstakingly licked and stuck together. The three of us are panda-eyed with Miner's navy-blue eyeshadow. Donna is thinner and Tess is taller, her long dark hair emerging in pigtails from a cloche hat she'd made from an old, green velvet party dress, using her mother's sewing machine.

I turn another page, and wham, there we are right in the middle of that incredible and ultimately tragic summer of 1976, baking in the sun by Christoff's swimming pool. There are only two photos. The first shows a collection of shadowy faces blinking at the camera. The poor quality of this shot hides the discomfort some of us felt at having to wear swimsuits and being forced to reveal our usually hidden bodies. The second photo is a head and shoulders shot of Ade. He's in the pool and his dark, floppy wet hair is brushed back, away from his forehead. He isn't at all embarrassed about his body, and his smile is broad and confident. The photo doesn't pick up the sheen of water coating Ade's pale shoulders or the droplets that have gathered in his hair or his default facial expression, which was sardonic as though he was in a permanent state of quiet amusement. But then, I don't need memory aids to conjure up any of that.

I lean back in my chair. My back aches and I feel slightly nauseous. Too many memories, more than I can cope with in one go. I shut the album and hide it under my book and the pile of magazines on the table by my chair, and I close my eyes.

I don't open them again until Bartosz walks into the kitchen, carrying a box with a handle and a mesh front. Something inside the box is wailing.

'Company for you. I nipped over to yours. Took me a while to find her. But here she is.'

He sets the contraption down in front of me and opens the door. We watch as Lesley stays in the box and does a very good impersonation of a cat that would rather be absolutely anywhere else in the world, including a nuclear war zone, than here with me. She refuses to be coaxed out until Bartosz tempts her with a hypoallergenic cat treat that looks like a pink oxo cube. Once she's gobbled it down, she gives me a hard stare, then stalks over to the sliding door and mewls to be let out into the garden.

'We should keep her inside for now. Otherwise, she might try and get back home,' Bartosz says.

'Let her out. She won't be bothered about getting home.'

Leslie hangs about in the garden. If I look out at her through the big window and catch her eye, she hisses at me. I'm not surprised. She's never shown me much affection, and our relationship broke down completely after I'd watched one of those cucumber versus cat videos and couldn't resist the temptation to put a rolling pin on the floor behind her while she was eating her kibble, just to see what would happen. All four paws left the ground at the same time. I hadn't realised she could jump so high. I watch as she menaces the poor alpacas and mooches around the bird table. I wonder if Bartosz and Gawain would mind if I leave her here when I go home.

Perhaps I'll leave the album here, too.

10. Michael

Michael unlocks his front door and enters the gloom. He's greeted by the grandfather clock, which seems surprised and possibly a bit put out to see him. Reese inherited the clock from an uncle, and Michael used to think it had a smiley face, as though the thing it loved most in the entire world was to be looked at. But now every tick seems like a criticism and its second and minute hands frame its face like a pair of angry eyebrows.

The clock has a point. Michael is in the wrong place at the wrong time. At ten past eleven on a Tuesday morning he should be in his office, pen in hand, with his laptop open in front of him, pretending to be doing something important. But here he is, at home, a canvas bag-for-life from Lidl in one hand and his briefcase in the other. His hands tremble as he rummages through the stuff in the bag. It doesn't amount to much, considering the number of years he's spent in that office: a hardback notebook, a large plaster bust of a youth with an abundance of curly hair but no arms, two cacti, a photograph of himself frowning imposingly with the cast of Ghost Search, and the contents of his snack drawer, which turned out to include two packets of jam sandwich creams, a box of tea bags and a half-eaten bar of surprisingly delicious white chocolate from the discount supermarket near the station.

The Vice Chancellor is a man Michael has been on first name terms with for years. But when Jeffrey described the act of casting out his friend as the granting of a temporary leave of absence for recouperation and evaluation purposes, and suggested he should take a chill pill and enjoy the festive season with his family, Michael got up and left his office without saying a word. Nobody was around when he walked back down the corridor to his own study. Even Pauline was absent, having gone to the cash and carry to pick up coffee and tea supplies. He imagines Jeffrey having a quiet word with her, telling her the Prof hasn't been coping for some time and is taking some leave. After all, Jeffrey will probably say, he can't come to work and sit behind his desk all day staring into space and having seizures whenever someone tries to talk to him. It's just not on.

So Michael packed up his belongings and left quietly without any fanfare. The trains were on time for once, and the walk from the station to his house only took ten minutes, even though he'd had to walk more slowly than usual because of the bust, which was astonishingly heavy. Within an hour, he was home.

He dumps everything in the hall and goes through the living room to the kitchen at the back of the house. His porridge bowl and spoon are on the draining board next to the sink, where he left them earlier that morning, at a time that now feels like a different epoch, an era when he expected not to enjoy his days exactly, but to get through them and arrive at bedtime in a state of muted sorrow, but with his dignity intact. Now even that coping mechanism has gone, and he's so rattled he doubts he'll ever be able to eat breakfast again. He shifts his gaze up from the draining board and looks out of the window behind the sink. The low November sun doesn't make it to the lawn, because the laurel hedge has grown very high, and the green rectangle is clumpy, more moss than grass. Reese was the one who tended the garden. The lawnmower is in the shed at the side of the house, but Michael can't bear to go in there, because he knows Reese's tattered old straw hat is on the workbench, where he left it one day in the spring, not knowing he'd never wear it again.

What on earth is he going to do, he wonders. Not in the long term, not even for the rest of the week, but today, in the hours between now and bedtime? He could go out again, for a walk or to the supermarket, but really, what's the point? He wanders into the living room and picks up each of the items on the mantlepiece, one by one. The Staffordshire dogs, with their inane grins were Reece's, too, as was the clock in the shape of an aeroplane propeller and the envelope addressed to a charity, that Michael has never got round to posting, as if the action of putting in the letterbox will finally put an end to the fantasy that Reese will return one day and post it himself. During this pointless mental torment, an armchair seems to creep up behind Michael until it nudges his calves. He drops into it and switches on the TV, something he hasn't done for a very long time. The screen becomes animated by a very camp man and a giggling woman who are both attempting to assist a celebrity chef as he prepares a vegan thanksgiving dinner. Thanksgiving, in England, Michael says to the invisible Reese in the other armchair. And how can you have a thanksgiving dinner without turkey?

Michael channel hops for a while and ends up tuning into a station that dedicates its existence to endless episodes of a programme about doing up your house and selling it. He's not the least bit interested in DIY and never has been, but the chap presenting the programme is quite buff in a chirpy, working-class kind of way, and Michael is confident that hammering, plastering and valuations by estate agents won't lead him into dangerous mental territory. He switches his phone off, stares at the screen and allows himself to be lulled into numbness by the world of house renovation and men with big beards and muscled arms bulging out of T-shirts with capped sleeves.

Dusk falls and he realises he's been sitting in his chair for several hours without moving. The TV, ignored when it put out an automated enquiry about whether anyone was still watching, has switched itself off. He gets up, makes a cup of cocoa and takes it upstairs, groping about in the shadows because he doesn't want to switch on any of the lights. He shuts the curtains, takes his jumper and shoes off and gets into bed. By sipping very slowly and swishing it around in his mouth before swallowing, he manages to get through half of the milky drink. Then he gazes over at the opposite side of the bedroom and suspects he can see a dark mass beginning to gather in the corner nearest to the door. He wonders if might be Reese, transformed into a shadow person, making a brief visit to check up on him, and he can't quite convince himself that this would be lovely rather than terrifying, so he sinks down under his covers and shuts his eyes.

At three thirty-five in the morning, he wakes with a jolt, and his thoughts gravitate back to yesterday's conversation with Jeffrey, which has become a bit of a blur now. Did Jeffrey really accuse him of doing absolutely nothing from early morning to late afternoon every single day? Had he really used that awful American word, zilch? Michael had tried to argue his case. He said he wasn't doing nothing, far from it. He was planning a new book, marking out the subject areas and dividing it into chapters in his head. Jeffrey shook his head at him sadly and went on to mention the recent weekend at Talbot Way. Michael had let things get out of control, hadn't he? Stacks of books appearing in the middle of the floor, for God's sake. And as for the new postgrad, what's his name? Jacob, that's it. What must he be thinking?

So who played the role of Judas? One by one, Michael considers the people who spent that last weekend at Talbot Way. It can't have been Ben. It won't be all that long before he has completed his PhD, and he doesn't need much more than light supervision these days, so he has little to gain by complaining. The same could be said of Kirsty. Jamie is a bit more confrontational. It might have been him. On the other hand, Matt is relatively new and not sufficiently entrenched in the ethos of the department to be in awe of Michael's reputation. He has made it clear on more than one occasion that he wants to make his own decisions and run his own research projects without interference. But now a senior academic from another department will be drafted in to oversee Matt's work and will interfere a great deal more than Michael ever would. And as for Pauline, well she's been his secretary for years and she's never been anything other than totally loyal and always on his side. Since Reese passed, she's baked a coconut sponge, a lemon drizzle cake or a batch of chocolate butterfly buns for him every single week. Most of them have ended up in the bin, because his appetite isn't what it was, but that isn't the point.

The only other contender is Jacob. Please don't let it be him, Michael thinks. The possibility that this golden angel of a boy might have betrayed him feels like another loss, a damping down of the tiny flutter of hope Michael had felt in the boy's presence. But students these days, particularly postgrads with dazzling first degrees, often wear cloaks of entitlement despite being so ignorant they have no idea how little they actually know. The boy is personable and well read, but he doesn't have the first clue about the work involved in studying for a PhD, and that won't change unless he gets some decent supervision. Admittedly, he hasn't had much of that so far, but surely he wouldn't go and complain about it behind Michael's back. Michael had been under the impression they'd formed a kind of bond both at Talbot Way and afterwards, on the drive home, when Jacob was so open with him and so charming about his family. No, Michael decides, Jacob isn't the two-faced, calculating type. He's one of life's innocents, the kind of boy who will always expect everybody else to be as honest and decent as he is himself and will be dismayed over and over again when this doesn't turn out to be the case.

Without putting on his slippers, he gets out of bed and fumbles his way downstairs in the darkness. Once in the kitchen he flicks on the dim light under the extractor fan, puts the kettle on and reaches into the carrier bag he brought home from his office for the jam sandwich creams. He opens one of the packets and posts a biscuit into his mouth. The best-before date on the wrapper is July fifth, and the biscuit is stale and slightly hard. He doesn't care. It will soon soften up if he dips it into his tea. Through the arch, in the shadowy living room, chairs hulk silently like sleeping cattle. The idea of sitting on one and watching TV, like he did for almost the whole of the previous day, seems outlandish now. The clock on the mantlepiece ticks quietly until its gentle sound is drowned out by the boiling of the water in the kettle. Once he's squished the tea bag against the side of his cup and added a splash of UHT milk, he opens the back door and steps outside onto the small patio.

The night has reached its most silent hour, that dead time when the main road at the other side of the canal is quiet, when even the earliest of the early morning commuters are still in bed. There are no stars and no moon, and the sky is the vague orange colour clouds adopt when they find themselves hovering over streetlights. Take a few months off, Jeffrey said. Get help. Review your situation. Go somewhere nice. Catch up with family. Michael deals with each of these points in turn. Get help. There isn't anyone to get help from. Review your situation. Done that. His situation is completely hopeless. Go somewhere nice. He can afford to buy tickets to anywhere he fancies. A Hawaiian beach lined with palm trees would be wonderful if he could only escape from himself and his predicament when he got there. And as for catching up with his family, his colleagues at the university are the only family he's got. Okay, there's Colin, his cousin, who he sometimes chats with on Facebook. He lives in New Zealand and he's suggested Michael flies over for a visit more than once. But he doesn't mean it. The two of them have nothing in common and haven't set eyes on each other since Uncle Roland's funeral, which must have been at least twenty-five years ago. No, Colin would be horrified if Michael turned up on his doorstep.

One of the canal's resident duck population suddenly lets out one of those long series of quacks that sound like laughter. Michael smiles a little and begins to wonder whether things would be easier to cope with if he became a nocturnal animal, a creature of the night. He goes upstairs to fetch his dressing gown, then he tops up his tea and settles himself on a bench in the garden. It takes a while for the cold to get to him. When it does, he returns inside and gazes out of his bedroom window, wearing the curtains around his head and shoulders like a cloak.

He doesn't go back to bed until he spots the first hints of grey in the eastern sky.

11. Suzy

The doorbell rings, which is odd, because it's after midnight. The first week of the summer holidays is nearly over and I've only just turned my light off. In September I'll be in the lower sixth. I've opted to do Biology, Chemistry and Physics, which was a bittersweet decision for me. My teachers say I'm definitely best at science, but it means I'll be saying goodbye to English Literature forever, which makes me sad, so I've decided to embark on an ambitious reading programme for the holidays. I spent the best part of the last three days trying to get beyond the first page of Ulysses. I failed, just like everyone said I would, so I've moved onto Iris Murdoch, and Doris Lessing is next on my list. It's all been a bit of a chore so far, and if I'm honest, I'm dying to sink back into The Railway Children or Tom's Midnight Garden or Enid Blyton's Mystery series, with Fatty and his friends, who spend every school holiday solving an endless series of unlikely crimes.

I switch my light back on and the doorbell rings again, twice. It sounds urgent. I go out onto the landing and Dad shuffles past me in his slippers, tying his dressing gown at the same time. I want to tell him to hurry, but he'd move at the pace of a tortoise even if the house was on fire. When he finally makes it to the front door and switches on the porch light, I lean over the banister to get a closer look. Davey emerges from his room and joins me.

'Sorry to bother you. It's only me.'

A tall and lanky boy with longish black hair is hopping about on the doorstep. He's wearing jeans, but nothing on his top half and nothing on his feet.

'I think there's someone in my house, Mr Fylde. Or some*thing*. Please could you come and have a look?'

It takes me a few second to realise the boy is Adrian from across the Crescent. He's way taller than the last time I saw him and his voice is deeper and scratchier. Davey goes back into his bedroom, but I creep downstairs and stand behind and slightly to one side of dad so I can scrutinise Adrian more closely. His hair flops over his eyes and he flicks it back with a sudden movement of his head that extends his neck and reveals his Adam's apple. The lower half of his face is shadowy, as though he could grow a beard in a matter of days if he wanted to.

Dad clears his throat.

'I thought you'd moved in with your grandad,' he says.

I've had nothing to do with Adrian for years and none of us has seen him since before Christmas when his parents were killed in a collision with a lorry on the A31. Adrian wasn't with them at the time, and afterwards he moved in with his grandfather, on the other side of Larchford. The house he used to live in, on the opposite side of Fieldgate Crescent to ours, has been empty since then.

'I did, but he's cramping my style.'

Adrian looks down and brushes the sole of one foot across the doormat. Then he looks up at my dad again.

'Anyway the probate's completed and the house is mine now, so I decided it was time to move back in and do my own thing.'

Dad's back and shoulders go all stiff and rigid. As far as he's concerned, having your style cramped and doing your own thing are concepts that belong in a shady and dangerous realm populated by drug addicts, drop outs, bearded wonders and for some reason, students training to be teachers. I glance over Adrian's shoulder. Lights glimmer cheerfully through the trees in the little circular garden in the centre of the crescent. They must be coming from his parent's house, or rather *his* house.

'Can you do that, Adrian?'

I squirm in mortification, but Adrian doesn't seem offended by Dad's question.

'I'm eighteen, so yeah. I can do what I want, as Alice Cooper says.'

Dad gawps at him. I do the same. I have no real idea who Alice Cooper is, but I think she might be connected to Emily Dickinson in some way. Tomorrow morning, I'll go to the library and see if they have any collections of her poetry.

'And I prefer to be known as Ade now, Mr Fylde.'

'Oh,' Dad says, faintly, as though he's never heard anything so outrageous and is wondering what's happened to his smelling salts. Me, on the other hand, I just think *wow*, and when Dad tells me to stay at home because Davey will be left on his own in the house if I don't, I ignore him and pad across The Crescent in his wake. I wish I was wearing actual clothes and not my pink pyjamas and matching slippers.

'What was it you heard, exactly?' Dad asks.

'It sounded like footsteps in the cellar or the loft, or both. I'm not sure. They started as soon as it got properly dark, at around ten. Running around all over the place. Proper freaked me out.'

His house is detached and much bigger than our semi. Like all the other residences in Fieldgate Crescent, as well as those that run along the avenue round the corner, it was built in the thirties on land that was once part of the Fieldgate Hall estate. Ade's garden backs onto the remaining grounds of Fieldgate Hall. I've been inside his house, and his garden, but not for a long time, not since we were at primary school, when our mothers were in and out of each other's homes all the time.

'How long have you been back?' Dad asks.

'Since lunchtime.'

He leads us along the brightly lit hall. The staircase is on the right and the hall is on the left, with three doors opening out onto it. The middle door leads to the cellar. Ade opens it and switches on the light at the top of the narrow, linoleum covered stairs. Then he steps back.

'After you,' he says.

Dad releases another of his mortifyingly pompous, ostensibly throat-clearing harumphs and heads down the stairs. I follow closely behind, but Ade stays at the top. For a moment, I wonder if it's a trap and Ade is going to lock us in and hold us hostage. Something similar formed part of the plot of a children's detective story I'd once read, not an Enid Blyton, but a book aimed at older children. But what would be the point of that? Davey would have to pay the ransom, and he'd only be able to stump up three pounds and seventy-six pence. I know that for a fact, because he'd told me he was flat broke in an attempt to extort money from me only yesterday, and I'd made him empty his Yogi Bear piggy bank in front of me.

Thankfully, Ade doesn't lock the door behind us, and Dad looks around carefully and makes sure the little half-window is secure. The ceiling is too low for Dad and Ade to stand up properly and there isn't a lot to see, just a few old packing cases, a set of shelves containing drink cans and bottles and a rusted metal contraption with a big handle. Dad says it's a mangle and you don't see those very often these days. We go back up to the hall.

'No sign of a break in. It might have been mice or rats. Or squirrels. They can make a racket, particularly if they get into the roof space. Like clog dancers. You'd be amazed. I'll ring the vermin people at the council tomorrow and get them to come round.'

Ade thanks Dad but still looks worried, so Dad says he can come and sleep in our house, in the boxroom, if he likes.

He flicks his hair away from his eyes again.

'Really? That's so cool of you. It would only be for tonight. I'll be okay after that.'

I wonder vaguely what's going to be different about tomorrow night that means he'll be alright, unless he's assuming the rat catchers from the council will have already been by then. But I don't dwell on it. I'm too busy rushing back to rummage about in the airing cupboard for spare sheets that don't have pictures of ballet dancers or rabbits on them. I make up the bed for him in the box room and when I show him where the bathroom is, he says he remembers and smiles at me. Or rather, down at me because he's so much taller than I am. And that smile. It's not the broad gap-toothed grin of the boy who used to trundle round the Crescent on his scooter. It's more of an amused twitching, an ironic and intimate pursing of the lips, as though he's sharing a private joke with me.

When I return to my own bedroom, I make a gap in my curtains and glance out across the square to Ade's house. It's all in darkness now. Before locking up and leaving, we went into every room, made sure nobody was there and turned the lights off. It was tidy inside, apart from the unmade double bed and an unpacked suitcase in what must be the guest bedroom. The house smelled fusty and unlived-in, and it still felt as though it belonged to his parents.

In the morning, I toast bread and pile it up on a plate, which I put on the kitchen table with a plastic container of Blue-Band margarine and a jar of marmalade. I pour boiling water onto loose tea leaves in the teapot and put that on the table, too, with milk and sugar. We never take sugar in our tea, but Ade might. Dad left early as usual to open the shop and Davey is still in bed. Ade sits at the table and watches as I move around the kitchen. I feel horribly self-conscious, as though my limbs have turned to wood and are being operated by a remote part of my brain via an awkward set of cogs. I drop a cup on the floor. It smashes into several pieces and makes him jump out of his chair.

'Don't cut your fingers,' he says, as he helps me to clear up the mess.

That look flashes across his face again and I suddenly feel brave enough to ask him a question.

'Do you remember when we used to play out in the crescent?'

'Of course I do. You were in charge of the time.'

All the neighbourhood children played together. Adrian, me, Tess, Donna and a group of other boys who also went to the local primary school. We'd devised a game called Ambush, where we dashed around the crescent as quickly as we could on bikes, scooters, skates and pogo sticks, and even stilts one time, when Adrian was given some for his birthday, until each of us had slipped and ended up with their blunt, wooden ends rammed painfully into our armpits. After two minutes, someone, usually me, because I had a Timex watch that I was very proud of, shouted *Ambush* and we all had to drop whatever means of transport we were using and pick up someone else's. But all that stopped even before we left primary school, and once Ade had gone up to the grammar, our only contact was a mumbled and embarrassed *hi* whenever we accidentally came within each other's orbit, which, by design, didn't happen very often.

'I still see Kev and Anthony. We all stayed on in the sixth form,' he says.

'Graham's still at the farm. His mum works in my dad's shoe shop now. He's just done his O' levels at Larchford Rise. I think he's keen on Art School, but his dad wants him to go to agricultural college so he can take over the farm.'

'That sounds a bit heavy. I'm lucky in that way. Free to do what I like.'

'Sounds amazing.'

And possibly terrifying, I think. I wonder if I should say something about his parents, how sorry I am and all that. But everyone said that to me after Mum died and it didn't help much. It was a just little speech they felt they had to make, a hurdle that needed to be clambered over before normal conversation could resume.

'What about you. Are you free to do what you like?'

He folds his arms and looks at me from across the table.

'Up to a point. As long as I'm in at six for supper. Dad likes us to eat together.'

I can hear the defensive tone my voice has taken on. He must think I'm pathetic. Even when I am actually out, I'm only ever at

Tess's house or Donna's, or wandering around the shops with them. It's not as though I've ever tested any boundaries.

'That's so sweet.'

He puts his head on one side and scrunches up his lips at me again.

'When I first saw you last night, I thought you were still that little scrap of a thing with the loud voice. I was wrong, though, wasn't I?'

A hot pinkness blooms in the area around my collarbone.

'Were you?'

'I don't know.'

He leans forward, put his elbows on the table and stares at me. Bravely, I stare back, torn between wanting him to stop whatever it is he's trying to do and wanting him to keep doing it forever. It feels as though a part of him has broken away so it can burrow into me.

'You've fined down. That's it. You have these really delicate features, now. Like a porcelain statuette.'

'Do I?'

'Yeah. But look, I don't want to embarrass you.'

He shrugs and stops speaking while he spreads marmalade on a slice of toast. Then he takes a bite and starts again.

'Do you have Graham's number? I'm going to ring everyone and get them round. You girls can come as well if you like. I've got the new King Crimson album. We can listen to that and hang out.'

'When?'

'This afternoon?'

'I have to work in the shoe shop this afternoon.'

'That's a drag.'

'I know. It's so *boring*.'

'But you get paid?'

'There *is* that. I don't have to beg my dad for pocket money.'

'I'm going to sign on. You can when you're eighteen. And I've got an allowance from my parents' estate, until I'm twenty-five. Then it all becomes mine to do what I like with.'

'That's so freaky.'

'Come tonight, after you've had your dinner.'

I nod. I'm not at all sure what Dad will say about me going to Ade's when his parents aren't around anymore, so I decide not to tell him. I won't hide it exactly, I just won't say anything about where I'm going. He'll assume I'm off round the corner to Tess's house or Donna's. Ade smiles at me again, but more broadly this time. Now he looks more like the little boy I used to know.

'This summer's going to be fab, Suzy. It's not even the end of June, yet. We've got more than two months before term starts. That's like forever.'

A vista of endless, sunlit days rolls out in my mind and doesn't stop until it reaches a distant, possibly non-existent horizon. And none of those days will be marred by my usual sense of seething frustration about the world being an exciting place for other people but not for me. What an unexpected miracle. At Mum's funeral, I overheard someone in the church say you never know what's round the corner. It made me think back to the time before she became sick, how happy we'd all been, and how blind and clueless we were about the horrors to come. Now I realise it can work the other way. Sometimes a really good thing can arrive out of nowhere.

Ade gets up from the kitchen table and stretches. The weather is very warm and he's only wearing a sleeveless top with his jeans. The top is bright red and slightly too small for him. When he raises his arms over his head, you can see his midriff. I gaze at him, taking in the flatness of his stomach, the narrowness of his hips and the little patches of black hair under his arms. He lowers his arms again and I look away, quickly.

I don't think he noticed.

12. Suzy

After he's gone, I rush upstairs to look at myself in the bathroom mirror. I can't see a single hint of any fining down process, just my piggy-blue eyes with their gingery eyelashes looking back at me and the drift of pale freckles across my cheeks and my nose. I pluck my eyebrows again, even though I've already fashioned them into high, disdainful arches, which are meant to make me look sophisticated. And I shampoo my hair, twice, because Patricia Rumbelow says my sebaceous glands secrete so much oil you could fry chips on my head.

My afternoon stint at the shoe shop goes on forever. The shop is carved out of an old terraced house at one end of Larchford High Street. Customers sit on a line of hard-backed chairs opposite the front door in what was once the living room. Dad goes in early each morning to vacuum the carpet with its pink and green swirls, otherwise it releases little clouds of mouldy dust into the air and makes everyone sneeze. Once, he hired a huge contraption to steam clean it, but the entire place ended up smelling like wet dog. The room catches the afternoon sun and the windows don't open, so when I arrive it feels as though most of its oxygen supply has been used up. I prop open the front door with one of the chairs. Breakfast with Ade seems a long time ago now. I wonder what he's up to, whether he's managed to get in touch with everyone and invite them round. Perhaps they're all at his place now, lounging about on the back lawn, the French windows propped open so they can hear King Crimson from the record player in the living room.

Dad is selling a pair of Green Flash tennis shoes to a young man with blonde curly hair and a foreign accent. I make an effort to clear my face, so Dad can't see the resentment simmering just beneath the surface. It must work, because his moustache bristles and his blue eyes twinkle when he spots me coming through the door, as though he didn't expect me to turn up, not really, but here I am and he's over the moon about it. I tell him to go make a cup of tea and take a chair out to the little yard at the back of the shop for ten minutes.

The rest of the afternoon is busy with more people wanting tennis shoes, and several other customers who desperately need sandals for their holidays in Spain, so I don't have time to brood about Ade. It also means I'm firmly in Dad's good books, and when we sit down at teatime to eat our fish fingers, chips and peas, with big blobs of salad cream, he focuses his attention on Davey. My mind wanders and I start to worry about the evening. What if Ade and his mates might have already bonded during the afternoon and formed one of those cliques like the ones at school that repel all incomers? Also, I have no clue what to wear, and I think my roots have become greasy again during the long, hot afternoon, so I'll probably have to wash my hair again.

 Dad's interrogation of Davey develops into an entertaining spectacle, the way such things often do when you're an onlooker instead of the target. Dad went home unexpectedly in the middle of the afternoon, after I'd arrived at the shop, to change his shirt, only to discover that Davey was still in bed. Dad has an idealized image of the way a young lad should spend his school holidays that involves games of cricket in the park, building go-karts out of bits of string and planks of wood, and going on long bike rides with a pack of sandwiches and a bottle of pop, preferably with other twelve-year-old boys from the grammar school. But my brother prefers to mope about in his room, or hang out on one of the benches in the park, with a group of older teenagers from Larchford Rise Secondary Modern. And worst of all, he has a girlfriend called Sharon, who is a year older than he is, which translates into a much bigger age gap when you consider the difference in maturity between boys of twelve and girls of thirteen. The other problem, as far as Dad is concerned, is that Sharon lives in a council house on an estate at the other side of the High Street, and her father is a binman.

 Dad goes on and on until Davey loses his temper and calls him a bloody snob who thinks he's still living in the fifties. As a result, my brother is made to both wash and dry the dishes, while Dad stands there, arms folded, still droning on, although now he's moved onto another of his favourite topics, namely Mum and how upset she would be to hear him use that kind of language. It's cruel of Dad to guilt-trip Davey like that, but I don't hang about to stick up for him. Instead, I run up to my room, fluff up my hair with little puffs of dry shampoo and change into a clean T-shirt and jeans. As I exit the house I shout *see you later* and before Dad has a chance to ask where I'm going, I'm half way to Donna's.

Donna wasn't around in the afternoon either, so it's her first time at Ade's, too and we agreed to arrive together. She hasn't made any extra effort with her appearance. She's just wearing her usual jeans, and a tee-shirt adorned with badges taken from her denim jacket, which she's left behind for once because of the heat, and she must have applied her customary eyeliner long ago and then forgotten about it because it's gone all smudgy. If Tess was here, she'd probably get her little mirror out of her cloth, patchwork handbag and offer it to both of us, in a discrete attempt to get Donna to sort herself out. Donna would then make a point of not caring about the state of her make-up and Tess would be miffed.

When Ade answers the door, he's smoking small roll-up that smells like the annual church barbecue.

'You remember Donna?'

'Of course! Hi, Donna.'

Ade bows. Then, with the joint or whatever it is still firmly clamped between his lips, he stands back to let us in. As I pass him he looks down at me. I think he might be doing that scrunched up smile again, but I can't be sure, because of the roll-up.

'The girls are here,' he announces as he shows us into the living room.

Two enormous half-men, half-boys are sitting on the floor, propped up against the sofa. They stand up when we walk in and shake hands with us, as though Ade's parents are present in spirit and expect us all to behave the way they would have done at our age. It's only then that I realise the fair one is Kev. Now I know it's him, I see the only thing that has changed since the days when his mum dropped him off in The Crescent with his pogo stick is his size, which is now considerable. I'd never have recognised Anthony, though. He used to be a scrawny kid with big mournful eyes and a tendency to slope off in a huff when things weren't going his way. Now he's all hair. His dark locks are a pair of curtains, parted at the centre and tucked behind his ears, and he has a spectacular moustache that grows downwards on either side of his mouth until it joins forces with a shaggy beard. Anthony has morphed into one of Dad's bearded wonders.

When they speak, their voices are deep and manly, and echo off the walls, as though they're communicating through megaphones. Donna and I plonk ourselves on two armchairs facing the sofa and Kev and Anthony flop down onto the floor again, apparently exhausted. We all stare at Ade as he hovers about.

'What do you think?'

He waves his arms vaguely around the room.

'You've been busy,' I say.

Last night when I was here with Dad, this was an unremarkable living room, with the tedious décor favoured by seventies parents everywhere.

'I've changed a few things around.'

The room has been transformed into a large, downstairs version of a teenager's bedroom, but with a three-piece suite instead of a bed. Ade has stuck posters to the glass fronts of his father's hunting prints. Now instead of hounds and horses tearing about the countryside, the walls are mostly covered with depictions of rock bands. The posters are longer than the frames they've been stuck onto and when the door opens, their lower halves flutter in the breeze. Another picture, showing the semi-naked rear view of a female tennis player, who seems to have forgotten her knickers, has been fastened directly onto the back of the door. I've seen that one before. It makes me squirm with embarrassment as though it's my bum that's on show, larger than life, for everyone to see.

Ade notices me looking at it.

'Sorry about that,' he says. 'It's a bit much, isn't it? Christoff bought it for me, so I thought I'd better put it up somewhere. Don't want to hurt his feelings.'

Anthony and Kev laugh uproariously. I'm beginning to notice they laugh at most things Ade says. I don't understand what was so funny about Ade's comment, and I don't know who Christoff is, but I take an instant dislike to him. Of course, I don't mention this out loud, and I can't think of anything remotely positive to say about the poster, so I get up from my chair and explore the rest of the room. A stack of LPs has been placed next to the music centre, progressive rock mostly and a few records by TRex, Elton John and Queen. The collection of Reader's Digest classics on the bookshelves has also been replaced. Weird titles I'd never heard of jump out at me: Zen and the Art of Motorcycle Maintenance, The Doors of Perception and The Occult.

'Those are mine. I've shoved all my parents' stuff into a cupboard. Have you read any of them?'

'I'm more into novels. But not Ulysees. I've tried, but I can't get the hang of it.'

Ade smiles.

'Same. Although someone read bits of it to me once. It makes more sense hearing it out loud.'

Gosh, I think. What must it be like to know someone who reads Ulysses to you?

'Have you read any Lawrence?'

'He's on my list, just below Thomas Hardy.'

Ade disappears upstairs. When he comes back he hands me a tattered copy of Lady Chatterley's Lover. As I take it, he scrutinises me closely, eyebrows raised. I know what this book is about, but I've never read it, and I get a sense of deja-vu, as though I'd already foreseen that he would give me this particular book to read at this particular time. I watch as he flicks his hair away from his face again, and I wonder if he's teasing me. Somehow I manage not to blush. Maybe I'm getting used to him, learning not to over react to everything he says and does. Perhaps I'm already becoming more sophisticated, more adult.

Ade claps his hands and walks back into the middle of the room.

'This summer is going to be one long party!'

He sounds massively enthusiastic, like one of our teachers telling us about a lesson plan or the itinerary for a school trip.

'The only thing we need is more people. And booze. Although, there's some in the cellar. We can drink that for now.'

We all troop down to the narrow steps and bring back cans and bottles left there by his parents. Ade opens a cabinet in the living room, to reveal a big space containing glasses of different shapes and sizes, as well as a soda syphon, red plastic cocktail sticks and jars of olives and maraschino cherries. Underneath is a shelf containing half empty bottles of Cinzano and Martini and a small flask of Angostura bitters. Donna and I exchange a glance that conveys our agreement not to mention we are almost complete novices when it comes to alcohol. Donna's father made her a small snowball at Christmas, but she didn't like it much, and Davey and I decided to explore our drinks cabinet one evening not long ago, when Dad went to one of his Rotary Club meetings. It was full of liqueurs that had been there since the time before Mum became ill, when they used to have friends round and entertain them with cine films they'd taken on their holidays. After one too many swigs of Crème de Menthe laced with Cointreau, Davey puked a big blob of green stuff onto the carpet and I struggled not to match it with an offering of my own. When Dad came in we managed to convince him it was a stomach bug, but since then, the thought of alcohol has always made me want to throw up.

'Is there any lemonade?' I ask, thinking I could take a can of beer to make weak shandies for Donna and me.

'No. Sorry. We'll have to get some.'

'In that case, I'll have one of these.'

Resolutely, I pick up a can of cider and open it, trying to make it look as though this is something I do all the time. Donna grabs a can, too and we sip our drinks slowly, and watch the boys knock back beer and lager with Southern Comfort chasers.

Kev gets out a tin of leaves.

'Cool, man,' Anthony says.

Kev makes roll-ups for all of us, and we all sit there with them sticking out of our mouths as Ade goes round the room and ignites them with his parents' fancy cigarette lighter, which looks is fashioned out of an enormous lump of quartz. Donna and I have both smoked before, with Tess, just once, in the woods at the back of the netball courts. If they'd caught us, we'd have been expelled on the spot. I didn't enjoy the experience much. It really hadn't been worth the risk. When Ade lights Donna's roll up she laughs in an artificial, high-pitched way. We both manage to take a few puffs without choking, but each time I inhale, my forehead feels as though it's pulsating, not throbbing like a proper headache, but going in and out slightly, like a small paper bag inflating and then deflating again.

After a while, Ade produces a set of tiny glasses from the cabinet and a bottle of something that's mainly orange, apart from a brown sediment at the bottom. 'From Portugal. Or Madeira. Can't remember. The sediment is coffee beans. Or chocolate. Or maybe mud. Who cares?'

His words slide into each other and he grins. Of course, the other boys roar with laughter. Ade pours an inch of the orange liquid into each of six glasses. Its flow is thick and slow, like engine oil.

'Why six glasses?' Donna asks.

'What? Oh. Because of Christoff. He'll be here in a minute.'

'Who is this Christoff?' Kev asks.

'He's from the big house. Someone else lived there when we all used to play in the Crescent, so you probably don't know him.'

'Is he one of the Schneider boys?' Donna asks. 'My dad's their doctor. They're Swiss.'

Donna's father is a local GP and a good source of local gossip.

'That's right,' Ade says, shooting a finger at her, like a gun.

'Something to do with banking?'

'Yep. They have a house on Lake Geneva, too, and another in Antibes.'

'Bankers!' Kev yells suddenly.

He and Anthony roll onto their backs in a fit of hysterics. I don't get the joke, and I don't think Donna does either, but she produces that bizarre fake laugh again. Ade smiles round at everyone. The perfect host. When I'm sure nobody is looking, I decant my glass of orange stuff into the soil around a more than half-dead yucca plant, which is conveniently situated on a small table, between Donna and me, and I manage to bury what remains of my roll-up in the same place. Donna knocks her glassful back in a single mouthful and the boys do the same. I manage to finish my cider, though. At first I'm sensible and only take small sips, but once a small amount of alcohol has blurred the edges of my brain, which doesn't take long, I don't care anymore and I gulp down the rest in a matter of minutes.

The evening passes in a kind of frantic and noisy haze. Ade plays his records and we stand up and dance about as though we're on Top of the Pops, which is stupid because it's not really the kind of music you can dance to like that. At ten pm, Christoff still hasn't arrived and I'm clear headed enough to realise Donna and I need to go, otherwise we'll risk being grounded, which would be a major disaster now there actually is something to go out for. On the way home we agree that we need to negotiate later curfew times as a matter of urgency, otherwise the entire summer will be a dead loss. Ade escorts us both to our front doors. At first he walks between us and holds our hands, but then Donna breaks away, runs into the small circle of trees in the middle of The Crescent and starts making Tarzan noises, which isn't like her at all.

13. Suzy

On Saturday nights Dad likes us to stay in and watch telly with him. He usually makes a cake or a pudding, like Angel Delight with Dream Topping and sprinkles, which we're allowed to eat in front of the TV, while the Generation Game or Summertime Special is on. Even Davey, who would much rather hang about with Sharon and her mates in their usual Saturday night venue, the bus shelter on Larchford Green, stays in. Usually, I don't mind, but tonight I'm nearly bursting with frustration. I'm terrified they'll all go through a special, Saturday night kind of blood brotherhood ritual, and I'll miss out and be permanently excluded. If I have to spend the rest of the summer watching from my bedroom window as Ade's friends troop across the crescent to and from his house, I'll die.

I needn't have worried, though, because late on Sunday morning, there's a knock on the kitchen door. I answer it to find Ade standing on the back doorstep, shoulders hunched and hands stuffed in the pockets of his jeans, as though he's cold.

'Fancy a walk? I thought we could try and rustle up Graham.'

'Is anyone else coming?'

'Kev and Anthony can't come out till after Sunday lunch.'

'And Donna has to go to church.'

'So it's just you and me.'

'What about Christoff?'

'God, no. Christoff's not a morning person.' He smiles. 'How was the shop?'

'Full of idiots wanting sandals and tennis shoes.'

'Oh no! I didn't realise tennis shoes were only worn by idiots!'

I look down at his feet. They are encased in an extremely grubby pair.

'I didn't mean you.'

He put a hand on my shoulder.

'Don't sweat it. I'm only teasing.'

When he removes his hand, each finger leaves behind a separate burning sensation. I try to pretend I'm not swooning like a heroine in one of my books, while he goes to thank Dad, who is sitting in the living room reading the Sunday Express, for contacting the council. It's definitely squirrels, he says, in the loft. Baits and traps have been laid and the pest controller will have to come back again, possibly twice. Ade feels bad about doing away with the poor animals, but the noise is more than he can bear. We walk round the corner to the newsagent's on East Parade, where we buy a bottle of pop, two bags of crisps and a packet of Nice biscuits. Ade stashes them in his rucksack, and we go back round the corner, cross Fieldgate Lane and set out on the tinder track that leads through the fields to the farm where Graham lives.

The day is burning hot, so hot the sky has turned from clear blue to a kind of glaring white, and Ade is wearing sunglasses, or mirror shades, as he calls them, with rectangular lenses. I don't like them much because I can't see his eyes, which makes it even harder to work out when he's being ironic. I don't own any sunglasses. Tess has a couple of pairs. I wish I'd borrowed one now, before she went to Italy. When we reach the shady area under the big trees along the lane to Arrow Farm, he keeps them on. Graham's home isn't called Arrow Farm because it was built on the site of a historical skirmish fought by bowmen, which is what I used to think, but because it used to be owned by the Arrow family. The tinder track is just a footpath really. Cars and tractors wouldn't get very far if they used it to try to reach the farm. The official entrance connects up to the road on the other side. Graham's family are Hopgoods. They bought the farm from the Arrows after the war, and the fields they plough, harvest and rear sheep on come right up to the edge of Fieldgate Lane, which means that the row of houses on the opposite side of the avenue, where Donna and Tess live, have a view of nothing but countryside from their front windows, whereas from the back bedrooms, all you can see are acres of rooftops and gardens stretching towards Larchford town centre and beyond.

The first part of the track is straight as a Roman road. Close to where it starts, we have to walk around the burnt out wreckage of a car that has been there since April, and the ditches on each side are littered with stuff people can't be bothered to take to the tip. Today we pass a heap of old cushions, a broken pedal car, a ripped bag of old clothes and the rusting cage of a presumably dead budgie, with a thin slice of off-white cuttlefish still wedged through the bars.

I pick up my pace, but Ade grabs my arm.

'Slow down, what's the hurry?'

'I don't like this bit. A gang of boys used to have a den over there.'

I point to the ditch on the right.

'They used to jump out and block the way with their bikes.'

'I remember them. They wouldn't let you through until you said the right password. Nobody knew what it was, so you couldn't go until they got bored.'

'They were horrible.'

'But that was years ago. One of them works in Fine Fare now.'

'Andrew Dorridge? I've seen him on the till. He doesn't ask for a password now.'

Ade laughs.

'Have you started Lady Chatterley yet?'

I knew he was going to ask me that. As soon as Saturday TV with Dad and Davey was over, I went up to bed. It was too hot to sleep, so I decided to lie on top of my bedspread and read a couple of pages of the book before going back to my Iris Murdoch, just so I could tell Ade I'd started it. Usually it's a chore to read books recommended by someone else, but two hours later, I was three quarters of the way through. I got up at that point, opened my bedroom window and leaned out. The upstairs lights at Ade's house were still shining through the trees, but I couldn't hear music or voices. I went back to bed and didn't sleep until I'd finished it. The entire book.

'I read a bit of it last night. Just the first few pages.'

He gives me a sideways glance. He knows I'm lying.

'Did it shock you?'

Shocked isn't the right word. Astonished is more accurate, like being thrown through a door into a world I didn't realise existed.

'I'm not surprised it was banned for so long.'

'I know,' he says.

Gradually, the discarded contents of people's homes become more scattered, then they disappear completely and the track narrows and begins to feel much more rural and isolated. Apart from the occasional dog walker, residents of the Fieldgate Lane area, even kids on bikes, rarely come as far as this. Cars driving down the avenue can no longer be heard, and if it wasn't for the crunch of our shoes on loose stones and the cawing of a single, angry-sounding rook, it would be completely silent. Golden-yellow glimpses of ripening barley flash through gaps in the hedgerows on each side, and eventually a spread of red brick outbuildings with black corrugated iron roofs comes into view. The path opens out again and merges a metalled drive, which leads to a yard with a gate. Two border collies with crazed eyes leap up and bark at us through the wooden bars. The house is further down the drive. It looks like a child's drawing, square and symmetrical, with sash windows and a yellow front door. The front garden is long and bisected by a path lined with lavender bushes. A recently shorn sheep with little horns chomps at the lawn as though it hasn't eaten in ages.

'A living lawn mower.'

'I could do with one of those. Having a garden to take care of is such a drag.'

'What will you do with it when you go to university?'

'I'll come back for weekends sometimes.'

'Where are going?'

'York at the moment, but I'm thinking of switching to London, which would be nearer for cutting the grass.' He shakes his head. 'Anyway, all that's ages away. No point worrying about it now.'

The farmhouse door doesn't have a bell. Instead, there's a big metal knocker in the shape of a fist grasping a dagger, ready to strike. Ade lifts the fist and lets it fall against the door with a loud bang, which sets the dogs off again. After a few seconds, Graham's mum appears. She's in her Sunday best, white stilettos and a summer dress covered in red poppies. A look of alarm passes over her face when she sees me.

'Is everything alright, Suzy?'

After Mum died, Mrs Hopgood took us under her wing. She brought us meat and potato pies and stews in Tupperware containers, and one time, a tin of home-baked ginger biscuits with faces on them for Davey. He opened the tin, took one look at the biscuits with their happy expressions and comical pink hair and then ran up to his room, sobbing. He said he couldn't bear to think someone else's mum had made them and not his. That set me off, too, but when were about to go into the crematorium for the funeral, Mrs Hopgood took me to one side and told me I mustn't cry, for Davey's sake. No point spreading misery around, she said. I was proud of myself when I made it through the ceremony dry eyed. It wasn't easy. I had to dig my fingernails into my palms and tune everything out, but I did it. I stood there blank faced and paid no attention to the arrival of the coffin, the sentimental hymns or the awful, beyond-terrible way Dad and Davey were clinging to each other and weeping.

'Yes thanks, Mrs Hopgood. We're going for a walk and we've were wondering if Graham wants to come.'

She looks Ade up and down and a little line appears across her forehead.

'This is Adrian from The Crescent,' I say. 'Do you remember him?'

'I think so.'

Mrs Hopgood stares at him doubtfully, as though she thinks she remembers him, but not like this and not with me in tow. But she shouts up the stairs to Graham and invites us in, and we hover in the living room, drinking glasses of orange squash and making polite conversation until Graham appears. I haven't seen him for ages. He's in the same academic year as me, but at Larchford Rise Comp, not the grammar school. It turns out he's as freckly as ever and his brown hair is still straight and spiky, but he's much taller and thinner now. His white shirt is freshly ironed and he's wearing it with the sleeves rolled up, showing his arms, which are tanned and muscled from working on the farm.

'I can't hang out with you now. I've got to go and see Gran.'

'I thought she lived with you?'

'She's had to go into a home. She kept wandering off in the middle of the night.'

He speaks with the local burr, the one Ade never had. The one I did have once, but lost quickly when I started at St. Ursula's.

'Never mind, mate,' Ade says. He doesn't usually call people mate. I hope Graham doesn't think Ade is talking down to him. 'I'm home again now. Got the house to myself. When you're free, just turn up. Any time, day or night. There's usually a few of us hanging out. If we're out, I'll leave a note on the front door saying where we've gone.'

'Great,' Graham says, nodding eagerly. 'Thanks. I will.'

It must be lonely for him, stuck out here. He scribbles the farm phone number down on a scrap of paper and hands it to Ade.

'I don't feel like going back yet, do you?' Ade says when we're back on the metalled drive.

We keep walking until a stile appears. When we clamber over it, we find ourselves on a narrow path that winds between stinging nettles and tall bramble bushes. I'm wearing shorts, so the outer sides of my thighs end up covered in little patches of itchy blisters. The path opens out into a wide, grassy space with a big pond in the middle.

'Don't scratch! Wait here.' Ade runs over to the other side of the pond, where there's a small coppice of trees and some undergrowth, and comes back with a handful of dock leaves. He hesitates for a second or two before handing the bouquet of foliage over to me. Then he sits back and looks at the pond. The water is brown and opaque, and a solitary moorhen is scuttling off in a panic, trying to get as far away from us as she can.

'I'd forgotten about this place,' he says.

We sit at the edge of the pond, take our shoes off and dip our feet in. The water feels muddy and kind of therapeutic, like a face pack for feet. We drink the fizzy pop and eat our salt and vinegar crisps.

'Have you ever been skinny dipping?'

'No.'

I hate how flat and boring my voice sounds.

Ade stands up and grins at me. He flings off his sunglasses and throws them onto the grass. Then he pulls his T-shirt over his head and takes off his jeans and underpants, almost in a single movement. Naked, he wades quickly into the water, like some long-legged aquatic bird. He tips himself backwards with a screech and floats on his back with his arms stretched out. I don't want him to see that I'm watching. But I am. I can't help it.

He swims across to the far side of the pond, then back again, and lifts his head out of the water to look at me, arms splashing gently to keep himself afloat.

'What are you waiting for? You *can* swim?'

I don't know what to do. I'm longing to get into the water with Ade, but stripping in front of a boy is a big step, not because I'm self-conscious about my body. I've never been like Donna and Tess, who are always looking at various parts of themselves in the mirror from different angles and trying to rub away cellulite with plastic hand mitts. My skinny frame is a sexless thing, a generic version of an adolescent teenage girl's, like a diagram in a biology text book, and I don't really care who sees it, because there isn't much to see. But my underwear is another matter. This morning I slung on a very old and faded pair of flowery knickers and a nasty looking bra that was once white but is now dishcloth grey. If I'd known we were coming here, I'd have worn my black, school swimming costume under my clothes.

In the end, I decide I'm not prepared to sit here like an idiot while he's splashing about enjoying himself, so I take my shoes and socks off and slip into the water fully clothed. It feels wonderful and my nettle rash stops stinging instantly.

    He doesn't comment on my failure to undress, and afterwards, we lie next to each other, flat on our backs, in the long grass. He reaches for my hand and entwines his fingers with mine. I turn my head to look at him. His eyes are closed, as if he's fallen asleep, and he hasn't put his clothes back on. I'm lying next to a naked boy, I think to myself. I want to stare and stare at him, but I turn my head back so it's flat on the grass again and I look up at the sky instead. When he lets go of my hand and his cool, muddy fingers slide under my shirt, onto my stomach and then down, beneath the waistband of my shorts, I don't tell him to stop. I split my focus between the movements his fingers are making and the gentle hum of a bee in the purple clover, close to my left ear. The rest of him remains perfectly still and he keeps his eyes closed. Afterwards, he turns onto his side, props himself up on his elbow and smiles down at me, pleased with himself and with me, I think. I smile back and wait for him say something incredible or lean over and kiss me. But he doesn't. He just flicks his hair out of his eyes and stands up to pull his clothes on. Once dressed, he sits down next to me again and gazes into the distance.

    'What are you looking at?' I ask.

    'That hill.'

    We both peer at the mound in the distance that rises so steeply above the flat landscape of fields and woodland it looks artificial, a pyramid with sides covered in shrubbery and a flattened top that sprouts tall trees like hair. St Augusta's Hill, but locals call it Elfbarrow Hill or The Elfbarrow.

    'We should go there.'

    'What, now?'

    'Not now! We need to make a proper plan. Get everyone else involved. Take tents and food, make a camp, light a fire. Stay all night.'

    'It's meant to be cursed or haunted or something. People used to do black magic there and witches had covens.'

    I realise my words sound idiotic and childish even before I've got them out, but he nods in agreement.

    'Joseph Dixon and Craig Benton from the year above me at school went last summer. They were going to stay the night and sleep under the stars, but they said they heard loads of weird noises and then Craig thought he saw a really tall man without a face looking at them from the edge of the trees. They freaked out and ran away. They left all their stuff behind. Joseph's mum had to drive them back to fetch it the next day, to collect it.'

I wonder how they could tell the man was looking at them if he didn't have a face, but I don't say anything.

'Sounds scary.'

'It wouldn't be if a lot of us went. We could do rituals. Contact the dead.'

'I don't know any rituals.'

'I don't believe you. I bet your ancestors were witches.'

I laugh, but at the same time I wonder what made him say that. Is he joking or does he genuinely think I'm weird? 'There's a Ouija board at the back of the cupboard in our dining room.' It's a hateful object. I don't even want to go near it, but it seems I'll say anything to impress him.

'Oh my God, that would be amazing! Have you used it?'

'Once with Tess and Donna, a long time ago.'

'Did anything happen?'

'The planchette thing kind of moved around on its own and spelled out words when we asked questions.'

We'd each rested a forefinger on the planchette and it skimmed over the board as though it had a mind of its own. I knew I wasn't pushing it. And I didn't think Tess or Donna were exerting any pressure either, but surely one of them must have been?

'What questions did you ask?'

I hug my knees and hesitate before answering.

'We started off with obvious things like *is there anybody there*? When it said *yes* we asked what its name was.'

'What did it say?'

'I've forgotten. It was so long ago.'

It said it was called Amy, which was my mum's name. I wondered whether Tess was responsible. She might have thought it would be nice for me to get a message from my mum. But it wasn't nice. It was creepy and morbid. I went along with it, even so, because I was curious, and we asked this Amy, whoever she was, all sorts of questions. A few of the answers made sense, but most didn't, and it didn't feel to me as though my mother was responsible for any of them. On top of the dining room sideboard there was a photo of Mum and Dad at their wedding. It's still there now. When I put the Ouija board away again, I felt like turning the picture to the wall.

Ade looks me in the eye.

'What sorts of questions did you ask it?'

'Stupid things, like who was going to die next. Things you shouldn't ask.'

'Did it respond?'

I nod.

'You don't like talking about it, do you?'

'It felt like we'd summoned something up we couldn't control. I had to sleep with the light on for ages.'

'Did Tess feel the same?'

'Not really.'

'She's not like you, is she? Unless she's changed.'

'What do you mean?'

'She just gets on with life. Doesn't brood over things?'

This comparison between me and Tess makes me despise myself. It hurts all the more, coming from Ade, particularly after what just happened. He's hardly seen Tess for years, but he's right. Tess is spontaneous, colourful and wild and I'm cautious, beige and boring. I jump up from the grass and walk off.

'It's getting late,' I say.

It isn't, not really, but I start to run and don't look back. Before I've even reached the stile, he's right behind me. He puts his arms around my waist and kind of crams himself against me, another thing that no boy has ever done to me before. I stand still and let him nuzzle my damp hair.

'I didn't mean anything. Don't be angry with me,' he murmurs as he reaches down and kisses the side of my neck.

I know the right thing would be to swivel around in his arms so I'm facing him and we can embrace properly. That's what Tess would do. But I stand there, rigid and immobile, like a dummy in a shop window. In the end he detaches himself, grabs my hand and leads me towards the stile, apparently not minding my inability to act like a normal girl. The pond seems further away from home than it had on the way out, and it's too hot to walk slowly. We don't talk and the silence soon becomes unbearable, but I can't think of a single thing to say.

Suddenly he stops and turns to face me.

'I didn't mean to compare you to Tess like that. It came out all wrong.'

'You were right. Tess engages with life, whereas I hide away from it.'

'That's not true. Look what just happened. You embraced *that*. You were amazing.'

'Was I?'

'Spectacular,' he says, laughing.

I laugh, too. He thinks I'm spectacular. How freaky is that? The awkwardness between us shakes itself free and soon we're talking over each other in our eagerness to get our opinions across.

'So when are we going to do this camping trip?' I ask him.

'In a fortnight?'

'Donna and I will have to work out how to sell it to our dads.'

'You could say we're camping on Arrow Farm land. It might be on their land. I don't know. Pretend you're sure it is.'

After that we argue about how many tents we'll need, or if the weather stays hot and dry, can we sleep under the stars? Could we get away with lighting a fire or will someone see it and call the fire brigade? I wonder whether we should bring food to cook or if it be will easier to stick to sandwiches and flasks of coffee, whereas Ade's main concern is the logistics involved in transporting crates of beer and cider to the top.

By the time we get back to Fieldgate Crescent, it's late afternoon, but still very warm. We step into the musky darkness of Ade's hallway and as soon as we've shut the front door behind us, he catches hold of my wrists, pushes me against the wall and kisses me on the lips. I panic for a second. He stops and tells me to relax, so I do.

'Today's been incredible," he says. 'You're so sweet.'

We continue with the kissing until I feel as though I'm falling backwards through the wall.

Then I hear a sharp burst of laughter. I open my eyes to see a boy standing behind Ade's right shoulder. His arms are folded and he has a look of surprised amusement plastered across his face. It's the customer with the foreign accent who was buying tennis shoes at the shop when I arrived on Friday afternoon. His dark blonde hair tumbles down to his shoulders in waves, like a lion's mane. His face is also lion-like, quite fierce, and he's shorter and more thickset than Ade, and a tiny bit older, I'd say. His hair is wet and he's wearing nothing but swimming trunks and flip flops, which have left a trail of droplets behind him on the hall carpet.

I wonder how long he's been standing there watching us with his arms folded like that.

'Sorry to disturb you,' he says. His words sound oddly precise and formal, as though he's making a TV or radio announcement.

Ade jumps away from me. For a second, I think he's going to swipe the back of his hand across his mouth. He shoves his hands in the back pockets of his jeans and turns towards the blonde boy.

'This is Christoff,' he says.

14. Suzy

Tess returns from her holiday and the sun continues to blaze down. It's too hot to do anything much, and we start spending most of our time lazing about by Christoff's swimming pool. His parents are in Geneva at the moment, but his older brother, Karl, is around, together with Alain, who does the gardening and some of the driving, and his wife, Jeanette, who cooks and looks after the house. Alain and Jeanette have been with the family for a very long time, and live in a flat over the garage. Jeanette dotes on Christoff. While we're hanging out in the garden, she brings out endless jugs of lemon barley water, plates of sandwiches and bowls of crisps, even though we could easily fetch them for ourselves. We never walk round to Christoff's front door and ring the doorbell. In fact, during that exceptionally hot summer, I don't think we go inside his house once, not until the end, anyway. We let ourselves onto the property via Ade's back lawn, through a connecting gate in a brick wall that has been there since the houses of Fieldgate Crescent and Fieldgate Lane were first built, when Ade's house was occupied by the gardener and his family.

The first time Tess joins us, she's wearing a white dress, big sunglasses and a straw sunhat, all of which she bought in Italy, which was mind blowing, she says. Her parents ran art classes at a holiday resort and she went off on to the beach on her own every day and flirted with the Italian boys. Tess is more experienced than either Donna or me when it comes to the opposite sex. During the May half term, when she was at guide camp, she had what she called *intimate interactions* with two different boy scouts on consecutive days. She told Donna and me what had taken place in minute detail, and from then on, she referred to that trip as her weekend of love. She didn't go all the way with either of them, but she went a lot further than either Donna or I had ever been. I was impressed and shocked at the same time. Later, when we were alone, I told Donna I couldn't imagine myself doing any of it with one boy, let alone two. Donna just shrugged.

Tess's dress has a crocheted yolk and you can see her bikini straps and her fantastic tan through the little gaps. I meet her in the Crescent and show her the short cut through the gate in Ade's garden, via the path at the side of his house. When we get there, everyone is sunbathing. I quickly remove my denim shorts and stripey T-shirt, then I flop down onto my towel in my school swimsuit, hoping none of the boys are watching me. I needn't have worried. They're all too busy leering at Tess, who says *hi* to everyone, peels off her dress, flings her hat to one side like a frisbee and jumps straight into the pool in her skimpy bikini.

Ade dives in after her. We watch for a while as he lifts her out of the water by the waist and plunges her back in again, then we all jump in, too. When we get out, he rubs sun oil into her arms and shoulders, taking care to lower the straps of her bikini so she won't get white marks. Then he comes up to me and does the same. After Tess's arrival, this kind of thing happens a lot, as though Ade has decided to share himself between us. Sometimes he holds my hand and kisses me on the cheek in front of everyone, but then he makes sure to do the same to Tess. He doesn't ask me to become his official girlfriend, but then he doesn't ask Tess either, so I assume he wants to keep his options open. I don't like it, but at first I tell myself his admiration for Tess is an act, that he's playing to the gallery, like Mr Rochester did with Blanche Ingram, and that Tess is just flirting with him. I told her what had happened between Ade and me as soon as she'd got back from Italy, hoping she wouldn't throw herself at him, for my sake. I reassure myself that when I'm alone with him again, he'll be like he was that Sunday at the pond. But since Tess got back, Ade and I have never been alone.

We swim and sunbathe and then swim again. The cheap brown suntan oil from the chemist's shop on Larchford parade that we smear over our legs, arms and shoulders doesn't offer much protection from the relentless sun, and when our skin grows tight and itchy, particularly mine, we move to the shade of the lawn under the elm trees by the grass tennis court. After we've cooled off and eaten marmite and cucumber sandwiches, Christoff usually rustles up a partner for tennis, or three of us for doubles, and we play while the others watch and half-heartedly cheer or jeer.

It goes on like this for a couple of weeks. More than that, even. Afterwards, I'm not sure why I put up with it for so long. Maybe I was trapped in a kind of enchantment or perhaps I still believed Ade saw me as plain on the outside, but fascinating on the inside, like

Jane Eyre. On the day I snap out of it, we're all sitting in the shade by the tennis court again. Jeanette has just wheeled out jugs of iced tea and plates of egg sandwiches and chocolate digestives on a big, creaking trolley. The chocolate on the digestives is already starting to melt. Tess and I are sitting next to each other, then Ade shoves himself between us and sits on the grass with one arm round Tess's shoulder and the other round mine. His fingers caress the skin at the top of my arm. I can't see, but I know he'll be doing exactly the same to Tess with his other hand. Christoff has been inside to get changed and now he's strolling towards us from the rose garden, wearing his tennis whites, carrying a tube of tennis balls.

'What's going on Ade?' He says in his cautious, stop-start voice. 'Are you starting a harem? If so, what about Donna? She must be feeling left out. But then, you've only got two arms, I suppose. Perhaps she'll get a turn later, yes?'

Anthony and Kevin guffaw loudly at this, of course, and Gaz, the new addition to the group, looks at me and then at Tess, and smirks. I don't much like that smirk. I have no idea where Ade found Gaz. He looks about ten years older than the rest of the boys, his light brown hair has been plaited into dreadlocks and his beard looks like a habitat for small creatures. Most of the time, he seems to be in a kind of stupor, induced by drugs or idiocy, or both. Everyone seems to accept him as part of the group, though, with the exception of Christoff, who ignores him. Ade laughs at Christoff's comment, too, but Graham gets up without saying a word, takes two of the rackets and the tube of balls from Christoff and holds his hand out to help Donna up. They stride over to the tennis court together.

That's when I realise Ade isn't interested in me at all. I've been behaving like a pathetic fool, grateful for any attention he cares to bestow on me, because I'm desperate. I have to stop letting it happen before it's too late. I don't say or do anything to mark this mental transition. I intend to continue hanging out with them. I don't want to miss out on anything, particularly the camping trip, so I decide to remove myself from girlfriend status, or whatever it is I am to him, but still bask in Ade's charisma, just like the others, as though he's some kind of superstar or cult leader.

When the afternoon comes to an end, I go home, change, wring out my swimsuit and have dinner with Dad and Davey. I feel sad, but it's disappointment more than anything else, and perhaps a vague sense of humiliation. Overall, I decide I'm just the same as I was before, intact as a pearl (almost), but maybe a little wiser.

Later, all of us, apart from Christoff, regroup in Ade's living room. Ade suggests there should be a beverage of the day, which we all have to drink. Tonight it's bloody Marys, laced with Worcester sauce. Ice cubes optional. He's always generous with the booze and he makes sure he pours a decent slug of vodka into each glass. I drink mine very quickly and it goes straight to my head, but instead of coming over all mellow and laid back, I feel hyper-aware, as though there's a buzz of discomfort in the air, an electrical charge, like the atmosphere before a storm. The other thing we've started to do is play games, and the more we drink the crazier the games become. Twister is a favourite, as is forfeits, and a slightly dangerous version of hide and seek invented by Ade, with complicated rules. Everyone apart from the seeker has to hide, and the seeker wears a blindfold and tries to find people before they creep up behind him and tap him on the back. It creates a lot of suspense and the seeker is usually a hysterical wreck by the end of it.

This particular evening, during a game of Twister, Ade and I become entangled, and he tries to kiss me. I remove myself from his reach and ruin the game. He doesn't say anything, but I can tell he's got the message, and from that point onwards, he glues himself exclusively to Tess.

Donna and I leave at eleven. We've both managed to persuade our dads that we're sensible girls and our curfews can be extended without us coming to any harm. I wanted midnight, but eleven is better than nothing. The others have later deadlines, and Tess, of course, can stay out as late as she likes. But Ade always chucks everyone out at midnight anyway. He says he doesn't want to disturb the neighbours too much in case they cause trouble. Reading in bed, I usually hear their noisy departure and sometimes I run to my window to watch as they walk across the crescent. What I'm really doing, sad individual that I am, is making sure Tess leaves. So far, she always has. Usually, she's accompanied by Graham who then cycles off down the farm track, which is almost exactly opposite her house. Donna lives next-door-but-one to Tess in a house that also faces the Arrow Farm fields. I wonder if she looks out of her bedroom window, too, to make sure Graham leaves Tess at her own front door. Soon afterwards, though, Graham starts walking Donna and me home at eleven, and Tess stays at Ade's house with the others.

One night as she passes, she looks up at my window and when she sees me, she waves and lets herself into our front garden. I go down to meet her. We sit together on the grass, hidden from the rest of the crescent by Dad's carefully trimmed holly hedge, not that there's anyone around.

'We've got something to tell you,' she whispers.

'We?'

'Me and Ade. We thought you should know up front. Before the others, so you don't, you know, humiliate yourself.'

She can't stop grinning. Her entire face must ache.

'Know what?'

'We're together. It's the real deal. We're mad for each other. We've talked it all through and we've agreed we both feel the same. The thing is, I know he likes you, too. But only as a sort of friend. He's worried he misled you and made you think it was something else.'

'I didn't think that. I'm not stupid.'

'Okay, well that's good.'

She looks at me as though she's waiting for me to thank her for telling me. When I don't, she continues.

'Anyway, you know when we go to Elfbarrow? That's when it's going to happen. Under the stars. Isn't that freaky?'

'Freakiest thing ever.'

The sarcasm in my voice doesn't reach her.

'Ooh, I nearly forgot. I've got something else to tell you!'

I cringe. I don't want to be told anything else.

'Christoff really fancies you. He told Ade.'

'Even freakier.'

I get up and go inside to bed, leaving her sitting on my Dad's neatly mown front lawn with its precise little border of alternating clumps of white alyssum and dark purple lobelia. After Tess's revelation, I keep my distance from Ade, and I try to shut my ears when Tess goes on about him. Every so often, I accidentally catch Christoff's eye and he responds by giving me these really bold stares until I have to look away.

The main topic of conversation is the camping expedition. The boys are still worried about how they're going to get all the booze up there. Christoff is the only one with access to a car, an ancient mini clubman held together with bits of rotting wood. It belongs to his older brother. Unfortunately, last summer, Karl got himself banned for a year when he drove the car into a ditch after driving after drinking eight pints of lager at the White Hart. Now Christoff's parents won't let either of the brothers use it in the evenings, and certainly not on overnight trips. Ade soon comes up with a plan, though. The road that passes the main entrance to Arrow Farm goes round a wide bend to the left, after which there's a lay-by. It's not all that near to Elfbarrow, but it's as close as you can get by car. And on the map it looks as though a bridle way leads from the lay-by to the foot of the hill, through a plantation of conifers. On the morning of the camping trip, Ade, Christoff and Kev pile into Christoff's car, with two crates of beer, a crate of cider, two bottles of vodka, one of whiskey and a few of lemonade, pull up at the lay-by and drag it all through the plantation and up a steep track. They hide it in some gorse bushes close to the flat area at the top of the hill. After that, they drive the car back to Fieldgate Hall, and we all make our way to the hill on foot.

It takes us ages to get there. The stuff to we have to carry, the tents, cushions, groundsheets, blankets, as well as the packs of sandwiches, fairy cakes and sausage rolls made by Donna and me that morning, slows us down, and by the time we reach the pond, we're hot and sticky. The girls decide to stop for a quick dip, but the boys, who are terrified someone will find the alcohol stash before they get there, press on. When we finally reach the top of the hill, the lads are sitting in a circle around the crates and bottles under the tall beech trees that crown the centre of the hilltop. Donna and I amble around the perimeter of the summit, trying to find the best place to pitch the tents. We keep stopping to take in the amazing view of patchwork fields, little squares of woodland and the winding road Christoff drove up and then back down again.

A loud burst of laughter from the direction of Kev and Anthony breaks the silence. It makes me realise how lonely this place is. It's the weekend and the sun is shining, but we didn't see a single other person walking along any of the tracks and footpaths that lead here, and the view on all sides gives the impression that there's no human habitation, no houses, farms or anything, for miles and miles. We set up camp in a small flat area not quite under the beech trees, one tent for the girls and two for the boys. By the time we've finished, the shadows are starting to lengthen and I keep thinking I can hear music jangling intermittently from somewhere far away, travelling along air currents generated by the unusual heat. It creeps me out a bit, probably because I can't identify either the song or its source. I tell myself it must be one of the ice cream vans that patrol the streets of Larchford, but up here it's difficult to believe either in Larchford or the vehicles that drive down its roads.

    We have a brief argument about whether or not we should light a fire. Ade and Kev are worried that people might see it and call the fire brigade. Graham points out that without a fire, it will be pitch black once the sun has gone down, because it's the dark phase of the moon, and we've only got a couple of torches, which Ade grabbed from his cellar at the last minute, with no idea how much life is left in the batteries. So a fire is lit and when it takes hold it definitely acts as much needed source of light. Kev walks around the edge of the hill, along the ridge where it begins to slope downwards, to check whether the fire can be seen. He says not, because of all trees and holly bushes. The only problem is that the fire casts everything else into almost complete darkness, and my shoulders keep twitching as though something or someone I can't see is standing behind us, watching. I look round a couple of times, but I can't make anything out. I begin to wish I hadn't brought the Ouija board.

15. Aunty Susan

Amanda was meant to be driving me home this morning. I packed up my belongings last night, so I'd be ready. The plaster has been removed and my ankle is on the mend. The next stage is up to me, they said at the hospital. As long as I attend my physio appointments and do the exercises they've prescribed, I'll make a full recovery. But that was yesterday. Today, as I get out of bed, an excruciating pain creeps from my neck to my waist and then stays there, turning one side of my back into an inferno. I can tell at once that this is a sinister and unusual symptom of something nasty, not simply an ache from a strained muscle, but I still hope it will fade away to nothing if I move around a bit. and ignore it. Gawain, who is never around during the day, is sitting at the kitchen table, tapping away at his laptop and drinking coffee. I'm so taken aback I have to stop and rest one hand on the back of his chair.

'What are you doing here?'

'Study leave for my exam. They've given me a single day to get through a year's worth of work, which is incredibly generous of them. I'm so grateful.'

I wander away and attempt to lower myself into my usual chair as though nothing is wrong, apart from my slightly stiff ankle, but I can't get comfortable, however much I shuffle around. Gawain looks up from his laptop.

'Are you sitting on an ant's nest?'

The pain still hasn't diminished. If anything, it's intensified. Now my back feels as though someone has put a match to it and set it alight. Little beads of sweat have formed on my forehead and under my arms. I panic, which isn't like me at all.

'I think I've got kidney failure,' I blurt out.

He rushes across to me and perches on the arm of my chair while I try and describe my symptoms.

'Shingles, most likely,' he says, calmly. 'It's incredibly common at your age.'

'I don't think I've got a rash.'

'How do you feel in yourself?'

'Alright, I think. A bit more tired than usual, perhaps.'

He takes my temperature and measures my pulse in a workmanlike way.

'I'm pretty sure it's shingles. It can affect the nerve endings just under the skin without causing a rash. Either that or the rash hasn't appeared yet. If you start taking anti-virals quickly, it might stop it in its tracks.'

So here I am, still at Gawain and Bartosz's house, with set of symptoms that are almost a mirror image of the ones I had before. Walking isn't much of a problem now, but resting is almost impossible. It hurts like hell when the affected area comes into contact with my bed or the back of a chair, and over the counter pain killers barely take the edge off it. Amanda got another doctor at her health centre to prescribe antivirals, as well as a particular type of antidepressant that they use for this condition, which helps me to sleep. But it's still bloody grim. And worst of all, I'm stuck here now here for goodness knows how long, with nothing to do but think about that wretched summer. If I'd managed to get myself home and resumed my usual activities, I'd have been able to let it fall away by now and sink to the back of my mind, with all the other forgotten dross that must be lurking there. But here I am, inwardly seething at my fate, hovering on the edge of what used to be an extremely comfortable chair, mooning over the damn photo album, completely unable to shove the thing back on the shelf in the hall where it belongs.

Tonight it's Bartosz's turn to cook. The only absentee at the table is Jacob. He's been closeted away in his room since he returned from his meeting with Matt, apart from brief, monosyllabic forays into the kitchen for food and coffee.

Gawain goes to the foot of the stairs and shouts 'Food!'

No reply.

'Bartosz has cooked. Get your sorry arse down here now!'

Jacob mooches into the kitchen and collapses heavily into a chair at one end of the table. He's even paler than usual and he has the same bruise-like, purplish shadows under his eyes he used to have when he was a small boy and was sickening for something. He pulls his hood over his head and rubs his eyes.

'What?' He demands when he realises everyone is staring at him.

'What do you mean, *what*? Nobody's seen you for days. Are you ill?' Gawain asks.

'No!' He lengthens the word out, making himself sound like a badly-done-to adolescent.

'What's wrong with you, then?'

'I'm screwed.'

'Wine,' Bartosz declares in a hearty, *brook-no-argument* voice. He empties an entire bottle into four glasses and passes them round. Then he sits down opposite Jacob.

'Your meeting didn't go very well?' Gawain asks.

Jacob takes a cautious sip of his wine and then scrutinises it through the glass.

'The prof's gone on extended leave and Edinburgh Matt's turned into a maniac.'

Silence.

'He hates me. I don't know what to do.'

He swallows and looks at Bartosz and then at his brother, as though he's decided to throw the problem over to them to sort out.

'What makes you think he hates you?' Bartosz asks.

'He gave me a huge bollocking. Like a proper Hitler rant. It was well harsh. He tore my proposals to shreds. I mean literally. I'd printed out a copy for him and he ripped it up in front of my eyes. He said it was pants. Apart from Point Seven. He liked that. Or rather, he didn't hate it as much as the other points. He said if it hadn't been for Point Seven, he'd have chucked me out of his office there and then.'

Jacob puts his head in his hands and looks through his fingers at us.

'He told me to use Point Seven as my starting point and rewrite the entire proposal. I've also got to read a load of books. Really long, boring ones.'

'Well then, that's what you have to do. I don't see what the problem is,' Gawain says.

Jacob folds his arms and shakes his head.

'No way. I'm done with being spoken to like that. I'm going to pack it all in and get more hours at the supermarket.'

'Stop being such a knob.'

Jacob hurls a shocked and wounded expression in his brother's direction. He looks as though he's about to burst into tears. Both of my nephews used to cry a lot when they were teenagers, particularly when they argued. I could never understand why, and I had no clue how to deal with it, particularly when they fell out completely after Gawain left school and Jacob refused to speak to his brother for what amounted to several years in the end. Displays of emotion like that didn't happen when I young. I put it down to the touchy-feely times we live in, that and the Italian genes they inherited from their mother.

'What's Point Seven?' I ask, in an effort to calm him down.

'Oh my God,' Jacob groans.

'Don't be rude,' Gawain says. 'Auntie's only showing an interest.'

'Sorry, Aunty S. It's just, I don't know anymore. I had a flash of inspiration about the circularity of time and I kind of suddenly grasped how it can't be linear. And I was wondering if paranormal activity, and UFOs and all the rest of it have something to do with the true nature of time and the fact that we don't understand that it doesn't really exist in the way we think it does. It sounds stupid now.'

'Not necessarily,' Gawain says, carefully.

'Yeah, well. All these ideas came bubbling out of somewhere inside my brain. I thought they made sense when I first wrote them down, but now Matt's bigged up Point Seven and made out it's the key to my entire thesis, I've lost the thread. I've read what I wrote over and over again, but it sounds like utter crap now. I can't write a proposal from an abstract concept that I don't understand, and I certainly can't do three years of research on it. I'm totally fucked.'

'Don't be such a drama queen,' Gawain says. 'Sleep on it. Read the books, then go back to your proposal and break the whole thing down into smaller parts. Then you might start to find a way through.'

'It's not just my proposal, though. He hates me, too. While he was yelling his head off, he got my CV up on his laptop. He said just because I'd sailed through my degree and got a first, it didn't mean things would automatically be easy for me from now on. My first degree means nothing, it's what I do with it that counts.'

'That's true, though, isn't it?'

'Yeah, I know that. It just pisses me off that he thought he needed to spell it out. And.'

Jacob stops, takes a large gulp of wine and looks down at the table.

'And?' I say, after a while.

He takes a deep breath. 'He asked me why there was such a big gap in my CV between leaving school and going to uni.'

The tears in his eyes start to spill over. He brushes them away, angrily. Bartosz hands him a paper napkin.

'Well that's tough for you, but from his point of view it's a valid question.'

'Whose side are you on, G?'

'I'd want to know if I was going to be your supervisor. What did you say?'

'I told him I'd gone out to the US to work in a church community with my mother for my gap year, but ended up staying longer. Then he asked why I did that. Was I some kind of religious fanatic? I didn't know what to say, so I got up and stormed out.'

'You didn't. Jesus, Jacob,' Gawain says.

'What would you have done, Mr Perfect?'

'I'd have sucked it up and explained.'

'But the way he shouted at me. It was well out of order!'

'Maybe it was, but you can't expect everyone to be kind to you all the time.'

'Oh really? I didn't know that. Thanks for the info.'

'It might be a good sign that he shouted at you. Maybe he thinks you're worth the effort, but you need a wake-up call?' Bartosz suggests.

'Nah. He despises me. He said he knows my type. I'm nothing but a feckless womaniser, apparently. Just because I hooked up with Aimee.'

We all look at him as we try to work out how to respond to this bombshell. If he wasn't so upset, we'd probably all laugh. I make a supreme effort not to wade in and tell him to pull himself together, and Bartosz focuses intently on his glass of wine. Jacob eyes each of us in turn, as though he's wondering who's going to crack first.

'Then he said if I didn't get a grip, I'd be up that well known creek without a paddle. I didn't understand what he meant. What creek?'

'The shit one,' I can't help saying.

'Eh?'

'Shit Creek? You'll be up it without a paddle.'

'What are you actually on about, Aunty?'

He looks at me, bewildered. The poor boy seems lost. And he looks a total mess, frankly. His fair, curly hair is all over the place, like a dandelion clock. If he doesn't get a grip, he'll blow away in the wind.

The next morning, as I alternate between hovering on the edge of a chair and pacing up and down, waiting for my next dose of painkillers to kick in, my mind turns to Elfbarrow again, and what happened to Tess. The album is open on the table in front of me, on the page with the swimming pool photos. There aren't any pictures of the trip to Elfbarrow because Tess was so excited about the trip, she forgot to bring her camera. I'm about to slam the album shut and put it back on the bookshelf, when Jacob appears with his laptop under his arm and falls dramatically onto the sofa in front of the stove, his legs caving in beneath him, cartoon-like, as though someone invisible has sneaked up behind him and whacked him on the head.

'I thought I'd keep you company,' he says gloomily. 'Sorry about last night. And sorry about your *thing*.'

'My shingles thing?'

'Nobody told me. If I'd known, I wouldn't have been such an arse at dinner. Or I'd have tried not to be.'

'Is there no way you can salvage your PhD?'

'Dunno. Gawain told me to e-mail Matt and apologise. He said what have I got to lose? I've done that. Now I'm waiting for him to reply. Or not.'

'So you're a bit on edge at the moment?'

'Yeah, a bit. But it's not just that.'

'Oh?'

He pulls the album towards him and looks at the swimming pool photo.

'I had another look at these photos after you'd gone to bed last night. I hope you don't mind. You're obviously the little ginger girl. But who's he?'

He points to the picture of Ade in the water.

'That's Ade. Why?'

'He's living his best life, isn't he? You, not so much. Or maybe you're frowning because of the sun. It's difficult to tell. These photos are pretty rubbish.'

'No,' I say.

'You weren't living your best life?'

'I had been. That summer started brilliantly, and it carried on being fantastic for a while. But by the time that photo was taken, everything had changed.'

He leans back in his chair and folds his arms.

'What happened?'

'Are you sure you want to know?'

'It would take my mind off the Matt thing.'

I look at him. Maybe unburdening myself about all this to someone else might help me, as well. He makes coffee and I begin to tell him. Of course I gloss over what happened between Ade and me at the pond. How could I go into detail about something like that with my twenty-four year old nephew? Before long, I've reached the point when night has just fallen at Elfbarrow.

'This must seem be very tame for someone from your generation?'

'No way. I'm fascinated.'

I think he means it. I'm about to ask him if he's *really* sure he wants me to go on, but he's staring at his screen.

'Matt's replied.'

Jacob opens the e-mail and reads it. I'm relieved he's heard from Matt, because my tale is about to take a darker turn, and I'm not sure I want him to know what happened next. If I go on with my story and leave gaping holes in the parts of the narrative that reflect badly on me, he'll notice immediately. I've come to realise he has almost the same capacity for radar like perception as his brother. God knows where he gets it from. Not from me, that's for sure.

'Bad news?' I ask him.

'I don't know. He doesn't mention me storming out of his office and he's ignored everything I said in my apology e-mail. It's mainly about two other books he wants me to read. They're relevant to Point Seven, apparently.'

'That sounds promising.'

'I suppose so. The only thing is, both books are out of print and they don't have them in the library. But there are copies of them on the shelves at Talbot Way.'

'The haunted house?'

'Yeah. The fifth most haunted. In England. Or the sixth. Depending on who you speak to.'

He frowns and runs a hand through his hair.

'Do you have a key?"

'The Prof gave me one before he vanished.'

'So what's the problem?'

He sighs and looks out of the window at the alpacas who are standing in their enclosure, gazing at nothing, heads held high, with satisfied little smirks on their faces, as though everything is peachy in the mind-space occupied by South American camelids.

'I don't like the idea of going in there on my own,' he admits eventually.

'Why ever not?'

'I know it sounds totally lame, but that night I was there, all sorts of things happened. The others said it was one of the most eventful nights they'd ever had. They thought it was me, the new boy mucking everyone about, playing tricks. It wasn't. I didn't do anything, but what if I acted as some kind of focus and something in the house reacted to something in me, because I'm not like other people?'

'What on earth do you mean?'

'I don't know. It's like something went into my head when I was in the house, and it's still there. It has this mocking voice and it says I'm wrong about everything. I was so confident when I did my first degree. All that's gone now. I'm right back where I was when I came out of the church. After I'd let myself become such a victim.'

'That's rubbish Jacob. You're miles away from where you were back then. And you didn't let yourself become a victim. The nutjobs in New Sunrise did that to you. You're just giving in to your tendency to catastrophise.'

'Am I?'

'You are.'

He looks down at the swimming pool photos again and shakes his head.

'Anyway, what does this voice think you're wrong about?' I ask him.

'Doing a PhD. The merits of Point Seven. What happened in the past, particularly when I was with Mum in the church. Everything, really.'

'And none of those feelings about past events were in your head before?'

"They were there, I guess, but more hidden? I thought I'd stopped letting all that bother me. But now it's kind of been dragged out into the open again. It won't ever go away. I'll always be the boy who got himself whipped. The whipping boy.'

He's never opened up to me like this before.

'You're not weak. You're just young and uncertain. We were all like that once. And most of us still have doubts and fears. I certainly do. All we can do is find a way to live with them.'

I say this with confidence, because it's mostly true, but if I'm honest, his words have pulled me up a bit. He's managed without knowing it, to describe exactly how I felt as that night on Elfbarrow Hill unfolded, and the next day, and for the rest of that summer, and afterwards when it all ended so badly. And I still harbour the same doubts now, about whether I'm remembering it all correctly, and what the hell made me do what I what I did, or do what I *think* I did, which of course makes me wonder what sort of a person I really am.

I don't know. Either I'm interpreting what Jacob said in a way that fits with my own insecurities, in a kind of subconscious shoehorning exercise, or it's a bizarre coincidence. A sign. But I've never believed in signs and portents. The shingles must be affecting my brain.

I make a decision.

'Do you want some company?'

'Really?'

'I'll come with you. I've been stuck inside for days. And the ghosts won't stand a chance when they see *me* walking through the door.'

16. Aunty Susan

Jacob doesn't make an enormous fuss like Gawain would have done, but he does throw me a sausage-shaped cushion from the back of his car and suggests I put it behind me to prop myself forward a bit so my painful areas don't come into contact with the back of the seat. It works quite well. I sit there, hunched forward slightly with my walking stick by my side and my handbag on my lap. I'm reasonably comfortable and excited as hell to be going out. I'd be happy to go anywhere after being cooped up for so long. Even a shopping trip to the nearest supermarket would be a thrill. But a visit to a supposedly haunted house, well at least it will give me something to tell Molly and June. Before we set off, he chooses some music with me in mind, Tony Bennett and Frank Sinatra accompanied by big band arrangements. This sort of thing was more popular in my parents' era than in mine, of course, but I appreciate the thought. And it's better than the usual electronic stuff he plays, long zig-zags of jerks and pops that repeat the same, tentative idea over and over again, and never move towards a satisfactory conclusion.

Jacob doesn't speak until we pull onto the motorway and he's adjusted himself to the rhythm and flow of the traffic.

'We should be there in about an hour,' he says. 'That'll give you plenty of time to tell me what happened on your hill.'

'I was hoping you'd forgotten about all that.'

'Well, I haven't. In fact, I'm dying to know.'

'It's probably not what you think,' I say.

'Which is what?'

'Strange rustlings in the trees, ghostly goings on, spirits summoned up by the Ouija board? Although, the Ouija board was scary, I have to admit.'

'Wow. Why?'

'It kept spelling out the same thing over and over again. Stupid, really. And most of us were pissed as farts by the time we got started. Myself included.'

'What did it say?'

'Two words, again and again. *Tess* and *not*. There wasn't any pattern to it. Sometimes we got *Tess* four or five times in a row, then there would be a *not*. We all swore we weren't doing it on purpose.'

'You know about the theory that subconscious micro-muscular movements can make fingertips move planchettes or upturned glasses?'

'I didn't. But it makes sense and I did suspect Tess. Making it spell out her name was exactly the kind of attention seeking thing she'd do. The *not* was more difficult to explain, though.'

'Maybe that was down to you. She spelled out *Tess* and some really deep part of your subconscious responded with *not*.'

'Could be. But she was still my friend, despite everything. I didn't want anything to happen to her.'

'I didn't mean you wished her harm. Why would you think that? I just meant, maybe you wanted her to stop with all the *me, me, me*?'

Did I want her to come to harm? Was there something about conditions on Elfbarrow that night, a malign atmosphere lingering from times gone by when witchcraft rituals were practised up there, or a peculiarity about the combination of people who had their fingers on the planchette that led to the surfacing of unacknowledged truths? As I consider this disturbing and unwelcome possibility and chide myself at the same time for even giving a single concession to such superstitious claptrap, the subdued pain in the part of my back affected by my shingles, the region Gawain refers to as the dermatome, suddenly flares up. I fidget in my seat and try to focus on Frank Sinatra asking to be flown to the moon. I don't want to think about Elfbarrow anymore. Jacob gives me a suspicious, sideways look.

'Are you transitioning into one of your Highly Indignant States?'

'No I am *not*.'

'You sound quite indignant.'

'Well, I'm not.'

'I wasn't trying to interrogate you. I was just curious. Tell me to butt out if I ask too many questions.'

'I will, don't worry.'

'Cool, but there's one more thing I need to put on the table.'

'Such as?'

'You know Ade?'

'I do.'

'It's been really bugging me. I should have said something earlier. This might be another of my wacky theories, like Point

Seven or the mocking presence at Talbot Way. On the other hand, it might be true.'

'Go on.'

'What if the Prof and Ade are the same person?'

'Eh? Why on earth would you think that?'

'The photos. Ade looks exactly like you'd expect a younger version of the Prof to look. Also, he was obviously interested in the paranormal back then, from what you've said.'

'So were a lot of people.'

'And when he found out my name was Fylde, not Field, he asked who my father was. I said he was the author, David Fylde. That was when he had the seizure.'

When Davey grew up, he was a university professor up in Hull and accidentally became known as the male Germaine Greer when he wrote a book about feminism from a male perspective.

'That's not much to go on. Anyway, I thought you said your Prof's name was Michael.'

'He might be using his middle name.'

'He had a couple of middle names, if I remember rightly. One of them was Gregory, I think.'

'What about his surname?' Jacob asks.

'Gossland.'

Jacob nearly swerves into the side of a milk tanker. Horns beep furiously. We're on the M25, not far from Heathrow, in five lanes of traffic. At the best of times it's like being in a car park moving at eighty miles per hour, and now Jacob's little car is lost in the middle of a stream of enormous lorries.

'Fuck me!' He yells. 'Fuck. Fucking hell. Jesus!'

I close my eyes and wait for death to come. Luckily, by the time we turn onto the M40, he's calmed down a bit. I make him pull off the motorway at the first service station we come to. We sit across from each other with a cup of tea and a couple of those enormous empire biscuits, round shortbread things, as big as beer mats, with white icing and a cherry on the top. We need the sugar.

'It can't be him. It's too ridiculous for words,' I say.

Jacob summons up Google Scholar on his phone.

'Professor Michael A. G. Gossland,' he says. 'I can only find only one Professor Michael Gossland. There's a Professor Stephen Gossland, but he's in Papua New Guines and he's into algae, not ghosts.'

'Adrian must be one of his middle names, then.'

'He must have decided to switch to Michael later on.'
'For a fresh start, perhaps.'
'Why would he need a fresh start?'
'It doesn't matter.'
Jacob googles Ade Gossland, then Adrian Gossland.
'Nothing,' he says.
'But Ade might not be noteworthy enough to come up on google. He could be dead, even.'
'I know. But still. It's more likely to be him than not, isn't it? Gossland must be a very uncommon name, surely?'
I nod.
'My blood sugar levels can't cope with this,' he says.

He gets up from the table and goes and buys himself another empire biscuit, which he eats on the way to the car. We leave the motorway services via the petrol station. He fills up his tank and I pay.

'Why didn't you say anything sooner?' I ask him once we're back on the motorway.

'I don't know. It seemed like such a mental coincidence. I thought you'd tell me off for letting my imagination get the better of me.'

I don't reply. My head is reeling.

'Are you ok, Aunty?' He asks.

Of course I'm not bloody ok. I'm stunned. Gobsmacked. Appalled. I never saw him again after that summer. I knew he went to one of the colleges that made up the University of London in those days, and I think someone said he went backpacking during the next summer holiday, but after that I lost contact with everyone who knew him, apart from Donna and Graham. And now he's reappeared. Just like that. He knows Davey is Jacob's father, so he'll have worked out that I'm his aunt. Christ almighty. What if Jacob's arrival in his department stirs up old memories and he decides the time has come to wake up those sleeping dogs that have been left in peace for so many years? Ade was the only other person who was there when Tess died. Nobody knows that apart from me. I could end up in prison.

The satnav on Jacob's phone instructs us to turn off the motorway at the next junction.

'What's he like?' I ask. 'You say he had a seizure and he's a bit eccentric, but how lucid is he?'

Jacob contemplates my question.

'One minute he's on another planet, then the next minute he's totally back, holding court, making jokes, telling anecdotes, discussing theories. I think he plays on the nutty professor thing a bit, but why shouldn't he? In the paranormal world he's a superhero.'

'You approve of him, then?'

'I do. I was incredibly lucky to be picked as his next PhD student. There were loads of other candidates. That's partly why I was so gutted when I found out he'd gone on leave and left me with Edinburgh Matt.'

'Maybe I'd better stop telling you all this stuff up from the past,' I say. 'It doesn't seem fair on you, somehow. Or him. He was only eighteen at the time, after all.'

'What? No don't stop, please.'

'He doesn't come out of it very well.'

But then, neither do I. In fact, I come out of it very badly indeed. I glance across at Jacob's navigation app. We've still got ten minutes until we arrive at Talbot Way.

'You're a man of the world, aren't you?' I ask him.

'Meaning?'

'You've had relationships with girls? Or boys, I suppose. If you're like your brother.'

"Exclusively girls so far. And mostly it's been friends with benefits, not relationships. Apart from Ruth at New Sunrise.'

'Ruth was his long-time girlfriend in the church, the daughter of the Chief Elder. She was the reason he got whipped. Someone discovered them together and reported him.'

'I'm not like my brother. He mates for life. Like a lobster.'

'I hope you treat these friends of yours with respect?'

'I'm a gentleman at all times, Aunty.'

'Glad to hear it.'

'Why do you ask?'

'Because Ade wasn't. Not that night on Elfbarrow Hill.'

'What did he do?'

'It's not a pretty story.'

'I *think* I'll be able to cope.'

I decide to continue, but I won't tell him everything.

'Where was I up to?'

'The Ouija session.'

'Ok. We all got to a point where we were too freaked out to continue. I put the Ouija board away in my backpack and the group seemed to disperse. My head was spinning from the alcohol, so I drank some lemonade and grabbed a ham roll. I sat by the fire and started to feel a bit better. Then Christoff appeared from nowhere. He sat down by my side and put his arm round me. And he started groping my leg.'

'From the tone of your voice, I'm guessing you weren't up for that?'

'His breath smelled of eggs and over the preceding few days he'd grown this horrid little collection of pale whiskers in the middle of his chin. I hesitate to describe it as a beard. His hand started to make its way upwards to the hem of my shorts, and his fingers were all coiled up, in a kind of fist, as though he was some kind of animal with paws instead of hands.'

'What did you do?'

'I almost panicked. I could see most of the others, but they were all quite a long way away at the other side of the fire, and I wasn't sure they could see us, or if they could, that they would be sober enough to come to my assistance. Ade and Tess had vanished altogether. Anthony and Kev were laying on the grass, propped up on their elbows, knocking back cans of lager and vodka chasers in little glasses they'd brought with them from Ade's drinks cabinet. We didn't call them shots then. Donna and Graham were rolling about in the doorway of our tent, snogging, and Gaz had taken all his clothes off and seemed to be howling at the stars. Not the moon, because there wasn't one, as I said.'

'The state of you all.' Jacob laughs.

'I know. I got hold of Christoff's fist, removed it from my leg and stood up. Then I ran over to the other side of the fire. Christoff got up, too and started lurching after me like Frankenstein's monster, but I sat myself down between Kev and Anthony, who greeted my appearance with riotous applause, as though I was a long lost hero who had suddenly appeared after an extended interval. They offered me a can of beer and poured me a chaser. It's all a bit of a blur after that. Christoff stood looking down at us for a while, I think, but then he must have sloped off somewhere. I don't remember seeing him again that night. But I *do* remember singing songs with Kev and Anthony. Tie your kangaroo down, I think it was, with those choruses about various forms of bestiality. Have a shag with a nag, and all the rest of it.

'Have a screw with a roo. Have a snog with a dog. Have a fuck with a…'

'Duck. Yes, that's the one. Well done, Jacob.'

'Sorry.'

'I must have crawled back to the girls' tent, because next thing it was morning and I was in my sleeping bag next to Donna and Tess, who were both dead to the world. Sunlight was seeping through the green canvas, the birdsong outside was practically deafening and I was desperately thirsty. I crept out for a wee and as I squatted behind a bush I glanced across at the boys' tents. No signs of life there. The embers of the fire were still glowing red, and empty bottles and cans were scattered about all over the place. I fumbled about until I found a three-quarters full bottle of lemon and lime. I knocked most of it back in one go. When I went back to the tent, Tess was sitting up. She looked as though she'd been crying, and she said she wanted Donna and I to pack our stuff and leave before the boys woke up. I asked her why, but she wouldn't tell me, so I said no, I wasn't going to do that. Donna said the same. We'd brought sausages, eggs, tins of beans and a little gas stove, and after we'd had our big breakfast we were going to hang out up here at least until lunchtime and maybe go swim in the pond again on our way back. I was looking forward to all of that and I didn't see why Tess should ruin the entire day just because for once in her life, something hadn't gone her way.'

We leave the motorway, enter a big roundabout and take the third exit onto a dual carriageway.

'How long before we're there?'

'About five minutes. What was Tess so upset about?'

'I'm getting to that. She got dressed and went home on her own before the boys were awake. Donna and I didn't see her until the next day, when we went round to her house to make sure she was ok. She looked at us with big mournful eyes and took us up to her bedroom via the outside staircase. That was when she told us she'd gone ahead and slept with Ade as planned. She'd made such a big thing of it beforehand and she'd looked forward to it so much I was steeling myself for the aftermath, her triumph about being the first of us to go all the way, how wonderful it was, how good she and Ade were together and all the rest of it. But she didn't say any of that and she wasn't jubilant at all, just pale and rather subdued.'

'At first I assumed it must have been a bit of a let-down. Cosmopolitan magazine always warned us girls not to expect too much the first time.'

'But it wasn't that?'

We're driving through a town, now. I didn't notice the name on the way in, but it's a dismal sort of place, all concrete brutalism, with slip roads, office blocks and car parks. A scant drizzle is falling.

'Her deflowering, as she put it, had taken place on the other side of the hill, in the trees, well away from the tents.'

'And?'

'It wasn't just Tess and Ade. It was Tess and Christoff, too.'

'Oh, right.'

We pull into the driveway of a small semi-detached house constructed from red brick. The front garden is paved over and the window frames are freshly painted. It doesn't look like a haunted house. It looks more cheerful and better maintained than all of the other houses in Talbot Way put together.

'You don't sound very shocked.'

'She might have been up for it. Or, if she wasn't, maybe she didn't make it clear.'

'But she'd never have been up for that. And she was drunk. It was totally wrong of Ade and Christoff to assume she'd be ok with it. Surely that's obvious?'

'Some girls send out confusing messages, though. It's hard to work out what they want. And if you get it wrong you can end up in some serious shit.'

'She said she couldn't get away. One of them held her down and watched while the other did it, and then they swapped. They were both really cold and clinical. It felt planned, she said, as though they were carrying out an experiment.'

'Jesus. Obviously that sounds like serious sexual assault. If it's true.'

He frowns and switches off the car engine.

'On the other hand, she could have made it all up. Things might not have gone quite the way she intended, but she went along with it because she was wasted. Then, when she sobered up she couldn't believe what she'd got herself into, so she invented the part about being held down to make herself feel more like a victim. Get herself off her own hook, kind of.'

'Even if that's true, they still took advantage of her.'

'Maybe.'

'You don't sound too sure?'

'When I was at school, I went through a phase when I shared a girl with one of my room-mates. One of us was allocated the half above the waist and the other the half below.'

'At the same time?'

'Yes. Then we'd change ends. It sounds awful. Exploitative. But she was up for it.'

'Good Lord, Jacob. How old were you?'

'Fifteen.'

'Who was the girl? Do I know her?'

'I'm not saying. We're still friends.'

'You wouldn't arrange to see a girl and then bring a friend along at the last minute, though, without consulting her first?'

'No, I'd never do that.' He stares out through the windscreen. 'Although, to be fair, I might have done when I was younger. All sorts of stuff went on at school. There was a big space under the stage, where they kept the gym mats, and an old classroom on the top floor, full of ancient typewriters. But if the girl had objected, I'd have stopped.'

'Well, thank goodness for small mercies.'

I don't want to talk about it anymore. But Jacob has a point when he says Tess could have made it all up. She'd always been a confabulator, a teller of tall tales. Her stories were influenced by the books we'd read, like the time she told us there was a tiger living in a cage at the back of her garden. It had come to tea, apparently, but had got out of control, so it had to be locked up until the zoo could come and fetch it. Another time, she told us to be very quiet when we went up to her bedroom, because there was a family of small pixies living in her airing cupboard. When we were a bit older, she'd often claim to have met famous people, through her parents. One of the earliest of these was Twiggy. She was quickly followed by the tennis star Chrissie Evert, then David Cassidy, and later, slightly unfortunately, Gary Glitter. It wouldn't be accurate to say Donna and I believed these claims. Not exactly, anyway. It was more that we pretended they were true. I think we could both see that Tess's compulsive fibbing made her seem vulnerable. We were irritated by her lies, but we felt sorry for her, too and we protected her feelings by going along with all the preposterous stories she made up. Also, it was very entertaining. Tess and her capacity for make believe were great *fun*. I must never forget that.

I stare at the house in front of us. All the curtains are closed. It looks like a sleeping face and the front door is grey and modern, one of the new, easy to maintain composite versions. I know, because I've got one myself. And I can't see any cobwebs or skeletons peeking out of windows. Jacob gets out of the car, slams his door shut and comes round to my side. He holds my hand and helps me out of my seat.

17. Aunty Susan

We make our way down a narrow passage at the side of the house. My progress is slow, but Jacob is very patient. He hooks my elbow around his arm, and rummages in his back pocket of his jeans for the key to the kitchen door at the same time. It seems very dark when we get inside and the door leading out into the next room is closed.

'I'm sure the curtains and blinds were all open when we left. I didn't think anyone had been here since,' he says.

'Maybe the spirits shut them?'

He doesn't respond. The kitchen is small but tastefully decorated in a minimalist style, and it feels very warm. I can hear the hum of a boiler and the buzz and tick of a fridge freezer, but I can't see any evidence of either. They must be hidden away behind cupboard doors. A gigantic, state of the art coffee machine that looks as if it would be more at home in a café, stands to attention in one corner. Jacob sees me looking at it.

'When the department kitted this place out they got told off for spending too much money on trivialities. You practically have to be a trained barista to get coffee out of that thing.'

He fills the kettle and puts it on.

'There's some instant.'

'Do they keep the heating on full when nobody's here?'

'They're not meant to. I thought it was set to come on for two hours in the evening and two in the morning just to keep the edge off. And you can't do it remotely. You have to set up the system manually, when you're actually here.'

He pours boiling water onto instant coffee granules in two large mugs, finds a jar of whitener and spoons some in. We wrap our hands round our mugs. I'm glad the heating is on. The journey in Jacob's car was damp and chilly because his radiator is on the blink and he can't afford to get it fixed.

'Can I have a look around?'

'Sure. I'll give you the guided tour. It won't take long. Then I'll find the books and we can get out of here.'

'It doesn't feel particularly spooky.'

'It's not too bad during the day. Nothing kicks off properly until after everyone's gone to bed. The current theory is that people have to be asleep for it to gather up its energy.'

He smiles and raises his eyebrows when he says this, as though he's joking. But I'm not sure he is. I find it hard to understand how he can possibly believe all the banging and knocking sounds they heard that night indicated the presence of anything other than floorboards and walls creaking as they cooled down for the night. I'd like to wager the rest of the kerfuffle was caused by the others playing tricks on the new boy, including the part where the books supposedly stacked themselves up in the middle of the room. It worries me that Jacob is so disturbed by it all. His mother was mad as a box of frogs, and one of my greatest fears has always been that Jacob or his brother, or even Amanda, will start to show signs they've inherited her mental instability.

'I know you think all this haunted house stuff is bonkers,' Jacob says, reading my mind. 'And you probably think I'm borderline insane, too. But your perceptions change after dark, particularly when you've been asleep. It's difficult to explain.'

'Yes, well.'

After that feeble retort, I open the stripped pine door that leads to the next room. The curtains must have black out linings, because I can't see much of anything at first. Soon, though, my eyes become used to the dark and I can make out a long space, separated into two halves by a set of folding doors. The area closest to me contains a dining table and an entire wall of bookshelves, from floor to ceiling. Jacob walks over to the side window opposite the bookshelves, and opens the curtains, letting in the late November light, which is already starting to fade, even though it's barely lunchtime. Through the window, you can see the alleyway we just walked down, and the pebbledash wall of the house next door, which looms surprisingly close, so close you could probably hear any loud noises that were made in the rooms behind it, particularly in the quiet of the night. Mystery solved, perhaps.

'This is the dining area and the library type thing,' Jacob says, pointing to a wall full of books from floor to ceiling. 'Some of them are rare and difficult to get hold of. They're categorised alphabetically according to subject. I'm looking for two really old books that have a go at conflating the nature of time with poltergeist activity.'

'Noisy spirits.'

'Yep.'

As Jacob tries to find his books, I potter off towards the other half of the long room, still holding my cup. I reach the archway and look through. It's still extremely dark in there, despite the open curtains in the dining area, but I can make out the hulking shapes of two sofas at right angles to each other, and something else, something lighter in colour than the sofa cushions. I blink. The scant visual data that passes through my eyes and into my brain generates an image I wasn't expecting. My heart starts to bang in my chest. Sitting in the chair furthest away from me is what looks like an enormous ventriloquist's doll. I try very hard to tell my mind it has construed this vision from a few fragments of light, and that if I calm down and wait a few moments, the true identity of the thing will pop out at me. Perhaps it's a lanky soft toy, a kind of rag doll, or maybe it's a long, slim package from Amazon, containing a curtain pole or a rolled up rug that someone has carried in from the front doorstep and left propped up in a chair.

But my brain is having none of it. It continues to insist that the thing has both a human form and a face. When my eyes become completely accustomed to the dark it pops out at me, as clearly it would if I'd put the main light on. It can see me too, and it's looking right at me. I take a step backwards. I'm not thinking clearly, but my plan, in as much as I have one, is to get back to where Jacob is standing and pretend I've seen nothing, that everything is fine and that my blood pressure isn't approaching a level that would cause Gawain's measuring implement to explode. But I can't tear myself away. The doll, or whatever it is, is sitting there with its legs crossed, right over left. Doggedly, I stare at it and continue my stupid attempt to pretend it's not alive. Unfortunately, this becomes impossible because it decides to swap its legs round, so they're now crossed left over right. I think it lets out a sigh, too, but I'm not sure, because I'm too busy screaming.

I try to leap backwards, but my ankle fails me and I end up on my backside. Jacob runs over from the bookcase, pulls me up, walks me back into the dining room and pushes me down into one of the chairs. I bounce up and he pushes me down again. Twice.

'What the hell? Sit there and don't move for a bit. I'll get you more coffee or maybe tea would best? Sweet tea. I don't know if there are any tea bags, though. They all prefer coffee.'

The coffee from my cup is splashed over the floorboards near the archway and I'm as out of breath, as though I've just run a marathon.

'Should I call an ambulance? Tell me what to do, Aunty.'

'I'm fine, Jacob. I've just had a shock.'

'Why are you whispering?'

'There's someone through there.' I stand up and point to the archway. 'Just sitting there, staring. I don't know who he is, but I'm off. Give me your keys. I'll go and sit in the car.'

I make for the kitchen. When I get there, I turn to make sure Jacob is following me. But he's heading in the opposite direction, through the archway, towards the entity. He switches on a light.

'Whoa!'

The surprise in his voice takes the edge off my own fear. I'm not going crazy. He can see it, too. I turn round and lug myself and my stiff ankle back to the archway, where I stand, partially hidden by my nephew. Sitting stiffly in the chair is an old man with closely cropped white hair that forms a neat helmet around his head. His face is a grey face and his cheeks are circular, as though they've been carved from wood. I'm as certain as I've ever been about anything that this oversized ventriloquist's doll is Ade, Michael, the Prof or whatever he wants to call himself. Who else could it be? He's dressed quite smartly, in beige chinos and a V-neck jumper with a shirt and tie underneath it. The jumper looks soft and is a pale, duck egg blue. It makes him seem incredibly vulnerable. I don't want him to be vulnerable. I was happier when I was scared of him. My eyes sting and I clear my throat to force the feeling away.

He stares across at us, his mouth open in what looks like a surprised but silent *oh*. As I look more closely I notice that his entire body is twitching steadily, like Davey's pet rabbits used to do. Suddenly, his mouth takes on a more rectangular shape, in what could be a smile, as he contemplates us, or rather Jacob.

Jacob puts his hands in his pockets and scuffs the polished floorboards with the toe of his right trainer. Then he strolls over, sits down right next to the old man and looks at him. The Prof reaches over and grabs his hand. He clutches it tightly and strokes the back of it, as though it's a small mouse.

'My angel,' he says.

He gazes around for a few seconds as though he's looking for something or someone. When he doesn't find them or it, he bursts into a rendition of While Shepherds Watch Their Flocks By Night.

Despite his enfeebled appearance, his voice is sonorous and rich, and the entire spectacle is both absurd and ghastly at the same time. He looks at Jacob as though he's singing the carol specially for him, although I can't for the life of me fathom why on earth he would do this, and as he booms out the words, he continues to caress Jacob's hand. Jacob frowns at him and then across at me. This hideous situation continues until the professor has stumbled his way through all six verses of the carol and gone on to sing the infant school version about the shepherds being tuned to ITV until the angel of the Lord comes down and switches to BBC.

I want to laugh. I turn away to compose myself. It's not funny. He can't be allowed to go on like this. We need to do something.

'Would you like a cup of tea? The kettles just boiled.'

I realise I'm shouting at him as though he's deaf, but I really, really want to make sure he hears me in the hope it will stop him launching into another Christmas carol.

'Polly,' he says in the voice of an orator quoting Shakespeare. 'Put the kettle on.'

I waste a couple of brain-dead seconds wondering if this is in fact a Shakespeare quote. A lot of quite unexpected sentences and phrases do turn out to have been penned by the Bard. Jacob looks across at me again, his expression intent and full of meaning, as though he thinks there are specific words I should be saying and he's trying to beam them across to me by telepathy.

'This is Professor Gossland,' he says, eventually, when it becomes clear I won't be saying anything at all unless prompted.

'Call me Michael or Prof. Whichever suits.'

'I'm Jacob's Aunty Susan. Pleased to meet you.'

'Enchanted, Polly. White, two sugars.'

I trip back to the kitchen like a trained poodle to make the tea. My hands are trembling so much I biff everything about as though I'm wearing oven gloves. I must be in shock. Somehow I manage to put the kettle on again, and I find some tea bags stashed away at the back of a cupboard. Then I grope inside my handbag for my ibuprofen. I need to take some, quickly. My ankle is starting to throb slightly and the almost unbearable zing of the shingles pain is digging its tentacles into my back. Even so, I still want to laugh. I'd like nothing more than to throw my head back and cackle hysterically for a very long time, like a madwoman. What's wrong with me? I'm behaving as though *I'm* the one in the middle of a mental health crisis.

Jacob appears and shuts the kitchen door behind him.

'What are we going to do?' He asks in a kind of stage whisper. 'We can't just leave him here in this state. I don't get it. What's he even doing here?'

'There must be someone you can call,' I say. 'Ghostbusters, perhaps?'

'I'm stuck in a haunted house with two mentalists.'

He decides to ring Matt. But when Matt answers, all you can hear is a baby screaming so loudly Jacob has to hold the phone several inches away from his ear. After a bit of shouting from Matt's end, Jacob terminates the call.

'Matt can't think straight because Winnie hasn't stopped crying for the past twenty-four hours, more or less, and is still going strong. And when Winnie does stop, if that ever happens, the only thing he's got planned is to sleep until it starts again, which it will before long. He said don't ever think about having kids. Like ever. And the best thing would be to ring Pauline.'

As he explains the situation to Pauline, it sounds even more ridiculous and implausible than it did when he related it all to Matt, particularly the bit about the singing. I wonder if Pauline believes a word of it. I'm not sure I would.

'There must be someone who can come over, like a friend or a relative?' He asks.

Kind but negative sounding murmurs emanate from Jacob's phone.

'Ask who his next of kin is,' I suggest.

He does. Then he shakes his head and ends the call.

'It's still Reese, according to their records. Pauline says we should ring for an ambulance.'

Jacob dials 999. When he's finished describing the state the Prof is in, we both expect the woman at the other end to say an ambulance will be with us in a few minutes. But instead she says the service in the area is overstretched and in the scheme of things, this is a relatively low level emergency. As such, it will be at least three or four hours before they can get to us, and in any case, it sounds more like a mental health situation than anything else, and they are dealt with via a different route. She doesn't tell us what this route is or how we can access it. Then Jacob says he thinks the Prof might have had a stroke, and the woman on the other end accuses him of being aggressive and terminates the call. Jacob stares at his phone.

'What did I say? And what exactly is a low level emergency? Either it's urgent or it isn't. I'll ring G. He'll know what to do.'

But Gawain doesn't answer. He's at work and probably as overstretched as the paramedics. Jacob leaves a message and we both creep back into the living room. The Prof is singing that song from the Phantom of the Opera now, the one where the soprano has to hit those really high notes. This rendition isn't as good as the previous one. In fact, it sounds like a frog being attacked by a cat. But, as with the carol, he knows all the words.

'We'll have to take him to hospital ourselves, then. Can you sit with him while I go and look for his shoes?'

Reluctantly, I perch on the edge of the other sofa, where he can't reach me. He continues singing and I focus my gaze on the carpet. Then he stops and I can feel him staring at me. I look up and meet his gaze.

'Fiery little ginger creature,' he says appraisingly. 'Dangerous, if wound up the wrong way.'

'Hello, Ade,' I say.

His lips twist into what might be an ironic smile and his eyes flash with amusement in what comes across as a grotesque parody of the way he used to look at me when he was eighteen. I can't even begin to process the mixture of emotions this elicits in me, but none of them are good. Luckily, the smile soon fades and his eyes close.

'He must have been staying here,' Jacob says when he reappears, what seems like ages later. 'The main bedroom's in a right state and the toilet's completely bunged up. Looks as though it hasn't been flushed for a week. Someone's going to have to clear it all up. Me, I expect. Anyway, I've found his shoes. And a coat.'

The Prof opens his eyes, but refuses to cooperate and kicks his legs about when Jacob tries to get his shoes onto his feet.

'Can you help?' Jacob asks me.

'I'm not a mental health nurse.'

'Neither am I.'

It's a dreadful business, almost as humiliating for us it must be for him, or would be if he was in his right mind. He's tremendously strong and when waves his arms and kicks his legs about, it almost turns into a fight. Jacob has to grab each leg in turn and hold it still, while I shove his feet into ankle boots and tie the laces, and then he does the same with his arms as I push them into the sleeves of a green, quilted jacket. I'm not sure the jacket belongs to him. It seems too small.

'He looks like Wurzel Gummidge in his Sunday best,' I say, when the task is completed.

'Where's my book?' The Prof asks, when he realises he's going somewhere.

'Which book?'

'My book of angels. I need my lovely angels.'

He points across the floor.

'Over there. Under the chair, Suzy-Polly.'

'You didn't tell me he called you Suzy,' Jacob says.

'Everyone did back then.'

'Oh my God,' Jacob says, as though this latest snippet of information is the icing on a very unpleasant cake.

I find a large book half hidden under the other armchair. On the front cover is a large photograph of a sculpture. It looks like one of those big books full of art that people who live in Hampsted or Islington put on their coffee tables when their house is being photographed for a spread in a Sunday supplement. I hand it to him and he flicks through it. It appears to be full of photographs of naked men, flesh and blood versions, not sculptures. Most of them seem to be in a state of excitement, and as to whether or not they represent art, well that could be a topic for a lengthy debate.

'Let's get him into the car,' Jacob says.

He throws me the car keys. I go and unlock the it, and he lifts the professor out of his chair, walks him outside, and folds him into the front seat as though he's made from a sheet of cardboard with creases in convenient places. As I cover his legs with an expensive-looking mohair blanket that was on top of the sofa, he beams up at me.

'Wonderful to see you again,' he says.

According to Google Maps, the nearest A&E department is some distance away in the opposite direction to home, so we decide to take him to the big hospital closer to where we live, the one where Gawain is working at the moment. The Prof chatters away throughout the entire journey, as though he's enjoying the ride and the company. At first Jacob and I listen and try to follow his thread, but eventually we realise there isn't one. Jacob finds Classic FM on the car radio and I sit hunched forward in the back of the car, holding the book of men in my lap, my feet nestling in the middle of a boyish clutter of cricket pads, dirty socks and empty cans of Red Bull. Jacob wanted to put the prof in the back and me in the front, but I didn't like the idea of him sitting behind me where I couldn't see him.

    I try to zone out as he witters on about angels and shepherds and people with luminous skin and the reassuring usefulness of Pollys who are not really Pollys at all, he emphasises, but who make a decent cup of tea, amongst other things.

18. Jacob

I deposit Aunty S with Bartosz, then I grab a couple of paracetamol from the medicine cupboard in the kitchen, pour myself a large glass of water and run up the stairs two at a time. I shut my bedroom door and huddle under my duvet as I wait for the tight band around my head to loosen its grip. I had the metal staples taken out last week, but it feels as though they're still there. And I'm as rattled as a jar full of plastic beads all moving in different directions.

Apart from ringing the hospital from the car, which was helpful to be fair, because she actually managed to get through to someone and they were waiting for us when we got there, Aunty Susan was a total nightmare. Maybe she was in shock. I suppose that makes sense. First she discovers my Prof is her Ade, and minutes later, before she's had a chance to absorb that astounding development, there he is, having some kind of crisis. And I know she hates hospitals, but while we were there, she was just plain rude. The nurse showed us to the waiting room and said someone would come and fetch us when they'd got him settled. I asked her if my brother was around. She said he was in Resus, but it was complete bedlam in there, so he wouldn't be able to come out for a chat if that's what we were hoping. We perched on vibrant chairs moulded from single pieces of orange plastic.

'What a lard-arse!' Aunty said, as soon as the nurse has gone. 'The power's gone to her head. Of course Gawain would come and see us if he knew we were here.'

'He's busy. It doesn't matter.'

I say this in a whisper, hoping it will make her realise she's shouting. It doesn't.

'Stupid cow. They think they're as good as the doctors with their crappy nursing degrees. Any moron can get in to do nursing. All they do is gossip and eat biscuits.'

'What are you talking about? They're rushed off their feet.'

'It's an act. As soon as they get back through those doors, where the public can't see them, they slack off and head for the cake tin.'

'Keep your voice down, Aunty.'

'The doctors are the real heroes. They're the ones who make the difference.'

'Particularly Gawain, eh?'

'At least he contributes.'

Whereas I just piss about with mad professors in haunted houses.

'He really is totally nuts, your Prof.'

'He's a bit eccentric and he had that seizure, when I was in his office, but I don't think he's ever been as bad as this.'

'At least I know for certain it's him. And he recognised me, too, despite all that Polly crap.'

Her voice cuts through the stifling atmosphere of the waiting room. Other patients are starting to look at us in dismay. Some of them must have been here for hours. Aunty Susan's high volume declarations will be the final straw. The beginnings of a dull ache start to build behind my right eye. I tell Aunty S I'm going to the loo. Instead, I walk to the external doors and breathe in the rainy air for a few minutes. On the way back I notice a vending machine. I get us both another coffee and a packet of chocolate digestives. Gradually, she comes out of combat mode.

'Would you have recognised him if you hadn't been primed?'

'Not at first. He used to be so handsome. And charismatic. He drew us all into his sphere of influence that summer. He was the flame and the rest of us were mere moths fluttering about in his light.'

'He's like that in the paranormal world, too. Really witty and charming. Eloquent. Great value for money on TV shows and podcasts. Gives fantastic talks. Everyone's number one ghost hunter. Or he used to be.'

'I've never seen him on TV. But then I don't watch that type of thing.'

"You should read some of his books. They're brilliant. Particularly the ones about time. That's where I got my inspiration for Point Seven from. I can't remember his exact words, but he thinks time is a fabric that's already there when we're born. It wraps itself around us, and every thought we ever think and everything we ever do, good or bad, gets woven into the material of the fabric.'

'So if you do something terrible, it's always a part of you?'

'Like a stain you can never wash away. And it's the same if someone hurts you badly. Either way, the fabric is tainted for the rest of your life. You might not think about it much. You might even forget about it completely. But it's always there, kind of surrounding you.'

'In that case, I'm screwed. Big time.'

'Are you? What have you done?'

'Mind your own business.'

I assumed she was referring to her life behind the iron curtain, which she's not allowed to talk about, so I didn't push her. She went quiet after that, which was blissful for me and probably for everyone else in the waiting room. The nurse let us see him eventually, but he was sedated and unresponsive, and nobody would tell us anything because we're not relatives. Then Pauline turned up, so we left. Of course, she's not a relative, either, but she's the next best thing, so hopefully she'll be more use to him than we were.

My plan was to hide under my duvet and process the events of the day, but I fall asleep instantly and sink into a dream that I can't recollect later, but I know involves a long swim in an inky-dark sea that is restful and completely silent. Then something cat-like lands on my bed with a gentle thud and wakes me. I'm just about to turn over and float back down again when my bedside light clicks on. I open my eyes. G's face is about three inches from mine. He's peering at me through half-closed eyes. He does that a lot, as though he thinks I'm an interesting but puzzling curiosity, which is stupid because he knows me better than anyone else on this earth. I don't puzzle him at all.

'It's macaroni cheese. And jacket potatoes.'

'Thanks but I'm not hungry.'

'When did you last eat?'

'What's that got to do with anything?'

'You can't not eat.'

G is always on at me about eating. I was seriously underweight when I came out of the church, although I wasn't aware of it at the time, and I have this rapid metabolism which means I need to pack away a huge amount of calories, otherwise I turn into a stick man.

'I had two empire biscuits in a café on the M40. And a packet of digestives in the hospital.'

I sit up and rub my eyes. I'm still in my clothes. I hate sleeping in my clothes.

'Anyway, why are you having supper at midnight?'

'It's only eight thirty.'

I scramble for my phone to check the time.

'I feel as though I've been asleep for hours.'

'Well you haven't.'

'I wanted to stay at the hospital, but Aunty was being, you know, difficult.'

'Highly Indignant State?'

'Deluxe version. I managed to subdue it a bit, but you could tell it was still there, lurking under the surface. I know she's not well, but even so.'

'She's sitting up in bed now, with her supper and a large whisky on a tray.'

'I'm sorry I got her involved. It was just that I had to go to Talbot Way to pick up some books and I felt bad for her, being stuck in the house on her own all the time, so I asked if she'd like to come. She jumped at the chance. I never thought for one minute the Prof would be there. Minus his marbles.'

'I wouldn't worry. She can't wait to tell Molly Beasley and that devil's disciple woman.'

'June Stanford.'

I pull my tee-shirt down over my jeans and I really wish I'd taken my trainers off before getting under my duvet. I try to ignore how minging I feel. But it's only G. He's just done a long shift at the hospital and I can tell he hasn't showered or changed his clothes yet. Several different hospital-related odours waft across to me from him in waves, including cabbage, floor polish, sweat and something else I'd rather not think about, and he has a small crust of dried blood close to the centre of his forehead. I lean up on my elbow, too, so I'm mirroring him.

'I don't know what's going on with Aunty S. She got really antsy when we found the Prof. She didn't seem to give a shit about the state he was in.'

'You know what she's like. When she gets rattled or upset she puts on an act.'

'Yes, but there's loads more to it than that. They used to hang out together.'

'Who?'

'Aunty and the Prof. Back in the Dark Ages. The seventies, when they were teenagers. They lived near each other.'

'They didn't.'

'They did.'

'That's crazy. No wonder she was taken aback. And to find him in that state.'

'It was a complete shitshow. I didn't know what to do. I rang you loads of times.'

'Yeah, sorry. It was manic. I don't think I looked at my phone once. You did the right thing, though. It's what I'd have told you to do.'

'Did you see the Prof?'

'He wasn't my patient, but someone told me you'd brought him in.'

'How's he doing?'

'He hasn't had a stroke or anything like that.'

'So it was a mental health thing, then? The person I spoke to when I tried to call an ambulance said it might be, but she didn't tell me what to do.'

'Partly it's a urinary tract infection. Older people can get really disoriented from those.'

'That's not so bad, is it?'

He doesn't reply.

'There's more, but you're not meant to tell me?'

'Close relatives only.'

'He doesn't have any of those, I don't think.'

'OK, well I still shouldn't say anything, but when they did the CT scan, they found a mass. The neurologists haven't confirmed what it is yet, but they think they know what it is.'

He looks at me and scratches his head, as though he's not sure if he should go on.

'And?'

'They think it's a glioblastoma or something similar. Stage four.'

'Oh, man.'

'You know what that is?'

'I did a module at uni. Will they tell Pauline?'

'Who?'

'His secretary. She kind of looks after him.'

'They might. If they do, when you speak to her, can you pretend you don't know?'

G pats me on the arm so lightly there's almost no sense that he's touching me at all. He says he's sorry about the Prof. Instantly, my eyes fill with tears, for the second time in as many days. Damn him.

'How long has he got?'

'Difficult to say. Could be months, but it's more likely to be weeks.'

'What's he going to do? There isn't anyone to look after him.'

'He might not be able to leave the hospital again. If he does, social services will sort out a care package. It's not your problem, sweetheart.'

I kind of feel as though it is my problem, but I don't say anything.

*

Two days later, I return to Talbot Way. I don't want to go anywhere near it ever again, particularly on my own. But I have to, partly because I left those books behind last time, and also because I feel like I should do something about the mess before anyone else turns up and sees what the Prof did to the place. It's still dark when I hit the motorway, but as I speed eastwards I can see the grey beginnings of the winter dawn starting to appear in my rear view mirror, so it will be light when I get there, and hopefully after such an early start I'll be on my way home long before darkness falls again. I switch to an indie rock station and I try really hard to focus on the music and nothing else. If I empty my brain, maybe all the thoughts and assumptions that were thrown up into the air by yesterday's events and the things Aunty Susan told me will fall back into some king of order and I'll be able to stash them all away.

I could do without all this. Seriously. I've been more or less fine for over three years now. The last thing I want is to go back to the way I was when they first got me out of the church. I was a total wreck then, and I continued to be one for a few months after that. It was rough. Also, Gawain and I had a lot of issues to settle. He was the reason I'd started going to stay with Mum at New Sunrise in the first place. I'd discovered he'd been sleeping with our beloved, father-substitute housemaster since he was fifteen, just after Dad died, three years previously, and had never once said anything to me about it. I didn't even know he was gay. In the end, we worked it out and I was able to see things from his point of view and accept he hadn't done anything wrong, just fallen in love. And we flipped back to the way we'd always been before our quarrel, which was life-saving for me. Also, Bartosz helped me develop coping strategies and got me to face up to what had happened to me in the church. Then I went to Uni, had a blast, got a First and wrote to Professor Gossland with a courageous (for me anyway) research proposal. I was accepted out of God knows how many applicants to study for a PhD. I thought the road ahead was clear. All I had to do was work hard and hold on to my sense of perspective. And now it's all falling apart and I'm falling with it, crying when my brother taps me on the arm my, second guessing myself all the time, reverting back to the damaged oddball I used to be.

The rush hour traffic isn't too bad for once, and I reach the house quickly, too quickly for me to prepare myself and sort my head out properly. The sun is shining and we left the curtains open yesterday, so the place is almost ridiculously bright inside, much cheerier and more welcoming than a haunted house should be. In the library area, a couple of books have tipped out onto the floor from the shelves. I jump backwards and cry out when I see them, and I have to make a fairly big effort to get a grip. They were probably there yesterday, I tell myself. I must have pulled them out by accident when I was looking for the other books and not noticed because of everything else that was going on. But what if they are the two books I'm looking for, and some hidden force in the house has seen into my mind, knows which volumes I want, and has saved me the job of searching for them? If that turns out to be the case, I'll take the books and get the hell out. Pauline can hire a cleaning company to sort out the bathroom.

They turn out to be Beano annuals from the 1960s, their covers decorated with vivid and totally unscary illustrations featuring Plug, Billy Whizz and the rest. I suppress all speculation about what on earth they were doing in the middle of a paranormal collection and I ignore the fact that I can't see any gaps on the shelves to show where they were situated before they fell out. Then it occurs to me that the Prof must have brought them with him. That'll be it. I shove them horizontally on top of a row of hardbacks on mediumship, and before I think or do anything else, I locate the dusty tomes I've come for, take them out to the car and lock them securely in the boot. Now, if anything unforeseen happens and I need to leave in a hurry, at least I won't have to come back again.

I re-enter the house and dash upstairs to the Prof's room. I open the windows wide, rip the sheets off the bed, pick up the clothes scattered about on the floor and sling everything in the washing machine on a rapid cycle. That way, I should be able to get them cleaned and dried, and put the sheets back on the bed, before I leave. I walk back towards the stairs and notice a kind of farmyard smell. I sniff about until I realise it's the sofa cushion where the Prof had been sitting. I spray detergent all over it and scrub the bejeesus out of it with a hard-bristled brush in the shape of a hedgehog I found hiding under the sink. Each time I move the brush over the leather, it makes a loud swishing noise, and I start to suspect my scrubbing is masking another sound, that of footsteps upstairs, walking up and down the landing. But when I stop, I can hear nothing but silence. Then, when I start again, the floorboards above my head creak. I tell myself it's in my head. I'm letting the house freak me out. When I've finished, I wipe the seat dry with a cloth and sniff it. It smells of swimming pools now and the black leather has faded to dark grey where I've scrubbed it. Never mind, it's better than it was.

I steel myself to tackle the bathroom. As I creep slowly up the stairs, I definitely don't hear the sound of small feet rapidly scampering away towards the bedroom at the far end of the landing. Or rather, I do hear something that sounds exactly like that, but it has to be coming from the road outside. I look at my watch and see it's still early enough for little kids to be walking home again after dropping off older siblings at school. It must be that. After all, I'm not familiar with the natural acoustics of the house, the perfectly ordinary noises you'd hear from inside it on a normal weekday morning.

I decide to play some music on my phone and I sing along to drown out any other sounds, real or imaginary. Unblocking the toilet is a challenge, but I'm an expert. I do a lot of cleaning at G and B's house, to help pay my way, and I went to boarding school from the age of six. The pupils lived in various houses, in mixed age groups, and we were all expected to do housekeeping chores. On top of that, in the Church of the New Sunrise, we were physically punished if we didn't pull our weight domestically. I put rubber gloves on, roll my sleeves up and remove several handfuls of solid filth and waterlogged loo roll. I'm not sure what to do with it all, so I chuck it into plastic bin liners and decide to dump it somewhere on my way home. I sink the plunger into the water and thrust it up and down. I manage to clear the blockage and I shout *yay* when the toilet flushes properly for the first time.

My voice is too loud. It shatters the silence and leaves an echo, which bounces back at me, and gives the impression that the original sound wasn't made by me, but by someone else in another part of the house. I switch my attention to cleaning the sink, the bath and the rest of the room, and I polish the taps and the mirror above the sink until they sparkle. I take the disgusting bin liners downstairs and leave them outside by the kitchen door. Completing all these tasks fills me with a huge sense of achievement and now I'm so relaxed, I pause to make myself a cup of coffee. I drink it as I wait for the washing machine to finish its cycle. When it does, I throw the laundry into the dryer and go back upstairs to finish tidying the Prof's bedroom. I pull back the curtains and a shaft of weak sunlight illuminates something under the bed. A leather wallet. I pick it up and open it. A passport-size headshot of a bloke, younger than the Prof and with a shaved head, beams out at me. Reese, I suppose. The wallet is bulging with twenty pound notes. I put it in the back pocket of my jeans and text Pauline to tell her I've got it. It sounds paranoid, but if I hold onto it without saying anything, I'm worried Matt or one of the others will accuse me of theft. Pauline replies instantly, thanks me for letting her know and says she's just about to go to the hospital again.

Then I really do hear someone moving about. They seem to be in the room I slept in that weekend, at the far end of the landing. Feet make their way slowly across the carpet, in a series of softened but heavy steps, and the person clears his throat. It sounds like a young boy. Matt and the others all have keys. One of them must have let themselves into the house through the front door when I was in the kitchen and brought a child with them. I wonder why they haven't come to say hello. Even if they didn't hear the washing machine, my car's in the drive, so they'd know I'm here. The Prof's team are all a bit socially dysfunctional, apart from Pauline, but surely none of them are that weird?

And why are they striding up and down in that particular bedroom? I decide to Rambo it. I shout *hello*, march down the landing and push open the door. The curtains are half open, and a boy is standing there with his back to me. He's staring out of the window with his head tilted slightly to the left, as though he's looking down the road, towards the T-junction at the end, waiting for someone to turn the corner and come into view. I say *hello* again, more quietly this time. I fully expect him to turn towards me, but he just sighs impatiently and hops from foot to foot, as though he can hear me, but doesn't want to be distracted from his vigil at the window. I wonder who he is. Does Matt have older children? Maybe he's brought one of them to the house to give them a break from screaming Winnie. But if that's the case, where's Matt?

As I stare, my eyes become accustomed to the semi darkness and I realise the boy is constructed from shadow, like a homogencous cut-out with no variations in colour or texture. I tell myself he looks like this because he's backlit by the window, not because he's one of those shadow people who lurk in corners and are captured on film and put on social media. I squeeze my eyes shut and open them again. The figure is still there, but he's no longer a shadow. His details have been filled in. I can see his fair hair, his red T-shirt and his baggy jeans and his cheap trainers. If I say *hi*, he'll turn to look at me this time. Instead, I blink once more and when I look again, he's taller and thinner and dressed in grey from head to foot. I watch as he transforms himself into a shadow again and becomes broader and more diffuse, as his edges bleed into his surroundings and he fades away.

    The word *no* runs through my mind. *No, no, no* and *no*. I turn and walk slowly back along the corridor to the Prof's bedroom. Quietly and calmly, I gather up the rest of the Prof's bits and pieces and put them all in a plastic carrier bag with the cleaning products. As I walk down the stairs and through the living room to the kitchen a tiny voice inside my head tentatively offers me congratulations for being so cool-headed. I thank the voice, but I tell it I'm putting on an act, one I won't be able to keep up much longer. The drying isn't finished yet. I was planning to put the sheets back on the bed when they were done. Instead, I pull out the damp laundry, put it a plastic basket and take it with me.

    In less than forty-five minutes I'm driving through the gap in the hedge and parking up outside our house. I can't remember a single thing about the journey. A speeding fine will probably arrive in the post in a few days. Bartosz's car is on the drive. I pull up next to it, clamber out and gaze about. It must have rained while I was out, and then stopped. It feels as though everything has been washed clean. The air is full of the scent of wood smoke. A watery sun is setting behind the bare branches of the trees on the other side of the track and the lantern above the front door is already switched on. I must have been at the house longer than I thought. A robin is singing, too, and I can hear the alpacas clip clopping about in their enclosure round the back of the house, and behind that, the hum of the motorway I've just driven down. Presumably.

    I open the boot. The books are here, together with the laundry basket. I put my hand over the back pocket of my jeans to make sure I haven't lost the Prof's wallet. None of the toilet related rubbish is here. For an instant, I wonder where it is, then I remember. I crammed it all into one of the bins at Talbot Way as I left. There were three bins, a brown, a blue and a green one and I wasn't sure which to put them in, so made a guess and went for the brown one. I don't suppose the council provides a bin specifically for the contents of blocked toilets. I wheeled it to the end of the drive. I expect it will probably get tagged by the council, and the house will be bin-shamed.

I run through the kitchen to the utility room, casting a brief glance and a curt hello in the direction of Aunty Susan, who is reading something on her kindle and eating a crumpet. I put the damp washing in the utility room dryer to finish it off, then I sink onto my knees and allow myself the luxury of a discrete meltdown, as I watch it going round. Bartosz strolls in and plonks himself down next to me. Now that Aunty Susan is using his office as a bedroom, he's put his desk behind an upstairs window of a spare bedroom that faces onto the parking area. I must have accidentally left my face naked when I walked up to the front door, and he must have looked out and noticed. We sit together, listening to the whirr of the drier and watching the swirling sheets. Eventually, he turns to look at me and leans over so he can give me a friendly nudge with his shoulder. A judder goes right through me. He yelps.

'What the hell was that?'

'I don't know. It's like I was full of electricity and you earthed me.'

'Blimey.'

'I've just had a really weird few hours. I think I was in an altered state of mind and you just woke me up.'

'I saw you getting out of your car. Your face was odd.'

'Like I'd seen a ghost?'

'Not exactly. You looked kind of grey and vacant. As though you'd left your body and gone somewhere else.'

'I've been to a place where time doesn't exist. Or rather, it does exist, but something made it collapse.'

Bartosz turns so he's facing me, piercing me with those blue eyes. I need to stop saying mad things and explain what happened, as much for my own benefit as for his.

'I saw a shadow person in one of the upstairs windows. Then I realized it was me, when I was six.'

'What the hell? You should stop going to that house. It's not good for your mental health.'

He's probably right, but then I'm right, too. It was definitely me standing there staring out of the window. Time collapsed and there I was, peering out through the grubby glass on the last Tuesday of the last Easter holidays, at the front garden of the house where I lived with Amanda, G and Dad, long, long ago, down a road with lots of trees, in a village big enough to be a town, close to the University where Dad worked. I tried to balance one foot on the edge of G's hip and use it like a step so I could climb up and see further down the road. He groaned and said I was hurting him. I moved down and wedged my feet between the curve of his spine and the back of the sofa. At least he's warmed up now, I thought. He was shivering before, but now I could feel the heat of his body through the backs of my heels.

'Is that better?' I asked in a whisper. I couldn't get my voice to go any louder.

'Don't move again without warning me.'

My brother was all bashed up. He couldn't breathe without making horrible wheezing sounds, like the ones I made when I was having an asthma attack, and I had to stay close to him or he'd die. I held one hand out in front of me and pressed it against the window with my fingers splayed. When I moved it again, I saw I'd left an outline on the glass. I thought about a thing we'd done at school with Mrs Parsons. We had to draw round our hands with a crayon and think of five facts about ourselves and our families, one for each finger and a big one for our thumbs. I used a purple crayon and it was easy to think of five facts. I did it again then, in my head. The five facts were still the same. I have a sister. I have a brother. I have a dad. My mum doesn't live with us. And I like football. The biggest fact, was the one about my brother. But it felt different now. Kind of wrong, as though someone had snatched it away and broken it.

The day before, was my birthday. Dad was home, and I was allowed three friends from school. He cooked his special fried chicken and chips and we had strawberry birthday cake and ice cream for pudding. My main present was two sets of mini-goalposts, the kind you can carry around and put away when it's raining. I also got the latest Hull City shirt, a new football from G and a pair of orange and black football socks from Amanda. After tea, we put the goalposts on the back lawn and G and Amanda joined in, so we almost had two proper five-a-side teams. Dad was the referee. He had a whistle in his pocket and he kept taking it out and blowing it for silly reasons, which made us laugh. Later, after my friends went home, I watched videos with G. I was allowed to choose all of them and we had a carton of caramel popcorn, even though I was already full of cake and ice cream. Dad said I had hollow legs.

    His car woke us up when he left for the airport the next morning. My Power Rangers clock said five-thirty, but it was already light. We slept in the bedroom up in the attic, my brother and me. There was a big space at the end of our beds, with bean bags and a table and chairs, and loads of shelves full of books, because Dad said reading was vital. We ran to the window and watched as he loaded his suitcase and cabin bag into the boot. He must have sensed our eyes burning into his back, because he looked round, smiled up at us and waved.

    G was ok then. His dark, corkscrew hair was wild like it always was when he'd just got out of bed and his eyes were bright. He jumped and skipped across the room and back into his bed again. I did the same. Later, we got ourselves to school and back home again afterwards, like we always did when Dad was away. G changed out of his uniform, said he was going out and did I want to come? I knew where he was going, to the ruined farm buildings on the new housing estate that never got started, never mind finished, at the back of our house. I didn't like it there, so I said no and he went on his own. He wasn't gone all that long, but when he came back, every bit of him was shaking, from the top of his head to the ends of his toes. His left eye was closed and his hoodie was ripped and hanging open at the front. He onto the sofa and curled himself up into a ball. I looked down at him and the floor caved in under my feet. I tried to gasp, but I couldn't get the air into the bottom of my lungs. It was like when Jonathon Pargiter in Year Six, thumped me in the middle of my back for no reason when I was standing in the playground trading Pokemon cards and minding my own business.

    'Don't worry,' G said. 'It looks worse than it is. I'll be alright in a minute.'

    I wanted to ask him how, when he was shaking so much, but I couldn't get the words out.

    'I'm cold, that's all. Please could you go and fetch my duvet?'
I nodded.

    'And while you're up there, get your puffer from your bedside drawer and have a couple of goes at it.'

    When I came back, I threw the duvet over him and climbed underneath it with him. He wrapped his arms and his legs round me, as though I was a giant hot water bottle, and I stayed there for ages, trying to warm him up. I didn't move, not once. I didn't even fidget.

Then, he fell asleep. I could tell because his breathing got really slow and heavy. I think I fell asleep, too, because I didn't hear when Amanda walked in. She was just there all of a sudden, screaming her head off and saying *oh my God* over and over again. I tumbled out from the duvet onto the floor and sat there cross legged, with a finger over my lips, like we did in assembly, to stop her being angry with me.

But she was looking at G, not at me. He shuffled round slowly until he was on his back and he pushed a hand through his hair. He wanted to rub his eyes. That's what he usually did when he woke up. But he remembered about his closed eyelid just in time.

'Please can you try and stop screaming, Amanda. It's not really helping all that much,' he said.

His words ran into each other and his eyes were dreamy, as though he was only pretending to be awake. Amanda got onto her knees so she could look at him more closely.

'Dotty Lotty was in the cellar. She didn't like me being there and she smashed me against the wall.'

Dotty Lotty was a crazy woman who used to hang about in the village, looking for food in bins outside the shops and shouting at children in the park. She was ginormous, but everyone said she was harmless.

'I'm fine. Just don't touch me.'

'I'll phone for an ambulance.'

'Dad said to call Aunty Susan if anything happens.'

'Only because he didn't think anything would happen. He didn't mean it.'

But when she went into the little cubby hole in the hall where the landline is, G and I could hear her crying into the phone. G said she was getting hysterical. Then we heard Aunty Susan shouting, trying to get her to calm down.

'Oh Lord,' G said.

I climbed back onto him. He told me where it was ok and where it wasn't ok for me to put my hands and feet. I pressed my face into the front of his T-shirt through the rip in his hoodie and wrapped the torn edges around my head.

'She's coming,' Amanda said.

I moved my head so I could look at my sister. She had black lines running down her face from her eyeliner, but at least she'd stopped crying now.

'What colour's her car?'

'I don't know. Who cares?'

I scrambled over G again so I could see out of the window.

'There's no point looking for her yet,' Amanda said. 'She'll be at least four hours. Way more if the traffic's bad. And it'll be dark by then. Past your bedtime.'

After ninety-two cars, eighteen double decker buses and seventeen vans had gone past, plus one ambulance with its lights flashing and its siren going, Amanda said she'd got her shit back together. She gave Gawain two paracetamol and sat him up so he could swallow them with a glass of water, then, without any warning, she reached across and grabbed me. I struggled and kicked, but she was loads bigger than me and I couldn't do anything to stop her when she dragged me upstairs, pulled my school clothes off, stuck me under the shower, dribbled shower gel over me, scrubbed me with the sponge shaped like an elephant's head, dried me and dressed me in my clean Gruffalo pyjamas. This was child abuse. I knew that for sure. We'd been told about it at school. But I didn't scream, because nobody would hear me apart from G, and he wouldn't be able to do anything. When I went downstairs again, I was scared he might be dead or in a coma or something. But his eyes were open and he kind of half smiled at me. I climbed over him and went back to looking out of the window. Apart from one trip to the toilet, I didn't move again. Amanda brought me a cheese sandwich and a carton of juice. Then, aeons layer, long after the streetlights had come on, A car turned into the drive. It was metallic grey.

I crawled back over G and tried to get to the front door before she rang the bell, but by the time I got there, she'd rung it four times, in a short, stabby way, and she was rapping her knuckles on the glass. I let her in. At first she didn't see me. Then she looked down.

'You don't remember me, I bet?'

I shook my head. Her hair was orange and her lipstick was bright red, and her trousers and jacket were tangerine mixed with brown. She looked like the pictures we made at school in the autumn from leaves collected in the playground and glued onto paper.

'Where is he?'

She swept past me, heels clicking on the parquet floor. Amanda appeared and took her into the front room. I followed. When Amanda told Aunty Susan about my brother, I wanted to join in, but the words wouldn't come out. G's eyes were closed. He'd been asleep for ages, but now he was dead, because I left him alone to answer the door.

'Good God,' Aunty said, in a voice loud enough for the people next door to hear.

She knelt on the carpet in front of him and said his name over and over again. Amanda folded her arms and shuffled her feet. She thought he was dead too, I could tell. I stopped breathing. But then he opened his good eye and blinked at Aunty Susan. He told her what happened. It took ages because he had to keep stopping to breathe. He tried not to wince but you can tell it hurt because his eyes filled with tears. Mine did, too. When he finished telling her, he closed his eyes again.

Aunty Susan turned to Amanda. 'Is all this true or is he hallucinating?'

Amanda shrugged.

'He *does* go to the old farm all the time. He's not meant to. And he's not making Dotty Lottie up. She's real.'

'You say your dad's gone to New York. When did he leave?'

'First thing this morning. Before we were awake.'

'And this happened, when exactly?'

'After school,' Amanda said.

'Are you sure?'

'I saw them leave the house this morning in their uniforms. Gawain was fine then, wasn't he, Jacob?'

I stared at Aunty Susan and I nodded and put on my sensible face, the one I used at school to show Mrs Parsons I was listening after she'd told me off for day-dreaming.

Aunty looked at me and then at Amanda.

'Is he special needs?' She asked.

'He's just spazzing out, because of Gawain.'

'Does Davey often go away like this?'

'He has to because of his book.'

'But who looks after you? I thought you had a nanny.'

'We look after ourselves. We don't need anyone else.' Amanda frowned and her eyebrows, which are darker than her hair made her look scary.

'If anything goes seriously wrong, we're meant to call you,' G added.

'First I've heard of it.'

Aunty Susan squatted down again and put her hand on his forehead.

I jumped forward and grabbed hold of her fingers, so I could stop them touching my brother's head. Amanda pulled me away. I kicked at her legs and tried to scream, but nothing came out. Aunty Susan barked at me like an angry fox, and said things in a voice so pointy it hurt my teeth. I wanted to tell her to leave us alone and go home. But she didn't. She drove G to the hospital and made Amanda and me go along, too, saying she didn't dare leave us on our own *again*. They asked a lot of questions and got the police in. They kept G in overnight, but the next day he was home and curled up on the sofa again, sleepy with painkillers, waiting while Amanda and me packed bags and got bossed about by Aunty Susan. She took us to her house, which was in a place called Down South. It was a long drive, and we'd never been there before.

Three weeks later, Dad appeared. G was almost ok and I could speak again, just about. I was really happy when I saw Dad had brought my new goals to put out in her back garden, and two big cases full of our stuff. Then I realised. I already knew we were going to boarding school. Our new uniforms were hanging in wardrobes upstairs, we'd had hair-cuts, and we'd met the head last week, Mrs Hopgood. She was terrifying, like Aunty, but we were also introduced to Liam, our form tutor, who was totally cool and was in charge of Cherry Tree House, where we were going to live. It was a proper house, with bedrooms and bathrooms upstairs and a big room downstairs where you could watch TV, plus a study for the older ones to do their homework in, although they call it prep. I was more or less ok with it. At least G and Amanda would be in Cherry Tree, too. But I thought we'd go back home in the holidays. Then Dad said he had to sell the house to pay his share of our school fees.

'So we won't be going home again. Like ever?' G said.

Dad did a sad face and shook his head.

'By the time I get back from my next book tour, which is in Australia, the house will be sold, with a bit of luck. I've already lined up a little flat in Beverley by the Minster, as a pied-a-terre. There won't be room for you to stay, I'm afraid.'

G's eyes filled with tears, until there was no more room and they flowed out. But he didn't make any crying noises and his face stayed the same.

Amanda scowled. And as for me, at first I couldn't breathe, and then all I could do was scream and cry. Dad pulled me onto his knee. I hit him in the chest with my fists.

'Crikey,' Aunty Susan said. 'Is he having a fit?'

Dad held me tight and rubbed my back until I stopped. Then he dabbed at my eyes with his hanky. 'You'll be much better off here, with Aunty S. I can't look after you properly with all my travelling. And anyway, we'll still see each other. I'll come down at Christmas and when you have your…what are they called?'

'Exeats,' Amanda said. 'We get two per term, from Saturday morning to Sunday evening.'

'That's it. I'll book a hotel and come and fetch you. We'll have a marvellous time. Cream teas and lashings of ginger beer.'

'I don't like ginger beer,' I said.

'Lemonade then.'

"So in the proper holidays we'll stay at Auntie's house?' Amanda asked.

'Yes, but also sometimes at cottages by the seaside, with me.'

'It won't be so bad, will it?' Aunty Susan said in that voice adults use when they want you to stop making a fuss.

Amanda and G looked at her and shook their heads, politely. I squeezed my eyes closed, pressed my head against Dad's chest and tried to feel safe. He smelled like he always did, a mixture of aftershave and mints. But he wasn't even staying for dinner. When he left, G went off for a lie down, and I wandered out into the garden with my football and set my goals up. Aunty Susan came to the back door and said she'd drown me in her water butt if I damaged any of her plants.

I've gazed from plenty of other bedroom windows since then. The worst was probably the narrow rectangle at the top of the wall of in the room I slept in when I was back in England with New Sunrise, just before Bartosz and G got me out. I used to fetch boxes full of religious pamphlets from the basement room outside my door, pile them up on my bed and balance on top of them, just so I could see the sky, the plane tree in the car park, and most of all, the street where ordinary people went about their business in that other world, the one I'd been removed from. I thought I'd never get back into that world. I wasn't even sure I wanted to at that point. I was so zombified, I'd never be able to cope.

I need to stop this. Dwelling on the past is pointless and I can see plenty from my bedroom window at G and Bartosz's house without having to stand on boxes, including the alpacas, the green lawn, my car, the gap in the hedge and the trees on the other side of the lane. And I can walk into all of it whenever I like.

Bartosz stands up, pulls me up by my armpits and propels me away from the tumble drier and into the kitchen, as though his main role in life is to conduct me in the right direction. He gives my shoulder a little shake and pushes me into a chair at the kitchen table.

19. Jacob

If Bartosz hadn't been there, I'd have sloped off and hidden in my room again, like I did last time, mainly because Aunty Susan is lurking in the kitchen. She's sitting in her chair by the window. I can feel her eyes boring into the space between my shoulder blades.

'There's no crumpets left,' she says in a flat and vaguely menacing voice.

She's been in a bad mood since we got back from Talbot Way. Really quite vicious. Particularly to me.

'There were loads this morning,' I say.

'Not loads. Some. You need to keep an inventory. Then you'd know exactly how many. It's all about efficiency.'

Bartosz, who is just about the most efficient person on the planet, after being in the army for several years, makes tea and toasts the last few remaining slices of brown bread. All the white bread is long gone. When he sits down at the table, Aunty Susan joins us.

'There's no jam left, either,' she says.

'We've got enough mince and potatoes to make a shepherd's pie for tonight and that's about it, apart from a few bits. I'm planning to do a supermarket run tomorrow morning,' he says.

'I'll come with you,' I say.

Food shopping has become something Bartosz and I often do together. We use the supermarket where I work, because I get ten percent off. I pay and Bartosz or G transfers money to my account. I realise I'm starving, and I try to get up and nip across to the fridge for the cheese, but Bartosz thinks I'm making a run for it. He intercepts me and pushes me back into my seat again. He goes to the fridge and the cupboards and comes back with cheese and peanut butter, which he plonks down in front of me.

'Eat,' he says in a growly voice.

I shovel several slices of toast with various toppings down my neck and wash it down with two cups of tea while they sit and watch. The mammoth intake of calories gradually jostles me back into normal mode. Bartosz and Aunty S seem to be waiting for me to explain myself. I don't really feel like bothering, but maybe I should try. Bartosz says I shouldn't bottle things up, and anyway, it might be good to get their take on it all.

'You'll think I'm mad if I tell you what happened,' I say, tentatively.

'We think you're mad anyway, darling,' Aunty Susan says.

'It's Talbot Way. It messes with your head.'

I look down at my empty plate.

'What did it do to you *this* time?' She asks.

Her tone is full of exaggerated concern, totally sarcastic, as though she thinks I'm a toddler. She really has undergone a complete personality transplant. When we were on our way to the house, she was confiding and happy to show her vulnerable side. I thought we'd made a breakthrough. But on the drive to the hospital, she reverted to her default setting, the one where the only snowflake in the room is me, and she's been like that ever since. In fact, she's doubled down and is behaving like an extreme version of her every day, hard-baked self. I get that it must have been a hell of a shock to bump into the Prof, or Ade, like that and she probably regrets telling me all that stuff about nineteen seventy-six. But even so. I'd like to pour the dregs from the teapot over her head. Then she'd have to go and clean herself up, and I could have a private conversation with Bartosz, and get his take on the whole thing without her unhelpful interruptions. I plough on and try to pretend she isn't here.

'There was someone else in the house. I heard them clearing their throat and walking up and down in the green bedroom, which is at the other end of the landing from the bathroom, where I was. It has a reputation, that room, but I slept in it that weekend when I stayed overnight and it seemed ok then. Anyway, when I went to investigate, I saw a little boy. He was staring out of the window, as though he was waiting for someone.'

'What did you do?' Bartosz asks.

He sounds as though he believes me. I'm so grateful, I get all emotional. I have to take a moment to suck it all up. Aunty Susan rolls her eyes and tuts.

'I stared at him for a while. I don't know how long. It was like I was mesmerized or something. Then I calmly gathered everything together, left the house and got into my car. Once I'd reversed out onto the street, I stopped and looked up at the window. The curtains were closed and there was no little boy.'

'Did you really think there would be?' Aunty Susan asks.

'No. I don't know. Maybe.'

'The person clearing their throat was obviously someone walking past, outside. Living here, in the middle of nowhere, you forget how sound carries in ordinary houses where there are roads and pavements.'

She sounds as though she's never been so certain about anything in her entire life. But she could be right.

'I definitely saw a little boy.'

'You thought you did,' Aunty Susan says. 'Your imagination was playing tricks with you. You know what you're like.'

'No, Aunty. I don't know what I'm like. Please tell me.'

She takes a breath as though she's getting ready to deliver one of her character assassinations. But Bartosz gets in first.

'Describe the room,' he says.

'It's long and narrow, and the window doesn't let in much light, even when the curtains are wide open. And they were only half open.'

'Is there anything on the walls?'

'There's a big poster on the wall by the side of the bed, a kind of pagan calendar type thing.'

'Maybe when you opened the door, light came in from the landing and bounced off the poster. You saw it and your mind made it into a figure standing in the window.'

'But I saw him clearly as I'm seeing you now. It was me, when I was six. And the curtains were open.'

'How long did you look at him for?'

'I don't know. Felt like ages.'

'I bet you didn't do much more than glance into the room,' Aunty Susan says, as though she's making a pronouncement that can't be disputed. 'In that time, you put a few beams of stray light together in your mind and made them into yourself in the form of a small boy. You decided it was you, then your brain made you see yourself.'

'But I was so certain. I don't know how to describe it. I kind of went into him and entered his time.'

'Not that rubbish again,' Aunty says.

She'd seemed to understand about the time thing when we talked about it before. She *did* understand. I feel betrayed.

Bartosz tries to rescue me. 'Something like that happened to me in Afghan, after I got hit,' he says. "I'd seen so many of my mates get blown up, I was kind of waiting for my turn. One minute, I was sitting at the side of the road waiting to be picked up, and next I was ten years old, getting told off for messing about during maths. It was like I was really there, in the classroom. Then I saw my grandad. He died when I was two.'

Aunty Susan dismisses Bartosz's narrative with a shake of the head.

'It's basic psychology, Jacob. You were in a state of heightened anticipation, partly because you have anxiety issues and partly because you were in a house you've been told is haunted. In situations like that, when you hear or see anything, you automatically make it into something it isn't. I expect it was the same when you were with the others and you heard all those knocking sounds.'

'So Talbot Way is just an ordinary house? Perhaps you could go along and discover the source of the noises. You could put your findings into a paper and get it peer reviewed and published, then the university could sell the house and use the money for something else.'

'You're really getting your knickers in a twist about this, aren't you? Man up, for God's sake.'

Her use of the word *knickers* in that context, as though I wear them, feels abusive and seriously pisses me off. I get up from the table.

'I'm going for a run,' I say.

I don't really want to go for a run right now, but Aunty Susan won't be able to come after me if I do, and it's not as though I'm dashing off to hide in my room, so it should satisfy Bartosz, too.

'I'll come with you,' he says.

We jog down the track to the main road and onto a narrow path that weaves through the woods on the other side, even though it's getting dark. At first I'm still slightly adrift, still trying to shake off all the old versions of myself, the boy who couldn't speak, the boy who was horrified at having to leave home and go to boarding school, the boy who was grief stricken when his dad died in a car accident a few years later, the boy who ended up making the biggest mistake of his young life, by seeking out his mother and joining New Sunrise, because he couldn't forgive his brother, who had probably only acted the way he did because he missed his father, too. The boy that behaves as though he wears *knickers* and gets them in a twist.

Eventually, though, I get my breathing into a rhythm and the endorphins kick in. We stop for a couple of minutes at the entrance to an old farm that's been converted into a collection of office buildings and a playgroup.

'You ok now?' Bartosz asks.

'Yeah. It's been a strange few days. But I'm manning up as we speak. Aunty would be proud of me.'

'It's not just you. Yesterday, she said it was a shame Gawain was gay because he'd make someone a lovely husband. I said he *has* made someone a lovely husband, but she shook her head and said you can't be a proper husband when you're a gay man.'

'Wow.'

Later, Bartosz makes the shepherd's pie. He puts Worcester sauce in the mince and adds cheese to the mash. It's utterly lush and there's loads of it. We all heap generous amounts of it onto our plates and add peas and broccoli.

'The potato's lumpy,' Aunty Susan says as the rest of us are practically slobbering as we spoon it into our mouths. 'Did you forget to mash it properly?'

'What's wrong with you? It's mint,' I say.

'Did you use a fork, Bartosz?' She persists.

'I used the thing.'

'The masher,' I say.

'Well, I think I'll go easy on the potato,' she says. I suggest you do the same, Bartosz.'

'What's that supposed to mean?'

She gives him a significant look and pats her stomach.

Without saying a word, G, who has been silent so far and looks completely wiped, like a person who has been working his arse off and would just like to eat his dinner in peace, gets up from the table. His mouth is set in a grim horizontal line that could be mistaken for a smile by people who don't know him. He squeezes a big blob of tomato sauce onto the side of his plate and leaves it on the table while he goes into the hall. When he returns, he's wearing his jacket and a woolly hat and he departs from the kitchen via the sliding door at the back, taking his plate and fork with him. Bartosz gets up and does the same. I'm tempted to follow them. But they want to be alone, and someone has to keep Aunty company, I suppose. We eat in a tense silence punctuated by bursts of distant laughter.

*

The next day, I fold all the Prof's clothes, including his pyjamas and dressing gown, pack them in a holdall with his wallet and toiletries, and take them to the hospital.

'My angel,' he says when he sees me.

He looks much better. His hair has been washed and looks more like a baby's bonnet than a helmet, and his cheeks are rosy and plump. You'd think he was in the best of health. At first I'm not sure he knows who I am. But then he uses my name and calls me his rescuer and his angel (again), and once he's calmed down we manage to have a normal conversation, more or less. He has good and bad days, he says. Or is it good and bad hours? When it's bad, he's not entirely sure who or where he is, but at the moment, he feels relatively ok.

'I know I'm about to conk out,' he says, casually.

I can't think how to respond to that. I've never had a conversation with a dying person before.

'It's turning out not to be awful as I expected it to be, this dying business. The drugs they give you help enormously, of course.'

I nod and he holds out his hand and stares into space until I reach out so he can wrap his fingers around my wrist. I realise he can't see me all that well.

'I'm glad. That it's not too bad, I mean.'

He squeezes my wrist.

'Less about me,' he says. 'And more about you. How are you getting on with Matt?'

'I don't know. Not very well?'

'Don't let his manner put you off. He can be an awkward sod. I don't know what's wrong with him exactly. Either he's on the spectrum as they all like to say these days, or he's just ill mannered.'

'He did spend ages going through my proposal with me, to be fair.'

'There you are then. It's all about Point Seven, apparently?'

'You've spoken to him?'

'I must have done. I can't really remember. My memory has become selective. It can only deal with small amounts of new information. It tends to focus on the important bits.'

'What did he say? Or was that one of the unimportant bits?'

'That was one of the most important parts of all. Now what was it he said?' He closes his eyes. 'I get tired. Things slip away from me. What were the words he used?'

'It doesn't matter.'

'It matters a great deal. Let me think. Restless, disturbed, oversensitive, too good-looking for his own bloody good, too distracted by girls.'

Thanks a bunch, Matt.

The Prof opens his eyes again. 'He also said you have a grain of originality hidden away somewhere inside your mind. A little piece of grit in the oyster. It all hinges on Point Seven. If you can get that right, you'll go far.' He removes his hand from mine and sinks down into the bed a little. 'At least, I think that's what he said.'

He seems to be fading, going somewhere far away. I want to ask him if he knows what Point Seven is about or if it's just something Matt's mentioned to him in passing. It would mean so much if he could give me some form of genuine, first hand endorsement. But I don't say anything more about it and neither does he. I'll just have to read the books and try to get there on my own.

'Thank you so much for bringing my things,' he murmurs.

His eyes close again. I think he's fallen asleep. I remember that his wallet is still in my pocket. As I stand up to go, I pull it out and put it in the top drawer of his bedside cabinet. I'm not really sure it will be safe there. I'll try and speak to one of the nurses about it on my way out. But as I step away, he speaks again. His voice is very faint. I go right up to him and put my ear next to his mouth. I realise he's talking about Talbot Way.

'Definite venue for spirits. Saw Reese in the green bedroom at the back, lying on the bed. He smiled up at me and said it wouldn't be long. The look on his face, it meant everything. That's why I wasn't bothered when they told me about the tumour. I saw a little boy at the window, once, too. Don't know who he was.'

I stagger back and crash down into his bedside chair. It makes an ugly scraping noise against the shiny plastic floor tiles, which attracts the attention of a senior-looking nurse. She comes marching down the ward towards us, as though she thinks I'm about to attack her patient.

'Sorry,' I say. 'I'm just leaving.'

'One more thing before you go.'

His fingers scrabble about, restlessly as though they're looking for something. I bend over and grab his hands in both of mine.

'What is it?'

'Polly. When I did all that spiel about putting the kettle on I was winding her up. Couldn't resist.'

His voice is louder again and clearer.

'Aunty Susan?'

'Is *that* what you call her?'

'Er, yes?'

'You look just like your father, apart from your borderline albinism and your very slender frame, of course.'

'I know you were friends back in the day. She told me all about you.'

I expect him to smile when I say this, but he doesn't.

'I bet she hasn't told you everything.'

'Probably not,' I concede.

Suddenly, he pulls me towards him. His grip is surprisingly strong.

'I'd be very careful around her, if I were you. We nearly ended up in prison because of her.'

Then he falls asleep.

20. Jacob

After shepherd's pie-gate, we all try our best to keep out of Aunty Susan's way. I've stopped setting up shop at the kitchen table to keep her company. Now I hide away in my room, where I can muse on Point Seven and plough through the two books from Talbot Way in peace. I'm making a big effort to get my head round everything. I don't just sit and read passively. I can't concentrate when I do that, so I make loads of notes on my laptop and highlight the important parts in bright green. Eventually, my brain starts to focus, but then a point comes where I can't go on any further without coffee.

'Where have you been?' Aunty Susan asks when I try to creep into the kitchen without her noticing.

'Upstairs, reading. Trying to get my proposal together.'

'I don't understand why you're still persisting with this psychic caper. You don't have to be a high achiever like your brother. Or your sister,' she adds after a short gap.

Poor Amanda, she's not really that much higher in Aunty Susan's estimation than I am. It's all about G, as far as Aunty is concerned.

'If I get through this PhD, I'll be a doctor, too. A proper one, not an honorary one like G. And anyway I got a First.'

Why am I even attempting to big myself up? I know it won't work.

'Ooh! Gosh!' She claps her hands like a demented seal.

'At Kings, London. Where G went.'

'But you went for the kind of subject you do when you can't get in to study medicine. You might as well have done Golfing Studies. Or aromatherapy.'

'What's wrong with Psychology and Neuroscience? It was what I wanted to do from the start. I never even thought of applying for medicine.'

'Only because your grades weren't good enough.'

My grades were ok, actually, but I don't say anything. What's the point? I stare at her with my mouth open and yet again, I wonder what the hell is wrong with her. Is she still regretting that she opened up to me about the past? If she is, I don't understand why. None of it matters now and anyway, I'm not going to judge her or tell anyone else. I try to beam some of this across to her, together with the idea that if she's thinking of shutting up any time soon, that would definitely be a good thing. But her antennae are firmly in the *off* position.

'You like working at the supermarket, don't you?'

'Er, yeah. It's ok. The people are a laugh, and I need the money.'

'Maybe that's more your thing. Long term, I mean. Shelf stacking is very calming, I imagine. Good for your mental health.'

I don't offer to make her a coffee and I don't try to stop myself when I start growling like an angry bear as I pour milk into my cup. I growl and I growl. It's wonderfully cathartic and it makes me feel kind of powerful. Eventually I build it up into a Tarzan-like roar that completely drowns out her tuts of disapproval. I hold my cup in one hand and thump my chest with the other, and I continue Tarzaning like crazy as I leave the kitchen and march upstairs.

'Well, really,' I think I hear her say.

Instead of putting me off, her ridiculous and totally irrational lack of faith in me drives me on. I keep on wading through the books and working on Point Seven. In the end, I manage to carve a narrow path through the dark thicket of complex philosophical arguments, the incomprehensible behaviour of subatomic particles, the nature of time and the ability of the observer to collapse the wave function and make events happen one way or another, and perhaps even both ways at once in certain circumstances. I get seriously bogged down with it all, but I can sense I've found a shred of meaning that I can hang onto. In the end, I've got the whole thing all broken up and reconstructed into an acceptable form. At least, I think that's what I've done.

On Thursday night, Bartosz is out doing his weekly all-nighter at the Samaritans, and my brother comes home slightly earlier than usual with pizza. Aunty Susan is watching Jaws in the man cave. We toss her a box containing a few slices, taking care not to include ones with pineapple, because she doesn't approve of those, and we retreat to the kitchen. While we're eating, G reads through my notes. He takes his time and he asks loads of questions. There is a lot to absorb, even for a mega-brain like his.

'Gosh,' he says when he's finished. 'I mean, I haven't read the books, but yeah. I get the essence of it. You've written out your argument clearly. It makes sense as far as I can tell, and I can see how there'd be three years of work to determine whether or not Point Seven is a thing. Then maybe you could write your *own* book. It's exciting, Jacob!'

'You don't think I should pack it in and do more hours at the supermarket, like Aunty suggested?'

He leans back in his chair and laughs.

'She's so mean to you.'

'It's not funny.'

On Saturday morning, I'm still asleep when my phone vibrates off my bedside cabinet and it continues ringing under my bed.

'Thank God, I thought you'd all died,' Amanda shouts.

'G's working a double shift. Practically the whole weekend.'

She screams.

'Amanda?'

'Can you come over?'

Bartosz and I scramble into his car half-dressed and speed off. I expect to find my sister doubled up in the bathroom standing in a pool of blood and water. I try to remember scenes in books and in films where babies arrive before the mother can get to hospital. All I manage to come up with is a black and white image of an astonished man wearing a flat cap, with a cigarette dangling out of his mouth, being told to fetch towels and boiling water, and maybe put newspaper over the floor. But she won't have any newspaper. She gets her current affairs from her phone, like everyone else, apart from Aunty Susan, who prefers the print version of the Telegraph.

'What are you looking at?' Amanda asks when she opens her front door.

'Nothing.' I realise, too late, that I'm staring at her legs. But my sister is her usual immaculate self. Her hair is tied back in a severe pony tail and she's fastening the belt on her raincoat.

'Tam!' She yells.

Tam runs into the hall.

'Get your shoes on, quickly.'

Tam sits down on the hall floor and does as she's told without a word, a sign that something serious is afoot.

Amanda looks at us both.

'Ok, so I was having contractions. I think they've stopped now, but my blood pressure's quite high, so I need to go and get checked out.'

She's packed a couple of bags, one for herself and one for Tam. Bartosz has brought the third bag, the one he and Gawain filled with things for the baby, just in case. But the delivery suite says they're Braxton-Hicks contractions, not real ones. They agree about her blood pressure, though, and they discharge her, with instructions to do nothing but rest, so she comes home with us. It's not a big deal. The plan always was for her to stay at our place towards the end. It's just been brought forward a bit.

When we get back to the house, Aunty Susan greets us at the door and complains that nobody tells her anything.

'Hello, Aunty,' Amanda says. 'Yes, I'm alright thanks for asking. Baby's fine, too. My blood pressure's a bit on the high side, though, so I've got to take it easy.'

Tam kicks off her shoes and chucks her coat on the floor. She was on her very best behaviour at the hospital, but now she bombs around the house at high speed, in and out of the kitchen and the man-cave and up and down the hall. As she runs, she sings the baby shark song, over and over again.

'Are you staying for dinner?' Aunty Susan asks.

'Bit longer than that.'

Amanda carefully lowers herself down onto the sofa in front of the kitchen stove. 'This is more comfortable than it looks. Not sure I'll be able to get up again anytime soon.'

'You're staying?' Aunty Susan stands over my sister, hands on hips, like some kind of grand inquisitor.

I wheel in Tam's toy kitchen and fetch the box of toys we keep under the stairs for her visits. She starts banging miniature metal pans and spatulas about. We have to yell to make ourselves heard above the racket.

'The only thing is,' Bartosz shouts at Aunty Susan, 'I think Amanda should have your bedroom. She can't be going up and down the stairs all the time in her condition. So would it be ok if we move your stuff up to one of the attic rooms?'

'You've planned this, haven't you?'

'It's been planned for ages.'

Bartosz senses that now would be a good time for him to leave us to it. He goes over to Tam and tells her he's starving. She takes plastic grapes, bread rolls, peppers and bananas out of a wicker basket and arrange them on little pink plates.

'We're not trying to get rid of you, Aunty,' I say.

'It looks that way to me.'

'You can stay as long as you like.'

'Can I, indeed? It's not up to you to say who's welcome or not. It's not your house. You're as much a visitor here as me. I bet they can't wait for you to grow up and move out, particularly now. They won't want a basket case like you here once they've got a real baby to look after.'

Bartosz terminates his brief attempt at not getting involved. He stands up and walks towards us, carrying a small bowl of plastic strawberries.

'This is his home, Sue. And he's not a basket case.'

'I am according to Auntie's criteria.'

'I can see you're all going to gang up on me,' Aunty shouts. 'You always did close ranks. No change there.'

Amanda staggers up from the sofa. 'You're being ridiculous, Aunty. Staying here, doing nothing all day long has addled your brain.'

'Rubbish.'

'Who's the prime minister?'

'For goodness sake,' Aunty Susan begins.

'Don't you know?'

She does, of course. Unasked, she goes on to the provide the names of the foreign secretary and the chancellor of the exchequer. And then the secretary of state for the environment. None of the rest of us know any of them, apart from the prime minister. Amanda has to check their names on her phone. Of course, Aunty gets them all right. Then she starts reciting a list of numbers.

'What are you doing?' I ask.

'Counting backwards in sevens.'

She started at a thousand, so it takes ages. We all watch. I don't know about Amanda and Bartosz, but I'm desperately trying to think of a way to make her stop, but coming up with nothing. Tam starts throwing plastic food items at us. Aunty Susan ignores her and carries on, past zero and into negative territory. Now, before each number she adds a minus. I visualise these numbers going on and on, in a never ending sequence, tumbling down and down into negative infinity.

Tam, annoyed at being deserted by Bartosz, hurls a plastic corn-on-the-cob across the room. It hits Aunty Susan squarely on the side of her head. Amanda tells Tam to apologise. Tam shakes her head, and flings a bunch of grapes and a small lamb chop in the same direction. I head over to Tam. I'll get her coat and wellies, I think, and take her outside to see the alpacas. Maybe I'll switch on the fairy lights, too. Make an event of it. But Aunty Susan has also set off across the room and she reaches Tam first. She grabs her by the arm and slaps her, leaving a bright red handprint on one side of her left thigh. It takes two chocolate biscuits and a bag of dinosaur shaped cheesy snacks to calm her down, followed by a long session in the damp garden, with the fairy lights flashing on and off and music blaring out of the outside speakers. We jump up and down and dance to pre-school top hits, like Wheels on the Bus and the Excavator Song, until my trainers and socks are soaked through. The alpacas had gone to bed, but when they heard the commotion, they got up again and came out to stare at us, puzzled dismay written all over their delicate features. By the time we come in, Aunty Susan has packed her bags and is in the hall, waiting for Bartosz to find his car keys.

Hours later, when G gets home, the house is at peace, apart from the usual surprised-sounding hoots coming from the owl that inhabits the trees behind the alpaca pen. Amanda and Tam are tucked up in bed, and Bartosz and I are huddled around the stove in the kitchen, drinking calvados in square, green-tinted glasses. I'm on my third glass and Bartosz is giggling because I've just done my best impersonation of Aunty Susan being indignant. I'm worried G might be annoyed about her sudden departure and somehow think it was my fault. But when he drifts into the kitchen, pale and insubstantial as a wraith, carrying the box that still contains the sandwiches Bartosz made for him this morning, he looks relieved. His shift should have ended four and a half hours ago.

'I only managed the satsuma. It was complete pandemonium from the get-go. Then there was a battle between two gangs in that park with the skateboard ramp, and three stab victims were wheeled in. Blood everywhere.'

He takes a large bite out of his almost day-old egg and marmite sandwich.

21. Aunty Susan

I look out of my bedroom window and notice a mysterious object sitting on one of the wing mirrors of my car. I can't tell what it is without my glasses, but I imagine it will be litter, discarded in an uncharacteristically imaginative way by some festive drunkard, rolling home from the station. I go out to look. It turns out to be a hand knitted creature, with a faceless head, yellow wings and a pink dress. Round its neck hangs a large, laminated label with the words *joy to the world* printed on it in an italic font. What a daft little thing. It must be one of those Christmas angels. I suspect Molly Beasley might be responsible. They all get together and make them at knit and natter sessions in a big room at the back of the craft shop. She asked me to come along once, but it's not really my cup of tea. The only items I can cobble together from wool are those hideous crocheted blankets that were all the rage when I was about thirteen, the ones that start life as a small square and grow outwards at an alarming pace until they cover you from waist to floor and you can't stand the sight of them anymore. The woolly creatures are rendered divine by being blessed in a special church service and then taken out into the neighbourhood and left in various places to be found by people who post pictures of them on Facebook and give them names, usually of family members they've lost. I don't do any of that with my one, but I do bring it inside. Now it's propped up next to the carriage clock on the mantlepiece.

    I haven't bothered sending Christmas cards this year. Every morning since I've been home, a few have landed on my doormat. I've opened them all and I've read them, but at the moment, they're piled up in the tray on top of my desk, with my other correspondence. Usually, I suspend them from little silver pegs on a string over the fireplace, but I can't be bothered with any of that now. Christmas Day is going to be low key. Just me and Netflix. No presents, no need to put on a big performance and pretend to be thrilled to bits about yet another silk scarf, comical mug or set of old-lady, lavender scented soaps. No false jollity whatsoever.

Not that I ever do much in the way of Christmas shopping or present buying. The shops are unbearable at this time of year, queues everywhere, and when you're sick and tired of the crowds and gagging for a coffee, there are no seats to be had in the M & S café or anywhere else for that matter. Then there are the carol singers, gathered in ghastly little clusters outside shops, rattling tins and polluting the air with their voices, which nobody apart from themselves wants to hear. As usual, I've avoided all that by buying something online for Tam and wrapping it in charity paper from the British Legion Christmas fete. The others will get the usual money transfers, which they seem to appreciate. At least, they normally do. Nobody has acknowledged the ones I've bestowed this year, not so far, anyway. Perhaps I'll get a few calls or texts later, when they've all had their dinner.

Gawain messaged me a few days ago, to invite me over. Come on Christmas Eve, he said, stay until Boxing Day. I told him I was busy. I expected him to ring again later and have another go. But he hasn't. I'm not complaining, though. Those old people who become dependent on their families are pathetic, expecting to be invited every Christmas, whining when they don't see their grandchildren as often as they'd like. Molly has got herself stuck in the routine of going up to Leeds on the train to stay with her son. They live miles away from the railway station, on a farm in the middle of nowhere, right up at the top of one of the dales, I forget which one, and they have to drive all the way down to fetch her, whatever the weather. June Stanford, on the other hand, has gone to stay with her daughter in South Africa for six weeks. Imagine that! They'll be wanting to throw her to the lions by New Year's Eve.

Almost ten months have passed now since I left my little office and walked down the long corridor to the discrete exit at the back of my big grey building for the last time. My staff formed a guard of honour and clapped politely as I marched past them with my garden centre vouchers tucked away in my handbag. Afterwards, I went for afternoon tea at the Dorchester with Donna to celebrate. It was Donna who egged me on to make the leap in the first place. She took early retirement years ago, and since then she's spouted the same clichés as every other pensioned-off person I've ever spoken to, about being so busy they can't understand how they ever found time to work. We sipped champagne and munched smoked salmon sandwiches and scones topped with whipped cream, and Donna told me about the recent trip she and Graham had made to Bolivia. Alaska next, she said.

My initial aim was to feel my way into retirement, let it evolve naturally. I tried a few different activities and failed at them all, including a pottery class where my sole achievement was bowl with compartments and access holes with different shapes for various types of nuts, which Gawain said looked like a nuclear bunker for mice, and a brief go at drawing, which made me wonder if there was something wrong with my brain, because everything I attempted seemed to come out all bunched up on the left hand side and elongated on the right. Also, I was in big demand as a babysitter for Tam, which was hard work, but worth it for the strangely addictive buzz off relief I always felt when Amanda came to pick her up. But I didn't really get the hang of retirement until Spring arrived. The garden came to life for one thing and once I'd joined the walking group and met Patrick, that was it. I hardly had a moment to spare. He sent me a card, by the way, a drawing of a battered old caravan being towed across the desert by three camels. On the inside he's put an enormous question mark. I added it to the pile on the mantlepiece. After Christmas I'll probably shred it, along with any other paperwork that needs to be permanently eliminated. And I'll have to think of other ways to fill my time.

My Christmas lunch is one of those turkey dinners from Waitrose, together with an individual Christmas pudding and a bottle of Chenin Blanc. I don't bother with a plate. I stick the food in the microwave, eat it, drink most of the wine and chuck away the plastic tray afterwards. Then I settle down in front of the telly with a tin of Celebrations. Before long, I'm asleep, and when I wake again, feeling slightly nauseous and desperate for a wee, night has fallen.

I decide to go for a short stroll before I batten down the hatches. I wind my way around the avenues, groves and closes of mock Tudor houses, and as I pass each one, I discretely glance at the windows, hoping the curtains will still be open and the lights on, so I can see inside and have a nose. When I reach my own road again, the Wilsons, who live in the five bed detached house on the corner, are sitting down to their Christmas dinner, eight of them, all wearing Captain Pugwash hats, like a gang of pirates.

Gawain and the rest will have finished their Christmas dinner by now, I imagine, and the table will be cleared, ready for the usual games session. Last year, Gawain wanted monopoly, but Jacob's preferred choice was Settlers of Qatan. An argument began, followed by a wrestling match on the kitchen floor. Gawain ended up on top of his brother, bouncing up and down on his stomach, stuffing bits of mince pie into his mouth to shut him up. Bartosz had to separate them. At least I don't have to put up with that kind of behaviour this year.

I turn down the road, towards my own house. I haven't bothered to drape the outdoor Christmas lights around the front porch. In fact, I haven't done that since the children grew up and moved out. But I left the outside light on when I went for my walk, and as I get closer to home, I see that someone is standing beneath it. Then I spot a battered old Fiesta parked outside my house.

Jacob starts walking down the road to meet me.

'Why aren't you answering your phone?'

'I switched it off.'

'Why?'

'So you lot would leave me in peace.'

'We've been ringing since lunchtime to say Happy Christmas. We thought something must have happened to you.'

He's starting to get a bit shouty, so I usher him inside.'

'I'm fine, as you can see. You've had a wasted journey.'

He stands in the hallway and gets his phone out.

'I'm messaging G to tell him you're ok.'

I take my coat off.

'Do you want a drink or something to eat?'

'Nope. We haven't had our Christmas dinner yet. Bartosz has put it on hold.'

He puts his phone away and stuffs his hands in his jacket pockets.

'I thought when you saw me standing outside your door, you'd be worried, in case I'd come with news about Amanda. But that didn't even occur to you, did it?'

'Why should I think that? I'm sure it will all go smoothly.'

'You're not bothered either way, though, are you?'

'It depends what you mean by bothered.'

'And you haven't even apologised for what you did to Tam.'

'We all got slapped when I was her age. Did us good. It wasn't a big deal.'

'Is that really what you think? I'm not sure Amanda will ever let you anywhere near her again.'

'Ah well, no more babysitting for me, then. And now you know I'm alright, you can leave.'

I try say this with some conviction, but he's such a life force, standing there in my hall. As he passes me and heads towards the door, I inhale a lungful of his scent, fresh air and rain, with an undertone of some kind of male fragrance product, a Christmas present, probably.

'Sorry you've had a wasted journey.'

He looks back at me and raises his eyebrows. Apology unaccepted, then.

After he's opened the door, he suddenly stops and turns back towards me. 'God, I almost forgot. How could I? The Prof wants to see you. He says there's something you both need to discuss.'

'Like what?'

'He wouldn't tell me. He said you'd know.'

'He's probably forgotten now, if he's so sick.'

'I don't think so. I've been with him nearly all day. He hasn't stopped talking about you. You should go. Like now. I'm going back again later, too. Pauline's with him at the moment.'

'He's probably just raving.'

Jacob shakes his head, steps outside and shuts the front door behind him without saying another word. I sit on the upright chair next to the hall table and listen to the sound of his car as he drives away.

22. Suzy

Donna and I are way out of our depth. Tess has had three showers since yesterday and has almost rubbed her skin raw with a nail brush. We hand her tissues, plait her wet hair and listen to her endless crying. At one point, I go to fetch glasses of lemon squash from the kitchen. Tess's parents are both in there when I go down, making sandwiches. I chat to them about their trip to Italy, and I gush about how jealous I am and how I'd love to go to Italy one day. You'd think nothing had happened from the way I go on and on. Her dad grins and scratches his shaggy beard, as though he's flattered by my words, and his mum, who looks beautiful as ever, but paint splattered, smiles vaguely into the air above my head. What idiots, I think. So talented at capturing their particular interpretation of world on canvas, but so completely useless when it comes to their own daughter. Tess doesn't want them to know what's happened to her, but even so, surely by now they should have noticed something is wrong?

Late in the afternoon, Tess falls asleep and Donna and I walk to the little supermarket on Larchford High Street to buy Lucozade and crisps. We go back via the war memorial gardens and sit on a bench for a few minutes.

'We should tell someone,' Donna says.

'Like who?'

'The police?'

The local police station is a small, square building run by PC Cardew, a friendly, porcine man with white hair who spends most of his time pottering about in the High Street and the park, chatting to shopkeepers and mums pushing prams. I don't think he's ever had to deal with any major crimes, only trivial incidents, like when someone set fire to the shed on the putting green where the golf clubs are kept. When he discovered it was one of the local boys, he went round to have a word with his parents. I've known PC Cardew since I was a baby. He usually winks when he sees me.

'He wouldn't believe us. And even if he did, he wouldn't be able to cope. What about your mum?'

Donna's mum has a good track record when it comes to knowing what to do. She was the one who sorted me out when my periods started and provided me not just with sanitary towels, but with paracetamol and chocolate, too.

'She'd be duty bound to tell Dad. And he'd have to do something official.'

'And anyway,' I start saying, then stop.

'Anyway, what?'

'I don't know. Ade, yesterday. He behaved as though nothing had happened.'

'So maybe nothing did? Is that what you're saying?'

After Tess had left the camp, Donna and I went back to sleep in our tent. We didn't wake up until much later, when we heard the boys kicking a football about. It was another hot, sunny day, but at first there was a heat mist suspended over the low lying land beneath the hill, making it feel like an island in the middle of a big expanse of nothing. Christoff had gone, too, but he'd already said he wouldn't be hanging around with us on the Sunday because his parents had guests staying who were something important to do with the motorsport industry, and he was expected to be there in the morning, so nobody read anything into his absence. We cooked eggs, sausages and tomatoes and rashers of bacon, on the little stove, in a single frying pan, and by the time we'd eaten, it was more like lunchtime, so the boys cracked open a few more beers. Ade joked about, like he always did, including us all in his banter, the perfect host, as though our encampment was an extension of his house. When we told him Tess had walked home earlier, he was concerned. Or he seemed to be.

'Is she ok? Should I go after her?'

'She'll probably be home by now,' I said. 'Sometimes she needs her own space.'

He looked at me in that way of his. I'd withdrawn myself from his attentions ages ago, like I said, because I didn't want to share him with Tess. But she wasn't here now, was she, and I know it sounds really bad, but the temptation to have him to myself was too much. For the rest of the day, I stayed close to him, willing him to focus on me. And he did, pretty much. Despite everything, I let him put his arm round me as we walked down the hill and when we stopped off at the pond again on the way back, I let him pull me into the woods and kiss me. We stayed by the pond until late afternoon, alternating between swimming and sunbathing in the long grass. The others left in dribs and drabs. Donna and Graham went first, because Donna had been invited to the farmhouse for tea. Then Kevin and the other boys sloped off, and it was just Ade and me.

Donna and I get up from the bench and start heading back to Tess's house.

'Do you think it was wrong of me to hang around with Ade after what had happened to Tess.'

'I don't know.'

There had been a couple of other times by then when Ade and I had found ourselves alone, and the secrecy, the snatched, private moments between us were exhilarating. Donna was the only other person who knew about those. I don't think she approved. But I couldn't seem to make myself care about the morality of it all.

'Do you think Tess is making it up?' She asks.

'Not exactly making it up. It's like there's two versions of everything. First, there's Tess's version, where people actually do what she wants them to do and things happen in real life the way she thinks they should happen. And then there's the other version, where people do what *they* want, and it isn't always the same as what Tess wants.'

'And there two versions of Ade,' Donna adds. 'The ok version when he's on his own and the other one who appears when Christoff's around.'

I hadn't really thought about that before, probably because I'm not much of a Christoff fan, so anything relating to him is only ever on the edges of my mental radar. But she's right. Ade *is* different around Christoff. I can't quite put my finger on how exactly, but it's got something to do with the dynamics of the group. When Christoff isn't around, Ade is top dog, but then Christoff appears and quietly assumes the role, with Ade as his deputy. Maybe it's because Christoff is the one with the pool and the tennis courts, the one with the wealthy family, the Lord of the Manor, doing the rest of us a favour by letting us hang out in his parent's fantastic garden.

'You and Ade aren't going to stop, are you?'

'I don't know.'

'Don't you think you should? What if he drags Christoff in and does the same thing to you?'

'He wouldn't. It's not like that between us.'

'How can you be sure?'

'I just am.'

'And it's two-timing.'

'I was there first.'

Donna doesn't say anything.

'Let's tell her we think she should talk to someone. If she says no, at least we'll have tried,' I suggest.

'But what if she does agree to talk to someone and it's all lies, and Ade's totally innocent? And anyway, there won't be any proof. She's had all those showers and baths now. And Christoff will probably deny it all, too, if he gets dragged into it. He'll say she consented and it will be impossible to prove she didn't. His word against hers.'

Despite our misgivings, we agree to have a go at Tess, but we've already convinced ourselves it's pointless, so our attempts at persuading her are pretty half hearted. And, as expected, she's totally and utterly adamant she doesn't want to speak to anyone. We stay with her until it's way too late to go over to Ade's house, like we would on a normal evening. I resent our enforced absence, but I don't say so, because I know how mean that would make me look. We get Tess to drink the Lucozade and eat a handful of crisps. After that, she seems calmer and happier, and we have another of our frequent conversations about contraception. Tess has already been on the pill for a while because she suffers from heavy periods, so an unwanted pregnancy isn't a concern for her. She even makes a joke about how awful it would be to fall pregnant and not know who the father is. I don't know about Donna, but the fact she can laugh about it adds to my suspicion that it didn't happen, at least not the way she said it did. Also, the disconnect between what she says took place and the way Ade behaved the day after is so enormous that unless Ade is a psychopath or very good actor, or both, it doesn't add up.

And unless I know for certain that he and Christoff did what Tess said they did, I'm not prepared to deliberately put an end to Ade and me. Why should I?

For the next fortnight, I have to work in the shop every single day apart from Sundays, because Mrs Hopgood has taken Graham and his little brother to Tenby. It could be worse, I suppose. Even though Dad's expecting the usual end of summer rush to build, as parents realise their children will need new shoes for the autumn term, the shop doesn't really get busy until eleven, so I don't have to go in until then.

After tea on Tuesday evening, everyone is in Ade's back garden, including Tess. We lounge about in deckchairs on the patio and drink today's beverage of the day, which is gin and bitter lemon. Someone starts a conversation about heading out to the pond again soon, but nobody can be bothered to pursue it. Tinny sounding music blasts out from a transistor radio on Kevin's lap and Ade makes a big production of running up and down with the lawn mower. He's wearing nothing but his red swimming trunks and couldn't look more glorious if he tried. Tess sits cross legged on the paving stones, watching Ade and laughing at his antics. I ask her how she's feeling. She says she's fine, in a surprised voice, as though she has no idea why I'm asking, which makes Donna and I exchange glances. We can hear Christoff's family and their important guests on the other side of the ivy-clad wall, enjoying themselves in and around the swimming pool. I keep expecting Christoff to pop his head through the gate and say hi. I'm a bit anxious about how I'll feel if he does this.

But it doesn't happen. And when I get up to leave, Tess runs after me and gets me on my own in the hallway.

'Ade and me are fine,' she says, smiling widely. 'I was only upset because it was such a big rite of passage. My tears were grief at the loss of my former self. You'll understand what I mean when it finally happens to you.'

'What about the part where he held you down, so Christoff could have a go? Was that a rite of passage, too?'

She shakes her head and smiles at me, her eyes full of pity, as though she's thinking that's exactly the kind of thing I'd invent, because I'm so envious of her and Ade. She's so convincing, I almost start to doubt that she'd ever said anything about Christoff. She goes back out to the garden, leaving me standing in the hallway, staring through the frosted glass panel in the front door, reluctant to open it and step out into The Crescent. Then Ade appears. He's barefoot and still in his swimming trunks. He's still thin as one of the reeds that blow in the breeze at the edge of the pond, but he has some muscle definition around his chest now. He must have been working out.

'Still here?' He grins as he opens the cellar door. 'We need more gin.'

He sounds more sober than he did when he was prancing around in the garden.

Now would be a good time to ask him what really happened on Elfbarrow Hill. But the sentence I start to formulate inside my head tapers away to nothing. It isn't really any of my business, I decide. And in any case, Tess has made it perfectly clear she's able to guide her own destiny without any help from either Donna or me. I think of the way she just spoke to me, the way she said *when it finally happens to you*. She didn't need to say *finally* like that. I move closer to Ade. I want to put my hand on his arm, but I've learnt that physical contact between me and him has to be initiated by him. My reserve and my apparent reluctance are the things he finds most attractive about me. He has to conquer me anew, each time, unlike Tess, who practically throws herself at him.

'Early start, tomorrow?' He puts his head on one side and looks at me.

'Not too early. I don't need to leave the house until about ten thirty.'

I take great care to toss this information at him casually, as though I'm merely stating a fact. I speak very quietly and as I'm saying it, I turn towards the door, in case my face is too blatant, my meaning too obvious.

'Goodnight,' I say, as I head for the door.

'Night, Suzy' he replies from half way down the cellar steps.

23. Suzy

Towards the end of August, the heatwave finally loses its grip. The evenings darken and thunderstorms chase away the sunshine. When the sun returns, it casts a mellow, more autumnal light and the temperature is often too low for swimming, either in the pool or the pond. I think back to the middle of June, when Ade said we had the whole summer ahead of us. To me, it genuinely felt as though it would never end. But now the winds of change are blowing for all of us. First Gaz stops coming round. Ade says he's gone off to Greece in a minibus with a group of other hippies. Then A' level results day arrives. Ade, Kev and Anthony all get the grades they need. Kev is going all the way up to St Andrews, Anthony is due to start training to be an accountant, at a firm in Guildford. Ade, on the other hand, has changed his mind. His parents were still alive when he filled in his university application form, which had a great deal to do with his decision to opt for a law degree. Now they're dead, he can do what he likes, so he's gone through clearing and got himself a place on a Psychology and Philosophy course in London.

When the O' level results come out, the following week, Ade is already filling in application forms for halls of residence in Kensington and Kev is actually starting to pack. His parents are driving him up to Scotland the weekend after next. Tess, Donna and I wait until the evening, then we gather in Tess's bedroom so we can open our envelopes together. I've already opened mine and sealed it up again, but I don't tell them that. I ran home from the shop at lunchtime to pick it up from the doormat. Dad opened the till and gave me twenty pounds when I told him I got seven A's and a B. The B is a bit of a shame, but it's only Religious Studies. Donna got the same grades as me and we're both going into the sixth form at St Ursulas, but I'm doing Maths, Physics and Chemistry, whereas her A' levels will be French, History and Latin. Graham did ok, too, well enough to go into the sixth form and avoid full time farming for another two years. And as for Tess, she got an A for Art, and the rest were B's and C's, so she's off to the Tech in Froehampton to study textiles and something else. She's not sure what exactly, but she'll speak to her course tutors about that when she gets there.

    The Kellers are hosting a big party on Saturday evening. For the last few days, we've watched fairy lights and wrought iron tables and chairs being set out by the pool, and a blue and white striped marquee being erected closer to the house. Christoff says they've put a dance floor in the marquee, and there'll be live band with swing music early on, followed by a disco. Most of the guests will be driving down from London, and a few are flying in from Switzerland and France. All the locals who live close by have been invited, too. Christoff's family went to the trouble of finding out who lives where, and invitations, in thick cream envelopes, personally addressed to each occupant, landed on the doormat of every house in Fieldgate Lane and The Crescent, as well as the big, Georgian dwellings along High Street, adjacent to Fieldgate Hall. Even Arrow Farm got one.

    Anthony and Kev have managed to find work with the catering company doing the buffet and drinks, but they're off duty from midnight, when the guests are expected to start leaving, and we're all bringing our swimsuits and stashing them behind the fence in Ade's garden, so we can dive into the pool for a chilly, late night swim. Davey was going to bring Sharon, but she's dumped him for someone older. He was gutted at first, but he soon bounced back and now he's hoping meet someone new at the party. As soon as the invitation arrived, he decided that if he started growing a moustache there and then, it would probably be a full handlebar affair when the night arrived. Dad sports a spectacular sweeping brush under his nose, and is acting as a role model for Davey in this endeavour, something that hasn't happened for a very long time, if ever. Since Davey turned ten and entered the hideous limbo of pre-puberty, he's regarded poor Dad as a source of personal shame and embarrassment, standing there in the shoe shop, as he does, in his long brown overall, clearly visible through the big glass window to all of Davey's friends when they happen to walk down the High Street. I tell him I've been to the library and done some research on factors that promote moustache growth. So far, I've managed to persuade him to eat a bowl of tripe and onions, drink an elixir made from liquorice and boiling water, and smear the contents of an old can of Crazy Foam over his face.

    Tess uses her mum's sewing machine to make a long dress from some material in buttercup-yellow she found on a stall in the market.

It has a satin-like sheen, although it isn't really satin, and she says it will accentuate her tall, willowy figure. Ade roots around in the wardrobes at his house and finds an old dress suit that belonged to his father. He tries it on, and parades up and down in front of us. The trousers are the right length, although the jacket is slightly loose, and he's wearing one of his school shirts with it, together with his school shoes and his dad's RAF tie. He jokes that his look is a bit cobbled together and he asks if we think he should cut his hair, which is now almost shoulder length. We all say he shouldn't. He looks handsome and kind of louche, but in a nice way.

    Tess offers to make me a dress, too, but I can't bear the thought of all that standing around while she measures me, sticks pins into me and leaves great conversational silences hanging in the air that she could, but won't fill with comments about my difficult hair colour, my inability to tan in the sun, the freckles on my shoulders and my almost total absence of boobs. And anyway, after my long and tedious stint working full time at the shop, I can afford to buy myself something to wear. I take Davey up to Oxford Street on the train to buy outfits for us both. We make a day of it. I try on a few dresses. When I emerge from changing rooms to ask him what he thinks, he makes a few embarrassed and non-committal grunts, and then continues with his obsessive and frankly painful ogling of the other female customers, all of whom ignore him completely. I feel sorry for him. It must be dreadful to be in thrall to your hormones to that extent. In the end I rely on my own judgement and opt for a knee length dress in pale blue cheesecloth from Chelsea Girl. I think it looks alright and it has the added bonus of being sufficiently modest to pass the Dad test, not that my body parts are in danger of tumbling out of any garment in a wanton manner. We manage to find a shirt in lime green for Davey and a pair of cream trousers that are jeans really, but which I think he'll get away with because you can't see the stitching unless someone bends down and gets within an inch of his legs, and that's not going to happen. Once we finish shopping, we buy sandwiches and eat them in Hyde Park. Then we have an ice cream as we walk across the still parched-looking grass and make our way back to Waterloo.

    Donna, Tess and I get ready for the party at my house. We were going to use Tess's bedroom, but Dad says why don't we all get ready here? The expression in his eyes makes me want to look away, because I know he's thinking, that the next two years will be over in a flash and then I'll be off, so he needs to make the most of Davey and me and the life we bring to the house while we're still here. I'm the first person in our family who'll be going to university, and instead of basking in his fatherly pride and scoffing at my eye-rolling brother, I just feel sad. For the first time, it occurs to me to wonder how they'll cope without me.

Dad puts on the immersion heater at lunchtime, which is unheard off, so we can all have baths and wash our hair. He lets us use the dining room to get ready and gives us a Do Not Disturb sign like the ones they have in hotels, to place on the door when we're not decent. As soon as we remove it, Davey pops his head round the door.

'Hi girls. How *are* you?' He says.

'Why is he speaking in an American accent?' Donna asks when he's gone.

'It's his new thing. He thinks it sounds cool.'

We take it in turns to blow dry our hair with Tess's new styling kit. Afterwards, mine looks every bit as limp as it had before I started, and Donna's sticks out all over the place in blonde spikes. Tess's hair on the other hand flows in gentle waves almost down to her waist.

'I'm not bothered,' Donna says, when she sees herself in the mirror.

Having managed to resist all her mum's attempts to make her dress like a girl, Donna is planning to wearing black trousers and a stripey shirt borrowed from one of her brothers. I persuade her to add a pair of dangly earrings though, and before we set off, she puts on eye shadow and matching lipstick in a bright plum colour.

'I wouldn't worry,' Tess says.

'I'm not.'

'No, well at least you've got Graham.'

She makes Graham sound like some kind of booby prize. Before Donna slaps her she turns her attention to me.

'I'll curl your hair for you if you like, and help you do your make-up. You need some mascara for those pale eyelashes. It's worth a try. You never know.'

'Never know what?'

'There might be someone really nice at the party. Someone new.'

'Some loser who doesn't mind flat chested girls with ginger hair?'

'I didn't mean it like that.'

She did, though. She's so full of crap tonight. I'm dismayed and kind of disappointed at how angry she's making me feel. I want to enjoy this evening, not just because it's such a big occasion, but because it marks the beginning of the end of what has been a truly remarkable summer. Soon we'll all be away at university or back at school. And Ade will be gone, perhaps forever. Tess says she's going to spend weekends with him in his halls, in London, but I don't suppose I'll see him again once he's left our little town. Unless he comes back to his house sometimes. Then he might turn up at my front door. You never know.

Dad brings in glasses of lemonade and bowls of crisps and iced gems.

'To line your stomachs before you start on the champagne.'

We all giggle. Davey comes in and helps himself to a lemonade. He's clean shaven now, all attempts at moustache growing abandoned, and he's made his hair go all flat, with a side-parting, like Hitler's. But he doesn't look too hideous for someone trapped between boyhood and manhood. We troop round the corner to Fieldgate Hall together, in an unruly gaggle, stopping off on the way to pick up Ade, who has promised not to sneak into the back garden via the gate in the fence, but to arrive like the rest of us by the front door. As he leaves his house, he holds hands with Tess and grins at the rest of us. When we reach the entrance to Fieldgate Hall, Tess removes her camera from the little clutch bag dangling from her wrist and takes photos. Me with Dad and Davey. Donna with Graham. And Ade with Christoff, Anthony and Kev. Then she gets Dad to take a few of her and Ade, standing slightly turned towards each other, his arm around her waist. Alain is dressed like a butler for the occasion. He stands at the door and announces us, one by one, remaining in character even when we all burst out laughing. Christoff, Karl and Mr and Mrs Keller are stand in a line in the hallway. They make us feel incredibly welcome, not at all like neighbours who have only been invited so we won't complain about the noise. We each take a glass of champagne from trays carried by Kev and Anthony, who tell us they've both already been reprimanded by the owner of the catering company for laughing too much. A couple of the guests though the boys were laughing at *them*, and complained.

Ade avoids my eye. I try not to mind, because, like I say, I really want to enjoy this party. But I'm longing to tell Tess that every morning, for the past two weeks, during the precious hour or so before I have to leave for the shop, Ade and I have fallen out of normal time and entered a different one. We've never spoken about it, either before or afterwards, not to each other or to anyone else. I don't know what it's been like for him, but each day, when he's left and I've gone to the shop, time and the universe have reverted to their usual states and I've found it difficult to believe he knocked on my door, I took him up to my room and we participated in what felt like a sacred ritual, fuelled by what? Submission on my side, and control on his. Definitely both of those, but also a pleasure that has been keen and raw.

 I've made a big effort not to get angry about the fact that Tess doesn't know, that she thinks she's the only one who has conquered Ade, that in public, they're the official couple. I try to tell myself it doesn't matter that she's so damned pleased with herself. Surely, I can let it go. After all Ade will be gone soon and it will cease to be a problem. But once they've finished posing together on the doorstep of Fieldgate Hall, all I want is to wipe that smug, condescending smile off her face and rip her entire evening apart.

24. Aunty Susan

Insomnia is so much harder to endure at this time of year. In summer, if you wake in the wee small hours it's a comfort to know the first blackbird will soon start heralding the dawn. But in the dead of winter, if you're tossing and turning at three in the morning, you've got another five hours of darkness to get through.

After Jacob has gone, I heat soup in the microwave, although I'm not really hungry, and I wash it down with a couple of glasses of port. Then I try to find a decent film to watch. Nothing takes my fancy, so I start a Scandi crime box set and pour myself a large gin and tonic. The drama is grim, lots of murders and a great deal of unpleasantness and tension, under a heavy, grey sky, but it's also compelling and complicated, and I'm forced to concentrate on the subtitles in order to understand what's going on. One episode runs into the next if you don't get your act together and click *exit*, and I finish the entire series in one go. By then, it's very late and I'm almost going cross eyed from deciphering the words at the bottom of the screen, so I go to bed, grateful that Christmas Day is over for me and that the next day won't be so loaded with the pressure to be happy. I read one page of my book, nod off, wake up again when my e-reader fall on my face, turn my light off and plunge into what promises to be a deep sleep.

It isn't. Before long, I'm back up at the surface, and I never go completely under again. My heart is beating faster than normal and the suspicion runs through everything in a subdued undercurrent that my blood pressure is through the roof, after all that unhealthy food and booze, and I really should be taking those tablets. Then I'm suddenly thrown into a dark sea, the colour of navy blue ink. A whirlpool pulls me down, even though I'm wearing a life jacket, tossed to me from a ship by Jacob. I hear his voice.

'There's more than one way to be a snowflake,' he says. 'And there's more than one way not to be a snowflake.'

I don't understand what he means and I don't have time to work it out because I'm sixteen again and flat on my back on the dining room floor with Ade. That particular day we were overtaken by lust before we'd even managed to get ourselves upstairs. Loud ticks from the clock on the mantlepiece split the air into clear intervals a second apart, but they seem to be coming from a long way away, and in any case, they are completely irrelevant because we've slipped out of time again. He stares into my eyes, his features illuminated by that smile, which is for my eyes only and is nothing like the one he uses for Tess. He throws textbook grins at her, as though he's on stage and has to present his affection for her in an exaggerated way, otherwise nobody will notice. It makes me feel as though I've won some kind of battle. An invisible person hands me several lengths of string, which are attached to balloons in bright colours. One of them, the biggest, has a white background overlaid with swirls of pink and blue, like the ones Mum used to put up by the front door for birthday parties when I was small. I realise they're also very similar to the ones they released at the Kellers' party on the stroke of midnight, except that those contained helium. The balloons pull me up into the air. Now I'm flying over Fieldgate Crescent, away from Ade's house, towards mine, then over the back gardens to Tess's house and her orange and white painted balcony. I let go of the strings and plummet to earth with a thud.

    My heart is racing. I get up and look out of the window. It's that time of night when the council turns the streetlights off to save money. Even the houses on the other side of the road, a stone's throw away, are veiled in darkness. I go back to bed and stare into the void. Scenes from the party run before my eyes, flickering like an old cine film that has been exposed to the light. Tess arm in arm with Ade, making an entrance, being photographed, dancing in the marquee, feeding him melon balls and prawn cocktail. The rest of are there, too, also dancing and eating, and drinking, but we seem shadowy and out of focus. The film continues in this vein until we notice Ade is no longer there. My brother takes advantage of the situation and asks Tess for a slow dance. She agrees, but when Ade still hasn't reappeared after *Three Times a Lady*, we start looking for him. We search everywhere, in the marquee, in the rooms of the house that the Kellers have made available to the party goers, in the pool, on the tennis court and in the rose garden where little tables and chairs have been arranged, but he's nowhere. Tess decides he must have gone home. He'd had a headache earlier, she says. I walk with her to the gate in the fence. She goes through and closes it behind her. I hover uncertainly on the other side. It's much quieter at that end of the Kellers' garden. The pool is only few metres away, at the other side of a cluster of shrubs, buddleia and bamboo mostly, and nobody is swimming at the moment, so when Tess screams I hear her. I stay where I am for a few seconds, waiting for something else to happen and trying to decide what to do. Then she screams again, but her voice is more distant this time. I think I hear the front door of Ade's house open and then slam shut.

I dash through the gate, across Ade's lawn, through his kitchen, along his hall and straight out of the front door. I see Tess at the other side of The Crescent, crying and shouting as she runs. Ade is there, too, trying to catch up with her. Apart from them, the Crescent is deserted. Most, if not all of the residents must be at the party. I try to work out what just happened. Did he tell her about us? Surely he wouldn't do that, not now, not on the night of the party?

I follow them as they run round the corner into Fieldgate Lane. Although she had a head start, by the time she reaches her house, Ade has caught up with her and I'm close behind. He's grabbing at her sleeve and she's telling him to let go. We all make our way down the path that winds round to the back of the house. He holds onto her round her waist from behind and whispers in her ear. From the way she's shaking her head, I assume he's begging her to do something she doesn't want to do. Or not do something. It could be either. They climb the outside stairs to the balcony. I do the same. As I make my way up, I shriek at her to stop being such a diva, but neither of them even notices me until I'm at the top, and when they do realise I'm there, they ignore me and continue tussling. Nothing I say or do has any impact. I might as well go back to the party for all the good I'm doing.

After that, my recollection is interrupted by little spaces, as though some external controller has looked at my personal script and redacted parts of it so completely that even now, all these years later, I have no memory of what happened during those intervals. One minute the three of us are standing together on the balcony, shouting at each other. Then the tape stops and starts again and Tess is on the paving stones below. I'm kneeling next to her and Ade is standing behind me, making horrible wailing sounds and generally freaking out. The hem of my dress has turned into blotting paper and a dark liquid is quickly seeping into it.

The next gap spans a much bigger leap in time. When it ends, I'm back at the party in a different dress, an older one that I don't like much, made from orange poplin with batwing sleeves. Ade is standing next to me. Anthony approaches with another tray of drinks. Ade takes a flute of champagne, knocks it back in one go and helps himself to another one. The fingers of his other hand are wrapped lightly around my wrist in a gesture that should, if it were being scrutinized, seem casual and friendly. But through this single point of contact, I can tell his entire body is shaking violently. I take a drink from Anthony and I smile at him. He giggles back at me. He thinks nothing has changed since the last time he approached us with his tray.

 I conduct a brief scan of my immediate surroundings and I use all my senses to seek out little details to focus on in an attempt to settle myself. Luckily, I find plenty. The bubbles in my champagne, the slightly chilly breeze around my knees and the thump-thwack of the disco beat coming from the marquee all help. I've got this, I think. I act super-calm, like an ice maiden. I wish I could tell Ade to get a grip, too, but I'd have to come out of character and openly acknowledge what just happened or might have happened, and I can't risk doing that. I stand really still and hold my arm rigid to resist the current his trembling body is trying to transmit to mine. I watch as Donna, Graham and my brother are ushered towards us by Christoff, who looks dashingly dishevelled in his white suit and black bow tie, which is unfastened. I search his face but can see nothing there but affability, the natural good manners of a host whose sole aim is to ensure that his guests should enjoy themselves.

 I ask myself why I'm so calm. I can't remember everything, but I know for sure when I was on the balcony with Tess and Ade I was utterly blinded by rage.

 'Everyone was wondering where you'd gone,' Christoff says to Ade and me. 'It's almost midnight. They're about to release the balloons and start the fireworks.'

 'What happened to your dress?' Donna asks.

 'Disaster. Time of the month. I had to go and change.'

 'Oh God, really? Poor you.'

 'I know. Such bad timing.'

 I don't sound like myself. My voice doesn't even feel as though it's coming from my own mouth. It seems to be emanating from an invisible ventriloquist's doll a few feet away. Once again, nobody else notices. I marvel at how good I am at acting, at lying to the people around me, my brother and my friends, people who know me really well. And I have no clue why I'm doing it.

 'Where's Tess?'

I can't remember who says this. It might be Anthony, who is still here, preferring to talk to his friends rather than circulate with his tray of glasses. But someone was bound to ask, and I have my lines ready.

'She went home. She wasn't feeling well.'

'I thought it was you that had the headache,' Anthony says to Ade.

'Me?' Ade says.

His eyes are wild. I start to say something else, to cover for him and at the same time garnish the fib I've already told and make it more credible, a mistake liars often make, particularly novices like me. But luckily, my voice is drowned out by the countdown to the balloon release, then cheering and fireworks fill the air, and I don't need to say anything else to anybody. Soon afterwards, I walk home with Dad and Davey. My brother is drunk and has enjoyed himself immensely. When we get inside, I go straight up to my room. I wait until Dad and Davey have gone to bed, then I wash out my other dress, the bloodstained one, in the bathroom sink and suspend it on a coat hanger above the bath. Trying to sleep is pointless. I can't even make myself lie flat on my bed. I open my bedroom window and stare out across the Crescent. All the lights are off in Ade's house. I want to sneak out again and make sure he's ok. But he won't be there. When we left, Christoff and his older brother were getting a group together to play poker, and Ade would struggle to avoid that. So I sit on the carpet with my back pressed against the wall beneath the open window and I stay there for the rest of the night, hugging my knees, listening and waiting.

Our house almost backs onto Fieldgate Lane, and our back garden is only separated from Tess's by two other properties. If Tess's mum screams when she discovers her daughter, I should be able to hear her. If not, I'll definitely hear the sirens when the emergency services arrive. Then, when the knock at the door comes, I'll be ready. Ready to act as though I'm shocked, ready to tell them I wasn't there when it happened. When she fell.

Forty years later, these memories are vivid and unaltered. I pull on underwear, cords, a long-sleeved tee-shirt and a Kashmir jumper, the first items of clothing that come to hand, and I go downstairs, slip my feet into my most comfortable ankle boots, don my green jacket with the fur hood, grab my bag and head for my car. It starts first time, even though I haven't driven since the accident, and I reverse out onto the road. My ankle seems fine, but even if it starts hurting like hell, I'm not planning to stop. Twenty minutes later I'm in Larchford. I park outside the parade of shops, which are all in darkness now, as you'd expect them to be before dawn on Boxing Day morning. After the house collapse, Bartosz drove Gawain here to pick up my car and drive it back to my place.

I haven't driven here to gaze at Tess's house again. Anyway, there's nothing to see. It's just a pile of rubble now. Instead, I decide to head over to the front of Fieldgate Hall and mooch about on the road outside. The entire area is deserted, so I can stand for as long as I like and stare at the place, like a complete wierdo, without attracting attention. The front garden used to contain an impressive display of rose bushes that curved along a drive running between two gaps in the old red-brick wall, one to enter by and the other to leave by. All of this has gone. The entire area is a car park now, plain and utilitarian, and by the door is a series of buttons with names against them. I don't know when the place was converted to flats. The Kellers still lived there when I was in the sixth form and when I came home from Oxford during the holidays, but I don't think any of them spent much time there after the summer of 'seventy-six, and they never held another party.

I walk round the corner and turn into Fieldgate Crescent. This has changed, too. The circle in the middle, the little garden we used to cycle, scoot and pogo round, used to be full of shrubs and bedding plants tended to by our next door neighbour, a retired district nurse, who would kneel in front of the flowerbeds, listening to radio 4 on a small transistor radio. Now this circle has been concreted over, apart from a small patch of soil in the middle, which has a single conifer growing out of it. I'm shocked to see Ade's house has gone, too, replaced by narrow turning into a road called Kingfisher Close, which has taken a considerable chunk out of the former back garden of the Keller house, and turns out to contain several expensive-looking modern houses with pointed gables and attractive little verandas. Nothing remains of the rose lawn, the tennis court, the swimming pool or the fence with the little door in it. But in the darkness I can still make out the roof of Fieldgate Hall looming up behind the new villas.

Pausing for a moment, I realise I'm shivering, so I put my hands in the pockets of my jacket, and take comfort from their fleecy linings. Then I turn, to face the other side of the crescent, the part where I used to live, wondering if my former home has disappeared too. Our house was one of a pair of semis, humbler and smaller than the other dwellings. I walk straight over the central circle, by-passing the tree, then I draw a deep breath. Our house and the one next door, with their postage-stamp sized lawns and neat holly hedges, have been replaced by a rectangular, three storey block. A Christmas tree with green and red lights flashes on and off through the full length window by the front door, even though it's five thirty in the morning, and a sign tells the world that this is the Fieldgate Court Rest Home. I glance upwards and realise I'm wrong. That window above the door used to be mine. I recognise its shape. The old semis are still there underneath, combined into a single building to which a third floor has been added.

So not only has Tess's house gone, Ade's has too, and mine is changed beyond recognition. All the physical reminders of that terrible September night have been completely erased. How ironic that the images in my head of Tess on the paving stones and all that followed, apart from the gaps in my memory, are more vivid than they've ever been.

25. Aunty Susan

After circling the Crescent one more time, staring into dark windows like some ghastly spectre of Christmas past, I change my mind and walk the short distance round the corner to Fieldgate Lane. Temporary metal fencing has been put up around the ruins, but I find a narrow gap and slip through. At the back, everything is the same as it was on the night the house collapsed, including the bed that sheltered Jacob so miraculously, which is still suspended over the shrubbery. I can't believe I left him there like that and crawled off to the shed. He could have had a bleed on the brain or God knows what else. And it was raining heavily, and freezing cold. My phone had died, which was why it took them a long time to find me in the shed, but I could see his, sticking out of his back pocket. I could have taken it and used it to call the emergency services. Luckily, someone else found him and he was rescued quickly. But why did I abandon him? Because I wasn't in my right mind? Or because I had to get away from those wretched paving stones?

 I can see bits of orange and white metal poking out from under the rubble. That balcony was always dodgy. I find it astonishing that parts of it are still in existence so many years after Tess's death. I get down on my hands and knees. The paving stones form of grid of differently coloured squares, and I can still remember exactly where her head was positioned. That night, the outside light at the back of the house was broken and there was no moon. When I clambered up the staircase after Tess and Ade, I could hardly see them, but I could hear them. Tess was hysterical and Ade was frantic and clearly had no clue how to make her stop. And as for me, I was as angry as I'd ever been, because Tess had claimed Ade, taken him away from me and now she was behaving like an idiot and screwing everything up between them as well. Ade didn't deserve it. I'd never have done that if he'd been my boyfriend. And I couldn't understand why Ade didn't just give up on her and walk away.

 The knock on the door didn't happen until the following morning. There were two of them, a man and a woman, both in uniform.

When the policewoman said the necessary words, I sat there, dry eyed. Dad, who was standing behind me, made some kind of exclamation, but I can't remember the words he used, and Davey flopped down onto the arm of my chair, briefly rested his head against my shoulder, then jumped up again and left the room. My brain sent a message to my face, telling it to look shocked. Then it sent another message to my hand, making it place itself over my mouth.

Dad trundled off to make everyone a cup of tea, and I was left alone with the police. They asked me, as I knew they would, when I'd last seen Tess. I told them she'd gone home on her own quite early in the evening, because she wasn't feeling well. I'd already calculated the risks associated with this lie. There wasn't much danger of being caught out. I was pretty sure I was the only one who saw Tess go through the gate to Ade's garden and I was almost one hundred percent sure nobody had seen the three of us crossing the crescent. I couldn't be certain the same was true when we'd returned from Tess's house, because I couldn't remember, but the police didn't ask about that. Nor did they ask why I'd vanished and returned to the party later wearing a different dress. I began to think I was safe, as long as Ade didn't crack under pressure and tell the truth, whatever that was. Later, I discovered the account he'd given was exactly the same as mine, and not only had the police not spoken to anyone else who'd been at the party, nobody had called them and volunteered any other information.

I did a reading at the funeral. Davey came up and stood next to me, so he could take over if I started to get upset. But I managed it easily, and I sang each of the hymns from beginning to end, in a loud voice. They were all Tess's favourites, ones we'd sung together at primary school and then at St. Ursula's, including He Who Would Valiant Be, which was one of my favourites, too. Afterwards, I went back to her house with everyone else, apart from Kev, who had gone up to St Andrews by then. His parents sent flowers on his behalf. At the wake, nobody knew quite how to behave. We were all shell-shocked, I suppose. Tess's father greeted everyone at the door and then disappeared upstairs to be with Tess's mother who had rushed up there as soon as she'd returned from the funeral. Ade cried during the ceremony and continued to do so during the wake. I wanted to comfort him, but I kept well away, in case it looked suspicious.

I get back in my car and start driving. I don't want to go home again with all these memories, or half memories boiling about in my head. It seems incredible to me now that until I saw that YouTube video, I'd been happy to consign all this to the past, a chapter that would never be closed, but one I could live with.

Seems I can't live with it now. Not anymore.

I end up in a car park half way up a hill on the North Downs. It's a place I've been to many times, particularly recently, with Patrick. I only feel an occasional twinge in my ankle as I climb to the top of the hill, which is quite steep. The rising sun casts a pinkish glow over the valley beneath me and I watch as the twinkling lights are extinguished one by one. A keen breeze is blowing, and I pace up and down the sandy path in front of the little hilltop church to satisfy both my restlessness and my need to keep warm.

I only saw Ade once more after the wake, just before he left for university. He went back to his grandfather's the day after the party, and his house was left in darkness again, until one night, after my school term had started, I looked across and noticed the upstairs lights were on. I went over and knocked. Nobody answered. But the next day, he appeared at my front door. He was back in Larchford to sort through the rest of his stuff, he said, and to decide what he wanted to take with him to university. I asked how he was doing. He shrugged and said he was ok, glad to be moving on. Me too, I said. We went for a walk down the track towards Arrow Farm, just as we'd done that Sunday at the beginning of the summer holidays, in that long ago time before Tess had returned from Italy, when he was mine and mine alone. Leaves fell sporadically from the big oaks along the lane and the fields had been harvested and ploughed over, so they didn't shine golden through the hedges anymore.

I thought Ade would want to talk about Tess and I was hoping he'd be able to fill in the gaps, tell me what really happened, reassure me that it wasn't my fault. We held hands and by the time we reached the pond, we'd covered a range of topics - what my sixth form was like, if I really was going to aim for Oxbridge entrance, his course at university, the pros and cons of the hall of residence he'd managed to get into, Davey's new girlfriend, whether Donna and Graham would keep on being an item or if it was just a summer fling. But every time I tried to ask him about the night of the party, he seemed to sense what I was going to say before I got started, and he stepped in quickly and began a conversation about something else.

It was way too cold to swim in the pond and it had been raining, so he spread his coat out over the wet grass under the trees. I started to protest, but he told me not to fret, it wouldn't change anything now, so why worry? I didn't need much persuading. Tess was dead, and even if she wasn't, why should she be allowed to stop us? How awful, though, how shocking for me to justify my behaviour like that. And yet, I'm glad I did, because it was the last time.

    A chill wind blew through those trees, and the sun didn't reach us through the leaves, so we didn't linger for long. On the way home, he put an arm around my shoulder, but neither of us had much more to say, and when we got to my house, he kissed me on the cheek and disappeared across the Crescent. Next morning, when I left for school, his grandad's car was parked in the drive of his house, the boot open and half filled with boxes and bags. I thought about going over, to say goodbye and wish him luck, but we'd already said our farewells the day before. I walked out of the crescent to the bus stop on Fieldgate Lane, and when the school day was over and I got off the same bus and walked back into the crescent again, his house was silent, the curtains closed against the September sunshine. All those summer gatherings might never have happened, and I didn't see him again.

*

    When I arrive at the hospital, it's still very early in the morning, but nobody challenges me as I walk through the foyer. Jacob gave me directions to the ward. You have to follow the yellow line that runs along the floor until you reach a pair of locked doors with reinforced windows and a bell. I ring the bell several times, but nobody comes to answer it. I wait for about ten minutes, then I ring it again. A nurse walks past. I tap on the window, but she doesn't even look at me. I resign myself to waiting until someone turns up who knows the keycode. But eventually, a doctor glances through the glass panel as he walks past. Unfortunately for him, he catches my eye. He pokes his head through the door.
  'Who are you after?'
  'Michael Gossland?'
  'You're a relative?'
  'His sister. I've driven a long way.'

Seems I'm still very good at telling lies with a straight face. He holds the door open for me and points.

'Down at the end. His son's with him. Been here all night.'

I didn't realise he had a son, I think, stupidly. I walk past a series of alcoves on both sides of a wide corridor, each containing four beds, all occupied by elderly patients who seem to be occupying a range of mental states, from sprightly awareness of their surroundings to zombie-like oblivion. I wonder where Ade will fall on this spectrum. I find him in an alcove on the left at the very end of the corridor, in a bed next to the window. His eyes are open and he's propped up in a half-sitting position, blinking at Jacob, who is holding his hand.

'Look who's here,' Jacob says when I appear.

Ade blinks and stares at me briefly. Then he focuses on Jacob again.

'His eyesight isn't great. Find a chair and sit close to him. I'd fetch you one, but he doesn't want to let go of my hand.'

It takes me a while to locate one and by the time I do, Ade's eyes are closed.

'He drifts off. But he always wakes up again. Or he has done so far.'

'How long do they think it'll be?' I whisper.

'Not long.'

'The doctor said you'd been here all night.'

'Pauline rang yesterday afternoon. Said he was asking for me.'

Jacob looks across at me. He has those purple blotches under his eyes again, but he seems calm and actually happy to be here. Me on the other hand, I have to grip the arms of my chair to stop myself getting up and running away. I've never sat and watched someone die. I slept through Mum's death. The first I knew of it was when the ambulance turned up the next morning and Davey ran into my room saying Dad had suffocated her with a pillow. I told him not to be silly, that would make Dad a murderer. But secretly, I did wonder. If he *had* done that, I wouldn't have blamed him. We put animals out of their misery, why not humans? Dad died from a heart attack when I was in East Berlin, and when Davey was killed, he was miles away, in Bridlington. I remember Jacob saying he'd have given anything to have been there when Davey died, that he'll always regret that he wasn't, and that if, heaven forbid, Gawain or anyone else he was close to was dying, he'd drop whatever he was doing to be with them. And I remember thinking, I'd do the opposite. I wouldn't be able to face it. I'd run a mile.

Ade's eyes and mouth pop open at the same time. He stares at me.

'Yes, it's really me,' I say.

He smiles, almost in the old way, and for a couple of seconds the eighteen year old boy I adored so deeply is right there in front of me. This is way more than I can cope with, so I make a start on the usual questions, the *let's pretend everything's going to be okay* ones. But he's having none of it.

'I'm dying, Suzy,' he says.

I start to object, but he waves his hands at me, releasing Jacob in the process.

'Don't fret. All will be well.'

He was always telling me not to fret. It was one of his stock phrases. *Don't fret.*

Jacob stands up and stretches.

'Do you mind if I go and get some air?'

'No,' I say.

But he's asking Ade, not me.

'Of course not, off you trot. I'm not going anywhere,' he says. 'At least, not yet.'

I have no choice but to stay with him. Reluctantly, I take off my coat and put it on the back of the chair. Ade reaches out a thin and veiny hand for me to hold. His breath smells acrid. I don't suppose he eats or drinks much now, if at all, and I try to shrug away the idea that the process of decomposition has already started. The young boy has vanished again now, and the man who takes his place seems very old, much older than sixty-six, which is no age at all these days. I don't want to touch him or move any closer to him, but I grit my teeth, shuffle forward in my chair and take his hand in mine.

'Jacob said you wanted to see me.'

'That boy,' he says. 'It shines out of him, doesn't it?'

'What do you mean?'

'My abstract nouns have all gone. I can't think of the word. But you know. From his eyes.'

'He's a good lad,' I say, despising the banality of the sentence as soon as it's left my lips.

'No,' Ade says. 'He's no better or worse than anyone else. He just has that thing, shining out from his eyes. Not many people have it. Its…'

'Rare?' I don't know what he's talking about, but I'm keen to help him finish his sentence.

He nods.

'That's it. You haven't got it. Nor I, at least not nowadays. I like to think I might have done once. I don't think Davey had it either. I've met very few, but he's one of them.'

I realise I do know what he means. Gawain has it. I've always been able to see it in him. Is it a subjective thing? Can an individual's charisma only be perceived by certain recipients? Gawain's inner light has always been visible to me, and now Ade can see the same thing in Jacob. Back in seventy-six, could he see something similar in Tess? Perhaps. And of course, everyone could see the magic that shone out of Ade.

His eyes close. Then they open again and he stares right at me.

'You should be …. I can't think of the word.'

He doesn't say anything more and I'm left dangling, speculating on what he would say if he could gather the vocabulary together. Arrested? Charged with murder and locked up? Made to live like a hermit in a cave, where I can't harm anyone else with my unkind words? Thrown into deep well and left there?

Jacob returns and nudges his way through the gap in the curtains.

'Has he told you the thing he wanted to say?' Jacob asks.

'He went on about you for a bit, and how marvellous you are. Then he started to say I should be *something*, but he went to sleep again before he said what it was.'

'He does that a lot. Starts to say things that sound really important, but drifts away before he finishes. It's incredibly frustrating.'

'Do *you* know what he wants to talk to me about?'

'No, but it was triggered by the photo album. I brought it in and he spent ages looking at the pictures, particularly the ones on the last page, taken at that party. Then he started mumbling something about priests and absolution. I asked him if he wanted to speak to the hospital chaplain. He said he didn't, but he'd very much like to speak to you.'

We sit together, the three of us, until dusk starts to gather over the hospital roofscape. Ade sleeps most of the time now and when he does wake up, he doesn't say anything, just casts his eyes about until they rest adoringly on Jacob. I don't think he can see him clearly, he just picks up the shimmer of his blonde hair in the overhead lights. When night has fallen and nurse comes to shut the blind, I beg Ade to wake up properly and speak to me. He opens his eyes and blinks at me, as though he knows I'm here even though he can't see me properly, and I'm sure he remembers the thing he wants to say to me. But words are beyond him now. I continue to berate him at regular intervals for a while, until Jacob tells me to stop. Ade frowns and sighs and smiles from time to time, but mostly he remains lost in sleep and the process of dying, and then a point comes when he doesn't open his eyes again. Slowly and gradually, his breathing changes. The doctor comes in he says it won't be long now and she makes an adjustment to the morphine drip.

I stand up.

'I'm not really up for watching him die.'

I pick up my coat and start to put it on.

'What are you doing?' Jacob asks.

'Going home.'

'You can't!'

'No need to shout. And I can do what I like, thank you very much.'

'You refused to turn up yesterday, when he was really, really desperate to have you here. The least you can do now is stay and bear witness to his passing.'

'Bear witness to his passing? What the hell does that mean?'

'It's something we did at New Sunrise. When a person was close to death, other members of the community had to surround the bed, three on each side. We prayed and sang hymns and held the person's hands until they'd passed. It was one of what they called The Duties. Most of The Duties were cruel and some were sick and just plain evil, but that one was a genuine act of kindness, not because the elders valued kindness as such, but because they thought God watched death scenes carefully, so they all wanted to be there and earn brownie points that would help them get into heaven when it was their turn.'

'How ridiculous!'

'The theory behind it was all wrong, but it helped the dying person, and afterwards it helped the bereaved.'

'I've never watched anyone die before.'

'It's nothing to be scared of. I've said before, I wish I'd been there for Dad.'

'But you were only ten.'

He shrugs.

'You feel you didn't have closure?'

He scrutinises me closely in case I'm mocking him. He knows how much I scorn phrases like that. Then he continues.

'I definitely had closure. I saw his coffin being lowered into the ground, remember? I just wish I'd been able to speak to him before he died and tell him I'd been appointed Captain of Junior sport at school.'

I had sole responsibility for the children after Davey died. Jacob was silent for weeks after his father's death, clinging onto Gawain like a life raft. Then, at the graveside, he had an enormous meltdown. I'm not sure how I'd have coped with that lost little boy if Gawain hadn't been there to look after him. I did what I could. I took them on holiday to places like Majorca and Florida, and I fed them, clothed them and paid their school fees. But I was rubbish when it came to their emotional needs. They had to rely on each other for all that. Then the boys fell out, and I was given another opportunity to demonstrate how useless I was, so useless that when Jacob left school he ran off to join his seriously unhinged mother and the Church of the New Sunrise in the US. Well done, me.

'I'm so sorry, Jacob.'

'Are you?'

'I am.'

'Oh, right. Okay. Thanks. Anyway, it was a long time ago. It doesn't matter now.'

'I'm sorry for what I said the other day, too. Comparing you to your brother. That was completely unfair. You've always been chalk and cheese. Nothing wrong with that.'

'We're not chalk and cheese. We're identical underneath. Different aspects of exactly the same thing. You've never been able to see that.'

He doesn't want to accept my apology, and who can blame him? Nevertheless, I decide to stay, for his sake more than anything else, so he doesn't have to carry out this vigil on his own. We alternate between superficial chit-chat and silence until, just after midnight, Ade's fingernails make scratching noises against at the crease where his sheet is neatly folded over the top of his blanket. Jacob leans forward and holds Ade's hands firmly in both of his again. He doesn't pray, but he talks to him. The words he uses would sound cringeworthy if taken out of context, but they seem appropriate now and I'm proud of him for saying them. I watch my old friend fade away, and my mind is full of his ironic little smile, his handsome face, his floppy hair, his narrow hips, the way he made that summer so amazing. The sheer bliss of him.

When the doctor comes in again, we both stand up and gather ourselves together. Neither of us wants to be there while he does all the tests necessary to certify a person as dead. Jacob takes one look at my face and walks round to my side of the bed. He holds his arms out and gathers me up in them. How assured he seems, how grown up, this nephew of mine, so strong and confident, despite all his tendencies towards uncertainty and self-doubt. I've never thought he resembles his father very much, except in that one photo, but right now he's exactly like him. A series of images of my brother rush into my head, Davey at the funeral after Tess's death, Davey grown tall at his eighteenth birthday dinner in a local Indian restaurant, Davey graduating from Cambridge with long fair hair and a gingery beard, Davey driving down to my house with the children's things, handsome and successful, sitting Gawain and then Jacob on his knee in the garden, trying to make everything alright for them again. It's all a bit much.

And I know for certain that in all the years I was responsible for Jacob, that lost little boy, I never did anything to deserve the kindness he's showing me now.

26. Jacob

I put my phone on silent while I was at the hospital and forgot to switch the sound back on again when we left. Now it's vibrating off the coffee table in Aunty S's living room, and she's tapping me on the shoulder, telling me to wake up.

'Where are you? I've been trying to contact you for bloody ages. I thought something had happened. Jesus.'

It's G. He sounds as though he's speaking with his teeth clenched together, which means he's in a state of extreme panic and is trying to hide it.

'I'm at Aunty Susan's.'

I stagger up from my chair and walk into the hallway, shutting the door behind me.

"What are you doing *there*?"

'The Prof died.'

'Oh shit. Sorry. Are you ok?'

'Just tired.'

'I don't get why you're at Aunty's house, though?'

'She was at the hospital, too. The Prof wanted to tell her something, but it was too late. When he died, she got really upset. Not indignant. She was crying and everything, G. When does that ever happen?'

I say all this in a whisper, in case Aunty can hear me through the door.

"Blimey. But I don't get it. Why did your Prof want to speak to Aunty Susan?"

'It's a long story.'

'You'll have to tell me later. Amanda's waters have just broken all over the kitchen floor.'

'What waters?'

'The fluid that comes out when the amniotic sac bursts?'

'She's gone into labour?'

'Not really. At least I don't think so. But if nothing happens after twenty four hours they usually induce because it's an infection risk.

She rang the labour suite and they said to come in, so I'm taking her in my car.'

'Oh my days. How's she doing? Is she giving you a hard time?'

'This is Amanda we're talking about. But look, can you get back here to look after Tam? Like now? Bartosz will wait for you, but be quick.'

I agreed ages ago that I'd babysit Tam when Amanda went into labour. I don't mind, but the timing couldn't be worse. I haven't slept properly for nearly three days and I don't want to leave Aunty Susan on her own. When I go back into the living room, she's sitting upright in her chair and staring at me. In my sleep-deprived state, it occurs to me she's using her eyes to convey the fact that she's being held at gunpoint by a person I haven't noticed yet.

'Did you hear any of that?'

'Yes. Just go. Send them my love.'

'Love?'

'You know what I mean.'

'Do you want to come with me? You could sleep in one of the attic bedrooms, now you can do stairs again.'

'Good God, no. Tam will be already be discombobulated. The last thing she'll want is the Wicked Witch of the West returning to glower down at her.'

By the time she's finished saying this, I've flung on my coat and I'm heading for the door. I turn back and give her another big hug, like the one I gave her in the hospital. I'm not sure I've ever done that to Aunty Susan before today, even when I was little, but she looks so diminished, as though she's been replaced by an even smaller version of herself.

'If you change your mind, call. I'll come and get you.'

'Don't be silly.'

I drive home as though I'm playing Grand Theft Auto. It's lucky the roads are so empty. When I pull up outside the house Bartosz dashes past me towards his car, carrying the holdall full of baby things.

'She's just thrown up,' he shouts as he unlocks his car.

'Who, Amanda?'

'Tam. Might be the excitement, but there's something doing the rounds at her nursery, so maybe not. I've left everything in a bit of a mess. Sorry about that.'

He jumps into his car and speeds off, tyres squealing.

I race across the kitchen and find Tam sitting on one of the kitchen sofas, bawling her head off. The front of her dress is covered by huge splat of vomit that looks like a lumpy green omelette, the liquid part of which has seeped down the side of her clothes into the gap between the sofa cushions. I wash her and face and hands, and switch her dress for a clean top and matching pair of leggings. Then I sit her down on the other side of the sofa from the puked-on area, wrap a big towel around her, put a plastic bowl in her lap and switch on the TV. When I've found a channel she's happy with, she quietens down a bit.

I scrub the sofa, the kitchen floor and the affected parts of the sofa cushions. Then I put Tam's clothes in the washing machine and meditate on why I seem to be the go-to person for clearing up other people's bodily secretions. I nodded off for a couple of hours at Aunty Susan's, but other than that I've been awake so long, I've passed through exhaustion and emerged on the other side, into a state of zombified acceptance that only option I have is to plod wearily on until someone makes it all go away. I sit down on the floor close to Tam, with a cushion against my back. She seems happy to watch a never ending series of seriously depressing stories about a family of weasels and badgers whose members keep getting get hit by cars, so I put the remote down and half close my eyes. After an episode in which the youngest weasel gets lost in a badger's set and they have to call the fire brigade, which only seems to employ guinea pigs, who are bigger than the badgers and too fat to cope with the tunnels, Tam throws up again. But she doesn't produce so much this time and only the towel suffers. I clean her up and I try to get her to drink some lemonade, but she won't, so I offer her water. This just makes her wail. I start to worry about dehydration and I have no clue how long this should be allowed to continue before it becomes a thing. I dig out the clinical thermometer. It's one of those you click on and place against your forehead. I press it against mine as a control. Then on hers. Hers is higher than mine, but I don't really know whether it's high enough to warrant calling for help. Of course, in normal circumstances, I'd call G.

I get out my phone and google what to do. As usual, there's loads of conflicting information and a discrepancy between US and UK websites, but infant paracetamol is mentioned more than once. I check our medicine cabinet. We have a bottle. I manage to persuade

Tam to swallow a carefully measured amount and keep my fingers crossed that she won't sick it back up again.

This wretched day has been going on for ever, but it's not even lunchtime yet. After a while, Tam says she's had enough of the badgers and weasels and her temperature has gone down a bit. I manage to get her to drink some lemonade and we sit on the floor together and play with her Barbies and Kens in a subdued way. Normally they have violent arguments and a splinter group forms and strides off, elongated plastic legs scissoring away in a state of high dudgeon, to set up camp at the other side of the room. But today, she just wants to brush their hair and make them try on different outfits. She pulls dresses over their heads and passes them over to me to force their rigid, unyielding little feet into plastic sandals or boots. Gradually, she becomes chattier, more like herself and less of a worry. I make a mental note to give her more paracetamol when the requisite number of hours has passed. When she's tired of the dolls, she retreats to the dry end of the sofa again and has a few more careful sips of lemonade.

'How are you feeling?' I ask her.

'Like a puddle.'

'Is that good or bad.'

'Don't know.'

'Would you like some toast?'

'I haven't finished vomiting yet. You can have some if you like.'

'Can I?'

She nods graciously.

I realise I could eat a mountain of the stuff. I put four slices in the toaster at the same time, then another four. I slather them in butter and go back to Tam. She's fallen asleep. I arrange a few cushions on the floor between the sofa and the wood-burning stove and settle myself so I'm lying on my side, facing Tam. My mind wanders back to the conversation I had with Aunty Susan on the way out of the hospital, after the Prof had died. It was more like a confession. Hers, not mine.

'Your mouth is open, Jacob,' she said when she'd finished.

'You really think you pushed Tess off the balcony?'

'It's more than likely. That makes me a murderer. And possibly a psychopath, when you consider that I went on to live my life without even thinking about her much, once that summer was over. I was worried about being pregnant for a while, but when that concern had passed, I moved on completely.'

'Generally speaking, people who worry about being psychopaths tend not to be. Let's see, what are the main symptoms? Lack of remorse or empathy.'

'I'm not very good at empathy.'

'You're pretty crap at showing it, but surely you feel it?'

She thought about that for a bit, for too long, really. Or at least long enough for me to start worrying that she really couldn't come up with an example of a single time when she'd felt someone else's pain.

'I felt really sorry for Gawain after you'd fallen out with him. He was devastated. You were completely wrapped up in yourself and so closed off. Gawain couldn't get through to you.'

'Ok, so you've experienced empathy. And if you knew for sure you'd pushed Tess off the balcony, you'd feel remorse, too. Wouldn't you?'

'I suppose so. It's hard to tell, when I don't actually know whether I did it or not.'

'Of course, the other thing about psychopaths is that they can be very charming and manipulative, whereas you always tell it like it is and bulldoze your way through tricky conversations.'

'Do I?'

I nodded and smiled at her.

'You've failed the psychopath test big time. On all counts. My diagnosis is that you are a normal person with feelings, but you're a genius at hiding them. Not just from other people, but from yourself, too.'

'How come you're such an expert on psychopaths?'

'I saw plenty when I was in the church. And half of my degree was Psychology, remember? Although you seem to equate that with – what was it you said? Macrame Studies or Yacht Sailing? Nowhere near as worthwhile as Medicine.'

'That was my shingles talking, not me. I was in bloody agony at the time. And I was in a state of shock about the Prof being Ade. Not that any of that is an excuse. I said some awful things. And I slapped Tam. I feel remorse about that.'

I didn't know how to help her. I wasn't sure she believed me about the psychopath thing. Aunty doesn't do uncertainty. She likes things to be sorted and placed in the appropriate compartments. And the only other person who knows what really happened on that balcony is dead. When we got back to her house, she was still visibly upset, but we drank tea, ate custard creams and tried to focus on practical matters.

'Who's the next of kin?' She wondered.

'I don't think he got round to changing his will after Reece died.'

'I've never been involved in a death where there wasn't a next of kin."

'Maybe there's a cousin somewhere.'

'There used to be. Perhaps the hospital has their names.'

'Hopefully. If not, Pauline will know what to do.'

'Good old Pauline.'

Aunty went off to have a shower and left her phone on the dining table. It buzzed and I picked it up. It was a text from Patrick. It read like an invitation and not at all as though he was in a serious relationship with the vicar's number one fan. I noticed several earlier messages, also from Patrick, but Aunty S hadn't acknowledged any of them. My fingers tingled. Eventually, the temptation to play cupid became too much. I typed out a friendly reply to the last text. Aunty will be furious when she finds out what I've done. But she's not very good with technology, so she might not realise.

When she reappeared she'd regrouped. She'd changed into her navy pyjamas and matching dressing gown and slippers and wore a towel, turban-like around her wet hair. I pointed an imaginary gun at her, as a kind of salute, a mark of respect for getting her shit together. According to the clock on her mantlepiece it was past midnight. Again.

'You should go home,' she said.

'Nope. Not leaving you till morning. If you want to go to bed, go ahead. I can crash out in my old room.'

'There aren't any sheets on the beds.'

'I'll get some out of the airing cupboard.'

'I'll sit down here for a bit,' she said.

I did the same. We settled ourselves in front of the gas fire and speculated endlessly about what might have happened during her memory gaps. In the end, I was so exhausted that forming words and getting them to leave my mouth became a struggle. I tried my best.

'It's possible one of you might have pushed Tess.'

'So you *do* think I'm a murderer?'

'Not necessarily. You might not have intended her to fall to her death. The real killer could have been the balcony rail.'

'Is that what you think Ade wanted to tell me?'

'I don't know. The day before he died, he was talking about priests and absolution? Maybe he wanted to grant you absolution, forgive you.'

'When you put it like that it makes him sound a tad arrogant.'

'It does, when you think about it. Unless I'm wrong about the absolution thing. But he doesn't come out of it very well in other ways, does he? Tess was crazy about him from all you've said. And there he was he was, you know. With you at the same time.'

'But then so was I, with him.'

'He was older than you, though and more experienced. You could argue that he played you.'

'I wasn't an idiot. I played back.'

'And also, why did you leave the scene? That must have been down to him. You'd never have done a thing like that. You'd have called the police and faced the consequences.'

'I would have. Hopefully.'

'So why didn't you? And why didn't he?'

'Perhaps he panicked. Perhaps we both did. Like when you run someone over and then drive off. There's no going back once you've done that, is there?'

'But it feels like there's something else. I can't pin it down.'

'I don't know what you mean.'

'Neither do I,' I said. 'But maybe that's not the point.'

'What is the point?'

'You're never going to know what happened now and you need to get back to the state of mind you were in before, the one where you could cope with not knowing.'

'How do I do that?'

'Stop dwelling on it. See people. Do stuff. Treat each day as though it might be your last.'

When I wake up, I've forgotten the part where I've driven home to look after Tam. Rustling sounds force me to open my eyes. Tam is perched on the sofa munching away at a packet of chocolate digestives and feeding bits of them to Barbie and her associates, who are sitting next to her in a row. Those biscuits are usually hidden away right at the top of one of the highest kitchen units. I get up and go over to the cupboard in question. She's used a stool to climb onto the worktop and then pulled the stool up onto the top of the worktop so she could reach them. She could have broken her neck.

I take the packet away from her and check the time on my phone. The afternoon is well underway. I've been asleep for hours, and there are no messages from the hospital.

'Jacob,' Tam says. 'the biscuits are coming out.'

'Where's the bowl?'

I find it under the kitchen table, but by then it's too late. I mop her up again and fetch some more clean clothes. Once I've got Tam settled, I'll tidy up the mess she's made and destroy the evidence that she ran amok while I slept. But before I make a start on any of that, the front door opens and Bartosz walks in, followed by Gawain escorting a furious looking Amanda, who waddles across the floor towards me, like an angry duck.

'They've sent me home.'

'Bummer,' I say.

'If nothing's happened by tomorrow morning, they're going induce me.'

'Sounds painful.'

'It's not funny.'

'I'm not laughing.'

'Perhaps you should go and lie down, Amanda?' G suggests in a carefully level voice.

'I've been lying down for bloody hours. I'd rather check in with Tam, thanks very much. Perhaps you can explain what's been going on, Jacob?'

She glances around at the chaos.

'Tam's been sick four times. She's had some flat lemonade and she got hold of a packet of biscuits while I was asleep. She was running a temperature this morning, but I gave her some Calpol, which brought it down a bit. I don't think it's serious. Just a bug.'

'I'll be the judge of that.'

'Right. Good. Off you go and judge, then.'

I leave the kitchen and go upstairs to bed.

27. Aunty Susan

After Jacob has gone, the sense of his absence is enormous, as though he's left a glaring abyss in the middle of the hall floor, like one of those street paintings of holes that are full of water or have steps going down into a cave. The concept is so vivid in my mind the soles of my feet tingle as I walk back towards the living room. I need sleep. That's why letting myself get carried away on stupid flights of fancy. When Jacob was dozing by the fire I should have covered him with a blanket and gone up to bed. But I knew I wouldn't be able to settle. Instead, I pottered about in my dressing gown, doing all the odd jobs around the house that I usually put off. I watered the cacti, cleaned out the vegetable compartment of the fridge, put out the recycling and mopped the kitchen floor. Then I had a good scout around online for baby gifts. As I was doing all these tasks, taking care to be quiet so I didn't wake Jacob, I pondered over his advice about moving on, getting myself out there and living my life again.

    I take myself up to bed and plunge into a deep slumber only to be woken by the sound of breaking glass. At first I think I'm being burgled, but then I notice daylight creeping in though a gap in the curtains and realise the bin men have arrived to collect the empty bottles. My bedside clock says eight thirty, which means I've slept for more than twelve hours. I pick up my phone and notice an extensive series of messages in the family What's App group. Attached to the first of these messages is a photograph of small, very alert creature, half wrapped in a towel, gazing at the camera with bright, wide-open eyes and a mop of dark hair. This is followed by photo of Bartosz doing the skin-to-skin bonding thing with said creature, the vibrant and colourful tattoos across his muscled torso making a dramatic backdrop for the baby, who is resting against his father's chest and being held as carefully as though he's made from glass.

    The final message says his name is Isaac and he was born at six-thirteen this morning. Nothing else. It's not enough. I want to know all the details. How much does he weigh? How is Amanda getting on? Has she left the baby with Gawain and Bartosz? But I tell myself to refrain from asking questions. I'll find out the details soon enough. I reply to Jacob's last message with a brief *Congratulations to all.* It sounds like a telegram. But then they won't know what one of those is, so it probably doesn't matter.

Actually, I'm chuffed to bits, so chuffed I don't know what to do with myself. I look at the photos over and over again, trying to see who he looks like. It's too soon to tell, but at the moment I can't see anything of Gawain, Amanda or Jacob in him, just Bartosz. I jump out of bed, go to the window and open the curtains slightly. Christmas lights still twinkle from windows along the road, brightening up the gloomy morning, and an inflatable snowman is bobbing about in the front garden of the house next door. It looks as though it's waving at me. I want to wave back and apologise for the fact that mine is the only house in the road where the festive season isn't being marked. I feel like Scrooge when he wakes up on Christmas morning. I'm a changed woman, and I'm bursting to tell someone, but I can't think who. In the end I decide to ring Molly Beasley. We haven't spoken since the last time she came to see me at Jacob and Bartosz's house, when she kept going on about Patrick and Lynda, and I ended up being quite abrupt with her. I'm not at all sure how she'll respond to an out-of-the blue phone call from me. I don't even know if she's back from spending Christmas with her son's family. Chances are she will be. Her daughter in law gets snippy and starts making sarcastic comments if Molly stays with them for more than two nights at a time.

Molly answers her phone immediately. After a few awkward seconds, she admits she *is* back in her own house, and as I ramble cheerfully on, she sounds more and more pleased to hear from me. I invite her round for lunch the next day and she accepts with gratifying enthusiasm. Next thing, I'm climbing up the ladder and rummaging around in the loft. I decide not to dig out the big tree, the one I used to put up in the hall when the kids were still living here. Christmas is nearly over, after all. Instead I opt for the smaller, newer one I've been in the habit of displaying somewhere in the house in more recent years. I position it on a table in front of the living room window and festoon it with an ancient set of lights in the form of stage coaches, and a few old decorations from my own childhood. Usually, I use a more recently purchased and much more tasteful set of silver lights and a combination of pale pink and silvery white baubles, but I find I'm craving a different, more colourful and nostalgic effect this time. When I've finished, I stand back to admire my handiwork. It's garish and possibly quite hideous in a seventies kind of way, but much less glacial than my usual efforts.

Today is one of those strangely normal weekdays between Christmas and New Year, so the supermarkets are fully open. I dash out and buy treats like smoked salmon, top of the range mince pies, an iced fruit cake and brandy butter, together with a left over box of Christmas crackers I find on the seasonal aisle, hiding among the mini eggs. When I arrange the crackers on the table the next day, I also make a centrepiece from a red candle and a few sprigs of holly from the garden, which I stick in the middle of a lump of oasis that has been lurking at the back of one of the kitchen drawers for at least the last ten years.

Molly turns up with a big carrier bag from Lidl. She doesn't live far away from me and she's walked round, which is good because the first item she pulls out of the bag is a bottle of the discount supermarket's best Polish, vodka, followed closely by a carton of premium, not-from-concentrate orange juice.

We fix ourselves a pre-lunch drinky-poo, as she calls it, and I show her the photos of my new great nephew.

'He's a handsome chap, isn't he?' Molly says.

'It's too soon to tell, surely?'

'No, I mean his dad. Look at him. All those tattoos and muscles. And that beard. So manly. Pity he's you know what.'

'Yes, well. No comment.'

Molly titters and takes a sip of her vodka and orange. I do the same. Then she reaches into her bag again and brings out a little package wrapped in tissue paper. I open it to discover two little knitted cardigans, one pastel green and the other buttercup yellow.

'Oh Molly, how adorable.'

'Obviously I didn't do them in blue or pink, because you didn't know the sex, and I've made them a bit bigger than newborn.'

'They're perfect.'

'I've made something else. Promise you won't laugh? I think the idea came from America originally.'

She dips into her bag again and pulls out what looks like a huge human head knitted in pinkish wool. She turns it round so I can see its face.

'Oh!'

It glares at me from protruding blue and white woollen eyes, and its raised black eyebrows make it look as surprised to see me as I am to see it. A clump of pretend hair, made from black ribbons, covers the top of its head and on its bottom half it's wearing a humpty-like pair of purple, green and orange trousers.

'You know those objects they make for people with Alzheimer's to fidget with?'

'No?'

'Yes you do. What are they called? Twiddle muffs, that's it.'

'What an awful name. But yes, I know what you mean.'

'Well these are called Fizzogs. You can get patterns for Mummy or Daddy ones. I made a Daddy version, because the baby has two dads.'

'Right, but…'

'There not just toys. The point is, you put one next to baby in his crib and he thinks it's real.'

'And is frightened out of his wits?'

'No! Babies find them comforting, apparently. They think their mum or dad has taken their head off and put it in the crib with them. It helps them to settle.'

She hands it to me.

'It does look remarkably like Bartosz.'

'It's meant to. And it's all done in materials appropriate for babies, so it's perfectly safe.'

'I'm sure they'll all love it.'

And if they don't, they'll have a good laugh about it, I think to myself. Then I feel mean.

'Thanks, Molly.'

She beams at me, and I feel a rush of affection for her that's not solely due to the vodka. I ask her how her Christmas went.

'Christmas Day was alright, but on Boxing Day evening, Jemma and Richard said they wanted to watch a film I wouldn't like, so they'd use the TV in their bedroom. And the kids both went out, so I was left downstairs on my own in the living room. I got a cab to the station the next day. There weren't any trains, but luckily there was a coach with a cancellation.'

'I was here on my own on Christmas day, and on Boxing Day I went to visit an old friend in hospital.'

'That can't have been much fun. Is your friend very ill?'

'He died.'

'Oh no! I'm sorry.'

I don't tell her much about Ade, apart from that I knew him a long time ago and he had a brain tumour. Luckily she's more interested in his brain tumour than the nature of his friendship with me, and she goes raring off along an illness-related tangent, which I'm happy to follow. There is something morbidly fascinating about discussing ailments we're not suffering from ourselves. I think it's due to fear mixed with relief that it's happening to someone else, combined perhaps in some cases with a hint of schadenfreude, although not this time. Not for me, anyway.

We sit down at the dining room table and start balancing little mounds of caviar on blinis. I don't usually buy caviar, but it was on special offer.

'You're supposed to use mother of pearl spoons. The metal is meant to affect the taste.'

'First world problems and all that. Tastes yummy to me. Where did you get it?'

She's surprised when I tell her it's from the local minimarket. We pour ourselves another generous round of drinks, more vodka than orange, and start on the gossip. I'm permanently banned from Facebook for airing my views in what I once believed was a free country, so Molly shows me the pictures June Sandford friend has posted from South Africa. There are several: June looking astonishingly glamorous, in knee length khaki shorts, a halter top and big sunglasses; June standing in what looks like a piece of scrubland with her daughter; June with her neck bent back at an awkward and jokey angle so she can look up at a giraffe; June driving a jeep; and June with her arm extended towards a big pond.

'What's she pointing at?'

'Look in the middle of the lake. There's a pair of ears sticking out.'

'Where?'

She enlarges the picture and sure enough, there they are.

'Oh yes! What do they belong to? Is it a hippo?'

Molly laughs so much she nearly falls off her chair.

'It's Leonard, having a swim!'

Leonard is June's husband. He's not a small man.

I bring out mince pies, cream, brandy butter and a small raspberry trifle. Then we sit in the living room with a cafetiere and a box of champagne truffles, watching the sun go down behind the beech hedge at the bottom of my garden. I'd forgotten what good company Molly could be.

'Today's beaten Christmas Day by a country mile,' I say.

'It's been lovely.' Molly beams at me. 'Look,' she says. 'I'm having a bit of a do at mine to see the New Year in. Come along if you're not too busy.'

'When?'

'New Year's Eve.'

'No, I mean, what time?'

'Oh! About eight-thirty? There's one thing I should tell you, though.' Molly makes a feeble attempt to look serious. 'I've invited Lynda.'

'Lynda, as in Patrick's latest squeeze? I didn't realise you knew her that well.'

'I didn't, but she joined the knitting group and I got talking to her. She's alright really, and she's not seeing Patrick as happens. They went out a couple of times, but it didn't work out.'

Molly pauses ominously.

'Go on.'

'Apparently, Lynda has issues with social anxiety, so she drinks too much when she goes on dates. Their first was at an Indian restaurant, which was ok, because the rice soaked up most of the alcohol. But on their second, she got pissed as a fart and made an exhibition of herself in the King's Head.'

'What did she do?'

"I'm not sure about the details. She was the one who told me and she couldn't remember all of it. I think it was karaoke night and she went up to sing, but there was a ticket-based queueing system, like the one in the post office, and it wasn't her turn, but she made a scene and refused to sit down until they let her do her number.'

'What did she sing?'

'That one from Titanic. She got booed.'

'Oh dear.'

'Patrick took her home and poured her through her front door onto her hall carpet. Lynda's words, not mine. She hasn't seen him since.'

'Poor Lynda.'

'She admits she's got a problem, which is a start, isn't it? She's going to try and do something about it in the new year.'

'Dry January? Rather her than me.'

Molly doesn't leave until late because we end up watching five episodes of Breaking Bad, a show neither of us has seen before. We enjoy it immensely, including all the violence, which makes us shout and cheer at the TV, and we agree to get together again soon to watch more of it. I walk her home. It's not far and I'm grateful for the fresh air. On the way back I award marks out of ten to each house for their Christmas decorations. The big dormer bungalow next-door-but-one has diamond shaped arrangements of lights fastened to an expanse of wall at the front. They flash on and off in time to Christmas music with a disco beat. The entire display is ghastly and life-affirming at the same time. I respect its creator for the way he's just gone for it without worrying about the aesthetics or potential accusations of vulgarity. He's reached out to the entire neighbourhood and given us all some festive cheer. Reaching out. That's what I did to Molly, so well done to me. And she'd already reached out to me by knitting those cardigans and that head thing, even though I'd been so unpleasant to her the last time we spoke.

Reaching out is a *thing*, as Jacob would probably say.

28. Jacob

I know I said I wouldn't go back to Talbot Way after the last time, when I scarpered like a total melt, but here I am, searching through the shelves for another rare book. The place is quiet, but everything feels normal. While I'm here, for the sake of my mental health, I need to go into that little bedroom again and prove to myself once and for all that nothing, apart from curtains, is hanging about in the window. My chest tightens slightly when I think about what I saw, even though I've told myself over and over again I imagined it, that because this house has a reputation for being haunted, you enter a kind of subdued state of red alert as soon as you walk through the door. Once you're inside, if you hear a noise you can't identify, you immediately go into panic mode, even though you know deep down it's probably just the floorboards contracting, or the central heating clicking or someone slamming a car door outside.

    I told Pauline I'd go and put clean sheets back on the bed in the polka dot bedroom. I went and bought some new ones in the end. I couldn't get the stains out of the others, even after two high temperature washes. Pauline told me to claim for them on expenses. She says the department need to keep the house ready for anyone who wants to stay, because now the Prof isn't around to object, the Uni has decided to rent it out to research groups and ghost hunters and the like. One of the TV channels is interested in doing a programme. It should be a big money spinner. When she says *we* need to keep the house ready, I hope she doesn't mean *me*. I don't mind helping out, but if it's going to become a commercial operation, they'll have to pay someone to do it. It might not matter, though. I probably won't be part of the team for much longer. I've read those first two books, twice, and made loads of notes, but my PhD proposal still feels like sand slipping through my fingers. Sooner or later Matt's going to want another one-to-one with me. I'm not sure what he's going to say. Obviously, he isn't as enthusiastic about me as The Prof was. Nobody else in the department likes me much, either, and the powers that be will listen to Matt more than anyone else. I'm still in my probationary period, so they could easily get rid of me.

On the other hand, if they do want me to stay, Matt will expect me to have re-written my proposal, using Point Seven as the starting point, and he'll also want to know about the road trip I'm meant to be planning, to visit victims of poltergeist-type hauntings all over the country, and ask them a set of specific questions from a detailed questionnaire I'm supposed to have put together. I haven't constructed a single question yet, and I can't get my head round the idea that I'll be knocking on people's doors in places like Newcastle and Aberystwyth and sitting in their living rooms, drinking tea and asking them about bangs on walls and pools of water on the kitchen floor, expecting them to take me seriously. I re-read my theoretical background to Point Seven last night. It might as well have been written by someone else for all the sense it made. It started off ok, but then it deteriorated into a long and rambling mess, and suddenly put itself out of its own misery with an abrupt and inexplicably random conclusion. The tortuous reasoning meant to link each part to the next didn't, and the final paragraph looked unfinished, as though I'd dropped my lap-top on the floor and it had switched itself off. Unless I'm the one who has switched off. I think my mojo died at the same time as the Prof.

I had intended to spend a serious amount of time working on my proposal during the Christmas holidays, but that didn't happen, because I ended up becoming a social worker. First there was Aunty Susan getting all upset about her issues relating to Ade, and then there was the drama around Isaac's birth. It's funny, really, because I'm meant to be the emotional runt of the litter. I'm the one who had to be rescued from a cult that almost killed me. I'm the one who refused to speak to his brother for years, the one who, since we made up, has been unable to function properly without G's close and continuous presence. And I'm the one who kept waking up in the night screaming, because I thought I was still at New Sunrise, and then spent months not being able to do anything at all, even get dressed or walk downstairs and sit in front of the TV, unless G or Bartosz did most of it for me.

They wanted Amanda to stay in hospital for the full twenty-four hours, but as soon as she was wheeled into one of the post-natal wards, she pulled the canula out from the back of her hand and discharged herself. I was at home, looking after Tam again, when she rang me. By the time I got to the hospital, my car filled with

Tam and all the belongings they'd both left at our house, Amanda was hiding on a bench behind a cluster of conifers in a little memorial garden just before the junction between hospital service road and the big roundabout.

She clambered into the passenger seat.

'Are you sure about this?' I asked her.

'Yes, thank you very much.'

'But are you fit to leave?'

'I'm fine.'

'But what if something happens?'

'Like what?'

Before Amanda rang, I'd managed to have a quick facetime with my brother and Bartosz. They were high as kites, completely smitten by this funny little creature that was in the process of crashing into their lives. They held him up to the camera so I could see his astonished face and his vertical mop of black hair. Everything had worked out according to the birth plan they'd devised between the three of them. Once they'd gone back into the hospital when Amanda started having proper contractions, which wasn't long after they'd all trooped home, it only took her two hours and ten minutes to push Isaac out. The two dads were both present. Amanda ended up on all fours, screaming her head off and saying she wished she'd never agreed to it. Bartosz got upset, but G reassured him it was normal for that stage of labour. When Isaac appeared, they gave him to Amanda for a few seconds, because of something I didn't really understand, about letting the baby confirm his sense of her smell, touch and voice, as he would already have had an inkling about those in the womb. Then she officially handed him over to G and Bartosz, who took him into a little room close by, where they were hanging out to make sure Isaac behaved like a newborn who is generally ok. Also, there was a small chance he could develop sepsis because of Amanda's waters breaking early, despite the fact that she'd delivered him within the recommended twenty-four hours and been given antibiotics as a preventive measure.

Once we were back at her cottage and I'd brought all their bags in, I wasn't sure what to do. I didn't really like the idea of leaving her and Tam on their own, so I hovered about in the hall for a bit, rattling my car keys in my trouser pocket.

'I'm going upstairs to lie down,' she said.

Her voice had a slightly shrill edge to it, so I decided to risk another question.

'Do you want me to stay?'

She shrugged. 'If you like.'

The first few days were a delicate balancing act. I went home briefly, to fetch my things. Amanda stayed in her room most of the time, and whenever I tried to speak to her she was bristly as a toothbrush. I took Tam to the local playground that same afternoon, and on the days that followed, I dropped her off at nursery and picked her up again later. And I bought food, cooked meals and sorted out laundry. G messaged me to ask why I was there and not at home. I told him Amanda needed a bit of help with physical stuff until she was back on her feet. He sounded worried and said he'd come round. I told him not to and that she was ok.

On the fifth day, the old Amanda was back. She rolled up her tatty old tracksuit, shoved in the washing machine, and there she was, sleek as a cat, in a short flowery dress with matching dangly earrings and black leggings, her gingery-blonde hair washed and tied back in a pony tail, and a look on her face that was beyond determined. She'd made a decision, she said. She could do with a bit of help from me, if that was alright, to hump boxes around and shift furniture, then she'd be on her way. I asked her where she'd be on her way to, but she didn't reply. I followed her instructions to the letter. I didn't dare do anything else. And soon the house was transformed into set of rooms with basic furniture and everything else a tenant would expect to find in a furnished property. The rest was either stashed in boxes to be collected by the storage firm she'd contacted or shoved into bags and suitcases. I was seriously worried she'd was suffering from some kind of brain storm, a postnatal mania, and I kept expecting her to suddenly see how crazy it was to make a decision like this so quickly, and come crashing down again. I'm still a bit worried about that, but it hasn't happened yet, as far as I know.

Once all the heavy lifting was done, I gathered up my few items of clothing, my laptop, which I hadn't switched on once, and the books I hadn't even glanced at, and went home. Amanda and Tam swung by later the same day, so Amanda could tell G and Bartosz face-to-face she was planning to take her fifty-two weeks of maternity leave and do something with it. They thought she was coming round to catch up with Isaac, who had been dressed specially for the occasion in his best sailor-suit onesie, but she was just dropping in to say goodbye. Gawain handed Isaac to her. I held my breath a bit as she inspected him and counted his fingers, but she seemed more like a friend or distant relative than a mother holding her own child for almost the first time. Isaac looked up at her with his now customary, astounded expression, and Tam stroked his hair. Then she looked up and told us all she'd left two sets of keys with an agent, because she was renting her house out for six months to start with, and maybe the six months after that, too. First, she was driving up to East Yorkshire, to our Aunt and Uncle's farm. They had converted some old farm buildings into holiday lets and put up some glamping pods, but none of them were booked until the beginning of April, so Amanda and Tam were going to stay there for a while.

'After that, I don't know. I might go up to Edinburgh. Catch up with Uni friends.'

G asked her about the disruption to Tam, taking her out of nursery, upsetting her routine.

'It'll be an adventure for her,' she said, 'before she starts proper school.'

She handed the baby back to Bartosz. G started to say something about how that wasn't what they'd agreed, that he'd understood they wouldn't share the parenting exactly, but that she'd be closely involved. She was the child's mother for God's sake. I told G to leave it, and my sister got up and said her goodbyes. We stood in the gap between the privet hedge, watching and waving until her car disappeared round the bend in the track. On the way back into the house, G burst into tears, then Isaac started to cry, too.

'Bloody hell,' Bartosz said.

A selection of random tapping noises begins while I'm putting the cover on the duvet in the spotty bedroom. I can't tell where they're coming from, and of course when I stop to listen, they stop, too. I hear them again when I go to the little bedroom, but this time I more or less manage to convince myself radiator half way down the landing is responsible. I stand in the doorway of the small bedroom and peer into the gloom. Just like before, I see someone standing in the window. But this time I can tell it's just a shadow, my own shadow, cast due to light from the landing window, which is directly behind me. This window has a blind. I close it and move back into the doorway of the little bedroom. The shadow has gone and the only version of myself remaining in the house is the real one.

29. Aunty Susan

I need to sit on a chair to pull on my black leather boots. They have zips at the sides and they come up to my knees. If I try to put them on standing up, there's a danger I might keel over like a skittle.

'We've got plenty of time,' Jacob says.

I haven't seen him for weeks. He seems to have grown taller and become more statesmanlike. This might be because he's wearing a suit. On the other hand, it could be because I've been spending a lot of time with Patrick recently, and he is shorter than Jacob and a good deal chunkier. I tell my nephew he looks very handsome and reminds me of his father. He looks surprised and half smiles. The usual soft pink bloom spreads across his porcelain cheekbones and then fades as quickly as it appeared. I pick up my coat, which is pastel green in colour, totally inappropriate for a funeral. Until I saw Jacob, resplendent in his charcoal grey apparel, I hadn't been worried. Now my confidence slumps slightly.

'Do you think this will be ok? Or is it too cheerful?'

'It's great.'

He takes it from me and holds it up to help me get my arms into the sleeves.

'It's meant to be one of those celebration of a life type funerals. People can wear what they want. I'm only wearing black because this is the only smart thing I own.'

'What about the scarf?' I pick up the silky item with its blend of pink, pale blue and green spirals and hold it up in front of him.

'Patrick bought it for me.'

'It's perfect. Go for it.'

I wind it round my neck.

He looks at me and laughs.

'What?'

'You look different.'

'How?'

He puts his head on one side and contemplates me. Then he grins.

'Rounder in the face? Kind of lush. Like a plum or something. Like you've been…God, what am I saying? Shut up, Jacob.'

He shakes his head quickly and laughs. I laugh, too. He's right, though. I have been. And I do feel a bit plum-like. On the way back from walking Molly home on Boxing Day evening, I was followed by a kerb crawler, who turned out to be Patrick, cruising around in his camper van. He said he was on his way to mine because I'd invited him over. I denied it, but I was still so full of vodka and wine, I wasn't sure what I'd said and done, so I asked him in. He told me he'd entered a competition in the Christmas issue of a magazine for the building trade. You had to answer a series of questions about dealing with asbestos, which was easy enough, because all the answers were embedded in an advertorial on the preceding two pages. But to clinch victory, you had to complete a limerick that started with *there once was a man with a hacksaw*. He can't for the life of him remember what he wrote, but it won second prize, a luxury weekend for two at a fancy hotel in the New Forest.

We travelled down in his camper van, which is his sole means of transport now, because he sold his car to pay for all the repairs it needed. When he turned up at my house, I suggested he parked on my drive and we took my car. He looked crestfallen and pointed out that the van had been resprayed and fitted with four shiny new wheels. I decided I didn't want to hurt his feelings again, and anyway, why waste time worrying what people think?

The hotel turned out to be an immense gothic mansion with extensive grounds, which were not at their best in early January. Perhaps that was why the car park was almost empty. Patrick parked the van right in front of one of the big bay windows. As soon as we reached the reception desk, a very young boy, dressed in gold and bottle green livery, like a Great Western train, appeared and said the hotel offered a car parking service, so if Patrick gave him the keys, he'd deal with it. It didn't say anything about a car parking service on the hotel website, and Patrick suspected the hotel wanted to put the vehicle somewhere round the back where other customers wouldn't be able to see it. In any case, he wasn't prepared to let anyone loose with his precious camper van, so it stayed where it was until we wanted to use it again.

It rained non-stop for the entire weekend. On the Saturday morning we made an effort and went for a drive. We had a pub lunch somewhere near Beaulieu, which Patrick refused to refer to as *Bewley*, but after that, we stayed in the room, in bed mostly, apart from mealtimes. We found a really good film channel on the smart TV and we talked a lot and made plans for the summer. I didn't tell him much about Ade, just that he was an old friend and by some unlikely coincidence, Jacob's PhD supervisor. I think he realised there was a lot more to it than that, but I told him I didn't want to talk about it, and he seemed happy with that.

Jacob stands behind me and takes a selfie of us in our smart clothes.

'Probably not an appropriate thing to do before a funeral, but never mind.'

We get into his car.

'You feeling anxious?' He asks when we're nearly there.

'I've got butterflies,' I say.

'Me too.'

'I'm not sure why I'm suddenly so nervous. All I have to do is stand at the back of the church with Donna and Graham, and pay my respects. What's the worst that could happen?'

'Hopefully, once it's over, you'll be able to move on properly.'

'And shove poor Tess to the back of my mind again?'

'It sounds harsh when you put it like that, but kind of.'

'I'm doing my best, but it's not easy. I keep dreaming about her. I think I'd rather know, even if it *was* me who killed her.'

'That must be tough.'

'Anyway, why are you so nervous?'

'Dunno. Social anxiety?'

'General or specific?'

'Both. Everyone from the Department will be there and they all hate me.'

'Are you stressed about doing your reading?'

Pauline had decided it would be nice if the Prof's oldest and youngest associates spoke at his funeral. Jacob hadn't liked to say no.

'It's not a reading. It's a few words I put together myself. Took me ages. I'm not sure I've got the tone right.'

'So that's the specific anxiety, what about the general?'

'Oh, I don't know. Just this feeling that I'm not like everyone else.'

'Imposter syndrome?'

'Maybe because of New Sunrise? It marks me out.'

'Nobody is the same as everyone else, Jacob. We're all imposters and we're all marked out one way or another.'

The car park is filling up rapidly when we arrive. Stewards in high viz jackets tell everyone where to leave their cars.

'It's going to be exactly like Dad's funeral, isn't it?'

He's got a point. Well known academic, ceremony in a large, imposing modern church, followed by burial in a large out of town cemetery a drive away, and a reception in one of the university's catering suites.

'Except that I won't be able to hide in my brother's blazer this time.'

'You don't need to hide. Come on, Jacob. Chin up, best foot forward and all that!'

When he gets out of the car, he walks round to my side, opens the door and helps me out. He escorts me down the path to the tall, open doors of the church and introduces us both to the vicar. It makes me glow with pride to see how confident he's managing to make himself look, even if he doesn't feel it, how polished and well turned out. He's right when he says he isn't like anyone else. He's better than most people. True, his time at the Church of the New Sunrise nearly ended in disaster, but it didn't, and because of it he's much more resilient than most other people his age. And Ade was right. A light does shine out of him.

A rush of almost physical gratitude, like a drenching in warm seawater, washes over me as I enter the church. I'm so thrilled with them all, with Jacob of course, but also with Amanda and her fierce independence, Gawain and his kindness and dedication to others, Bartosz and his gruff, soft hearted manliness, Tam and her wild eccentricity and of course, Isaac with his raised eyebrows, wide eyes, sticky-uppy hair. Gawain and Bartosz seemed pleased to see me when I turned up at their house without warning, after Amanda had left for the North. They brushed off my apologies, as though someone else had been responsible for the things I'd said and done, not me, and I handed over Molly's cardigans and the knitted head thing, plus a basket of baby-related goodies and chocolates from me. They loved the cardigans and fell about laughing when they saw the head. Isaac, who had actually been asleep for once, in his Moses basket, woke up and howled. Once he'd been placated, I held him and tried to decide who he takes after. Bartosz still, I think, but there's something of Gawain in the wildness of his hair, and he definitely has Amanda's stubborn chin.

I don't really believe in God, but maybe I'll say a little prayer of thanks to whatever *is* out there or in here, or both, while I'm here. I smile serenely at the vicar, but he doesn't notice because he's too busy grinning at Jacob. The place is filling up rapidly. The organ is playing Bach, candles have been lit and I think I can smell incense. I'm vaguely surprised that Ade would want a high church send off like this. But he'd love the pomp and ceremony, the drama of it all, even if it meant nothing to him on a personal level. Jacob's hand is still under my elbow. I spot a cluster of young people close to the front of the church. I can't see them properly in the dim light, but I assume they are the other members of the Department of Paranormal Psychology. One of them is flitting about more than the others, as though he's excited by the occasion. His clothes are very unusual. From where I'm standing he seems to be wearing what looks like a short, white shift and his legs are bare. Takes all sorts, I suppose. Aimee, the girl with from the video is with them. She spots Jacob and waves at him.

'You go and talk to your friends. I'll find a seat at the back.'
'You sure?'
'Of course.'

The boy in the shift jumps about when he sees Jacob approaching.

30. Jacob

The church is completely rammed. They're all here, academics, paranormal experts, celebrities and students, not just from the UK, but from all over the world, like a paranormal Who's Who. It makes me feel a bit starstruck and by the time I get to the front of the church, I'm bricking it. Matt nods and shakes my hand, as though he's meeting me for the first time. I'm glad to see he's suited and booted, too. Aimee, Ben, Jamie and Kirsty say hi, but they don't smile. Pauline also fails to smile when she sees but she rushes towards me, grabs me and kisses me on both cheeks.

'I need to speak to you,' she whispers in my ear. 'Can we grab a few minutes together, later? In my office, when we get back from the burial?'

That's it then. I can see it in her face, plain as anything. She's going to tell me the department is letting me go. An usher directs me to the front pew, where the other speakers are sitting. There are three of them, all at the other end of the age spectrum to me, although Aunty Susan says I think everyone over the age of forty-five is ancient. Each one is insanely famous. I've read everything ever published by all three of them, all their monographs and papers and popular books, and I've listened to their podcasts. One of them, Jenna Blakeney, has her own YouTube channel, which is a much more serious affair than Aimee's urbex meanderings. I'm a subscriber. I hope she hasn't spotted me sloping about like a ghoul on Aimee's urbex video. The other two speakers are grand old men of psychical research, a poltergeist expert from Brazil and the Prof's Icelandic friend, Einar Gunnarsson.

'Jacob,' he says, when I sit down next to him. 'I've heard about you.'

He's heard of me? I'm completely gobsmacked and have no clue whatever how to respond. I can't say I've heard about him, too, because obviously I have, same as most other people here. Luckily, the organ suddenly lets off a loud, throaty blast, like a ship announcing its departure from a dock, so anything stupid I might have said to him would have been drowned out anyway. We stand and I look round to see the procession entering the church, the clergy, the choirboys two abreast and the coffin. The pall bearers are dark suited and have professionally mournful expressions on their faces. They must be from the funeral company. The coffin is placed on a stand at the front of the church, very close to where I'm sitting. I glance at it quickly. One of the pall bearers puts a simple bunch of yellow roses on the top. I look away again, quickly. Memories of Dad's funeral spring into my mind as I knew they would. That terrible jolt when I first saw the coffin and realized he was definitely dead inside it, and the way I fell to pieces in the cemetery when they put him in the ground.

    I shake my head and do the mental trick Bartosz taught me, where I place all these unwanted recollections of former times into a big metal cylinder, paint it yellow, weld the lid shut and throw it off a cliff. It plummets to the bottom of the sea and stays there, slowly sinking into the sand. The first hymn is All People That on Earth Do Dwell. I'm too embarrassed to join in because I'm sitting next to Einar Gunnarsson. I hear him having a go. He doesn't know the melody and he keeps getting it wrong, but he doesn't care. I wouldn't care, either, if I were Einar Gunnarsson. When the Bishop welcomes the congregation, I start worrying about my speech. I think about Einar, Jenna and Hector Rodrigues, the Brazilian poltergeist guy, and imagine their eyes boring into me and wondering who the hell thought it was a good idea for me to speak. The other members of the department will be sending bad vibes in my direction, too, and hanging on my every word in the hope that I'll screw up. That trick about imagining the audience naked passes through my mind, but then I remember Aimee. She's seen me without any clothes on, too, so it's kind of reciprocal and won't work, at least not with her.

    Pauline is up first. She does a reading from the Prof's autobiography, which made the bestseller list. I've just finished re-reading the first part, because I couldn't remember what he says about his teenage years. Turns out he said nothing at all, and either Aunty Susan nor Tess get a single mention. I'm too nervous to listen properly to the humorous recollection of the first major haunting he was involved in, back in the eighties. Pauline smiles once or twice and several people in the congregation laugh. I feel sick. I'll never be able to follow that. I look at Pauline as she returns to the other end of the pew and I wonder if I could communicate to her that I'm unwell and won't be able to do my little speech.

The opportunity for gesticulating at Pauline passes without me doing anything about it, and that's it. I'm next, and everything I'd planned to say has dropped out of my head. I've shoved a sheet of prompts in my trouser pocket, but I don't want to stand there like a lemon, going through them out one by one. Amazingly, though, by the time I've walked to the front and stepped onto the little platform by the coffin all my nerves have drained away. Fuck it, I think. Fuck them. They're going to ditch me anyway, so why should I care what they think? I remember all the times at New Sunrise when I was forced to put together some stupid bollocks or other and churn it out at community services and how I got quite good at it and earned myself a few second chances, even though everything I said was total crap.

Then it strikes me that there is a big similarity between those eulogies and the one I've crafted for this occasion. The little speeches I composed for the New Sunrise congregations were artful, stuff I was forced to churn out in order to save my skin. The words I'm about to say now are just as disingenuous. Their sole aim is to make me look good and impress an international audience of academics who could easily influence my future career, one way or another.

I'm better than that, I decide. And braver. I lean forward slightly and grasp either side of the lectern with my hands, and I abandon the words I'd crafted so carefully. I talk about the impact the Prof has had on my life. I know he wasn't perfect and I don't lapse into blind hero worship, but my words come from the heart, and if the congregation don't like my earnestness or my callow lack of cynicism, and if they think the Prof favoured me solely because of my supposedly stunning good looks, that's their problem, not mine. When I finish speaking, my adrenaline surge ends abruptly and my blood sugar level plummets so rapidly, I'm surprised I make it back to my pew. Einar's next. He gets to his feet and before he walks up to the front, he pats me on the back. He murmurs something to me, but my focus is shot to pieces and I can't make it out. I stand and sit and mutter prayers when everyone else does, and I hold the order of service in front of me with shaking hands.

No family members are present at the burial, so his crew from the department and a selection of his closest friends and most illustrious colleagues take red roses from a wicker basket held out by one of the pallbearers and throw them down into the grave, where they land haphazardly on the top of his coffin. I hate this ghastly combination of sentimentality and gothic drama. It was this that finally did for me at Dad's funeral. G had to take me into the toilets at the reception to splash water on my face and remove my snot and tears from his school shirt with paper towels. Afterwards, I dreamt of bright red petals being crushed by soil, which led to nightmares about the weight of the earth pressing down on Dad. I force myself not to think about all that now, and when the priority candidates for the rose-throwing ritual have done their thing, there are still a few flowers left in the basket. The guy from the funeral home passes through the crowd, eyes discretely downcast, and offers them to anyone else who fancies chucking one in.

Aunty Susan steps forward and take one. She goes to the side of the grave and after she's despatched her flower she stands there with her hands clasped and looks down at the coffin. The expression on her face is serious, but not tearful. While she is still standing there, an oldish man I don't recognise approaches and throws a rose in, too. I'm not an expert on clothes that don't come from the cheaper end of the High Street, but I can tell his overcoat is expensive, and I could easily imagine his black leather shoes have been made for him specially. There's a word for that, but I can't remember what it is it at the moment. Yes I can. Bespoke. His silver hair is unusually abundant for a man of his age, as though he's paid for hair transplants or thickening treatments, and even his glasses, which are suspended around his neck from a lanyard, look exotic. Their frames are a tasteful blue-brown shade, like expensive paint, blended especially for spectacle frames instead of walls or woodwork. After he's thrown his rose in, he turns and nods at Aunty Susan, but she's so lost in her own thoughts she doesn't notice.

The traffic is light and it only takes us about fifteen minutes to reach the car park outside the suite of rooms the Uni hires out for occasions like this.

'Your little speech certainly hit the spot,' Aunty Susan says. 'Some people wanted to clap when you'd finished. I could tell.'

'And other people probably wanted to boo or heckle.'

'Those people are idiots, if they exist. I'm dying for a G & T.'

She sounds as though she's looking forward to the wake. I wish I felt the same. I'd hoped that once I'd done my little speech and got through the graveside bit, I'd be massively relieved and ready to pile my plate with slices of smoked salmon and roast beef. But that was before I was collared by the Prof's secretary.

'Pauline wants to speak to me. In her office. They're going to fire me, now he's gone."

'Did she say that?'

'No, but if it was anything else, she'd just say what it was in front of everyone, wouldn't she?'

'Not necessarily. They wouldn't leave it to the Prof's PA to tell you if they were turfing you out.'

I'm silent for a few seconds as I negotiate a right turn across a very busy dual carriageway.

'Who do you think they'd get to tell me, then?'

'The chap from Edinburgh. Your new supervisor. He'd do it.'

'I don't know, Aunty. People get sacked by text these days. Or worse, they only find out when someone posts it on social media.'

'That's still the exception, not the rule.'

I think she genuinely believes I'm not getting ditched, but I can sense indignation beginning to prickle somewhere in the back of her voice, a force in reserve, ready to be brought out at a second's notice on my behalf. It makes me smile and I'm grateful for her support. I escort her into a vast curtained room with parquet flooring and long velvet curtains. It looks like a school hall, but it has a bar at one end and is filled with adults rather than kids. I find her a table in a quiet corner away from the bar and I fetch her a double gin with ice, a slice of lemon and a dash of tonic. Then I make a trip to the buffet to set her up with a plate of quiche and little sandwiches.

When I come back, she's been joined by Donna, tall and imposing in a pinstriped jacket with white trousers and a bright purple shirt, and portly Graham is walking steadily towards them, carrying two pints of real ale on a tray. Of course, to me, Donna is still Mrs Hopgood, the headteacher from my boarding school, so and I'm overcome by a ghastly shyness. I might be every bit as much of a fully functioning adult as she is these days, but in her presence, I turn into the snivelling little six year old I was when I first started at the school. Nevertheless, I manage to stumble my way through a friendly conversation with her. She expresses amazement at the coincidence that their friend Ade should have been my PhD supervisor. I agree that it's insane and such a shame that he died, and I try to act as though I'm doing really well and not about to be sacked.

'Excuse me. I have to go and speak to some people,' I say, when there's a suitable gap in the conversation.

As I head out of the hall with Pauline, I don't notice that the man with the tasteful spectacles is making his way towards Aunty Susan's table.

31. Aunty Susan

A gentleman with a luxurious head of white hair strides up and asks if we mind if he joins us. Mr Whippy, I think to myself, remembering the face on the ice cream vans of my youth. I have to suppress a giggle. That's what happens when you neck a double gin with hardly any tonic on an empty stomach. Mr Whippy puts down a glass of sparkling mineral water, a fork and a plate with nothing on it but a couple of lettuce leaves and a slice of smoked salmon. We all make vaguely bewildered, but polite welcoming noises, expressing the general idea that we don't know who the hell he is or why he wants to sit with us, but we're nice people and we're sure he is, too, so yes, he should make himself at home. He bows slightly to show his gratitude. Then he takes off his expensive looking overcoat, hangs it carefully over the back of his chair and sits down. Beneath his coat, he's wearing a cashmere jumper in a bright lime green over a shirt with a matching tie, his contribution to the celebration of Ade's life, I suppose. He cuts his food into bite sized pieces and repositions each item slightly on the plate to form an orderly pattern. Then he clears his throat and looks at each of us in turn as though he expects some kind of reaction, but he only thing he gets from all of us is a blank, but friendly and expectant openness.

'None of you recognise me?'

We all shake our heads in unison.

He laughs warmly and he half stands up again. He has an accent and he talks a clipped and efficient way, as though he's previously written out everything he intends to say and the addition of any extra words would be a waste of energy and possibly bad for the environment. He reaches out to Donna and shakes her hand. He says her name and adds that she hasn't changed. He does the same to Graham, and then he turns to me.

'Ade's little firecracker,' he says.

I blush from the base of my neck up to the top of my head, as though I'm sixteen again, and I frown at him. He just shakes his head and laughs and he still doesn't introduce himself. We all watch as he sits down again, forks small bits of salmon into his mouth and chews each morsel rapidly, with his lips closed. I think it might be this, the way he eats that triggers a memory.

'Christoff,' I say.

'Good Lord,' Graham says.

'Yes, of course. Who else? I read about Ade's death in the Times. Usually, in January, I like to stay holed up at my house on Lake Geneva but I was deeply saddened, so I flew in. I had to come and say goodbye, pay my respects. You know?'

I watch as he dabs his mouth with a paper napkin. Deeply saddened is a quaint phrase to use, like something from an English language phrase book from the fifties. But deeply saddened is exactly how he looks. In the seventies, he spoke with an equally cultured, but much more English accent, probably due to years he spent at boarding school during term time, and in Larchford during the summer holidays, and if I remember correctly, which I might not, because I tried to ignore him as much as I could back then, he had a tendency to shout or over emphasize his words as though he thought we were all a bit stupid or deaf.

He had a point, though. We were both. All of us. And blind.

As I stare, probably quite rudely, at this vaguely exotic man, I reflect on how utterly dim I've been. We were all incredibly innocent in the seventies, so I can understand why I didn't see the truth back then. But things have changed considerably in the intervening years and I still didn't get it, even when Jacob told me Ade was mourning the loss of his partner, who was a man. Donna and I exchange a glance. She's remembering how much we disapproved of Christoff and how we distanced ourselves from him after Tess told us what he and Ade did to her on our camping trip. Graham, too, probably. Donna must have told him. But we never challenged Ade or Christoff about it. Then Tess changed her story, which muddied the waters, of course. And I kept on seeing Ade. The way he was during those encounters should have made me wonder, perhaps. I thought he was being a gentleman, focusing on my pleasure at the expense of his own.

I don't think I saw Christoff again after the night of the party. It didn't seem like a hardship at the time, and I'm not sure I ever gave him a moment's thought after that, except for the role he played in the overall narrative of that summer. But now I act as though I'm delighted to see him. Donna and Graham behave similarly, and we exchange potted life stories, just like any other old friends would do if they hadn't seen each other for decades. Even so, our conversation is a brittle thing skittering lightly across a reflective surface and never taking a dive into deeper waters. Donna tells him she was a head teacher until recently and Graham mentions their four grown-up kids. They both laugh self-mockingly about becoming grandparents. Christoff says he has no children, but his older brother has two sons, to whom he is absolutely dedicated. He seems disarmingly pleasant, self-effacing and even funny, a greatly improved version of his former self. If he goes on like this, he might charm us into liking him.

'My brother died a long time ago, in a car accident,' I say, when he asks about my family.

'Davey? How terrible. I'm so sorry.'

'The young man who spoke at the funeral is his son, Jacob.'

'The golden boy! But yes, there is a resemblance. You kept in touch with Ade, then? I didn't know. He offered your nephew a studentship?'

'No! We completely lost contact when he left Larchford. Jacob got his studentship on his own merits. Ade had no idea he was my nephew. And Jacob had no clue I'd known his prof all those years ago. It was a remarkable coincidence.'

'Ah,' he says.

I go on to tell Christoff how I took on Davey's kids when Jacob was only six. I also tell him I never married and I allude to my career in Whitehall and in Berlin during the Cold War, and with my usual cryptic and slightly ironic brevity, I make a bit of a thing about not being able to talk about it. Donna and Graham laugh politely. They've heard it all before, many times. Christoff laughs too, and it might be my imagination, but I think I detect a subtle change in the way he looks at me after that, as though in his eyes I've suddenly become more than a dull, old woman. We don't talk about the past very much, though. We mention Ade once, just to say what an unusual character he was and how he made that long, hot summer so memorable for us all, which is true, whatever else was going on beneath the surface. But it feels dangerous to continue because sooner or later, we'd have to talk about Tess.

Eventually, Donna and Graham get up to leave because this is one of the days when they have to pick up their youngest grandson from school. They offer me a lift, but I say I'll wait for Jacob. The crowd in the hall is thinning out a bit. I look over to the bar area. I can see some of his university friends sitting round a big circular table and starting to get a bit loud. The curly haired boy in the shift hasn't reappeared. I hope Jacob is ok and not hiding in his car because he's had bad news. I could easily have gone with Donna and Graham and messaged Jacob to let him know. But I need to speak to Christoff alone.

I get straight to the point.

'I didn't realise,' I say. 'About you and Ade. You hid it incredibly well.'

He doesn't look shocked or even surprised.

'Different times. We were very careful. We had to be. Ade was only eighteen. What we were doing was against the law and if we'd been discovered, nobody would have sympathized. Not in a place like Larchford. We'd have been regarded as some kind of abomination, and the shame would have been terrible for my parents. But even so, we were surprised none of you put two and two together, particularly you.'

He shakes his head and laughs quietly.

'That little gate in the fence was so very useful. I used to sneak through it when nobody was around, then creep back to my own bed again before breakfast. Nobody ever realised. Not my parents, not my brother, not the staff. Except perhaps the gardener. He saw me returning home once or twice. He never said anything. Perhaps he sympathized.'

I'm reminded of the gardener in Tom's Midnight Garden. He was the only one who could see the ghost of Tom, apart from Hatty, of course. It all adds up. It explains why Ade wanted everyone to leave his house at midnight, and why he said that strange thing I didn't understand, that first night when he slept at our house, about how he wouldn't need to stay in our spare room the following night or any time thereafter. Christoff must have been due to return home from university the next day. From that point, Ade wouldn't be spending the nights alone.

'Was it serious or was it just a summer fling?'

'He was my first love and I his. It started the summer before. Of course, it was more difficult then because Ade's parents were still alive. After 'seventy-six, we stayed together for several years. Ade went to university in London while I was still in Cambridge, which was an easy commute and we both had our own rooms, so privacy wasn't an issue. But it was still illegal until Ade was twenty one, so we had to be discrete. We didn't split up until after he'd completed his PhD. I'd got a job with an American bank by then, so I was in

New York most of the time, and he started a post-doc at a university in the middle of Wales, so he wasn't even near an airport. It became, I don't know, difficult, more complicated. Not quite so worth the effort, somehow. But we kept in touch and still met up sometimes, even when we were both in new relationships. And I followed his career avidly. I watched all the TV shows he was in. I was always incredibly proud of him.'

He sighs.

'I wish I'd known he was sick. I'd have come over sooner.'

'He went downhill very quickly. Some of his symptoms were masked by his epilepsy, so nobody realised how sick he was.'

'I hope someone was with him when he passed. I know Reese died a few months ago.'

'I was with him. I'd got to know Ade again through Jacob by then. He was there, too.'

'Ah, good. That's comforting to know.'

There's a pause as he takes in everything I've just said.

I wait a few moments.

'So the thing between Tess and Ade was part of the cover up?' I ask.

'I'm afraid so. It sounds dreadful, but she was so easy to use like that. She made a beeline for Ade as soon as she returned from Italy. All he had to do was go along with it.'

'What about me?'

'You were slightly different. We argued about you. He was more or less sure he preferred boys, but you intrigued him. I hid it pretty well, I think, but I was beside myself with jealousy about you that summer. I never felt like that about Tess.'

I don't know how to react to this revelation. I decide to store it away for now and think about it later. Christoff stands up and starts putting on his coat. I stand up too. I can't let him leave with so much left unsaid.

'Tess said you had sex with her while Ade held her down.'

I realise I'm being extremely ill mannered towards this courteous gentleman, throwing out accusations like this in a public place. But I need to know. After all, I probably won't bump into him again. At least I don't accuse him of rape. I wonder if I should have. We women have fought hard to be able to call serious sexual assault by its proper name.

'What?'

'On Elfbarrow Hill, in the tent?'

'Did Tess tell you that?'

'She was very upset.'

'I wouldn't dream of doing such a thing.' He wraps his tartan scarf around his neck and carefully knots it at the front. 'Why would I even want to? Ade was everything to me.'

'Why would she say you did, then?'

'Tess was a fantasist. She made up narratives to match the stories inside her head. If she was alive now, she'd be all over social media, marketing herself as a commodity, living off the advertising revenue.'

'That's a cruel thing to say, seeing as she's dead.'

'Accusing an innocent man of serious sexual assault is also rather unkind.'

He's got me there. If he's telling the truth, that is. He sounds earnest and I desperately want it to be true, because it would mean Ade was innocent, too. He'd still be guilty of deception against Tess, but his reputation as the zany, imaginative, wonderful person I fell in love with would be more or less restored. And Christoff was jealous of me. Think of that.

I'm on a roll now, with these difficult questions.

'On the night of the party, did Tess run off in floods of tears because when she went looking for Ade in his house and discovered the pair of you together?'

'Of course. She went apeshit, as my nephew would say.'

I don't want him to go. There are still things I need to know, things I can't go through the rest of my life not knowing.

'Let's find a footpath and walk for a while,' I suggest.

He nods in agreement and I let him help me on with my coat, but when we reach the outer door, it's getting dark and a fine drizzle is falling. We stand in the porch, looking out into the gloom. Christoff speaks into his phone. My German is a bit rusty these days, but still fluent enough after so many years in Berlin for me to understand that he's calling a chauffeur and asking for a car to be brought round.

'We'll drive you home.'

'There's no need. Jacob's coming to find me when he's ready.'

'There is every need.'

I text Jacob. I don't want to alarm him, so I tell him Donna and Graham have given me a lift home. Seconds later, a large black Daimler purrs quietly to a halt in front of the porch. The chauffeur gets out an opens one of the rear doors.

'Please,' Christoff says.

I get in. He goes round to the door on the other side and gets in next to me. We drive off through the campus, towards the exit.

'Where do you live? Not still in Larchford?'

I give the driver my address. He keys it into the Daimler's satnav. 'Thirty-five minutes,' he says.

The car is very warm. Christoff unties his scarf and unbuttons his coat.

'Where were we?' He says. 'Ah, yes. Tess came up to Ade's bedroom and found us in bed together. She became hysterical in an instant, completely out of control. We didn't know what to do. The bedroom windows were open. We could hear the party going on in the background. We could even hear the individual voices of people in my parents' garden, on the other side of the shrubbery near the fence. By the swimming pool, you know? If we could hear *them*, there was every chance *they* could hear Tess.'

'I heard her.'

'We guessed that. You were there when she ran out into Fieldgate Crescent.'

'I saw Tess running off across the crescent. Ade was chasing after her, pleading with her not to go.'

'It was lucky she didn't run in the opposite direction, through the gate and back to the party.'

'Lucky for you and Ade, maybe. For her, not so much.'

'No. No, of course not.'

I stare out of the window. I can't see anything but rain and darkness. No streetlights, no tail lights of cars ahead of us on the road, no traffic coming the other way. I'm in a car, in the middle of nowhere, with a man I haven't seen for years, who I don't know at all and who might have raped my best friend, however convincing his attempts to deny it.

'Did Ade tell you what happened when they got to Tess's house?' I ask him.

'He didn't need to. I was there.'

'No you weren't. I'd have remembered that!'

"But I was. Tess was running and screaming, Ade was trying to catch up with her and you were right with them, shouting at Tess, grabbing at her arm and telling her to shut up. I noticed you'd left the gate to our garden open, so I went to shut it. I peeped through into our garden, half expecting I'd be forced to dissemble to a crowd of guests standing there, wondering what was going on. But there was no-one. Nobody had noticed a thing. It would have been easy for me to step through the gate, back into the party, and act as though nothing had happened.'

'But you didn't do that?'

'Not then, no. I didn't trust the situation with Tess, so I decided should follow you and try to calm things down.' He stops and glances pointedly at the back of the chauffeur's neck. 'Look, Suzy, you were in Berlin. Shall we continue in German?'

I nod. At first, I'm a bit rusty, and I find his Swiss accent difficult to follow, but I soon get the hang of it.

'By the time you reached Tess's house, I'd caught up with you,' he says.

'I didn't see you.'

'You did, or you heard me. You turned round and told me to fuck off.'

'No I didn't.'

'You were so very angry. I thought you must have worked it all out.'

'I was incandescent with rage, but I hadn't worked anything out. It was Tess I was angry with, not you or Ade.'

'You grabbed her shoulders and started pulling her hair and scratching her face with your fingernails. We tried to pull you away, but your fury must have given you extra strength. It was as though you were glued together, and once you got up onto that rickety balcony it was an accident waiting to happen.'

'I don't remember that bit.'

'You must, surely?'

I lean forward and put my head in my hands. This is the moment when I'll find out for certain that I'm a murderer.

'I pushed her off the balcony, didn't I?'

I brace myself for his answer.

'Do you really not remember?'

'There's a gap. One minute I'm at on the balcony, so furious with Tess I can't think straight, the next minute I'm at the bottom of the wrought iron stairs, kneeling on the paving stones, the skirt of my dress covered in her blood.'

I try and take a deep breath. The air doesn't quite reach the bottom of my lungs.

'If I go to the police and hand myself in, will you be a witness?'

'What are you talking about?'

'I wasn't sure it was me that killed her. I suspected it might be, though. I've suspected it for years. And now you've confirmed it, I'll have to do the honourable thing. For Tess. There comes a point in life where you have to do what's right. Face the music, otherwise there's no point going any further.'

He grips my wrist with one of his gloved hands.

'Stop speaking in ridiculous cliches,' he says. He asks the chauffeur to pull into the side of the road as soon as it's convenient.

After a few minutes we drive into a lay-by. It's stopped raining and a gibbous moon has appeared low down in the night sky, casting sufficient light to make out a rubbish bin and a row of skeletal winter trees along the edge of the parking space. I recognise this picnic area. In the spring and summer a man sets up a stall here to sell flowers and punnets of strawberries. My house is only a couple of miles away, if that. Between our seats is a cabinet-type thing, made out of highly varnished wood, walnut, I think. He opens the lid and pulls out a half bottle of brandy and two huge, globe-shaped glasses. He pours us both an inch of the bronze liquid. I see the label on the bottle. It's expensive, the kind they serve in the first class cabin on flights to Quatar and places like that. I knock mine back quickly. Too quickly, if I'm honest, but I enjoy the warming sensation it makes as it goes down. He pours me another shot and sips his slowly. The chauffeur has discretely turned on the radio and is humming quietly to Michael Jackson, making a big show of the fact that he's not listening to our conversation. The only other sound comes from vehicles on the road. As each one passes, the car shakes.

He looks across at me and then at the remnants of his brandy, which he swirls around in his glass.

'You've lived all this time, how long? Over forty years, thinking you murdered your best friend?'

'I wanted to kill her. But I don't remember actually doing it. I must have blanked it out because it was too hard to face.'

'I don't think you're the kind of person that doesn't face up to things. Why didn't you ask Ade? I know you spent time alone together afterwards.'

'He refused to talk about it. And I was reluctant to force the issue.'

'The English can be so diffident.'

'Now you're the one talking in cliches.'

'It's true. If you'd pressed Ade, he'd have told you. Then you could have moved on and grieved for your friend without all this self-doubt.'

'What would he have told me, exactly?'

I'm ready to hear it. The brandy has warmed my face and my hands have stopped trembling. Everything he says makes sense, and I can tell he's not the type to make things up. When I have to stifle a sob, he strokes my arm and murmurs something kind and comforting in German. I don't catch what he says, exactly. Perhaps he's speaking in a Swiss dialect. But whatever the words mean, he's definitely not behaving like the monster I'd always thought him to be.

'I'm so glad we bumped into each other,' he says when the Daimler pulls up outside my house.

'Will you come in for a moment?'

'Thank you very much, but no. I'd love to, but I need to get back to Farnborough. I'm flying to New York this evening.'

'Farnborough? You have your own private jet? What a glamorous life you lead.'

'Not really. It becomes very ordinary when you do it all the time.'

He tells the chauffeur to wait until I've unlocked my front door and am safely inside. I turn and wave at him before I step into my hallway. As I kick my shoes off, I hear the Daimler accelerate away with a modest growl. I wonder if Mr Lilicrap's curtains twitched as it pulled up outside my house and he saw me disembark from it. I close my own curtains and switch on a few table lamps in the living room and the hall. The apricot lightbulbs make the house warm and welcoming. I'm grateful to be here, out of the drizzle and the darkness, in one piece, more or less. I decide to open a bottle of Pinot Noir and run myself a bath filled with bubbles. Then I'll put some music on and submerge myself. While I'm in there, I'll do a single mental re-run of what Christoff has just told me.

Then I'll put it all to bed for the last time.

32. Aunty Susan

Dad was in the shop when he had his heart attack, half-way up a ladder in the store room, trying to reach a box containing a pair of size five ankle boots in red, requested by a teenage girl. Minutes after he fell from the ladder, he died on the hard, wooden floor. He'd never been ill, or at least he hadn't mentioned anything to us.

When Davey rang to let me know, I was in Berlin, deeply submerged in my work to the exclusion of just about everything else. I was rising rapidly through the ranks. My bosses put my success down to my capacity for level headedness and my ability to remain cool and objective even in the most extreme crisis. There were always crises in the Service, cock-ups that were both idiotic and spectacular, and sometimes cost lives. I treated each one as though it was a minor problem, on a par with a loose button on a coat or a broken heel on a shoe. I loved working under the constantly shifting atmosphere of Berlin, with its permanent sense of hidden movement beneath the surface, and I adored all the clandestine visits to the Eastern half of the city, the tense car journeys away from the permitted route, to towns or villages Westerners were forbidden to enter without permission, which they had no chance of being granted under normal circumstances.

I've always assumed my tutor had recommended me for the service, via the old boy's network, which had existed forever at Oxbridge, and was just starting to be more inclusive towards women. Now, though, I wonder whether Christoff had something to do with it. Perhaps he'd also been recruited, at Cambridge, or maybe his father exerted some influence. When we were sitting in that lay-by in his hired Daimler, he asked me a couple of careful questions about my career in a manner that could easily have been interpreted as an attempt to communicate that he already knew the answers. After what he told me about my reaction to events on the night of the party, I can understand why he might have seen that kind of potential in me.

Once probate had been granted, Davey and I went through the contents of the various rooms in Dad's house. We poured bottles of semi-evaporated sherry down the kitchen sink, disposed of the few bits of food we found in the fridge and took most of what was in the cupboards, drawers and wardrobes to the tip. The majority of it was dreary, long forgotten rubbish - ice buckets shaped like pineapples, plastic cocktail sticks, PVC placemats, toilet roll covers with dolls' heads sticking out of the top, crocheted by female relatives who had been dead since before we were born, and the encyclopaedias Dad bought to help with our education, which still had pristine white pages because we'd hardly ever used them.

Davey took his wooden horse on wheels and his cars, which Jacob still has, I think, and the only things I wanted were Tess's floppy-brimmed hat, which she'd left at my house by mistake, and Dad's vast collection of handkerchiefs, bought for him repeatedly as birthday and Christmas presents because nobody could think of anything else he might like. We found boxes and boxes of them, all unopened. I removed them from their cardboard containers and took the entire lot back to Germany with me, where I washed, starched and ironed every single one of them, folded them into neat little rectangles and stashed them away. My favourites, the polka dot silk ones he'd been given by an eccentric great uncle we hardly ever saw, became frayed and full of holes eventually, but I still have the rest. I always carry one in my handbag for the same reasons most people carry a pack of tissues.

I still have Tess's velvet hat, too, in the bottom of a wardrobe in the spare room. I go fetch it now, and I sit on my bed, holding it in my lap. The poor thing is a bit threadbare, but it doesn't matter. I'm not planning to wear it. I just want to look at it and rub the faded material between my fingers. When the house and shop were finally emptied and put on the market, I never went back to Larchford again. And in all the years that I'd been coming back before then, to see Dad and even before that, when I was in the sixth form, still living at home, I never once walked round the corner to say hello to Tess's parents. What a despicable coward I was, for all my supposedly courageous gallivanting in East Germany.

Crying is a selfish and pointless exercise. You don't feel any better afterwards and it upsets everyone around you. A brisk walk is a much more effective method for dealing with excess angst, and since Mum died, over fifty years ago, I've manged to stay almost completely dry eyed. But these days, I can't seem to help myself.

First there was that awful exhibition I made of myself in the hospital after Ade died, then this evening I wept in Christoff's car, and now I'm at it again.

    I go over to the drawer in the dressing table where I keep Dad's handkerchiefs and I select one from the pale blue pile. Before long the thin piece of cloth is saturated with my tears and I have to go and get another one. I weep and I weep, for everyone and everything. For Jacob and the way he seemed so grown up and self-assured today, despite the terrible things he's had to deal with, for Ade and the sudden loss of his friendship and whatever else it was that flickered between us all those years ago and for poor Dad who still doted on me even when I was too busy to visit him for months at a time. But most of all, I weep for Tess, for all the good things about her, the way she stood up to the bullies at St. Ursula's, the fantasy worlds she created for us, her kindness to me after Mum's death and the way her parents didn't mind when I became an almost permanent fixture in their house. How could I not go and see them after Tess died and how could I not forgive her for taking Ade away from me and for rewriting bits of her day-to-day life to make it conform to the truths she preferred? God knows, it's not as though I haven't been a fantasist, too. For most of my life, I've presented a particular image to myself and to the world. Sue Fylde, tough cookie, nobody's fool, Highly Indignant State permanently simmering on the back burner, so watch out!

    What a joke. The truth is, I've been vile to people who deserved much more than that from me. I go through them one by one and think about how I could have made a difference to each of them by being empathetic instead of standoffish. I've treated all of them like caricatures or stereotypes rather than real people, even Gawain. I progress from quiet crying to manic sobbing and wailing, and the second handkerchief, which is a supposedly soothing turquoise colour that usually reminds me of holidays by the Adriatic, quickly becomes sodden. Then, all of a sudden I stop, or rather it stops, as though a tap has been switched off behind my eyes. I continue to sit on my bed and I gasp quietly for a bit. I'm broken. I'm a wreck. I've imploded. But I don't deserve sympathy. Everyone is wary of me, and it serves me right. I get up from the bed and go look at myself in my full length mirror. The spectacle is so ghastly it makes me want to laugh. Point zero, I think. Things can only get better. The only way is up.

I need to stop spouting cliches and get a grip, crack on with my bath. I'll play some seventies music, something that Ade used to play when we were round at his house. Camel springs to mind. And I'll take my bottle of wine with me and celebrate the magic of that summer and my friendship with Tess and mourn her death properly, now I know what really happened.

I fill the bath with bubbles and I'm just about to plunge in, when the doorbell rings. It keeps on ringing in the way doorbells do when someone presses them continuously. Then a tapping starts on one of the glass panels in the door. My heart starts to pound with annoyance and I wrap myself in a towel and hover at the top of the stairs where I can't be seen. I hope it's not one of those Nottingham knockers. I know they are doing the rounds in the area at the moment. They can be quite aggressive, these young blokes with their holdalls and sob stories about just being released from prison and how it will make all the difference to them if you buy a fake chamois leather or a set of ridiculously expensive sponges. On the other hand it might be that woman who pretends to be a Romany and tries to sell you white heather. People only buy it because they're afraid she'll put a curse on them if they don't, and she's not actually a Romany at all. She was in the same class as June at infants school. Her parents ran a haberdashery shop near the newsagents in Ash Grove. She's got a nerve pestering people at this hour when it's so dark outside you can hardly see your hand in front of your face.

There's no law that says I have to answer the door, either to her or to menacing young men with holdalls. If I ignore the knocking it will stop eventually. I turn away from the stairs and head back towards the bathroom, but the banging starts to sound more violent.

'Bugger off,' I yell from the top of the stairs in a croaky voice. 'I've called the police.'

Someone puts a key in the lock and turns it. The door opens and I watch from above as Jacob and Gawain tumble across the threshold, tripping over each other in their eagerness to get inside. I'd forgotten they still had keys to my house. I dash downstairs, holding the towel around me as best I can.

'What the bloody hell do you think you're doing?'

I nearly put my hands on my hips to strike an angry pose. Luckily, I realise just in time that if I do that my towel will fall to the floor, and it would horribly unfair to subject my nephews to a spectacle like that, even if they have just charged through my front door without permission.

'We've been driving around looking for you,' Jacob says. 'Like everywhere. We've even been back to our house in case you were there. Jesus, Aunty.'

'Why does it matter where I've been? I'm free to come and go as I please. Or I was the last time I looked. I haven't got an ankle tag and I'm not sodding well senile. Not yet, anyway.'

'We thought you'd been kidnapped,' Gawain says.

'Kidnapped? Why would you think that? Who the hell would want to kidnap *me*? Have you both gone completely doolally?'

'You said Donna and Graham were giving you a lift home, but I saw them leave without you, when I was looking out of the window in Pauline's office. Ok, I thought. You'd changed your mind. Fair enough. I'd catch up with you when I went back to the bar. But ten minutes later, I was still in Pauline's office and I saw you getting into a big black Daimler with that guy with the Farrow and Ball glasses and the hair. I texted you, to make sure you were ok, but you didn't reply. I texted like a thousand more times and got nothing. So I rang you. Still nothing. Then Gawain rang you. Nothing again.'

'I had my phone set to silent and I haven't looked at it since this morning.'

'Why would you *do* that?'

'I didn't want it to go off in the funeral, and after that I was talking to people. I'm not one of those idiot who keeps checking their phone all the time. You know my feelings about that kind of behaviour.'

'You could have glanced at it once in a while, surely?' Jacob says.

'Anyway,' Gawain says, 'Jacob and I met up here a while ago, but all the lights were off and there was no sign of you, so we rang the police.'

'You did what? They haven't got patrol cars out there looking for his Daimler, have they? He'll miss his flight or his slot or whatever they call it.'

'They said you were a grown woman and seeing as you don't have dementia, you'd probably turn up eventually, but if you didn't appear within the next twenty-four hours, we should call them again.'

'Thank goodness for that.'

'We also rang Patrick. He's still out there, driving around.' Jacob digs his phone out. 'I'll message him. Tell him you're ok.'

'You're not ok, though, are you?' Gawain says.

He looks at me sympathetically with his cow eyes and of course, his *making-people-cry* superpower kicks in immediately and I start blubbing again, like a complete nincompoop.

'Oh my days, what's happening?' Jacob says.

He puts both hands on the top of his head and stares at me. Then they both rush up and hug me. They're both being very sweet, and for a few seconds I rest my head against Gawain's shoulder. It's a comfort, until I remember I'm only wearing a towel. Then it's just awkward.

I detach myself from them.

'Shall I phone for an ambulance?' Jacob asks. 'Or call the police or what?'

'I'm ok. Just let me go and put some clothes on.'

'I'll come up with you,' Gawain says.

'I'm perfectly capable of dressing myself, thanks very much.'

'I'll stand outside your room and wait, just in case.'

'In case what? Am I on suicide watch?'

'Aunty, stop it.'

I sling on my usual underwear, joggers and fleecy top. Then I add a dressing gown and a pair of slippers, because I realise I'm really cold. I scrutinise myself again in the full length mirror. The state of me. My eyes are tiny and red. What's that expression? Piss-holes in the snow. I tuck a few wild strands of hair behind my ears and grab another handkerchief.

'Can I come in, now?' Gawain says from the hallway.

'Yes, if you must.'

He tells me to sit on the bed. Then he sits next to me, so close our thighs make contact. His shoulders are hunched and he doesn't look at me. Instead, he stares at his knees.

'I know something's been going on with you and Jacob. He won't say what is and obviously you don't have to tell me anything if you don't want to. But are you really alright? Did that man hurt you?'

'Of course he didn't.'

'Are you sure? You look awful, if you don't mind me saying.'

'I'm fine.'

Gawain lifts his head and looks at me. He's yet to be convinced and he's waiting for me to say more, doing that professional silence thing that forces people to talk.

'Christoff is an old friend. His chauffeur was driving me home, but when we were nearly here, we found we still had quite a lot to say to each other, so we parked up in that lay-by near the garden centre. Not the dogging one. The car he hired had a little locker between the seats with glasses and a bottle of brandy. It was all quite convivial.'

'Why didn't you bring him here?'

'I don't know. The lay-by seemed more appropriate. Neutral ground. Maybe because I hadn't seen him for years and before we had our talk I wasn't sure who he was exactly or how things were between us. I did invite him in later, when he dropped me off, but like I said, he had a flight to catch.'

'Who *is* this bloke?"

'A very old friend of Jacob's Prof. I knew him a long time ago.'

'*You* knew him?'

'Yes.'

'But he wasn't a friend?'

"Yes. No. Not really. Not then. He might be now.'

'What sort of friend leaves you in a state like this? I've never seen you so upset.'

Infuriatingly, I start crying again.

'I'm not upset," I manage to say eventually. 'It's raw emotion, that's all.'

He scrutinizes me again, very carefully, in exactly the same way doctors do in those fly-on-the-wall A&E series, when they know a patient is trying to hide something, but they can't work out what it is. It irritates me, but I feel a bit sorry for him, too. I bet he'd like to grab hold of my wrist and measure my pulse. In fact, he'd probably be much happier if I was wired up to a machine with a screen that provided details about my heart rate and oxygen saturation, immobilized so he could take blood from me for tests.

'And maybe I'm a bit squiffy,' I add. 'I had two huge gins at the wake and Christoff kept plying me with brandy in the car. Not sure how many units I've imbibed. All on an empty stomach, more or less. At the wake, I was so astounded when he turned up at our table, the only food I managed to eat was the crust from a slice of quiche.'

Gawain looks fractionally happier. He can do something with information like this.

'Get into bed and I'll fetch you a cup of tea.'

'Tea would be nice, but I'd rather go downstairs. I need to talk to Jacob.'

When he's bustled me down the stairs and fussed me into a chair, Gawain looks across at his brother, who is standing in the kitchen doorway with his arms folded, staring at us both. His eyebrows are raised. Stupidly, I comment to myself that they are higher in the middle than at each end, like one of those bridges that opens when a tall ship needs to pass through. I really need to get a grip.

'Kettle's boiling,' he says in a voice filled with fake heartiness.
Then the doorbell rings again.
'That'll be Patrick.' Jacob runs to open the door.

I stand up again and Patrick rushes towards me as though he's going to take me in his arms, but he suddenly comes to an abrupt halt a few inches away.

'You're ok then? Jacob says you went off with a strange man in a Daimler?'

'Sit down, Patrick,' I say.

He lowers himself, possibly reluctantly, into the other armchair.

'Not strange. Christoff. I knew him when I was sixteen.'

'The guy with the hair and glasses was Christoff?' Jacob says.

I nod.

'Oh wow!'

'Who the hell is Christoff?' Patrick asks.

'A businessman who spends most of his time in Switzerland and has a kind heart.'

'Christoff has a kind heart? What the hell?'

'He's also gay.'

'What's that got to do with anything?' Jacob leans against the door frame again, and he stares at me, his face a picture of bewilderment. Then it clears. 'Oh,' he says. 'Right.'

'I was wrong about so much,' I say.

'Shit,' Jacob says, thoughtfully. Then he retreats into the kitchen to finish making the tea.

A kind of pregnant pause follows, then Gawain says 'It would be really nice if you could tell the rest of us what you were wrong about, so we can decide whether you're ok or not, and if we need to do anything.'

Patrick grunts his agreement and I nod. I rally and order them all about. I ask Gawain to get the whiskey and glasses from the cabinet and I tell Jacob to get on with making that pot of tea and fetch the tin of M&S chocolate biscuits I bought for Christmas but never opened. Patrick take his coat off and I grab his hand and pull him down next to me in the armchair. It's a bit of a squash, but he puts his arm around me and pulls me towards him. He's still perplexed, but he seems much less prickly now he knows Christoff is gay. I get the boys to turn off all the lights apart from a single table lamp at the far side of the room, and I switch on the electric fire. It fills the room with a red glow and breathes warm air onto our legs.

'I'll explain everything. It might take a while, particularly to bring you two up to speed,' I say, looking at Gawain and Patrick. 'If you need to get home, Gawain, you should go. Jacob can always tell you it all later.'

'I'm not going anywhere. Bartosz is fine. His mum's come to stay for a bit.'

'Right then,' I say. 'Are you sitting comfortably?'

'Er, yeah, nearly. Hang on,' Jacob says.

He grabs a biscuit, sinks to the floor and stretches himself out in front of the fire, like a long, skinny cat.

'Good. Then I'll begin.'

I start way back, at the time when Mum had just died and Tess, Donna and I went to St Ursula's, and don't I stop until I reach the night of the party. I keep expecting one or other of them to interrupt me or start clicking at their phones, but none of them does. They all stare at me, apparently transfixed. Then there comes a point when their collective silence becomes a bit suspect.

'Am I boring you?'

'No!' They all say, shaking their heads.

Jacob takes the opportunity to dig out one of the foil-wrapped chocolate orange biscuits from the tin. He tries to open it quietly, but fails.

'Sorry. Continue,' he whispers.

When I reach the part where it all kicks off, I stop and take a deep breath because I'm worried I'll become emotional again. I can hear a faint catch enter my voice when I start to describe what happened on the balcony, but I manage to suppress it.

'There are two versions, the one in my memory, which is full of gaps, and the one Christoff has just told me. The first part is the same in both. Ade goes home, saying he has a headache, that he's going to get some of his painkillers and he'll be back soon. About half an hour later, he hasn't reappeared and Tess says she's going to go and make sure he's ok. I walk with her to the gate, then as I start making my way back to the rose garden, where everyone else is standing about, drinking champagne. Before I get to them I hear Tess scream. I'm the only one who hears her. Nobody else is close enough.

'As I run through the gate and cross Ade's garden, I hear Tess leaving the house by the front door and Ade running after her, shouting, so I go round the outside of the house and follow them. She dashes across Fieldgate Crescent, yelling like a maniac, calling Ade all manner of names - an abomination a vile, hateful monster, a pervert - things like that. We find out later that nobody witnessed our transit across the cul-de-sac and out onto Fieldgate Lane, probably because they were all at the party.'

'Why does that matter?' Gawain asks.

'Just let her talk,' Jacob says.

'You'll see why. Now I'm moving on to my version of events. Once we reach her house, we go round the back and up the metal staircase to her balcony. I'm so beside myself with rage, I'm actually shaking. How could Tess come back from Italy and take Ade away from me like that, and then act like such a bloody diva all the time? I want to kill her, I really do. Next, I'm grappling with Tess on the balcony. I want to slap her, pull her hair, hurt her in any way I can, but she's holding my hands, preventing me, which makes me even angrier. I sound awful, don't I?'

'Pretty bad,' Gawain says.

Jacob throws him a look. 'Because you behave perfectly at all times.'

'Anyway,' I cut in, raising my voice slightly. 'Suddenly, the scene shifts, exactly like it does in dreams, and Tess and I are both on the paving stones three floors down from the balcony. She's flat on her back and I'm crouched down by her side. My skirt is soaking up blood which seems to be seeping out from the back of her head. I hear an awful moaning noise. At first I think it's Tess, but then I realise it's coming from Ade who is standing behind me, and he's doing it because Tess is dead.'

I stop for a second, to give my audience a chance to react, but nobody says a word.

'Another gap in my memory follows, a bigger one this time. Then I'm back at the party, wearing a different dress, a smock-type one from the previous year. It's orange. I'd never choose to wear this dress, particularly to a party, because it's old fashioned and so short it exposes my skinny knees. But here I am wearing it, and I'm super calm, sipping a champagne cocktail by the pool, chatting to Graham, Donna and Christoff's brother, Karl, as though nothing has happened. Ade is standing right next to me, gripping my arm, underneath my elbow. His nails are digging into my flesh and he's trembling so much my entire arm is shaking. I move my glass to my other hand to keep it still and I say something about Tess having gone home because she felt unwell. Nobody bats an eyelid at this and nobody comments on the fact that at different times both Tess *and* Ade vanished from the party. And Christoff, as it turns out. The conversation quickly turns to train journeys, because Karl has spent the summer travelling around Europe with an inter-rail pass. I listen to him intently, and it's strange, but since then, my memories of that night have been intermingled with images of express trains hurtling down the tracks in places like France and Yugoslavia.

'Soon, Christoff approaches from the back of Fieldgate Hall, all debonair and spotless in his white suit, but with his bow tie unfastened, carrying a fresh bottle of champagne. He tops up our glasses and grins at us all. The perfect host. I don't know why at the time, but his appearance prompts me to explain to everyone that I had to go and change my dress because it was that time of the month and I'd had a disaster with the pale blue one. Donna is sympathetic and the boys give me that *too-much-information* look. I think I sound convincing.

Ade and I both know Tess is dead and that we mustn't say anything until we're told officially by the police. When this happens, we have to act shocked and surprised. I don't understand why we have to do this, but I accept it and understand how important it is that we do that. I seem to have been programmed to follow a specific set of instructions, like a robot, but I don't know where the orders came from.'

I stop and polish off the tea in my cup. I reach over and pour myself some more.

'So you thought you were responsible for Tess's death?' Gawain asks.

'From my point of view, it was the most probable version of events. Like I say, I was incredibly angry with Tess when we were on the balcony. She had her back to the balcony rail. I wanted her to die. It makes sense to think I pushed her.'

'But you're not the kind of person who loses it completely,' Gawain says. 'I mean, you get annoyed a lot, but you never go completely over the top.'

'I don't know. I've always had a temper and I was much younger then. More impetuous. And I'd been drinking.'

'But anyway, that's not what really happened?' Jacob says.

'Not according to Christoff.'

'Tess found him with Ade, didn't he?'

'She'd had no idea. None of us had. They were incredibly careful, until that last night. And really, there wasn't much of a chance anyone would find out. Christoff would sneak through the fence in Ade's garden when we'd all gone home. It was a secluded spot, not overlooked by the neighbours on either side of Ade's house and surrounded by shrubs on Christoff's side. Then he'd go home early in the morning, before anyone at Fieldgate Hall was awake. But that evening, he and Ade decided on the spur of the moment, to nip through the gate during the party when nobody was looking. If only they'd waited.'

'Maybe it was the excitement of the party and seeing each other all spruced up,' Gawain suggests.

'Perhaps. Anyway, I don't remember seeing Christoff, but he says he was there the whole time. He followed us across Fieldgate Crescent and when we got to Tess's back garden, Tess, Ade and I ran up the stairs to the balcony, but he stayed at the bottom. Or rather, by the time he'd made it to the paving stones, there was no point climbing the stairs because we'd both fallen.'

'Both of you?' Jacob says.

'Both of us. Christoff says we were wrapped around each other and Ade was trying to separate us. It all happened much more quickly than that sounds, though. While we were engaged in this ridiculous combat, we ended up leaning against the balcony rail. It gave way and down we both went, still holding onto each other. Tess broke my fall and died instantly. At first, they thought I was dead, too. I banged my head and was out of it for a bit, thirty seconds or so, he thinks. Apart from that, I didn't have a scratch on me.'

'Why didn't Christoff ring for an ambulance?' Jacob asks.

'He was scared, in case people found out about his relationship with Ade.'

'Even so, they should have called an ambulance.' Jacob says.

'Things weren't that straightforward in the seventies. Apart from anything else, they were committing a criminal act,' Gawain says.

'Christoff regrets it now. They didn't have to tell anyone why Tess was so upset and the chances of anyone guessing were minimal. But they panicked. Their first instinct was that we should go back to the party and pretend we didn't know she'd fallen to her death. Once we'd gone down that road it was impossible to go back and do the right thing. And also, it wouldn't bring Tess back from the dead, would it? At least that's what they told themselves.'

'It would have made a difference to you,' Jacob says. 'You wouldn't have had to spend the next forty years wondering if you were a murderer.'

'Yes, well. I don't think that occurred to anyone at the time. And if it had, it wouldn't have been a priority.'

'What happened next?' Patrick asks.

'Christoff took charge. He instructed Ade, who was a gibbering wreck, to go back to the party, through the gate at the back of his garden and tell everyone Tess had gone home, although I was the one who told them in the end, because he was incapable of stringing more than two words together. Everyone assumed he was off his face on alcohol and pain killers. Christoff escorted me back to my house. Once I'd changed into another dress, wiped my face, washed my hands and brushed my hair, he told me to head back to the party on my own, through the gate in Ade's garden, and act as though everything was fine. I was very calm, apparently. I did everything I was told to do without batting an eyelid. He waited in my house on his own for ten minutes, then he let himself out, crept home and entered Fieldgate Hall through the front door. I don't know if anyone saw him and what he said to them if they did, but he got away with it. We all did.'

'It must have been the knock on the head that made you so calm when you were back at the party,' Gawain says.

'I have this vivid memory of standing at the party thinking to myself, how strange everything felt. Tess was dead, probably because I killed her, but there I was, behaving as though she was at home in bed. It was as though Christoff had hypnotised me. I must have been stunned, I suppose. By the morning, it had worn off. I had a splitting headache, which I thought was a hangover.'

I take a gulp of my tea. It's stone cold now but my mouth is dry.

'Poor you,' Gawain says.

'Poor Tess, more like. And it's still my fault, really. That she died, I mean. If I hadn't been so angry with her, we'd never have fallen off the balcony like that.'

'Don't be so bloody silly,' Patrick says.

'That's bullshit," Jacob adds. 'You had no idea what was going on. Ade and Christoff misled you all. Particularly Ade. I mean, having sex with Tess and with you, to make it look as though he was straight. That was bang out of order.'

'You and Ade? Wow,' Gawain says.

They all stare at me.

'You needn't look so shocked. Queen Victoria had been dead for quite a number of years by then.'

'You were a bit of a goer, were you?' Patrick asks.

'No I bloody wasn't. I was very young and stupid. And completely besotted.'

I know I sound cross, but I'm relieved Patrick is amused. I was afraid he might be jealous of something that happened forty years ago.

Gawain stands up and stretches as he prepares to deliver his verdict.

'So, Tess's death was a tragedy. She died because you were both played by two boys who were caught in a difficult situation and couldn't think what else to do, and also because that balcony was sketchy and nobody had bothered to fix it. You could easily have been the one who died. Or you both could have. Stupid, random accidents like that happen all the time. People wake up one morning and have no idea that by the end of the day they'll be dead or in hospital with life changing injuries, because they fell off a ladder when they were scraping moss from the garage roof. Or they slipped in a pool of cat sick and banged their head on the edge of a mantlepiece. I see it every day. Alcohol's often a factor.'

'We *had* all been drinking.'

'You just as easily argue that the balcony rail was responsible for Tess's death. Or her parents. They should have got it fixed.'

'They said as much after the funeral.'

Gawain squats down next to me.

'So none of it was down to you. I'm not going home until you say you agree with me.'

'He's right,' Jacob chips in. 'About your part in it all. Ade and Christoff were bang out of order. But not you, Aunty.'

I still think it was partly my fault, but I appreciate their support, so I nod.

My eyes fill with tears again. Damn it.

33. Aunty Susan

Jacob answers the door wearing what looks like a tatty old trilby, made from pale yellow straw and full of holes.

'Where did you find that?'

'In the shed. I was just getting the lawnmower out. Come through.'

He leads me into a dark corridor that smells vaguely of damp and mould. The hall opens out into a surprisingly wide room with armchairs at one end and a dining table at the other, as well a small kitchen at the back. Jacob turns to me and smiles. He looks completely at home.

'Is it too warm? I put the heating on to check that it's working. And also because there's a kind of funky smell. I don't know where it's coming from.'

'You might need to get the house checked for damp.'

His face falls.

'Really?'

'Don't worry. It happens. You'll be able to sort it.'

'It's a bit of a responsibility, isn't it? Being a house owner, I mean?'

'There's always some problem or other, and you're the one who has to deal with it.'

'Yeah. Anyway, come on, I'll give you the guided tour. It'll only take about three minutes. Then we can have a coffee. I've got some of those chocolate macaroon things you like.'

A pair of wellies is parked by the French windows at the back of the room. He puts his feet in them and we head out to the tiny garden.

'You wouldn't know it, but the canal's on the other side of this hedge. It's a shame you can't see it from the garden, but if the hedge wasn't here, it wouldn't be very private. There's a path round the side of the garage that leads to the towpath. Come and see.'

I follow him. Our steps crunch on the gravel path that leads around the garage. At the back of the garage is a small grassy space on the water's edge.

'They've got, I mean *I've* got some deckchairs in the garage. It would be cool to get them out and you know, have a glass of wine and watch the coots.'

'It's a nice spot,' I say, looking up at the cloudless, early October sky.

Yesterday, Patrick and I were still on the road, heading home down the M1. I don't think I've ever been as grubby. My hair needed a proper wash, but the weather had turned chilly and at the last campsite we stayed on, the showers were in a concrete block with a force nine gale blowing under the cubicle doors, so I decided not to bother and I fluffed my hair up with talcum powder instead, like I used to do when I was a schoolgirl. On the way home, we stopped off at a camp site in the village where Bartosz grew up, for Isaac's christening.

I managed to have a quiet chat with Amanda after the ceremony, in the marquee the caterers had set up in the little paddock next to the church, but our conversation didn't stray very far beyond generalities. She said she'd moved out of the farm cottage and into an apartment in the village nearby, the one where she and the boys had lived until they moved in with me. The flat comprises the entire ground floor of a Georgian house, apparently, with a huge garden, which Tam loves. I already knew she was renting out her house in the south, but it turns out she's not on maternity leave anymore. She's doing locum work at a surgery in the village, and Tam has joined a new nursery nearby.

Jacob puts two mugs of coffee down on a table between the armchairs. Puffs of dust are displaced into the air as we sink into the cushions and a huge house spider scuttles down the leg of my chair and away across the carpet to the dark space beneath a chest of drawers. I could offer my nephew some advice about taking the cushions outside and bashing the dust out of them with carpet beaters, but I'm not that person anymore.

'Good coffee,' I say after taking a sip. 'I noticed the fancy machine in the kitchen.'

'It's the one from Talbot Way. I got it for a really good price. They thought it might end up getting damaged now the house is being rented out to strangers. The books have been moved, as well, to special section in the university library.'

Jacob smiles. His face and arms are a light honey colour and he seems to have filled out a bit. He spent the summer in Iceland where he split his time between travelling to remote areas to investigate poltergeist outbreaks and working in the same university department as the one the Prof visited last summer.

'I don't think I've ever seen you with a tan before.'

'I was in the sun a lot, what with the light evenings and everything. And I didn't have Gawain chucking bottles of Factor 50 at me the minute I stepped outside. Although he messaged me about it nearly every day.'

'You had a good time, then?'

'It was awesome. I can't believe they practically had to shovel me out of the house to get me to the airport.'

Jacob had been reluctant to leave home for such a long period of time, after his experience in South Carolina. He was particularly terrified about the end part, when he had to fly from Reykjavik to Seattle to attend a conference. Luckily, Gawain managed to convince him the chance of bumping into anyone from the Church of the New Sunrise was as low in Seattle as it was Iceland. And anyway, if he did, he'd cope.

'So what do you think? About the house?' He asks.

'It's a great little place.'

When Pauline invited Jacob to her office during the wake it wasn't to tell him he'd become surplus to requirements. Far from it. While he was gazing out of the window watching Donna and Graham leave and then seeing me get into a car with a strange man, Pauline, who is one of the Prof's executors, was taking him through some of the details included in the Prof's will. During one of his final periods of lucidity, the Prof had asked his solicitor to visit him in hospital so he could make some changes. Jacob explained it all to me at the christening.

'All his books and papers are going to be put into a special archive in the university library, and his financial assets have been left to the department. He's instructed them to set up a thing called the Michael Gossland Scholarship Fund, for PhD students mainly, and possibly research fellows. And he requested that the first scholarship should go to me.'

'Gosh, Jacob.'

'It's a real life saver. I only had enough funding to get me through the first year. And not only that, he's left me his house and everything inside it.'

'Good Lord.'

'I know! It's mortgage-free and everything. Of course, everyone else in the department hates me even more now.'

'Are you going to move here permanently?'

'I'm not sure, yet. I mean, I really like it. I don't even mind the furniture. Bartosz and a couple of his army mates are coming to strip the walls and the woodwork, and paint it all a kind of pale stone colour. Once that's done and the windows have been left open for a while, it'll be great. I'm not keen on the paintings, though. Too many owls.'

I look around the room. He's right. Owls everywhere.

'And as for that painting over there, I'll ask Gawain and Bartosz if they want it. Otherwise, I might try and sell it on e-bay.'

He points to a tastefully erotic painting of limbs, headless torsos and possibly other parts of the male anatomy entwined around each other.

'You should get it valued first.'

'You reckon?'

'You never know.'

'Anyway, I'd love to move in. I've stayed here a few nights on and off. It's great to have a place to entertain without having to deal with my brother the next morning and the way he makes such an obvious big deal about not asking me any questions. Until he can't help himself anymore and sort of bursts and starts going on about condoms and getting tested for chlamydia.'

'I can see it would be nice to get away from all that. But you'd miss him.'

'I know, but he's only down the road, isn't he?'

'Could you afford to move in?'

'That's the problem. It's mortgage-free, but there'll be bills to pay. I'm still an impoverished student, despite the scholarship. And I'm going to be travelling loads. I'm off to Canada soon, to another conference. Then I'm spending three weeks at a university in India. And I've planned a series of experiments for Talbot Way, so I'll be staying there a lot of the time, on and off.'

'On your own?'

'Nah. I've roped in a couple of third year undergrads to help me. They can use some of the findings in their dissertations.'

'So you're going to base yourself at Gawain and Bartosz's for now?'

'I think so. I'll probably rent this place out. Then I can move in later, if I want to. Or sell it. Who knows?'

'Sounds like a plan.'

34. Aunty Susan

I get up to leave and Jacob follows me to the door. When we get there he puts a hand on my arm.

'Aunty, I nearly forgot. Did you ever manage to find how those pictures from the party came to be in the photo album? And how it ended up in Tess's room.'

'Tess had her bag with her when she fell from the balcony. The zip at the top must have been open because the camera fell out onto the paving stones. Christoff picked it up and put it in his pocket. He took it back to Fieldgate Hall and hid it in his room.'

'That was risky. Imagine if the police had searched his room and found it, or someone in his household had come across it. And his fingerprints must have been on the bag.'

'The police assumed right from the start that Tess had been alone when she fell to her death and the sole culprit was the dodgy balcony rail. None of us were questioned about any of it and nobody at the party noticed anything that made them suspicious enough to phone the police. We were incredibly lucky. There were plenty of things a curious person might have wondered about. My change of dress for instance, and Christoff suddenly entering his own house through the front door when he was last seen at the other end of the garden.'

'What did he do with the film?'

'When he went back to Cambridge, he took the camera with him. He had the film developed there, where nobody knew anything about his home life or what had happened to Tess.'

'Why didn't he just destroy it?'

'He wanted to see what the photos were like. How incriminating they might be, whether some of the images had captured something of the truth between the two of them. That kind of thing. If any of them had, I think he might have kept them. But as it was, none of them did anything of the sort. They were a perfect disguise. All of them.'

'So how did the photos end up back in Tess's bedroom?'

'Tess had left her album at Ade's house in Larchford and Ade took it to London with him, when he went off to university. Christoff put the new photos in the album and told Ade he should go back to Larchford and give the album to Tess's parents.'

'That must have been difficult. Good for him.'

'He didn't, though. He said he couldn't face it. Christoff was angry with him for that. I think that was the first time a crack appeared in their relationship, although they still saw each other for a while afterwards. No, Christoff was the one who gave Tess's parents the album. He went round to their house with it one Saturday afternoon when he was home for the weekend. He told them that he'd found Tess's camera in the garden of Fieldgate Hall when they were clearing up after the party. It was under one of the chairs near the pool, where they'd all been sitting. He told them he hoped they didn't think he'd taken a liberty, but he'd had the film developed and added the new photos to Tess's album.'

'How did Tess's parents react?'

'They were grateful, overwhelmed. All they wanted to do was look at the photos and talk about Tess. Bring her back to life for a while. The house was a total mess, Christoff said, and Tess's parents were a mess, too, hair and clothes covered in paint, clearly immersing themselves in their work to the exclusion of everything else. They told Christoff they blamed themselves for the whole thing, that it wouldn't have happened if they'd bothered to fix the balcony. I suppose after Christoff had gone, they must have put the album in Tess's room and left it there with all her other possessions, like some kind of shrine to her memory. Then it must ended up on the floor and got kicked under the bed when the looters and urbexers turned up.'

'It was decent of Christoff to do that, wasn't it?' Jacob asks. 'Or did he only do it because he felt guilty?'

'Or to provide Tess's parents with irrefutable evidence that Ade had been her boyfriend right up until the end?'

'I reckon Christoff went round there out of kindness. He's not the ogre you thought he was, is he?'

'Not at all. He was very young and potentially in a great deal of trouble. And it's not as though he could have done anything to bring Tess back to life.'

'But Ade on the other hand. Deceiving Tess like that. And you.'

'People are complicated, Jacob. I'm not sure it was deception. Not entirely, anyway. Yes, he used me and Tess, but there was more to it than that. The time I spent with him was special. Magical even. It meant a lot to me. It still does, if I'm honest. And I think it meant something to him as well.'

Jacob hugs himself and looks down at the doormat. 'Maybe. He seemed like a decent bloke to me. That first weekend I spent at Talbot Way, before he got really sick, I felt we had a connection. And he went to the effort of changing his will. That was an act of kindness, wasn't it? Most people wouldn't have bothered. Basically, he was a good person who found himself in a difficult situation.'

I nod and give my nephew a peck on the cheek. Jacob has faced more than his fair share of problems in his young life, including a huge amount of unkindness from his own mother and the dreadful New Sunrise. He clearly needs to feel that in this new life he's carved out for himself, most people are as nice to him as he is to them, and that the decision to set up the scholarship and leave Jacob his house were acts of pure benevolence on the part of his professor, carried out because he liked his new student and saw a lot of potential in him. I wonder, though. I suspect Ade might have done it for a slightly different reason, because at the end of Ade's life, young Jacob with his carved cheekbones, his blue eyes, his long, slender limbs and his white blonde hair became his golden boy, the last in a long line of similar boys and men. Even so, does the precise way in which the Prof liked Jacob really matter? Changing his will like that could still be seen as an act of benevolence.

*

If you use the dual carriageway, it takes about twenty minutes to get from Jacob's house to mine, but I choose a less direct route that wends its way along narrow, hedgerow-bound B roads. As I drive, my mind goes back to that distant summer, yet again. I can't lie. I thought Ade was amazing. I was entranced by him and I remained infatuated after Tess had come back from Italy and staked her claim. And after she'd died and Ade and I spent that last afternoon together, I still felt the same way. As far as I was concerned, Ade was an angel and Christoff was an oaf, despite his wealthy background. But I've spoken to Christoff a few times since the funeral. I even managed to bring up the pawing incident on

Elfbarrow Hill. He was utterly mortified and apologised profusely. He didn't know what he'd been thinking. Yes, he'd had a few beers and Adrian was somewhere over at the other side of the woods with Tess at the time, which he found difficult to deal with, but none of that even came close to a decent set of excuses for his appalling behaviour. So, I was wrong. Christoff was a decent person in nineteen seventy-six, but like a lot of young people, he was too embarrassed to show it.

When I first found out about Ade and Christoff, I assumed the game they'd played with Tess and me had been a joint endeavour, to throw everyone off the scent about their own relationship. I wasn't angry with them. It happened too long ago to hold a grudge, and things have changed a lot since then. But now I can't help wondering whether the only person playing a game was Ade, not just with Tess and me, but also with Christoff. That summer, he took his pleasure wherever he wanted, regardless of the emotional consequences for the rest of us. What sort of a person did that make him? And was he really any different during the brief time when Jacob had known him?

But then, how can we ever know the true essence of another human being? Nobody is governed by a single character trait. Ridiculously, I think of the major tenets of quantum physics, which fascinated me at university, specifically the Copenhagen Interpretation, the way it says a quantum particle doesn't exist in one state or another, but in all of its possible states at the same time and that observation is needed to collapse the wave function and see the reality of the particle's state. People are the same. Their personalities are a complex and dynamic mass of potentialities and probabilities, flitting about all over the place at the same time. We cause other people to settle into the human beings we think they are by observing them. What's more, the data we extract by viewing another person is strongly influenced by the views we already hold about them and about ourselves. And interactions between two people are dynamic. They oscillate and shimmer between various probabilities and never really reach a steady state.

When I wake from this metaphysical reverie, I realise I've missed my turning by quite a distance. I drive on, down an extremely narrow lane, not knowing where I am until I reach a small roundabout with a white signpost on a grassy hump in its centre. If I turn left here and travel a further five miles, I'll be in Larchford. Instead of using the roundabout to turn round and head back the way

I came, I swerve off to the left without indicating. The car behind me beeps. I recognise this road, mainly because of the tree-covered hill I can see in the distance. This is the route that winds past Elfbarrow, the one Christoff and the others took when they carted the booze and camping equipment up there and hid it behind the shrubs.

I keep going and end up in Larchford, in Fieldgate Lane. I turn into the car park, and I get out and wander along one of the paths that thread between managed woodland, a playground containing tasteful wooden play structures for children, a picnic area with permanent barbeque equipment, and open grassy spaces for football. It's changed a lot since 'seventy-six.

Poor Tess. I wish there was a grave I could visit. I'd buy her some flowers and go there now. I'd talk to her as an equal, the balance of innocence and blame equally distributed between us. None of it was entirely her fault, or mine. My sins are cancelled out by hers and vice versa. But Tess was cremated, and as far as I know, her parents never claimed her ashes and sprinkled them anywhere. I stroll on. Suddenly, I feel tired and quite hungry. I flop down for a minute on one of the benches that line the path and I rustle in my handbag until I find the little tin of sugar-free mints I always carry around with me and pop one in my mouth. Revived, I stand up again and a bronze rectangular plaque on the back of the bench catches my eye as it glints in the sunshine. I put my reading glasses on. *In memory of Sandra Hopgood, who loved this lane when it ran between fields of golden barley*. This bench commemorates Graham's mum. I had no idea.

When I get home, Patrick's camper van is in my drive. It's clearly had a good clean and a polish. Once we've checked in with friends and family, sorted through our post, checked our plumbing for leaks, cut the grass, set up the heating to come on for an hour each morning and night, and completed any life admin that we can't do remotely by laptop, we're off again. This time we'll be heading West instead of North. He jumps down from the driving seat when he sees me pull up and looks at me in that way he has. Lunch now, perhaps, and soon afterwards it will be that period in the sleepy middle of the afternoon when we shut the bedroom curtains and collapse each other's wave functions.

'I thought it might be good if I came to stay with you until we head West.'

'Can't keep away, eh?'

'I woke up at three a.m. and you weren't there. It wasn't a good feeling.'

I unlock the front door and he wraps his arms around my waist and pushes me inside. As he removes my coat and turns to hang it up, an idea comes to me. I'll speak to Graham and ask him how you go about putting a memorial bench in Fieldgate Country Park. It can't be difficult and I don't care how much it costs. The hardest part will be coming up with the right combination of words to summarize Tess.

I'm sure I'll think of something.

Thank you!

Thank you so much for reading Aunty Susan and the Fabric of time. I hope you didn't find Jacob's aunt and the rest of his family too annoying! If not, I'd like to tell you about the first book in the Fylde series, Gawain and the Green Man, which focuses on Gawain and Jacob, their early life, the reasons for their massive quarrel, Jacob's time in the Church of the New Sunrise, and what happened afterwards.

The next book in the series will be about Gawain and Jacob's sister, Amanda, and the surprising direction her life takes when she moves back up North to the village where she spent her childhood.

If you enjoyed Aunty Susan's adventures, it would be amazing if you could leave a review on the platform of your choice, to help spread the word!

About the Author

Kate Laxen grew up in the North of England, but now lives in the South, in an area not too far from London, where footpaths wind their way between industrial estates and stretches of woodland, and canals form liminal spaces that separate rows of houses from green fields. Perhaps because of this, she prefers characters who don't live in the mainstream, but tend to occupy the borderlands and make their own way through life as individuals, not members of a crowd.

Printed in Great Britain
by Amazon